Collector's Library

Collector's Library

CLASSIC TALES OF THE MACABRE

CLASSIC TALES OF THE MACABRE

Selected and Introduced by
DAVID STUART DAVIES

Collector's Library

This edition published in 2011 by
Collector's Library
an imprint of CRW Publishing Limited
69 Gloucester Crescent, London NW1 7EG

ISBN 978 1 907360 27 5

Typeset in Great Britain by Antony Gray
Printed and bound in China by Imago

1

Contents

Introduction 7

About the Authors 13

MARGARET OLIPHANT

The Library Window 25

EDGAR WALLACE

The Black Grippe 81

ROBERT LOUIS STEVENSON

The Bottle Imp 103

ARTHUR QUILLER-COUCH

A Pair of Hands 141

EDGAR ALLAN POE

The Facts in the Case of M. Valdemar 157

W. F. HARVEY

The Beast with Five Fingers 170

PERCEVAL LANDON

Thurnley Abbey 205

WILKIE COLLINS

A Terribly Strange Bed 226

CHARLOTTE PERKINS GILMAN

The Yellow Wallpaper 249

W. W. JACOBS

The Monkey's Paw 271

AMBROSE BIERCE

The Damned Thing 285

BRAM STOKER

The Squaw 297

H. P. LOVECRAFT

The Horror in the Museum 314

RUDYARD KIPLING

The Mark of the Beast 353

BARRY PAIN

The Undying Thing 370

O. HENRY

The Last Leaf 400

Introduction

Looking up the word 'macabre' in my copy of *The Concise Oxford Dictionary*, I find that it is defined thus: 'grim, gruesome, grotesque'. This definition sums up with a splendid conciseness the flavour and the content of the stories you will find in this collection. The umbrella-like function of this wonderful word is to describe tales which may feature ghosts, ghouls, monsters, magic – everything and anything which is out of kilter with the norm and challenges the imagination, always relying on that special tingle of fear which is generated by uncertainty. In reading these stories it is as though one is looking at the world through a glass darkly.

Indeed, the aim of these exercises in the macabre is to unsettle, even shock, the reader with grim and indelibly vivid images and unnerving concepts that cannot be dismissed from the memory. Perhaps the most successful method used by some of the authors to entwine you in their nightmare world is to begin with apparent normality and then introduce some aspect of the unusual which grows in its strangeness until, like some monstrous weed, it entangles and overwhelms not only the central characters in the story but you, the reader, too.

This potent brew of macabre titbits has been concocted from a generous measure of well-known tales written by famous authors mixed with a selection of more obscure but no less juicy morsels from lesser known or neglected writers. The majority of the stories were composed in the Victorian era, that fascinating period when men were making magnificent strides in science and technology while at the same time becoming obsessed with the mysteries of death and the afterlife. Mediums and spiritualists of all hues and persuasions flourished during this period. They were visited not only by the lower orders but also by the great and the good. It was a time when the ghost story as a recognised form of literature became a popular source of entertainment. More than ever questions were being asked about life and death and, in particular, what happens after we have shuffled off this mortal coil. This concern was investigated, explored and, some might say, exploited by many writers of the time. Distinguished authors such as Charles Dickens, Wilkie Collins and Mrs Gaskell tried their hand at the genre.

This collection presents a variety of dark glimpses into the 'grim, gruesome [and] grotesque'. For true horror, concerning the power that life holds over death, there are grisly examples provided in Edgar Allan Poe's 'The Case of M. Valdemar', W. W. Jacobs's 'The Monkey's Paw', W. F. Harvey's 'The Beast with Five Fingers' and Barry Pain's 'The Undying Thing'. All these tales come with a warning – do not dabble in things you wot not of.

If your taste is for something less graphic but still ghostly, tales that lure you in through their gentle strangeness, you could not do better than the opening offering, 'The Library Window' by Mrs Oliphant, subtitled 'A Story of the Seen and Unseen'. This atmospheric and engaging tale begins almost like a mild domestic drama told in a gossipy manner. The situation seems a simple one: does the library window glimpsed across the street really exist or not? With consummate skill Mrs Oliphant shows how the narrator becomes obsessed with this strange window and the figure that appears in the room beyond. The realistic situation slowly takes on a surreal dreamlike quality. And yet we, the readers, are with the girl all the way as her obsession takes hold. The situation may be 'macabre' but it also seems so very real. It is this aspect of the tale that provides the reader with a strong sense of pleasurable discomfort.

Obsession leading to madness is explored in exquisite detail in Charlotte Perkins Gilman's 'The Yellow Wallpaper', a story which provides a fascinating insight into a mind slowly losing touch with reality so that the ordinary seems increasingly bizarre. The realism and accuracy of the process lends the narrative its power and chilling frisson.

Ghosts are always good value for money in the world of macabre fiction and we have a tale featuring a slow, insidious haunting, notably 'A Pair of Hands' by Arthur Quiller-Couch. The anecdotal tone lends the narratives credibility. For ghosts of a more visceral nature, Perceval Landon's 'Thurnley Abbey' serves up a special treat, as does Ambrose Bierce's 'The Damned Thing'. However, one may question whether the latter tale is in fact a ghost story. The vicious, destructive unseen agent is never quite explained. Is it a ghost or some strange elemental force? It is up to the reader to decide. That is the beauty of the macabre tale: there are no restrictions placed upon the nature of the narrative. All things strange may apply, from Robert Louis Stevenson's exotic 'The Bottle Imp' to Wilkie Collins's 'A Terribly Strange Bed', and you would expect nothing less than a classic from H. P. Lovecraft, one of the masters of supernatural fiction, with his weird and challenging 'Horror in the Museum'. For touches of furry menace you have Kipling's 'Mark of the Beast' (our sole offering in the realm of lycanthropy) and Bram Stoker's malevolent, revengeful feline in 'The Squaw'.

There are some stories which cannot really be shoehorned into any sub-category of the 'macabre'. A case in point is Edgar Wallace's 'The Black Grippe', which deals with an 'unnatural disaster' that threatens mankind. The style is a mixture of science fiction and thriller and there is even a surprise ending. Wallace, who cut his writing teeth in journalism, turning out the sort of sensational stories produced by Lord Northcliffe's *Daily Mail*, gives this one all the lively force of a tale delivered by the popular press.

With regards to surprise endings, the most consummate of writers with this trick up his sleeve is the American author O. Henry, and he does not disappoint in 'The Last Leaf', which demonstrates his wonderfully concise style and his ability to surprise even the most prescient reader.

I would make the point that all these stories work effectively not just because of their unusual content but also because they are so well written. Often tales featuring ghosts, the supernatural and macabre occurrences are looked down upon by certain critics and regarded as so much catchpenny pulp. Not so. The calibre of the writers and the quality of the writing in this volume prove otherwise. To use a modern expression, these stories are 'fit for purpose', and they excel in their intentions. This collection is designed to encourage you, the reader, to dip into it in a kind of sampling fashion, but I am sure that once you have sampled, you will hurry back for more.

About the Authors

Mrs Oliphant (1828–1897)

Margaret Oliphant was in the front row of the second rank of Victorian novelists. Due to the early death of her husband and the hardships that this brought about, she wrote principally as a means of earning an income. Her work varied from historical to domestic dramas, but perhaps her most successful narratives were her forays into popular supernatural fiction in which she was able to explore the psychological elements involved while presenting the ghostly trappings with great aplomb. 'The Library Window' is among her most successful efforts in this genre. It is one of the last stories she wrote and combines a disappearing room, the emotions of a young woman and a past romance.

Edgar Wallace (1875–1932)

Wallace was the most prolific of authors. He wrote at a prodigious pace, producing one hundred and seventy-three books (more than half involving crime and mystery) and seventeen plays during his lifetime. In essence he could and indeed would turn his hand to any kind of story. However, Wallace was attracted to fantasy and used many of the genre's central themes in his work, particularly in his short stories. He was especially fond of large-scale disasters and the effect they had on society. In 'The Black Grippe', which was first published in the *Strand Magazine*, we have a macabre tale that deals with a mysterious new disease that threatens mankind. The story is effective not just in its unusual theme but also in the clean and polished prose which seemed to flow effortlessly from Wallace's pen.

Robert Louis Stevenson (1850–1894)
A writer of adventure stories, possibly the most famous being *Treasure Island*, Stevenson was also a major figure in the horror genre as author of *The Strange Case of Dr Jekyll and Mr Hyde* as well as a number of other notable horror tales. Towards the end of his life, he lived in the South Seas and it was there at Apa in the Samoan Islands that he wrote 'The Bottle Imp'. The story is set in this exotic location and is full of local colour. Told as an anecdote, this tone of realism adds to its chilling quality. It is one of the most brilliantly uncomfortable tales ever penned.

Arthur Quiller-Couch (1863–1944)
British scholar and author (generally referred to as Q), Arthur Quiller-Couch is perhaps best remembered for collating and editing *The Oxford Book of English Verse 1250–1900* (1900). This volume had a very substantial influence on popular taste and the perception of poetry for at least a generation. Quiller-Couch was a noted academic and was an active supporter of and activist for the Liberal Party. He was knighted in 1910. However, he also wrote several novels in the romantic swashbuckling vein and a number of ghost stories. These supernatural sketches are charming rather than grotesque, but the elegance of his prose draws one

into the tales in a very seductive fashion. The author was born in Cornwall, a location which provides the atmospheric setting for 'A Pair of Hands', a gentle tale of haunting featuring the spirit of a child.

Edgar Allan Poe (1809–1849)

Born in Boston to two itinerant actors, Poe embarked on a literary career after a short stint in the army. He became the master of the macabre, and his influence on both the supernatural genre and the detective story is immense. A troubled soul in his personal life, he was able to inject his stories with his own powerful and dark poetical imaginings. Many of his tales concern death and an obsession with death and what happens after 'we pass the through the gate'. While many of his stories, such as 'The Fall of the House of Usher' and 'The Masque of Red Death', are imbued with a Gothic, dreamlike quality, 'The Facts in the Case of M. Valdemar' has a more realistic setting and as a result achieves a more profound sense of the macabre.

W. F. Harvey (1885–1937)

By all accounts, Yorkshire-born William Fryer Harvey was a good and gentle soul, a war veteran and a loving family man – and yet he found pleasure and success in creating a series of grim, disturbing and frightening tales. Harvey's stories are remarkable for their subtlety and restraint. Like M. R. James, he relies on the readers to pick up suggestions from the text to create their own horrid imaginings. 'The Beast with Five Fingers' is typical of Harvey's smooth and deceptive style, incorporating as it does sly moments of gentle humour among the dark and sinister shadows. One of his most effective devices is the way the author allows the reader to be one jump ahead of the main protagonist. The story is beautifully conceived and cinematic in its moments of climax.

Perceval Landon (1868–1927)

There are many writers of ghost stories and bizarre tales who engage in this pursuit for relaxation and amusement, as an antidote perhaps to a demanding career. Perceval Landon was one of these fellows. He led a crowded and fulfilling life, mainly as a journalist covering various conflicts and uprisings around the world. He travelled constantly from the age of twenty-one until his death, never settling anywhere for more than a few years at the most. Apart from 'Thurnley Abbey', his small fictional output has been forgotten but this story is a real classic. In the tradition of all the great chillers, the reader is kept guessing as to the actual nature and appearance of 'the thing' that threatens the central characters in that house of horror, Thurnley Abbey.

Wilkie Collins (1824–89)

In 1846, having spent five years in the tea business, Wilkie Collins entered the legal profession and read for the bar at Lincoln's Inn. It was here that he gained experience of the law, the practitioners of it and those individuals who fell foul of it, and from this he derived much of the material for his fiction. Collins was the first Englishman to write a full-length detective novel, *The Moonstone*. Probably his most famous work is *The Woman in White*, a mystery novel with the kind of bizarre elements and strange characters that particularly appealed to the author.

The same nightmarish quality which pervades much of this novel can be found in 'A Terribly Strange Bed', which is set in Paris in the middle of the nineteenth century. The oddness of the situation, the apparent innocence of the narrative and the growing sense of menace draw the reader into this deceptively simple but remarkably unsettling story.

Charlotte Perkins Gilman (1860–1936)
Born in Connecticut in the USA, Gilman was one of a new breed of women who wanted to be independent and to work for a living rather than simply accept a cosseted domestic life, relying solely on her husband's income. She campaigned hard for women's suffrage. Because of her strong views, she approached marriage with some apprehension. When she gave birth to a daughter, she fell into such a state of post-natal despair that her husband insisted on her seeking medical advice. The doctor recommended a complete rest from all activities and she was advised ' . . . never touch pen, brush or pencil as long as you live'. The strictures of the supposed cure drove this sensitive, artistic woman mad. When she emerged from the nightmare, she believed that her personality had changed irrevocably and that she was destined to live 'a crippled life'. Elements of this shattering experience inform the narrative in 'The Yellow Wallpaper', describing as it does a sensitive young woman's slow and seemingly inevitable descent into madness.

W. W. Jacobs (1863–1943)
William Wymark Jacobs was a British journalist, humorous writer and playwright who is remembered today principally for his dramatic tale 'The Monkey's

Paw'. It is a story that finds its way into many anthologies – and not without reason: it is one of the most powerfully tragic tales ever penned and therefore no excuses are needed for its inclusion in this collection. There is a dark, painful, creeping inevitability about the course of events that both fascinates and chills. Some critics have claimed that the story is about fate and the dangers in attempting to set one's will against it. While this is certainly true, the use of the dried-out monkey's paw that can grant three wishes adds a wonderfully surreal and macabre touch which elevates the story well above its anecdotal structure. Such is the power of 'The Monkey's Paw' that it has been dramatised several times for radio, television and the cinema, but still its most effective incarnation is on the printed page.

Ambrose Bierce (1842–*c.*1914)

Of all writers of ghost and horror stories, Ambrose Bierce is perhaps the most colourful. He was a dark, cynical and pessimistic soul who had a grim vision of fate and the unfairness of life which he channelled into his fiction. He was the author of the bitterly satirical *The Devil's Dictionary*, in which, for example, he defined the grave 'as a place in which the dead are laid to await the coming of the medical student'. He was also the creator of a large number of bizarre short stories which helped to establish him as an important figure in the evolution of horror fiction. His unusual approach in presenting a narrative, as though one were slowly pulling back a cloth to reveal a painting, is well demonstrated in 'The Damned Thing'. Only in the closing moments of the story do we glimpse the whole picture and the shocking implications thereof.

Bram Stoker (1847–1912)
Stoker is, of course, famous as the creator of the Gothic masterpiece *Dracula*, whose influence on the world of supernatural fiction and horror movies is incalculable. As a result, his other fiction has been overshadowed by this seminal work, which is a shame for while Stoker's other novels really do not match up to his masterpiece, he did create some very effective eerie short stories. 'The Squaw' is one of the best and is perhaps his most grotesque. The idea for the tale came to the author on a visit to Nuremberg where he was impressed by the medieval German city and its more bizarre relics. The determination of the cat in the story to wreak revenge has echoes of Poe's 'The Black Cat'.

H. P. Lovecraft (1890–1937)
Because of his unique approach and individual style in creating bizarre and macabre stories, Howard Phillips Lovecraft became one of the most important authors of supernatural fiction in the twentieth century. This is a remarkable fact for while he was alive he wrote entirely for pulp magazines or the amateur press and so had only a limited circle of readers. However, since his death, his work has achieved a much wider audience and he is now regarded as one of the masters of the genre. 'The Horror in the Museum' is a fine example of Lovecraft's power to chill and unnerve. While most of his tales are set in his native America, often in imaginary towns in the state of Massachusetts, this one is located in London and begins with the juicy premise of a wax museum boasting a new exhibit which no man has looked upon and remained sane . . .

Rudyard Kipling (1865–1936)
Kipling, the celebrated author of *The Jungle Book* and *The Just So Stories*, was also a master of the strange and macabre short story. He was born in Bombay (now Mumbai) in India, and while growing up in the atmosphere of a white middle-class artistic family, he was also steeped in the Indian culture on his doorstep. Indeed he was brought up by an ayah, his Indian nurse, who taught him Hindustani as his first language. The folk tales, fuelled by Indian mysticism, that he heard while a child influenced a great deal of his fiction. 'The Mark of the Beast' is one of the more graphically horrific of the author's tales and was written while Kipling was a young man in India. Among the first to see it was the important editor Andrew Lang, who recoiled with disgust on reading it. He commented: ' . . . this [is] poisonous stuff which has left an extremely disagreeable impression on my mind.' Nevertheless the story was published and was so successful that Kipling wrote a sequel, 'The Return to Imray'.

Barry Pain (1864–1928)
Barry Pain not only wrote well-wrought horror stories but, like his friend Jerome K. Jerome, was also a journalist and humorist; he was perhaps best known for the Eliza books, featuring stories about the comical trials and tribulations of a young housewife. Nevertheless, Pain's darker fictions, appearing in a series of strange stories, were equally accomplished. He seemed to take pleasure in presenting the reader with a scenario that was not quite a ghost story and not quite a supernatural tale, but certainly one that was macabre and unsettling.

'The Undying Thing' deals by implication with a kind of lycanthropy. One hundred and fifty years ago, Sir Edric's baby was 'marked' when its mother was frightened by wolves, and therefore was not wholly human. The baby was abandoned in the forest but it did not die. Now an adult, it is waiting to act!

O. Henry (1862–1910)

O. Henry was the pseudonym of the American William Sydney Porter, the king of short-story writers. His brief narratives were famous for their surprise endings; indeed, the twist in the tale was such a feature of his work that this device became known as an 'O. Henry ending'. He had a colourful life and spent some time in prison for embezzlement. He wrote sporadically from his youth, but the greatest bulk of his output was produced in the last eight years of his life when he had settled in New York. He wrote in many genres but the main subject matter of his tales was the folly, foibles and frailty of human nature. 'The Last Leaf' focuses on the belief of a girl who is dangerously ill that she can fend off death only until the last leaf has fallen from the tree she can see through the window from her sickbed. Watch out for a suitably bizarre 'O. Henry ending'.

The [illegible] dealt by implication with the kind of [illegible] hopes [illegible] one hundred and fifty years ago. [illegible] it [illegible] early [illegible] when its modern [illegible] was [illegible] and [illegible] was not wholly [illegible] The [illegible] in the [illegible] to all.

O. Henry [illegible]

O. Henry [illegible] William Sydney Porter [illegible] short-story writers. His [illegible] were famous for their surprise endings [illegible] the twist of the tale was [illegible] feature of [illegible] that this device became known as an O. Henry ending. He led a colourful life and spent some time in prison for embezzlement. He wrote [illegible] but the greater part of his [illegible] was produced in the last [illegible] in New York. He [illegible] of [illegible] was [illegible] The [illegible] who [illegible] until [illegible] she can [illegible] for a suitable [illegible] O. Henry [illegible]

CLASSIC TALES
OF THE MACABRE

The Library Window

MARGARET OLIPHANT

I

I was not aware at first of the many discussions which had gone on about that window. It was almost opposite one of the windows of the large old-fashioned drawing-room of the house in which I spent that summer, which was of so much importance in my life. Our house and the library were on opposite sides of the broad High Street of St Rule's, which is a fine street, wide and ample, and very quiet, as strangers think who come from noisier places; but in a summer evening there is much coming and going, and the stillness is full of sound – the sound of footsteps and pleasant voices, softened by the summer air. There are even exceptional moments when it is noisy: the time of the fair, and on Saturday nights sometimes, and when there are excursion trains. Then even the softest sunny air of the evening will not smooth the harsh tones and the stumbling steps; but at these unlovely moments we shut the windows, and even I, who am so fond of that deep recess where I can take refuge from all that is going on inside, and make myself a spectator of all the varied story out of doors, withdraw from my watchtower. To tell the truth, there never was very much going on inside. The house belonged to my aunt, to whom (she says, 'Thank God!') nothing ever happens. I believe that many things have happened to her in her time; but that was all over at the period of which I am speaking, and she was old, and very quiet. Her life went on in a routine never broken. She got up at the same hour every day, and did the same things in the same rotation, day by day the same. She said that this was the greatest support in the world, and that routine is a kind of salvation. It may be so; but it is a very dull salvation, and I used to feel that I would rather have incident, whatever kind of incident it might be. But then at that time I was not old, which makes all the difference. At the time of which I speak the deep recess of the drawing-room window was a great comfort to me. Though she was an old lady (perhaps because she was so old) she was very tolerant, and had a kind of feeling for me. She never said a word, but often gave me a smile when she saw how I had built myself up, with my books and my basket of work. I did very little work, I fear – now and then a few stitches when the spirit moved me, or when I had got well afloat in a dream, and was more tempted to follow it out than to read my book, as sometimes happened. At other times, and if the book were interesting, I used to get through volume after volume sitting there, paying no attention to anybody. And yet I did pay a kind of attention. Aunt Mary's old ladies came in to call, and I heard them talk, though I very seldom listened; but for all that, if they had anything to say that was interesting, it is curious how I found it in my mind afterwards, as if the air had blown it to me. They came and went, and I had the sensation of their old bonnets gliding out and in, and their dresses rustling, and now and then had to jump up and shake hands with someone who knew me and asked after my papa and mamma. Then Aunt Mary would give me a little smile again, and I slipped back to my window. She never seemed to mind. My mother would not have let me do it, I know. She would have remembered dozens of things there were to do. She would have sent me upstairs to fetch something which I was quite sure she did not want, or downstairs to carry some quite unnecessary message to the housemaid. She liked to keep me running about. Perhaps that was one reason why I was so fond of Aunt Mary's drawing-room, and the deep recess of the window, and the curtain that fell half over it, and the broad window-seat where one could collect so many things without being found fault with for untidiness. Whenever we had anything the matter with us in these days, we were sent to St Rule's to get up our strength. And this was my case at the time of which I am going to speak.

Everybody had said, since ever I learned to speak, that I was fantastic and fanciful and dreamy, and all the other words with which a girl who may happen to like poetry, and to be fond of thinking, is so often made uncomfortable. People don't know what they mean when they say fantastic. It sounds like Madge Wildfire or something of that sort. My mother thought I should always be busy, to keep nonsense out of my head. But really I was not at all fond of nonsense. I was rather serious than otherwise. I would have been no trouble to anybody if I had been left to myself. It was only that I had a sort of second-sight, and was conscious of things to which I paid no attention. Even when reading the most interesting book, the things that were being talked about blew in to me; and I heard what the people were saying in the streets as they passed under the window. Aunt Mary always said I could do two or indeed three things at once – both read and listen and see. I am sure that I did not listen much, and seldom looked out, of set purpose – as some people do who notice what bonnets the ladies in the street have on; but I did hear what I couldn't help hearing, even when I was reading my book, and I did see all sorts of things, though often for a whole half-hour I might never lift my eyes.

This does not explain what I said at the beginning, that there were many discussions about that window. It was, and still is, the last window in the row, of the College Library, which is opposite my aunt's house in the High Street. Yet it is not exactly opposite, but a little to the west, so that I could see it best from the left side of my recess. I took it calmly for granted that it was a window like any other till I first heard the talk about it which was going on in the drawing-room. 'Have you never made up your mind, Mrs Balcarres,' said old Mr Pitmilly, 'whether that window opposite is a window or no?' He said Mistress Balcarres – and he was always called Mr Pitmilly, Morton: which was the name of his place.

'I am never sure of it, to tell the truth,' said Aunt Mary, 'all these years.'

'Bless me!' said one of the old ladies, 'and what window may that be?'

Mr Pitmilly had a way of laughing as he spoke, which did not please me; but it was true that he was not perhaps desirous of pleasing me. He said, 'Oh, just the window opposite,' with his laugh running through his words; 'our friend can never make up her mind about it, though she has been living opposite it since – '

'You need never mind the date,' said another; 'the Leebrary window! Dear me, what should it be but a window? up at that height it could not be a door.'

'The question is,' said my aunt, 'if it is a real window with glass in it, or if it is merely painted, or if it once was a window, and has been built up. And the oftener people look at it, the less they are able to say.'

'Let me see this window,' said old Lady Carnbee, who was very active and strong-minded; and then they all came crowding upon me – three or four old ladies, very eager, and Mr Pitmilly's white hair appearing over their heads, and my aunt sitting quiet and smiling behind.

'I mind the window very well,' said Lady Carnbee; 'ay: and so do more than me. But in its present appearance it is just like any other window; but has not been cleaned, I should say, in the memory of man.'

'I see what ye mean,' said one of the others. 'It is just a very dead thing without any reflection in it; but I've seen as bad before.'

'Ay, it's dead enough,' said another, 'but that's no rule; for these hizzies of women-servants in this ill age – '

'Nay, the women are well enough,' said the softest voice of all, which was Aunt Mary's. 'I will never let them risk their lives cleaning the outside of mine. And there are no women-servants in the Old Library: there is maybe something more in it than that.'

They were all pressing into my recess, pressing upon me, a row of old faces, peering into something they could not understand. I had a sense in my mind of how curious it was, the wall of old ladies in their old satin gowns all glazed with age, Lady Carnbee with her lace about her head. Nobody was looking at me or thinking of me; but I felt unconsciously the contrast of my youngness to their oldness, and stared at them as they stared over my head at the Library window. I had given it no attention up to this time. I was more taken up with the old ladies than with the thing they were looking at.

'The framework is all right at least, I can see that, and pented black – '

'And the panes are pented black too. It's no window, Mrs Balcarres. It has been filled in, in the days of the window duties: you will mind, Leddy Carnbee.'

'Mind!' said that oldest lady. 'I mind when your mother was marriet, Jeanie: and that's neither the day nor yesterday. But as for the window, it's just a delusion: and that is my opinion of the matter, if you ask me.'

'There's a great want of light in that muckle room at the college,' said another. 'If it was a window, the Leebrary would have more light.'

'One thing is clear,' said one of the younger ones, 'it cannot be a window to see through. It may be filled in or it may be built up, but it is not a window to give light.'

'And who ever heard of a window that was no to see through?' Lady Carnbee said. I was fascinated by the look on her face, which was a curious scornful look as of one who knew more than she chose to say: and then my wandering fancy was caught by her hand as she held it up, throwing back the lace that dropped over it. Lady Carnbee's lace was the chief thing about her – heavy black Spanish lace with large flowers. Everything she wore was trimmed with it. A large veil of it hung over her old bonnet. But her hand coming out of this heavy lace was a curious thing to see. She had very long fingers, very taper, which had been much admired in her youth; and her hand was very white, or rather more than white, pale, bleached and bloodless, with large blue veins standing up upon the back; and she wore some fine rings, among others a big diamond in an ugly old claw setting. They were too big for her, and were wound round and round with yellow silk to make them keep on: and this little cushion of silk, turned brown with long wearing, had twisted round so that it was more conspicuous than the jewels; while the big diamond blazed underneath in the hollow of her hand, like some dangerous thing hiding and sending out darts of light. The hand, which seemed to come almost to a point, with this strange ornament underneath, clutched at my half-terrified imagination. It too seemed to mean far more than was said. I felt as if it might clutch me with sharp claws, and the lurking, dazzling creature bite – with a sting that would go to the heart.

Presently, however, the circle of the old faces broke up, the old ladies returned to their seats, and Mr Pitmilly, small but very erect, stood up in the midst of them, talking with mild authority like a little oracle among the ladies. Only Lady Carnbee always contradicted the neat little old gentleman. She gesticulated, when she talked, like a Frenchwoman, and darted forth that hand of hers with the lace hanging over it, so that I always caught a glimpse of the lurking diamond. I thought she looked like a witch among the comfortable little group which gave such attention to everything Mr Pitmilly said.

'For my part, it is my opinion there is no window

there at all,' he said. 'It's very like the thing that's called in scientific language an optical illusion. It arises generally, if I may use such a word in the presence of ladies, from a liver that is not just in the perfitt order and balance that organ demands – and then you will see things – a blue dog, I remember, was the thing in one case, and in another – '

'The man has gane gyte,' said Lady Carnbee; 'I mind the windows in the Auld Leebrary as long as I mind anything. Is the Leebrary itself an optical illusion too?'

'Na, na,' and 'No, no,' said the old ladies; 'a blue dogue would be a strange vagary: but the Library we have all kent from our youth,' said one. 'And I mind when the Assemblies were held there one year when the Town Hall was building,' another said.

'It is just a great divert to me,' said Aunt Mary; but what was strange was that she paused there, and said in a low tone, 'now'; and then went on again, 'for whoever comes to my house, there are aye discussions about that window. I have never just made up my mind about it myself. Sometimes I think it's a case of these wicked window duties, as you said, Miss Jeanie, when half the windows in our houses were blocked up to save the tax. And then, I think, it may be due to that blank kind of building like the great new buildings on the Earthen Mound in Edinburgh, where the windows are just ornaments. And then whiles I am sure I can see the glass shining when the sun catches it in the afternoon.'

'You could so easily satisfy yourself, Mrs Balcarres, if you were – '

'Give a laddie a penny to cast a stone, and see what happens,' said Lady Carnbee.

'But I am not sure that I have any desire to satisfy myself,' Aunt Mary said. And then there was a stir in the room, and I had to come out from my recess and open the door for the old ladies and see them downstairs, as they all went away following one another. Mr Pitmilly gave his arm to Lady Carnbee, though she was always contradicting him; and so the tea-party dispersed. Aunt Mary came to the head of the stairs with her guests in an old-fashioned gracious way, while I went down with them to see that the maid was ready at the door. When I came back Aunt Mary was still standing in the recess looking out. Returning to her seat, she said, with a kind of wistful look, 'Well, honey: and what is your opinion?'

'I have no opinion. I was reading my book all the time,' I said.

'And so you were, honey, and no' very civil; but all the same I ken well you heard every word we said.'

2

It was a night in June; dinner was long over, and had it been winter the maids would have been shutting up the house, and my Aunt Mary preparing to go upstairs to her room. But it was still clear daylight, that daylight out of which the sun has been long gone, and which has no longer any rose reflections, but all has sunk into a pearly neutral tint – a light which is daylight yet is not day. We had taken a turn in the garden after dinner, and now we had returned to what we called our usual occupations. My aunt was reading. The English post had come in, and she had got her *Times*, which was her great diversion. The

Scotsman was her morning reading, but she liked her *Times* at night.

As for me, I too was at my usual occupation, which at that time was doing nothing. I had a book as usual, and was absorbed in it: but I was conscious of all that was going on all the same. The people strolled along the broad pavement, making remarks as they passed under the open window which came up into my story or my dream, and sometimes made me laugh. The tone and the faint sing-song, or rather chant, of the accent, which was 'a wee Fifish', was novel to me, and associated with holiday, and pleasant; and sometimes they said to each other something that was amusing, and often something that suggested a whole story; but presently they began to drop off, the footsteps slackened, the voices died away. It was getting late, though the clear soft daylight went on and on. All through the lingering evening, which seemed to consist of interminable hours, long but not weary, drawn out as if the spell of the light and the outdoor life might never end, I had now and then, quite unawares, cast a glance at the mysterious window which my aunt and her friends had discussed, as I felt, though I dared not say it even to myself, rather foolishly. It caught my eye without any intention on my part, as I paused, as it were, to take breath, in the flowing and current of undistinguishable thoughts and things from without and within which carried me along. First it occurred to me, with a little sensation of discovery, how absurd to say it was not a window, a living window, one to see through! Why, then, had they never *seen* it, these old folk? I saw as I looked up suddenly the faint greyness as of visible space within – a room behind, certainly dim, as it was natural a room should be on the other side of the street – quite indefinite: yet so clear that if someone were to come to the window there would be nothing surprising in it. For certainly there was a feeling of space behind the panes which these old half-blind ladies had disputed about – whether they were glass or only fictitious panes marked on the wall. How silly! when eyes that could see could make it out in a minute. It was only a greyness at present, but it was unmistakable, a space that went back into gloom, as every room does when you look into it across a street. There were no curtains to show whether it was inhabited or not; but a room – oh, as distinctly as ever room was! I was pleased with myself, but said nothing, while Aunt Mary rustled her paper, waiting for a favourable moment to announce a discovery which settled her problem at once. Then I was carried away upon the stream again, and forgot the window, till somebody threw unawares a word from the outer world, 'I'm goin' hame; it'll soon be dark.' Dark! what was the fool thinking of? it never would be dark if one waited out, wandering in the soft air for hours longer; and then my eyes, acquiring easily that new habit, looked across the way again.

Ah, now! nobody indeed had come to the window; and no light had been lighted, seeing it was still beautiful to read by – a still, clear, colourless light; but the room inside had certainly widened. I could see the grey space and air a little deeper, and a sort of vision, very dim, of a wall, and something against it; something dark, with the blackness that a solid article, however indistinctly seen, takes in the lighter darkness that is only space – a large, black, dark thing coming out into the grey. I looked more intently, and made sure it was a piece of furniture, either a writing-table or perhaps a large bookcase. No doubt it must be the last, since this was part of the Old Library. I never visited the old College Library, but I had seen such places before, and I could well imagine it to myself. How curious that for all the time these old people had looked at it, they had never seen this before!

It was more silent now, and my eyes, I suppose, had grown dim with gazing, doing my best to make it out, when suddenly Aunt Mary said, 'Will you ring the bell, my dear? I must have my lamp.'

'Your lamp?' I cried, 'when it is still daylight.' But then I gave another look at my window, and perceived with a start that the light had indeed changed: for now I saw nothing. It was still light, but there was so much change in the light that my room, with the grey space and the large shadowy bookcase, had gone out, and I saw them no more: for even a Scotch night in June, though it looks as if it would never end, does darken at the last. I had almost cried out, but checked myself, and rang the bell for Aunt Mary, and made up my mind I would say nothing till next morning, when to be sure naturally it would be more clear.

Next morning I rather think I forgot all about it – or was busy: or was more idle than usual; the two things meant nearly the same. At all events I thought no more of the window, though I still sat in my own, opposite to it, but occupied with some other fancy. Aunt Mary's visitors came as usual in the afternoon; but their talk was of other things, and for a day or two nothing at all happened to bring back my thoughts into this channel. It might be nearly a week before the subject came back, and once more it was old Lady Carnbee who set me thinking; not that she said anything upon that particular theme. But she was the last of my aunt's afternoon guests to go away, and when she rose to leave she threw up her hands, with those lively gesticulations which so many old Scotch ladies have. 'My faith!' said she, 'there is that bairn there still like a dream. Is the creature bewitched, Mary Balcarres? and is she bound to sit there by night and by day for the rest of her days? You should mind that there's things about, uncanny for women of our blood.'

I was too much startled at first to recognise that it was of me she was speaking. She was like a figure in a picture, with her pale face the colour of ashes, and the big pattern of the Spanish lace hanging half over it, and her hand held up, with the big diamond blazing at me from the inside of her uplifted palm. It was held up in surprise, but it looked as if it were raised in malediction; and the diamond threw out darts of light and glared and twinkled at me. If it had been in its right place it would not have mattered; but there, in the open of the hand! I started up, half in terror, half in wrath. And then the old lady laughed, and her hand dropped. 'I've wakened you to life, and broke the spell,' she said, nodding her old head at me, while the large black silk flowers of the lace waved and threatened. And she took my arm to go downstairs, laughing and bidding me be steady, and no' tremble and shake like a broken reed. 'You should be as steady as a rock at your age. I was like a young tree,' she said, leaning so heavily that my willowy girlish frame quivered – 'I was a support to virtue, like Pamela, in my time.'

'Aunt Mary, Lady Carnbee is a witch!' I cried, when I came back.

'Is that what you think, honey? well: maybe she

once was,' said Aunt Mary, whom nothing surprised.

And it was that night once more after dinner, and after the post came in, and *The Times*, that I suddenly saw the Library window again. I had seen it every day and noticed nothing; but tonight, still in a little tumult of mind over Lady Carnbee and her wicked diamond which wished me harm, and her lace which waved threats and warnings at me, I looked across the street, and there I saw quite plainly the room opposite, far more clear than before. I saw dimly that it must be a large room, and that the big piece of furniture against the wall was a writing-desk. That in a moment, when first my eyes rested upon it, was quite clear: a large old-fashioned escritoire, standing out into the room; and I knew by the shape of it that it had a great many pigeon-holes and little drawers in the back, and a large table for writing. There was one just like it in my father's library at home. It was such a surprise to see it all so clearly that I closed my eyes, for the moment almost giddy, wondering how papa's desk could have come here – and then when I reminded myself that this was nonsense, and that there were many such writing-tables besides papa's, and looked again – lo! it had all become quite vague and indistinct as it was at first; and I saw nothing but the blank window, of which the old ladies could never be certain whether it was filled up to avoid the window-tax, or whether it had ever been a window at all.

This occupied my mind very much, and yet I did not say anything to Aunt Mary. For one thing, I rarely saw anything at all in the early part of the day; but then that is natural: you can never see into a place from outside, whether it is an empty room or a looking-glass, or people's eyes, or anything else that is mysterious, in the day. It has, I suppose, something to do with the light. But in the evening in June in Scotland – then is the time to see. For it is daylight, yet it is not day, and there is a quality in it which I cannot describe, it is so clear, as if every object was a reflection of itself.

I used to see more and more of the room as the days went on. The large escritoire stood out more and more into the space, with sometimes white glimmering things, which looked like papers, lying on it; and once or twice I was sure I saw a pile of books on the floor close to the writing-table, as if they had gilding upon them in broken specks, like old books. It was always about the time when the lads in the street began to call to each other that they were going home, and sometimes a shriller voice would come from one of the doors, bidding somebody to 'cry upon the laddies' to come back to their suppers. That was always the time I saw best, though it was close upon the moment when the veil seemed to fall and the clear radiance became less living, and all the sounds died out of the street, and Aunt Mary said in her soft voice, 'Honey! will you ring for the lamp?' She said honey as people say darling, and I think it is a prettier word.

Then finally, while I sat one evening with my book in my hand, looking straight across the street, not distracted by anything, I saw a little movement within. It was not anyone visible – but everybody must know what it is to see the stir in the air, the little disturbance – you cannot tell what it is, but that it indicates someone there, even though you can see no one. Perhaps it is a shadow making just one flicker in the still place. You may look at an empty room and the furniture in it for hours, and then suddenly there will be the flicker, and you know that something has come into it. It might only be a dog or a cat; it might be, if that were possible, a bird flying across; but it is someone, something living, which is so different, so completely different, in a moment from the things that are not living. It seemed to strike quite through me, and I gave a little cry. Then Aunt Mary stirred a little, and put down the huge newspaper that almost covered her from sight, and said, 'What is it, honey?' I cried, 'Nothing,' with a little gasp, quickly, for I did not want to be disturbed just at this moment when somebody was coming! But I suppose she was not satisfied, for she got up and stood behind to see what it was, putting her hand on my shoulder. It was the softest touch in the world, but I could have flung it off angrily: for that moment everything was still again, and the place grew grey and I saw no more.

'Nothing,' I repeated, but I was so vexed I could have cried. 'I told you it was nothing, Aunt Mary. Don't you believe me, that you come to look – and spoil it all!'

I did not mean of course to say these last words; they were forced out of me. I was so much annoyed to see it all melt away like a dream: for it was no dream, but as real as – as real as – myself or anything I ever saw.

She gave my shoulder a little pat with her hand. 'Honey,' she said, 'were you looking at something? Is't that? is't that?' 'Is it what?' I wanted to say, shaking off her hand, but something in me stopped me: for I said nothing at all, and she went quietly back to her place. I suppose she must have rung the bell herself, for immediately I felt the soft flood of the light behind me, and the evening outside dimmed down, as it did every night, and I saw nothing more.

It was next day, I think, in the afternoon that I spoke. It was brought on by something she said about her fine work. 'I get a mist before my eyes,' she said; 'you will have to learn my old lace stitches, honey – for I soon will not see to draw the threads.'

'Oh, I hope you will keep your sight,' I cried, without thinking what I was saying. I was then young and very matter-of-fact. I had not found out that one may mean something, yet not half or a hundredth part of what one seems to mean: and even then probably hoping to be contradicted if it is anyhow against oneself.

'My sight!' she said, looking up at me with a look that was almost angry; 'there is no question of losing my sight – on the contrary, my eyes are very strong. I may not see to draw fine threads, but I see at a distance as well as ever I did – as well as you do.'

'I did not mean any harm, Aunt Mary,' I said. 'I thought you said . . . But how can your sight be as good as ever when you are in doubt about that window? I can see into the room as clear as – ' My voice wavered, for I had just looked up and across the street, and I could have sworn that there was no window at all, but only a false image of one painted on the wall.

'Ah!' she said, with a little tone of keenness and of surprise; and she half rose up, throwing down her work hastily, as if she meant to come to me: then, perhaps seeing the bewildered look on my face, she paused and hesitated – 'Ay, honey!' she said, 'have you got so far ben as that?'

What did she mean? Of course I knew all the old

Scotch phrases as well as I knew myself; but it is a comfort to take refuge in a little ignorance, and I know I pretended not to understand whenever I was put out. 'I don't know what you mean by "far ben",' I cried out, very impatient. I don't know what might have followed, but someone just then came to call, and she could only give me a look before she went forward, putting out her hand to her visitor. It was a very soft look, but anxious, and as if she did not know what to do: and she shook her head a very little, and I thought, though there was a smile on her face, there was something wet about her eyes. I retired into my recess, and nothing more was said.

But it was very tantalising that it should fluctuate so; for sometimes I saw that room quite plain and clear – quite as clear as I could see papa's library, for example, when I shut my eyes. I compared it naturally to my father's study, because of the shape of the writing-table, which, as I tell you, was the same as his. At times I saw the papers on the table quite plain, just as I had seen his papers many a day. And the little pile of books on the floor at the foot – not ranged regularly in order, but put down one above the other, with all their angles going different ways, and a speck of the old gilding shining here and there. And then again at other times I saw nothing, absolutely nothing, and was no better than the old ladies who had peered over my head, drawing their eyelids together, and arguing that the window had been shut up because of the old long-abolished window-tax, or else that it had never been a window at all. It annoyed me very much at those dull moments to feel that I too puckered up my eyelids and saw no better than they.

Aunt Mary's old ladies came and went day after

day while June went on. I was to go back in July, and I felt that I should be very unwilling indeed to leave until I had quite cleared up – as I was indeed in the way of doing – the mystery of that window which changed so strangely and appeared quite a different thing, not only to different people, but to the same eyes at different times. Of course I said to myself it must simply be an effect of the light. And yet I did not quite like that explanation either, but would have been better pleased to make out to myself that it was some superiority in me which made it so clear to me, if it were only the great superiority of young eyes over old – though that was not quite enough to satisfy me, seeing it was a superiority which I shared with every little lass and lad in the street. I rather wanted, I believe, to think that there was some particular insight in me which gave clearness to my sight – which was a most impertinent assumption, but really did not mean half the harm it seems to mean when it is put down here in black and white. I had several times again, however, seen the room quite plain, and made out that it was a large room, with a great picture in a dim gilded frame hanging on the farther wall, and many other pieces of solid furniture making a blackness here and there, besides the great escritoire against the wall, which had evidently been placed near the window for the sake of the light. One thing became visible to me after another, till I almost thought I should end by being able to read the old lettering on one of the big volumes which projected from the others and caught the light; but this was all preliminary to the great event which happened about Midsummer Day – the day of St John, which was once so much thought of as a festival, but now means nothing at all in Scotland any more than any other of the saints' days: which I shall always think a great pity and loss to Scotland, whatever Aunt Mary may say.

3

It was about midsummer, I cannot say exactly to a day when, but near that time, when the great event happened. I had grown very well acquainted by this time with that large dim room. Not only the escritoire, which was very plain to me now, with the papers upon it, and the books at its foot, but the great picture that hung against the farther wall, and various other shadowy pieces of furniture, especially a chair which one evening I saw had been moved into the space before the escritoire – a little change which made my heart beat, for it spoke so distinctly of someone who must have been there, the someone who had already made me start, two or three times before, by some vague shadow of him or thrill of him which made a sort of movement in the silent space: a movement which made me sure that next minute I must see something or hear something which would explain the whole – if it were not that something always happened outside to stop it, at the very moment of its accomplishment. I had no warning this time of movement or shadow. I had been looking into the room very attentively a little while before, and had made out everything almost clearer than ever; and then had bent my attention again on my book, and read a chapter or two at a most exciting period of the story: and consequently had quite left St Rule's, and the High Street, and the College Library, and was really in a South American forest, almost throttled by the flowery creepers, and treading softly lest I should put my foot on a scorpion or a dangerous snake. At this moment something suddenly calling my attention to the outside, I looked across, and then, with a start, sprang up, for I could not contain myself. I don't know what I said, but enough to startle the people in the room, one of whom was old Mr Pitmilly. They all looked round upon me to ask what was the matter. And when I gave my usual answer of, 'Nothing,' sitting down again shamefaced but very much excited, Mr Pitmilly got up and came forward, and looked out, apparently to see what was the cause. He saw nothing, for he went back again, and I could hear him telling Aunt Mary not to be alarmed, for Missy had fallen into a doze with the heat, and had startled herself waking up, at which they all laughed; another time I could have killed him for his impertinence, but my mind was too much taken up now to pay any attention. My head was throbbing and my heart beating. I was in such high excitement, however, that to restrain myself completely, to be perfectly silent, was more easy to me then than at any other time of my life. I waited until the old gentleman had taken his seat again, and then I looked back. Yes, there he was! I had not been deceived. I knew then, when I looked across, that this was what I had been looking for all the time – that I had known he was there, and had been waiting for him, every time there was that flicker of movement in the room – him and no one else. And there at last, just as I had expected, he was. I don't know that in reality I ever had expected him, or anyone: but this was what I felt when, suddenly looking into that curious dim room, I saw him there.

He was sitting in the chair, which he must have placed for himself, or which someone else in the dead of night when nobody was looking must have set for him, in front of the escritoire – with the back of his head towards me, writing. The light fell upon him from the left hand, and therefore upon his shoulders and the side of his head, which, however, was too much turned away to show anything of his face. Oh, how strange that there should be someone staring at him as I was doing, and he never to turn his head, to make a movement! If anyone stood and looked at me, were I in the soundest sleep that ever was, I would wake, I would jump up, I would feel it through everything. But there he sat and never moved. You are not to suppose, though I said the light fell upon him from the left hand, that there was very much light. There never is in a room you are looking into like that across the street; but there was enough to see him by – the outline of his figure dark and solid, seated in the chair, and the fairness of his head visible faintly, a clear spot against the dimness. I saw this outline against the dim gilding of the frame of the large picture which hung on the farther wall.

I sat all the time the visitors were there, in a sort of rapture, gazing at this figure. I knew no reason why I should be so much moved. In an ordinary way, to see a student at an opposite window quietly doing his work might have interested me a little, but certainly it would not have moved me in any such way. It is always interesting to have a glimpse like this of an unknown life – to see so much and yet know so little, and to wonder, perhaps, what the man is doing, and why he never turns his head. One would go to the window – but not too close, lest he should see you and think you were spying upon him – and one would ask, Is he still there? is he writing, writing always? I wonder what he is writing! And it would be a great amusement: but no more. This was not my feeling at all in the present case. It was a sort of breathless watch, an absorption. I did not feel that I had eyes for anything else, or any room in my mind for another thought. I no longer heard, as I generally did, the stories and the wise remarks (or foolish) of Aunt Mary's old ladies or Mr Pitmilly. I heard only a murmur behind me, the interchange of voices, one softer, one sharper; but it was not as in the time when I sat reading and heard every word, till the story in my book and the stories they were telling (what they said almost always shaped into stories) were all mingled into each other, and the hero in the novel became somehow the hero (or more likely heroine) of them all. But I took no notice of what they were saying now. And it was not that there was anything very interesting to look at, except the fact that he was there. He did nothing to keep up the absorption of my thoughts. He moved just so much as a man will do when he is very busily writing, thinking of nothing else. There was a faint turn of his head as he went from one side to another of the page he was writing; but it appeared to be a long long page which never wanted turning. Just a little inclination when he was at the end of the line, outward, and then a little inclination inward when he began the next. That was little enough to keep one gazing. But I suppose it was the gradual course of events leading up to this, the finding out of one thing after another as the eyes got accustomed to the vague light: first the room itself, and then the writing-table, and then the other furniture, and last of all the human inhabitant who gave it all meaning. This was all so interesting that it was like a country which one had discovered. And then the extraordinary blindness of the other people who disputed among themselves whether it was a window at all! I did not, I am sure, wish to be disrespectful, and I was very fond of my Aunt Mary, and I liked Mr Pitmilly well enough, and I was afraid of Lady Carnbee. But yet to think of the – I know I ought not to say stupidity – the blindness of them, the foolishness, the insensibility! discussing it as if a thing that your eyes could see was a thing to discuss! It would have been unkind to think it was because they were old and their faculties dimmed. It is so sad to think that the faculties grow dim, that such a woman as my Aunt Mary should fail in seeing, or hearing, or feeling, that I would not have dwelt on it for a moment, it would have seemed so cruel! And then such a clever old lady as Lady Carnbee, who could see through a millstone, people said – and Mr Pitmilly, such an old man of the world. It did indeed bring tears to my eyes to think that all those clever people, solely by reason of being no longer young as I was, should have the simplest things shut out from them; and for all their wisdom and their knowledge be unable to see what a girl like me could see so easily. I was too much grieved for them to dwell upon that thought, and half ashamed, though perhaps half proud too, to be so much better off than they.

All those thoughts flitted through my mind as I sat and gazed across the street. And I felt there was so much going on in that room across the street! He was so absorbed in his writing, never looked up, never paused for a word, never turned round in his chair, or got up and walked about the room as my father did. Papa is a great writer, everybody says: but he would have come to the window and looked out, he would have drummed with his fingers on the pane, he would have watched a fly and helped it over a difficulty, and played with the fringe of the curtain, and done a dozen other nice, pleasant, foolish things, till the next sentence took shape. 'My dear, I am waiting for a word,' he would say to my mother when she looked at him, with a question why he was so idle, in her eyes; and then he would laugh, and go back again to his writing-table. But he over there never stopped at all. It was like a fascination. I could not take my eyes from him and that little scarcely perceptible movement he made, turning his head. I trembled with impatience to see him turn the page, or perhaps throw down his finished sheet on the floor, as somebody looking into a window like me once saw Sir Walter do, sheet after sheet. I should have cried out if this Unknown had done that. I should not have been able to help myself, whoever had been present; and gradually I got into such a state of suspense waiting for it to be done that my head grew hot and my hands cold. And then, just when there was a little movement of his elbow, as if he were about to do this, to be called away by Aunt Mary to see Lady Carnbee to the door! I believe I did not hear her till she had called me three times, and then I stumbled up, all flushed and hot and nearly crying. When I came out from the recess to give the old lady my arm (Mr Pitmilly had gone away some time before), she put up her hand and stroked my cheek. 'What ails the bairn?' she said; 'she's fevered.

You must not let her sit her lane in the window, Mary Balcarres. You and me know what comes of that.' Her old fingers had a strange touch, cold like something not living, and I felt that dreadful diamond sting me on the cheek.

I do not say that this was not just a part of my excitement and suspense; and I know it is enough to make anyone laugh when the excitement was all about an unknown man writing in a room on the other side of the way, and my impatience because he never came to an end of the page. If you think I was not quite as well aware of this as anyone could be! but the worst was that this dreadful old lady felt my heart beating against her arm that was within mine. 'You are just in a dream,' she said to me, with her old voice close at my ear as we went downstairs. 'I don't know who it is about, but it's bound to be some man that is not worth it. If you were wise you would think of him no more.'

'I am thinking of no man!' I said, half crying. 'It is very unkind and dreadful of you to say so, Lady Carnbee. I never thought of – any man, in all my life!' I cried in a passion of indignation. The old lady clung tighter to my arm, and pressed it to her, not unkindly.

'Poor little bird,' she said, 'how it's strugglin' and flutterin'! I'm not saying but what it's more dangerous when it's all for a dream.'

She was not at all unkind; but I was very angry and excited, and would scarcely shake that old pale hand which she put out to me from her carriage window when I had helped her in. I was angry with her, and I was afraid of the diamond, which looked up from under her finger as if it saw through and through me; and whether you believe me or not, I am certain that it stung me again – a sharp malignant prick, oh full of meaning! She never wore gloves, but only black lace mittens, through which that horrible diamond gleamed.

I ran upstairs – she had been the last to go and Aunt Mary too had gone to get ready for dinner, for it was late. I hurried to my place, and looked across, with my heart beating more than ever. I made quite sure I should see the finished sheet lying white upon the floor. But what I gazed at was only the dim blank of that window which they said was no window. The light had changed in some wonderful way during that five minutes I had been gone, and there was nothing, nothing, not a reflection, not a glimmer. It looked exactly as they all said, the blank form of a window painted on the wall. It was too much; I sat down in my excitement and cried as if my heart would break. I felt that they had done something to it, that it was not natural, that I could not bear their unkindness – even Aunt Mary. They thought it not good for me! not good for me! and they had done something – even Aunt Mary herself – and that wicked diamond that hid itself in Lady Carnbee's hand. Of course I knew all this was ridiculous as well as you could tell me; but I was exasperated by the disappointment and the sudden stop to all my excited feelings, and I could not bear it. It was more strong than I.

I was late for dinner, and naturally there were some traces in my eyes that I had been crying when I came into the full light in the dining-room, where Aunt Mary could look at me at her pleasure, and I could not run away. She said, 'Honey, you have been shedding tears. I'm loth, loth that a bairn of your mother's should be made to shed tears in my house.'

'I have not been made to shed tears,' cried I; and then, to save myself another fit of crying, I burst out laughing and said, 'I am afraid of that dreadful diamond on old Lady Carnbee's hand. It bites – I am sure it bites! Aunt Mary, look here.'

'You foolish lassie,' Aunt Mary said; but she looked at my cheek under the light of the lamp, and then she gave it a little pat with her soft hand. 'Go away with you, you silly bairn. There is no bite; but a flushed cheek, my honey, and a wet eye. You must just read out my paper to me after dinner when the post is in: and we'll have no more thinking and no more dreaming for tonight.'

'Yes, Aunt Mary,' said I. But I knew what would happen; for when she opens up her *Times*, all full of the news of the world, and the speeches and things which she takes an interest in, though I cannot tell why – she forgets. And as I kept very quiet and made not a sound, she forgot tonight what she had said, and the curtain hung a little more over me than usual, and I sat down in my recess as if I had been a hundred miles away. And my heart gave a great jump, as if it would have come out of my breast; for he was there. But not as he had been earlier – I suppose the light, perhaps, was not good enough to go on with his work without a lamp or candles – for he had turned away from the table and was fronting the window, sitting leaning back in his chair, and turning his head to me. Not to me – he knew nothing about me. I thought he was not looking at anything; but with his face turned my way. My heart was in my mouth: it was so unexpected, so strange! though why it should have seemed strange I know not, for there was no communication between him and me that it should have moved me; and what could be more natural than that a man, wearied of his work, and feeling the want perhaps of more light, and yet that it was not dark enough to light a lamp, should turn round in his own chair, and rest a little, and think – perhaps of nothing at all? Papa always says he is thinking of nothing at all. He says things blow through his mind as if the doors were open, and he has no responsibility. What sort of things were blowing through this man's mind? or was he thinking, still thinking, of what he had been writing and going on with it still? The thing that troubled me most was that I could not make out his face. It is very difficult to do so when you see a person only through two windows, your own and his. I wanted very much to recognise him afterwards if I should chance to meet him in the street. If he had only stood up and moved about the room, I should have made out the rest of his figure, and then I should have known him again; or if he had only come to the window (as papa always did), then I should have seen his face clearly enough to have recognised him. But, to be sure, he did not see any need to do anything in order that I might recognise him, for he did not know I existed; and probably if he had known I was watching him, he would have been annoyed and gone away.

But he was as immovable there facing the window as he had been seated at the desk. Sometimes he made a little faint stir with a hand or a foot, and I held my breath, hoping he was about to rise from his chair – but he never did it. And with all the efforts I made I could not be sure of his face. I puckered my eyelids together as old Miss Jeanie did who was short-sighted, and I put my hands on each side of my face to concentrate the light on him: but it was all in vain. Either the face changed as I sat staring, or else it was the light that was not good enough, or I don't know what it was. His hair seemed to me light – certainly there was no dark line about his head, as there would have been had it been very dark – and I saw, where it came across the old gilt frame on the wall behind, that it must be fair: and I am almost sure he had no beard. Indeed I am sure that he had no beard, for the outline of his face was distinct enough; and the daylight was still quite clear out of doors, so that I recognised perfectly a baker's boy who was on the pavement opposite, and whom I should have known again whenever I had met him: as if it was of the least importance to recognise a baker's boy! There was one thing, however, rather curious about this boy. He had been throwing stones at something or somebody. In St Rule's they have a great way of throwing stones at each other, and I suppose there had been a battle. I suppose also that he had one stone in his hand left over from the battle, and his roving eye took in all the incidents of the street to judge where he could throw it with most effect and mischief. But apparently he found nothing worthy of it in the street, for he suddenly turned round with a flick under his leg to show his cleverness, and aimed it straight at the window. I remarked without remarking that it struck with a hard sound and without any breaking of glass, and fell straight down on the pavement. But I took no notice of this even in my mind, so intently was I watching the figure within, which moved not nor took the slightest notice, and remained just as dimly clear, as perfectly seen, yet as indistinguishable, as before. And then the light began to fail a little, not diminishing the prospect within, but making it still less distinct than it had been.

Then I jumped up, feeling Aunt Mary's hand upon my shoulder. 'Honey,' she said, 'I asked you twice to ring the bell; but you did not hear me.'

'Oh, Aunt Mary!' I cried in great penitence, but turning again to the window in spite of myself.

'You must come away from there; you must come away from there,' she said, almost as if she were angry; and then her soft voice grew softer, and she gave me a kiss: 'never mind about the lamp, honey; I have rung myself, and it is coming; but, silly bairn, you must not aye be dreaming – your little head will turn.'

All the answer I made, for I could scarcely speak, was to give a little wave with my hand to the window on the other side of the street.

She stood there patting me softly on the shoulder for a whole minute or more, murmuring something that sounded like, 'She must go away, she must go away.' Then she said, always with her hand soft on my shoulder, 'Like a dream when one awaketh.' And when I looked again, I saw the blank of an opaque surface and nothing more.

Aunt Mary asked me no more questions. She made me come into the room and sit in the light and read something to her. But I did not know what I was reading, for there suddenly came into my mind and took possession of it, the thud of the stone upon the window, and its descent straight down, as if from some hard substance that threw it off: though I had myself seen it strike upon the glass of the panes across the way.

4

I am afraid I continued in a state of great exaltation and commotion of mind for some time. I used to hurry through the day till the evening came, when I could watch my neighbour through the window opposite. I did not talk much to anyone, and I never said a word about my own questions and wonderings. I wondered who he was, what he was doing, and why he never came till the evening (or very rarely); and I also wondered much to what house the room belonged in which he sat. It seemed to form a portion of the old College Library, as I have often said. The window was one of the line of windows which I understood lighted the large hall; but whether this room belonged to the Library itself, or how its occupant gained access to it, I could not tell. I made up my mind that it must open out of the hall, and that the gentleman must be the Librarian or one of his assistants, perhaps kept busy all the day in his official duties, and only able to get to his desk and do his own private work in the evening. One has heard of so many things like that – a man who had to take up some other kind of work for his living, and then when his leisure-time came, gave it all up to something he really loved – some study or some book he was writing. My father himself at one time had been like that. He had been in the Treasury all day, and then in the evening wrote his books, which made him famous. His daughter, however little she might know of other things, could not but know that! But it discouraged me very much when somebody pointed out to me one day in the street an old gentleman who wore a wig and took a great deal of snuff, and said, 'That's the Librarian of the old College.' It gave me a great shock for a moment; but then I remembered that an old gentleman has generally assistants, and that it must be one of them.

Gradually I became quite sure of this. There was another small window above, which twinkled very much when the sun shone, and looked a very kindly bright little window, above that dullness of the other which hid so much. I made up my mind this was the window of his other room, and that these two chambers at the end of the beautiful hall were really beautiful for him to live in, so near all the books, and so retired and quiet that nobody knew of them. What a fine thing for him! and you could see what use he made of his good fortune as he sat there, so constant at his writing for hours together. Was it a book he was writing, or could it be perhaps poems? This was a thought which made my heart beat; but I concluded with much regret that it could not be poems, because no one could possibly write poems like that, straight off, without pausing for a word or a rhyme. Had they been poems he must have risen up, he must have paced about the room or come to the window as papa did – not that papa wrote poems: he always said, 'I am not worthy even to speak of such prevailing mysteries,' shaking his head – which gave me a wonderful admiration and almost awe of a poet, who was thus much greater even than papa. But I could not believe that a poet could have kept still for hours and hours like that. What could it be then? perhaps it was history; that is a great thing to work at, but you would not perhaps need to move nor to stride up and down, or look out upon the sky and the wonderful light.

He did move now and then, however, though he never came to the window. Sometimes, as I have said, he would turn round in his chair and turn his face towards it, and sit there for a long time musing when the light had begun to fail, and the world was full of that strange day which was night, that light without colour, in which everything was so clearly visible, and there were no shadows. 'It was between the night and the day, when the fairy folk have power.' This was the after-light of the wonderful, long, long summer evening, the light without shadows. It had a spell in it, and sometimes it made me afraid; and all manner of strange thoughts seemed to come in, and I always felt that if only we had a little more vision in our eyes we might see beautiful folk walking about in it, who were not of our world. I thought most likely he saw them, from the way he sat there looking out: and this made my heart expand with the most curious sensation, as if of pride that, though I could not see, he did, and did not even require to come to the window, as I did, sitting close in the depth of the recess, with my eyes upon him, and almost seeing things through his eyes.

I was so much absorbed in these thoughts and in watching him every evening – for now he never missed an evening, but was always there – that people began to remark that I was looking pale and that I could not be well, for I paid no attention when they talked to me, and did not care to go out, nor to join the other girls for their tennis, nor to do anything that others did; and some said to Aunt Mary that I was quickly losing all the ground I had gained, and that she could never send me back to my mother with a white face like that. Aunt Mary had begun to look at me anxiously for some time before that, and, I am sure, held secret consultations over me, sometimes with the doctor, and sometimes with her old ladies, who thought they knew more about young girls than even the doctors. And I could hear them saying to her that I wanted diversion, that I must be diverted, and that she must take me out more, and give a party, and that when the summer visitors began to come there would perhaps be a ball or two, or Lady Carnbee would get up a picnic. 'And there's my young lord coming home,' said the old lady whom they called Miss Jeanie, 'and I never knew the young lassie yet that would not cock up her bonnet at the sight of a young lord.'

But Aunt Mary shook her head. 'I would not lippen much to the young lord,' she said. 'His mother is sore set upon siller for him; and my poor bit honey has no fortune to speak of. No, we must not fly so high as the young lord; but I will gladly take her about the country to see the old castles and towers. It will perhaps rouse her up a little.'

'And if that does not answer we must think of something else,' the old lady said.

I heard them perhaps that day because they were talking of me, which is always so effective a way of making you hear – for latterly I had not been paying any attention to what they were saying; and I thought to myself how little they knew, and how little I cared about even the old castles and curious houses, having something else in my mind. But just about that time Mr Pitmilly came in, who was always a friend to me, and, when he heard them talking, he managed to stop them and turn the conversation into another channel. And after a while, when the ladies were gone away, he came up to my recess, and gave a glance right over my head. And then he asked my Aunt Mary if ever she had settled her question about the window opposite, 'that you thought was a window sometimes, and then not a window, and many curious things', the old gentleman said.

My Aunt Mary gave me another very wistful look; and then she said, 'Indeed, Mr Pitmilly, we are just where we were, and I am quite as unsettled as ever; and I think my niece has taken up my views, for I see her many a time looking across and wondering, and I am not clear now what her opinion is.'

'My opinion, Aunt Mary!' I said. I could not help being a little scornful, as one is when one is very young. 'I have no opinion. There is not only a window but there is a room, and I could show you – ' I was going to say, 'show you the gentleman who sits and writes in it', but I stopped, not knowing what they might say, and looked from one to another. 'I could tell you – all the furniture that is in it,' I said. And then I felt something like a flame that went over my face, and that all at once my cheeks were burning. I thought they gave a little glance at each other, but that may have been folly. 'There is a great picture, in a big dim frame,' I said, feeling a little breathless, 'on the wall opposite the window.'

'Is there so?' said Mr Pitmilly, with a little laugh. And he said, 'Now I will tell you what we'll do. You know that there is a conversation party, or whatever they call it, in the big room tonight, and it will be all open and lighted up. And it is a handsome room, and two-three things well worth looking at. I will just step along after we have all got our dinner, and take you over to the pairty, madam – missy and you – '

'Dear me!' said Aunt Mary. 'I have not gone to a pairty for more years than I would like to say – and never once to the Library Hall.' Then she gave a little shiver, and said quite low, 'I could not go there.'

'Then you will just begin again tonight, madam,' said Mr Pitmilly, taking no notice of this, 'and a proud man will I be leading in Mistress Balcarres that was once the pride of the ball!'

'Ah, once!' said Aunt Mary, with a low little laugh and then a sigh. 'And we'll not say how long ago'; and after that she made a pause, looking always at me; and then she said, 'I accept your offer, and we'll put on our braws; and I hope you will have no occasion to think shame of us. But why not take your dinner here?'

That was how it was settled, and the old gentleman went away to dress, looking quite pleased. But I came to Aunt Mary as soon as he was gone, and besought her not to make me go. 'I like the long bonnie night and the light that lasts so long. And I cannot bear to dress up and go out, wasting it all in a stupid party. I hate parties, Aunt Mary!' I cried, 'and I would far rather stay here.'

'My honey,' she said, taking both my hands, 'I know it will maybe be a blow to you, but it's better so.'

'How could it be a blow to me?' I cried; 'but I would far rather not go.'

'You'll just go with me, honey, just this once: it is not often I go out. You will go with me this one night, just this one night, my honey sweet.'

I am sure there were tears in Aunt Mary's eyes, and she kissed me between the words. There was nothing more that I could say; but how I grudged the evening!

A mere party, a conversazione (when all the College was away, too, and nobody to make conversation!), instead of my enchanted hour at my window and the soft strange light, and the dim face looking out, which kept me wondering and wondering what was he thinking of, what was he looking for, who was he? all one wonder and mystery and question, through the long, long, slowly fading night!

It occurred to me, however, when I was dressing – though I was so sure that he would prefer his solitude to everything – that he might perhaps, it was just possible, be there. And when I thought of that, I took out my white frock though Janet had laid out my blue one – and my little pearl necklace which I had thought was too good to wear. They were not very large pearls, but they were real pearls, and very even and lustrous though they were small; and though I did not think much of my appearance then, there must have been something about me – pale as I was but apt to colour in a moment, with my dress so white, and my pearls so white, and my hair all shadowy perhaps, that was pleasant to look at: for even old Mr Pitmilly had a strange look in his eyes, as if he was not only pleased but sorry too, perhaps thinking me a creature that would have troubles in this life, though I was so young and knew them not. And when Aunt Mary looked at me, there was a little quiver about her mouth. She herself had on her pretty lace and her white hair very nicely done, and looking her best. As for Mr Pitmilly, he had a beautiful fine French cambric frill to his shirt, pleated in the most minute pleats, and with a diamond pin in it which sparkled as much as Lady Carnbee's ring; but this was a fine frank kindly stone, that looked you straight in the face and sparkled, with the light dancing in it as if it were pleased to see you and to be shining on that old gentleman's honest and faithful breast: for he had been one of Aunt Mary's lovers in their early days, and still thought there was nobody like her in the world.

I had got into quite a happy commotion of mind by the time we set out across the street in the soft light of the evening to the Library Hall. Perhaps, after all, I should see him, and see the room which I was so well acquainted with, and find out why he sat there so constantly and never was seen abroad. I thought I might even hear what he was working at, which would be such a pleasant thing to tell papa when I went home. A friend of mine at St Rule's – oh, far, far more busy than you ever were, papa! – and then my father would laugh as he always did, and say he was but an idler and never busy at all.

The room was all light and bright, flowers wherever flowers could be, and the long lines of the books that went along the walls on each side, lighting up, wherever there was a line of gilding or an ornament, with a little response. It dazzled me at first all that light: but I was very eager, though I kept very quiet, looking round to see if perhaps in any corner, in the middle of any group, he would be there. I did not expect to see him among the ladies. He would not be with them – he was too studious, too silent; but, perhaps among that circle of grey heads at the upper end of the room – perhaps –

No: I am not sure that it was not half a pleasure to me to make quite sure that there was not one whom I could take for him, who was at all like my vague image of him. No: it was absurd to think that he would be here, amid all that sound of voices, under the glare of that light. I felt a little proud to think that he was in his room as usual, doing his work, or thinking so deeply over it, as when he turned round in his chair with his face to the light.

I was thus getting a little composed and quiet in my mind, for now that the expectation of seeing him was over, though it was a disappointment, it was a satisfaction too – when Mr Pitmilly came up to me, holding out his arm. 'Now,' he said, 'I am going to take you to see the curiosities.' I thought to myself that after I had seen them and spoken to everybody I knew, Aunt Mary would let me go home, so I went very willingly, though I did not care for the curiosities. Something, however, struck me strangely as we walked up the room. It was the air, rather fresh and strong, from an open window at the east end of the hall. How should there be a window there? I hardly saw what it meant for the first moment, but it blew in my face as if there was some meaning in it, and I felt very uneasy without seeing why.

Then there was another thing that startled me. On that side of the wall which was to the street there seemed no windows at all. A long line of bookcases filled it from end to end. I could not see what that meant either, but it confused me. I was altogether confused. I felt as if I was in a strange country, not knowing where I was going, not knowing what I might find out next. If there were no windows on the wall to the street, where was my window? My heart, which had been jumping up and calming down again all this time, gave a great leap at this, as if it would have come out of me – but I did not know what it could mean.

Then we stopped before a glass case, and Mr Pitmilly showed me some things in it. I could not pay much attention to them. My head was going round and round. I heard his voice going on, and then myself speaking with a queer sound that was hollow in my ears; but I did not know what I was saying or what he was saying. Then he took me to the very end of the room, the east end, saying something that I caught – that I was pale, that the air would do me good. The air was blowing full on me, lifting the lace of my dress, lifting my hair, almost chilly. The window opened into the pale daylight, into the little lane that ran by the end of the building. Mr Pitmilly went on talking, but I could not make out a word he said. Then I heard my own voice, speaking through it, though I did not seem to be aware that I was speaking. 'Where is my window? – where, then, is my window?' I seemed to be saying, and I turned right round, dragging him with me, still holding his arm. As I did this my eye fell upon something at last which I knew. It was a large picture in a broad frame, hanging against the farther wall.

What did it mean? Oh, what did it mean? I turned round again to the open window at the east end, and to the daylight, the strange light without any shadow, that was all round about this lighted hall, holding it like a bubble that would burst, like something that was not real. The real place was the room I knew, in which that picture was hanging, where the writing-table was, and where he sat with his face to the light. But where was the light and the window through which it came? I think my senses must have left me. I went up to the picture which I knew, and then I walked straight across the room, always dragging Mr Pitmilly, whose face was pale, but who did not struggle but allowed me to lead him, straight across to where the window was – where the window was not; – where there was no sign of it. 'Where is my window? – where is my window?' I said. And all the time I was sure that I was in a dream, and these lights were all some theatrical illusion, and the people talking; and nothing real but the pale, pale, watching, lingering day standing by to wait until that foolish bubble should burst.

'My dear,' said Mr Pitmilly, 'my dear! Mind that you are in public. Mind where you are. You must not make an outcry and frighten your Aunt Mary. Come away with me. Come away, my dear young lady! and you'll take a seat for a minute or two and compose yourself; and I'll get you an ice or a little wine.' He kept patting my hand, which was on his arm, and looking at me very anxiously. 'Bless me! bless me! I never thought it would have this effect,' he said.

But I would not allow him to take me away in that direction. I went to the picture again and looked at it without seeing it; and then I went across the room again, with some kind of wild thought that if I insisted I should find it. 'My window – my window!' I said.

There was one of the professors standing there, and he heard me. 'The window!' said he. 'Ah, you've been taken in with what appears outside. It was put there to be in uniformity with the window on the stair. But it never was a real window. It is just behind that bookcase. Many people are taken in by it,' he said.

His voice seemed to sound from somewhere far away, and as if it would go on for ever; and the hall swam in a dazzle of shining and of noises round me; and the daylight through the open window grew greyer, waiting till it should be over, and the bubble burst.

5

It was Mr Pitmilly who took me home; or rather it was I who took him, pushing him on a little in front of me, holding fast by his arm, not waiting for Aunt Mary or anyone. We came out into the daylight again outside, I, without even a cloak or a shawl, with my bare arms, and uncovered head, and the pearls round my neck. There was a rush of the people about, and a baker's boy, that baker's boy, stood right in my way and cried, 'Here's a braw ane!' shouting to the others: the words struck me somehow, as his stone had struck the window, without any reason. But I did not mind the people staring, and hurried across the street, with Mr Pitmilly half a step in advance. The door was open, and Janet standing at it, looking out to see what she could see of the ladies in their grand dresses. She gave a shriek when she saw me hurrying across the street; but I brushed past her, and pushed Mr Pitmilly up the stairs, and took him breathless to the recess, where I threw myself down on the seat, feeling as if I could not have gone another step farther, and waved my hand across to the window. 'There! there!' I cried. Ah! there it was – not that senseless mob – not the theatre and the gas, and the people all in a murmur and clang of talking. Never in all these days had I seen that room so clearly. There was a faint tone of light behind, as if it might have been a reflection from some of those vulgar lights in the hall, and he sat against it, calm, wrapped in his thoughts, with his face turned to the window. Nobody but must have seen him. Janet could have seen him had I called her upstairs. It was like a picture, all the things I knew, and the same attitude, and the atmosphere, full of quietness, not disturbed by anything. I pulled Mr Pitmilly's arm before I let him go – 'You see, you see!' I cried. He gave me the most bewildered look, as if he would have liked to cry. He saw nothing! I was sure of that from his eyes. He was an old man, and there was no vision in him. If I had called up Janet, she would have seen it all. 'My dear!' he said. 'My dear!' waving his hands in a helpless way. 'He has been there all these nights,' I cried, 'and I thought you could tell me who he was and what he was doing; and that he might have taken me in to that room, and showed me, that I might tell papa. Papa would understand, he would like to hear. Oh, can't you tell me what work he is doing, Mr Pitmilly? He never lifts his head as long as the light throws a shadow, and then when it is like this he turns round and thinks, and takes a rest!'

Mr Pitmilly was trembling, whether it was with cold or I know not what. He said, with a shake in his voice, 'My dear young lady – my dear – ' and then stopped and looked at me as if he were going to cry. 'It's peetiful, it's peetiful,' he said; and then in another voice, 'I am going across there again to bring your Aunt Mary home; do you understand, my poor little thing, I am going to bring her home – you will be better when she is here.' I was glad when he went away, as he could not see anything: and I sat alone in the dark which was not dark, but quite clear light – a light like nothing I ever saw. How clear it was in that room! not glaring like the gas and the voices, but so quiet, everything so visible, as if it were in another world. I heard a little rustle behind me, and there was Janet, standing staring at me with two big eyes wide open. She was only a little older than I was. I called to her, 'Janet, come here, come here, and you will see him – come here and see him!' impatient that she should be so shy and keep behind. 'Oh, my bonnie young leddy!' she said, and burst out crying. I stamped my foot at her, in my indignation that she would not come, and she fled before me with a rustle and swing of haste, as if she were afraid. None of them, none of them! not even a girl like myself, with the sight in her eyes, would understand. I turned back again, and held out my hands to him sitting there, who was the only one that knew. 'Oh,' I said, 'say something to me! I don't know who you are, or what you are: but you're lonely and so am I; and I only – feel for you. Say something to me!' I neither hoped that he would hear, nor expected any answer. How could he hear, with the street between us, and his window shut, and all the murmuring of the voices and the people standing about? But for one moment it seemed to me that there was only him and me in the whole world.

But I gasped with my breath, that had almost gone from me, when I saw him move in his chair! He had heard me, though I knew not how. He rose up, and I rose too, speechless, incapable of anything but this mechanical movement. He seemed to draw me as if I were a puppet moved by his will. He came forward to the window, and stood looking across at me. I was sure that he looked at me. At last he had seen me: at last he had found out that somebody, though only a girl, was watching him, looking for him, believing in him. I was in such trouble and commotion of mind and trembling that I could not keep on my feet, but dropped kneeling on the window-seat, supporting myself against the window, feeling as if my heart were being drawn out of me. I cannot describe his face. It was all dim, yet there was a light on it: I think it must have been a smile; and as closely as I looked at him he looked at me. His hair was fair, and there was a little quiver about his lips. Then he put his hands upon the window to open it. It was stiff and hard to move; but at last he forced it open with a sound that echoed all along the street. I saw that the people heard it, and several looked up. As for me, I put my hands together, leaning with my face against the glass, drawn to him as if I could have gone out of myself, my heart out of my bosom, my eyes out of my head. He opened the window with a noise that was heard from the West Port to the Abbey. Could anyone doubt that?

And then he leaned forward out of the window, looking out. There was not one in the street but must have seen him. He looked at me first, with a little wave of his hand, as if it were a salutation – yet not exactly that either, for I thought he waved me away; and then he looked up and down in the dim shining of the ending day, first to the east, to the old Abbey towers, and then to the west, along the broad line of the street where so many people were coming and going, but with so little noise, all like enchanted folk in an enchanted place. I watched him with such a melting heart, with such a deep satisfaction as words could not say; for nobody could tell me now that he was not there – nobody could say I was dreaming any more. I watched him as if I could not breathe – my heart in my throat, my eyes upon him. He looked up and down, and then he looked back to me. I was the first, and I was the last, though it was not for long: he did know, he did see, who it was that had recognised him and sympathised with him all the time. I was in a kind of rapture, yet stupor too; my look went with his look, following it as if I were his shadow; and then suddenly he was gone, and I saw him no more.

I dropped back again upon my seat, seeking something to support me, something to lean upon. He had lifted his hand and waved it once again to me. How he went I cannot tell, nor where he went I cannot tell; but in a moment he was away, and the window standing open, and the room fading into stillness and dimness, yet so clear, with all its space, and the great picture in its gilded frame upon the wall. It gave me no pain to see him go away. My heart was so content, and I was so worn out and satisfied – for what doubt or question could there be about him now? As I was lying back as weak as water, Aunt Mary came in behind me, and flew to me with a little rustle as if she had come on wings, and put her arms round me, and drew my head on to her breast. I had begun to cry a little, with sobs like a child. 'You saw him, you saw him!' I said. To lean upon her, and feel her so soft, so kind, gave me a pleasure I cannot describe, and her arms round me, and her voice saying, 'Honey, my honey!' – as if she were nearly crying too. Lying there I came back to myself, quite sweetly, glad of everything. But I wanted some assurance from them that they had seen him too. I waved my hand to the window that was still standing open, and the room that was stealing away into the faint dark. 'This time you saw it all?' I said, getting more eager. 'My honey!' said Aunt Mary, giving me a kiss; and Mr Pitmilly began to walk about the room with short little steps behind, as if he were out of patience. I sat straight up and put away Aunt Mary's arms. 'You cannot be so blind, so blind!' I cried. 'Oh, not tonight, at least not tonight!' But neither the one nor the other made any reply. I shook myself quite free, and raised myself up. And there, in the middle of the street, stood the baker's boy like a statue, staring up at the open window, with his mouth open and his face full of wonder – breathless, as if he could not believe what he saw. I darted forward, calling to him, and beckoned him to come to me. 'Oh, bring him up! bring him, bring him to me!' I cried.

Mr Pitmilly went out directly, and got the boy by the shoulder. He did not want to come. It was strange to see the little old gentleman, with his beautiful frill and his diamond pin, standing out in the street, with his hand upon the boy's shoulder, and the other boys round, all in a little crowd. And presently they came towards the house, the others all following, gaping and wondering. He came in unwilling, almost resisting, looking as if we meant him some harm. 'Come away, my laddie, come and speak to the young lady,' Mr Pitmilly was saying. And Aunt Mary took my hands to keep me back. But I would not be kept back.

'Boy,' I cried, 'you saw it too: you saw it; tell them you saw it! It is that I want, and no more.'

He looked at me as they all did, as if he thought I was mad. 'What's she wantin' wi' me?' he said; and then, 'I did nae harm, even if I did throw a bit stane at it – and it's nae sin to throw a stane.'

'You rascal!' said Mr Pitmilly, giving him a shake; 'have you been throwing stones? You'll kill somebody some of these days with your stones.' The old gentleman was confused and troubled, for he did not understand what I wanted, nor anything that had happened. And then Aunt Mary, holding my hands and drawing me close to her, spoke. 'Laddie,' she said, 'answer the young lady, like a good lad. There's no intention of finding fault with you. Answer her, my man, and then Janet will give ye your supper before you go.'

'Oh speak, speak!' I cried; 'answer them and tell them! you saw that window opened, and the gentleman look out and wave his hand?'

'I saw nae gentleman,' he said, with his head down, 'except this wee gentleman here.'

'Listen, laddie,' said Aunt Mary. 'I saw ye standing in the middle of the street staring. What were ye looking at?'

'It was naething to make a wark about. It was just yon windy yonder in the Library that is nae windy. And it was open as sure's death. You may laugh if you like. Is that a' she's wantin' wi' me?'

'You are telling a pack of lies, laddie,' Mr Pitmilly said.

'I'm tellin' nae lees – it was standin' open just like ony ither windy. It's as sure's death. I couldna believe it mysel'; but it's true.'

'And there it is,' I cried, turning round and pointing it out to them with great triumph in my heart. But the light was all grey, it had faded, it had changed. The window was just as it had always been, a sombre break upon the wall.

I was treated like an invalid all that evening, and taken upstairs to bed, and Aunt Mary sat up in my room the whole night through. Whenever I opened my eyes she was always sitting there close to me, watching. And there never was in all my life so strange a night. When I would talk in my excitement, she kissed me and hushed me like a child. 'Oh, honey, you are not the only one!' she said. 'Oh whisht, whisht, bairn! I should never have let you be there!'

'Aunt Mary, Aunt Mary, you have seen him too?'

'Oh whisht, whisht, honey!' Aunt Mary said: her eyes were shining – there were tears in them. 'Oh whisht, whisht! Put it out of your mind, and try to sleep. I will not speak another word,' she cried.

But I had my arms round her, and my mouth at her ear. 'Who is he there? – tell me that and I will ask no more – '

'Oh, honey, rest, and try to sleep! It is just – how can I tell you? – a dream, a dream! Did you not hear what Lady Carnbee said? – the women of our blood – '

'What? what? Aunt Mary, oh Aunt Mary – '

'I canna tell you,' she cried in her agitation, 'I canna tell you! How can I tell you, when I know just what you know and no more? It is a longing all your life after – it is a looking – for what never comes.'

'He will come,' I cried. 'I shall see him tomorrow – that I know, I know!'

She kissed me and cried over me, her cheek hot and wet like mine. 'My honey, try if you can sleep – try if you can sleep: and we'll wait to see what tomorrow brings.'

'I have no fear,' said I; and then I suppose, though it is strange to think of, I must have fallen asleep – I was so worn-out, and young, and not used to lying in my bed awake. From time to time I opened my eyes, and sometimes jumped up remembering everything; but Aunt Mary was always there to soothe me, and I lay down again in her shelter like a bird in its nest.

But I would not let them keep me in bed next day. I was in a kind of fever, not knowing what I did. The window was quite opaque, without the least glimmer in it, flat and blank like a piece of wood. Never from the first day had I seen it so little like a window. 'It cannot be wondered at,' I said to myself, 'that seeing it like that, and with eyes that are old, not so clear as mine, they should think what they do.' And then I smiled to myself to think of the evening and the long light, and whether he would look out again, or only give me a signal with his hand. I decided I would like that best: not that he should take the trouble to come forward and open it again, but just a turn of his head and a wave of his hand. It would be more friendly and show more confidence – not as if I wanted that kind of demonstration every night.

I did not come down in the afternoon, but kept at my own window upstairs alone, till the tea-party should be over. I could hear them making a great talk; and I was sure they were all in the recess staring at the window, and laughing at the silly lassie. Let them laugh! I felt above all that now. At dinner I was very restless, hurrying to get it over; and I think Aunt Mary was restless too. I doubt whether she read her *Times* when it came; she opened it up so as to shield her, and watched from a corner. And I settled myself in the recess, with my heart full of expectation. I wanted nothing more than to see him writing at his table, and to have him turn his head and give me a little wave of his hand, just to show that he knew I was there. I sat from half-past seven o'clock to ten o'clock, and the daylight grew softer and softer, till at last it was as if it was shining through a pearl, and not a shadow to be seen. But the window all the time was as black as night, and there was nothing, nothing there.

Well: but other nights it had been like that: he would not be there every night only to please me. There are other things in a man's life, a great learned man like that. I said to myself I was not disappointed. Why should I be disappointed? There had been other nights when he was not there. Aunt Mary watched me, every movement I made, her eyes shining, often wet, with a pity in them that almost made me cry; but I felt as if I were more sorry for her than for myself. And then I flung myself upon her, and asked her, again and again, what it was, and who it was, imploring her to tell me if she knew? and when she had seen him, and what had happened? and what it meant about the women of our blood? She told me that how it was she could not tell, nor when: it was just at the time it had to be; and that we all saw him in our time – 'that is,' she said, 'the ones that are like you and me.' What was it that made her and me different from the rest? but she only shook her head and would not tell me. 'They say – ' she said, and then stopped short. 'Oh, honey, try and forget all about it – if I had but known you were of that kind! They say – that once there was one that was a scholar, and liked his books more than any lady's love. Honey, do not look at me like that. To think I should have brought all this on you!'

'He was a scholar?' I cried.

'And one of us, that must have been a light woman, not like you and me – But maybe it was just in innocence; for who can tell? She waved to him and waved to him to come over; and yon ring was the token; but he would not come. But still she sat at her window and waved and waved – till at last her brothers heard of it, that were stirring men; and then – oh, my honey, let us speak of it no more!'

'They killed him!' I cried, carried away. And then I grasped her with my hands, and gave her a shake, and flung away from her. 'You tell me that to throw dust in my eyes – when I saw him only last night: and he as living as I am, and as young!'

'My honey, my honey!' Aunt Mary said.

After that I would not speak to her for a long time; but she kept close to me, never leaving me when she could help it, and always with that pity in her eyes. For the next night it was the same; and the third night. That third night I thought I could not bear it any longer. I would have to do something if only I knew what to do! If it would ever get dark, quite dark, there might be something to be done. I had wild dreams of stealing out of the house and getting a ladder, and mounting up to try if I could not open that window, in the middle of the night – if perhaps I could get the baker's boy to help me; and then my mind got into a whirl, and it was as if I had done it; and I could almost see the boy put the ladder to the window, and hear him cry out that there was nothing there. Oh, how slow it was, the night! and how light it was, and everything so clear, no darkness to cover you, no shadow, whether on one side of the street or on the other side! I could not sleep, though I was forced to go to bed. And in the deep midnight, when it is dark dark in every other place, I slipped very softly downstairs, though there was one board on the landing-place that creaked – and opened the door and stepped out. There was not a soul to be seen, up or down, from the Abbey to the West Port; and the trees stood like ghosts, and the silence was terrible, and everything as clear as day. You don't know what silence is till you find it in the light like that, not morning but night, no sunrising, no shadow, but everything as clear as the day.

It did not make any difference as the slow minutes went on: one o'clock, two o'clock. How strange it was to hear the clocks striking in that dead light when there was nobody to hear them! But it made no difference. The window was quite blank; even the marking of the panes seemed to have melted away. I stole up again after a long time, through the silent house, in the clear light, cold and trembling, with despair in my heart.

I am sure Aunt Mary must have watched and seen me coming back, for after a while I heard faint sounds in the house; and very early, when there had come a little sunshine into the air, she came to my bedside with a cup of tea in her hand; and she, too, was looking like a ghost. 'Are you warm, honey – are you comfortable?' she said. 'It doesn't matter,' said I. I did not feel as if anything mattered; unless if one could get into the dark somewhere – the soft, deep dark that would cover you over and hide you – but I could not tell from what. The dreadful thing was that there was nothing, nothing to look for, nothing to hide from – only the silence and the light.

That day my mother came and took me home. I had not heard she was coming; she arrived quite unexpectedly, and said she had no time to stay, but must start the same evening so as to be in London next day, papa having settled to go abroad. At first I had a wild thought I would not go. But how can a girl say I will not, when her mother has come for her, and there is no reason, no reason in the world, to resist, and no right! I had to go, whatever I might wish or anyone might say. Aunt Mary's dear eyes were wet; she went about the house drying them quietly with her handkerchief, but she always said, 'It is the best thing for you, honey – the best thing for you!' Oh, how I hated to hear it said that it was the best thing, as if anything mattered, one more than another! The old ladies were all there in the afternoon, Lady Carnbee looking at me from under her black lace, and the diamond lurking, sending out darts from under her finger. She patted me on the shoulder, and told me to be a good bairn. 'And never lippen to what you see from the window,' she said. 'The eye is deceitful as well as the heart.' She kept patting me on the shoulder, and I felt again as if that sharp wicked stone stung me. Was that what Aunt Mary meant when she said yon ring was the token? I thought afterwards I saw the mark on my shoulder. You will say why? How can I tell why? If I had known, I should have been contented, and it would not have mattered any more.

I never went back to St Rule's, and for years of my life I never again looked out of a window when any other window was in sight. You ask me did I ever see him again? I cannot tell: the imagination is a great deceiver, as Lady Carnbee said; and if he stayed there so long, only to punish the race that had wronged him, why should I ever have seen him again? for I had received my share. But who can tell what happens in a heart that often, often, and so long as that, comes back to do its errand? If it was he whom I have seen again, the anger is gone from him, and he means good and no longer harm to the house of the woman that loved him. I have seen his face looking at me from a crowd. There was one time when I came home a widow from India, very sad, with my little children. I am certain I saw him there among all the people coming to welcome their friends. There was nobody to welcome me – for I was not expected; and very sad was I, without a face I knew; when all at once I saw him, and he waved his hand to me. My heart leaped up again; I had forgotten who he was, but only that it was a face I knew, and I landed almost cheerfully, thinking here was someone who would help me. But he had disappeared, as he did from the window, with that one wave of his hand.

And again I was reminded of it all when old Lady Carnbee died – an old, old woman – and it was found in her will that she had left me that diamond ring. I am afraid of it still. It is locked up in an old sandal-wood box in the lumber-room in the little old country-house which belongs to me, but where I never live. If anyone would steal it, it would be a relief to my mind. Yet I never knew what Aunt Mary meant when she said, 'Yon ring was the token,' nor what it could have to do with that strange window in the old College Library of St Rule's.

The Black Grippe

EDGAR WALLACE

Dr Hereford Bevan was looking thoughtfully at a small Cape rabbit; the rabbit took not the slightest notice of Dr Hereford Bevan. It crouched on a narrow bench, nibbling at a mess of crushed mealies and seemed perfectly content with its lot, in spite of the fact that the bench was situated in the experimental laboratory of the Jackson Institute of Tropical Medicines.

In the young principal's hand was a long porcelain rod with which from time to time he menaced the unconscious feeder, without, however, producing so much as a single shiver of apprehension. With his long ears pricked, his sensitive nostrils quivering – he was used to the man-smell of Hereford Bevan by now – and his big black eyes staring unwinkingly ahead, there was little in the appearance of the rabbit to suggest abnormal condition.

For the third time in a quarter of an hour Bevan raised the rod as though to strike the animal across the nose, and for the third time lowered the rod again. Then with a sigh he lifted the little beast by the ears and carried him, struggling and squirming, to a small hutch, put him in very gently, and closed the wire-netted door.

He stood staring at the tiny inmate and fetched a long sigh. Then he left the laboratory and walked down to the staff study.

Stuart Gold, his assistant, sat at a big desk, pipe in mouth, checking some calculations. He looked up as Bevan came in.

'Well,' he said, 'what has Bunny done?'

'Bunny is feeding like a pig,' said Bevan, irritably.

'No change?'

Bevan shook his head and looked at his watch. 'What time – ' he began.

'The boat train was in ten minutes ago,' said Stuart Gold. 'I have been on the phone to Waterloo. He may be here at any minute now.'

Bevan walked up and down the apartment, his hands thrust into his trousers pockets, his chin on his breast.

Presently he walked to the window and looked out at the busy street. Motorbuses were rumbling past in an endless procession. The sidewalks were crowded with pedestrians, for this was the busiest thoroughfare in the West End of London and it was the hour of the day when the offices were absorbing their slaves.

As he looked, a taxi drew up opposite the door and a man sprang out with all the agility of youth, though the iron-grey whiskers about his chin and the seamed red face placed him amongst the sixties.

'It is he!' cried Hereford Bevan, and dashed from the room to welcome the visitor, taking the portmanteau from his hand.

'It is awfully good of you to come, professor,' he said, shaking the traveller warmly by the hand. 'Ever since I telegraphed I have been scared sick for fear I brought you on a fool's errand.'

'Nonsense,' said the elder man, sharply; 'I was coming to Europe anyway, and I merely advanced my date of sailing. I'd sooner come by the *Mauretania* than the slow packet by which I had booked. How are you? You are looking bright.'

Hereford Bevan led the newcomer to the study and introduced him to Gold.

Professor Van der Bergh was one of those elderly men who never grow old. His blue eye was as clear as it had been on his twentieth birthday, his sensitive mouth was as ready to smile as ever it had been in the flower of his youth. A professor of pathology, a great anatomist, and one of the foremost bacteriologists in the United States, Bevan's doubts and apprehensions were perhaps justified, though he was relieved in mind to discover that he had merely accelerated the great man's departure from New York and was not wholly responsible for a trip which might end in disappointment.

'Now,' said Van der Bergh, spreading his coat-tails and drawing his chair to the little fire, 'just give me a second to light my pipe and tell me all your troubles.'

He puffed away for a few seconds, blew out the match carefully and threw it into the grate, then before Bevan could speak he said: 'I presume that the epidemic of January has scared you?' Hereford Bevan nodded.

'Well,' said the professor, reflectively, 'I don't wonder. The 1918 epidemic was bad enough. I am not calling it influenza, because I think very few of us are satisfied to affix that wild label to a devastating disease which appeared in the most mysterious fashion, took its toll, and disappeared as rapidly and mysteriously.'

He scratched his beard, staring out of the window.

'I haven't heard any theory about that epidemic which has wholly satisfied me,' he said. 'People talk glibly of "carriers" of "infection", but who infected the wild tribes in the centre of Africa on the very day that whole communities of Eskimos were laid low in parts of the Arctic regions which were absolutely isolated from the rest of the world?'

Bevan shook his head.

'That is the mystery that I have never solved,' he said, 'and never hope to.'

'I wouldn't say that,' said the professor, shaking his head. 'I am always hoping to get on the track of first causes, however baffling they may be. Anyway, I am not satisfied to describe that outbreak as influenza, and it really does not matter what label we give to it for the moment. You might as truly call it the Plague or the Scourge. Now let's get down to the epidemic of this year. I should like to compare notes with you because I have always found that the reports of this Institute are above suspicion. I suppose it has been suggested to you,' he went on, 'that the investigation of this particular disease is outside the province of tropical medicines?'

Stuart Gold laughed.

'We are reminded of that every day,' he said, dryly.

'Now just tell me what happened in January of this year,' said the professor. Dr Bevan seated himself at the table, pulled open a drawer, and took out a black-covered exercise book.

'I'll tell you briefly,' he said, 'and without attempting to produce statistics. On the 18th January, as near three o'clock in the afternoon as makes no difference, the second manifestation of this disease attacked this country, and, so far as can be ascertained, the whole of the Continent.'

The professor nodded. 'What were the symptoms?' he asked.

'People began to cry – that is to say, their eyes filled with water and they felt extremely uncomfortable for about a quarter of an hour. So far as I can discover the crying period did not last much more than a quarter of an hour, in some cases a much shorter time.'

Again the professor nodded.

'That is what happened in New York,' he said, 'and this symptom was followed about six hours later by a slight rise of temperature, shivering, and a desire for sleep.'

'Just the same sort of thing happened here,' said Bevan, 'and in the morning everybody was as well as they had been the previous morning, and the fact that it had occurred might have been overlooked but for the observation made in various hospitals. Gold and I were both stricken at the same time. We both took blood and succeeded in isolating the germs.'

The professor jumped up.

'Then you are the only people who have it,' he said, 'nobody else in the world seems to have taken that precaution.'

Stuart Gold lifted a big bell-shaped glass cover from a microscope, took from a locked case a thin microscopic slide, and inserted it in the holder. He adjusted the lens, switched on a shaded light behind the instrument, and beckoned the professor forward.

'Here it is, sir,' he said.

Professor Van der Bergh glued his eye to the instrument and looked for a long time.

'Perfect,' he said. 'I have never seen this fellow before. It looks rather like a trypnasome.'

'That's what I told Bevan,' said Stuart Gold.

The professor was still looking.

'It is like and it is unlike,' he said. 'Of course, it is

absurd to suggest that you've all had an attack of sleeping sickness, which you undoubtedly would have had if this had been a trypnasome, but surely this bug is a new one to me!'

He walked back to his chair, puffing thoughtfully at his pipe. 'What did you do?'

'I made a culture,' said Bevan, 'and infected six South African rabbits. In an hour they developed the first symptoms. Their eyes watered for the prescribed time, their temperature rose six hours later, and in the morning they were all well.'

'Why South African rabbits?' asked Van der Bergh, curiously.

'Because they develop secondary symptoms of any disease at twice the rate of a human being – at least that has been my experience,' explained Bevan. 'I found it by accident whilst I was in Grahamstown, in South Africa, and it has been a very useful piece of knowledge to me. When I wired to you I had no idea there were going to be any further developments. I merely wanted to make you acquainted with the bug – '

The professor looked up sharply. 'Have there been further developments?' he asked, and Bevan nodded.

'Five days ago,' he said, speaking slowly, 'the second symptom appeared. I will show you.' He led the way back to the laboratory, went to the little hutch, and lifted the twisting, struggling rabbit to the bench under a blaze of electric light. The professor felt the animal gingerly.

'He has no temperature,' he said, 'and looks perfectly normal. What is the matter with him?' Bevan lifted the little beast and held his head toward the light.

'Do you notice anything?' he asked.

'Good heavens!' said Van der Bergh; 'he's blind!' Bevan nodded.

'He's been blind for five days,' he said.

'But – ' Van der Bergh stared at him. 'Do you mean – ' Bevan nodded.

'I mean, that when the secondary symptom comes, and it should come in a fortnight from today – '

He stopped.

He had replaced the animal upon the bench and had put out his hand to stroke his ears when suddenly the rabbit groped back from him. Again he reached out his hand and again the animal made a frantic attempt to escape.

'He sees now,' said the professor.

'Wait,' said Bevan.

He took down a board to which a paper was pinned, looked at his watch, and jotted a note. 'Thank God for that,' he said; 'the blindness lasts for exactly one hundred and twenty hours.'

'But do you mean,' asked Van der Bergh, with an anxious little frown, 'that the whole world is going blind for five days?'

'That is my theory,' replied the other.

'Phew!' said the professor, and mopped his face with a large and gaudy handkerchief. They went back without another word to the study and Van der Bergh began his technical test. For his information sheet after sheet of data were placed before him. Records of temperature, of diet and the like were scanned and compared, whilst Bevan made his way to another laboratory to examine the remaining rabbits.

He returned as the professor finished.

'They can all see,' he said; 'I inspected them this

morning and they were as blind as bats.' Presently the professor finished.

'I am going down to our Embassy,' he said, 'and the best thing you boys can do is to see some representative of your Government. Let me see, Sir Douglas Sexton is your big man, isn't he?'

Bevan made a wry face.

'He is the medical gentleman who has the ear of the Government,' he said, 'but he is rather an impossible person. He's one of the old school – '

'I know that school,' said the professor, grimly, 'it's a school where you learn nothing and forget nothing. Still, it's your duty to warn him.'

Bevan nodded and turned to Stuart Gold.

'Will you cancel my lecture, Gold?' he said; 'let Cartwright take the men through that demonstration I gave yesterday. I'll go down and see Sexton though he wither me!'

Sir Douglas Sexton had a large house in a very large square. He was so well-off that he could afford a shabby butler. That shrunken man shook his head when Dr Bevan made his enquiry.

'I don't think Sir Douglas will see you, sir,' he said. 'He has a consultation in half an hour's time and he is in his library, with orders that he is not to be disturbed in any circumstances.'

'This is a very vital matter and I simply must see Sir Douglas,' said Bevan, firmly. The butler was gone for some time and presently returned to usher the caller into a large and gloomy room, where Sir Douglas sat surrounded by open books.

He greeted Bevan with a scowl, for the younger school were not popular with the Sextonians.

'Really, it is most inconvenient, doctor, for you to

see me at this moment,' he complained. 'I suppose you want to ask about the Government grant to the Jackson Institute. I was speaking to the Prime Minister yesterday and he did not seem at all inclined to agree to spend the country's money.'

'I haven't come about the grant, Sir Douglas,' replied Bevan, 'but a matter of much greater importance.'

In as few words as possible he gave the result of his experiment, and on the face of Sir Douglas Sexton was undisguised incredulity.

'Come, come,' he said, when Dr Bevan had finished, and permitted his heavy features to relax into a smile. 'Now, that sort of stuff is all very well for the Press if you want to make a sensation and advertise your name, but surely you are not coming to me, a medical man, and a medical man, moreover, in the confidence of the Government and the Ministry of Health, with a story of that kind! Of course, there was some sort of epidemic, I admit, on the 18th. I myself suffered a little inconvenience, but I think that phenomenon could be explained by the sudden change of wind from the south-west to the north-east and the corresponding drop in temperature. You may have noticed that the temperature dropped six degrees that morning.'

'I am not bothering about the cause of the epidemic,' said Bevan, patiently. 'I am merely giving you, Sir Douglas, a rough account of what form the second epidemic will take.'

Sir Douglas smiled.

'And do you expect me,' he asked with acerbity, 'to go to the Prime Minister of England and tell him that in fourteen days the whole of the world is going blind?

My dear good man, if you published that sort of story you would scare the people to death and set back the practice of medicine a hundred years! Why, we should all be discredited!'

'Do you think that if I saw the Prime Minister – ' began Bevan, and Sir Douglas stiffened.

'If you know the Prime Minister or have any friends who could introduce you,' he said, shortly, 'I have not the slightest objection to your seeing him. I can only warn you that the Prime Minister is certain to send for me and that I should give an opinion which would be directly contrary to yours. I think you have made a very grave error, Dr Bevan, and if you were to take the trouble to kill one of your precious rabbits and dissect it you would discover another cause for this blindness.'

'The opinion of Dr Van der Bergh,' began Bevan, and Sir Douglas snorted.

'I really cannot allow an American person to teach me my business,' he said. 'I have nothing to say against American medicines or American surgery, and there are some very charming people in America – I am sure this must be the case. And now, doctor, if you will excuse – '

He turned pointedly to his books and Bevan went out.

For seven days three men worked most earnestly to enlist the attention of the authorities. They might have given the story to the Press and created a sensation, but neither Bevan nor Van der Bergh favoured this method. Eminent doctors who were consulted took views which were extraordinarily different. Some came to the laboratories to examine the records. Others 'poohpoohed' the whole idea.

'Have you any doubt on the matter yourself?' asked the professor, and Bevan hesitated.

'The only doubt I have, sir,' he said, 'is whether my calculations as to the time are accurate. I have noticed in previous experiments with these rabbits the disease develops about twice as fast as in the human body, but I am far from satisfied that this rule is invariable.'

Van der Bergh nodded.

'My Embassy has wired the particulars to Washington,' he said, 'and Washington takes a very serious view of your discovery. They are making whatever preparations they can.'

He went back to his hotel, promising to call on the morrow. Bevan worked all that day testing the blood of his little subjects, working out tables of reaction, and it was nearly four o'clock when he went to bed.

He slept that night in his room at the Institute. He was a good sleeper, and after winding the clock and drawing down the blind he jumped into bed and in less than five minutes was sound asleep. He awoke with the subconscious feeling that he had slept his usual allowance and was curiously alive and awake. The room was in pitch darkness and he remembered with a frown that he had not gone to bed until four o'clock in the morning. He could not have slept two hours.

He put out his hand and switched on the light to discover the time. Apparently the light was not working.

On his bedside table was a box of matches, his cigarette holder, and his cigarettes. He took the box, struck a light, but nothing happened. He threw away the match and struck another – still nothing happened.

He held the faithless match in his hand and

suddenly felt a strange warmth at his fingertips. Then with a cry he dropped the match – it had burnt his fingers!

Slowly he put his legs over the edge of the bed and stood up, groping his way to the window and releasing the spring-blind. The darkness was still complete. He strained his eyes but could not even see the silhouette of the window-frame against the night. Then a church-bell struck the hour . . . nine, ten, eleven, twelve!

Twelve o'clock! It was impossible that it could be twelve o'clock at night. He gasped. Twelve midday and dark!

He searched for his clothes and began to dress. His window was open, yet from outside came no sound of traffic. London was silent – as silent as the grave.

His window looked out upon the busy thoroughfare in which the Jackson Institute was situated, but there was not so much as the clink of a wheel or the sound of a pedestrian's foot.

He dressed awkwardly, slipping on his boots and lacing them quickly, then groped his way to the door and opened it. A voice outside greeted him. It was the voice of Gold.

'Is that you, Bevan?'

'Yes, it is I, what the dickens – ' and then the realisation of the catastrophe which had fallen upon the world came to him.

'Blind!' he whispered. 'We're all blind!'

Gold had been shell-shocked in the war and was subject to nerve-storms. Presently Bevan heard his voice whimpering hysterically.

'Blind!' he repeated. 'What a horrible thing!'

'Steady yourself!' said Bevan, sternly. 'It has come!

But it's only for five days, Gold. Now don't lose your nerve!'

'Oh, I shan't lose my nerve!' said Gold, in a shaky voice. 'Only it is rather awful, isn't it? Awful, awful! My God! It's awful!'

'Come down to the study!' said Bevan. 'Don't forget the two steps leading down to the landing. There are twenty-four stairs, Gold. Count 'em!'

He was halfway down the stairs when he heard somebody sobbing at the foot and recognised the voice of the old housekeeper who attended to the resident staff. She was whimpering and wailing.

'Shut up!' he said, savagely. 'What are you making that infernal row about?'

'Oh, sir,' she moaned. 'I can't see! I can't see!'

'Nobody can see or will see for five days!' said Bevan. 'Keep your nerve, Mrs Moreland.' He found his way to the study. He had scarcely reached the room before he heard a thumping on the door which led from the street to the staff quarters. Carefully he manoeuvred his way into the hall again, came to the door, and unlocked it.

'Halloa,' said a cheery voice outside, 'is this the Jackson Institute?'

'Thank God you're safe, professor. You took a risk in coming round.'

The professor came in with slow, halting footsteps, and Bevan shut the door behind him.

'You know your way, I'll put my hand on your shoulder if you don't mind,' said Van der Bergh. 'Luckily I took the trouble to remember the route. I've been two hours getting here. Ouch!'

'Are you hurt?' asked Bevan.

'I ran against an infernal motorbus in the middle

of the street. It had been left stranded,' said the professor. 'I think the blindness is general.'

Stuart had stumbled into the room soon after them, had found a chair and sat down upon it.

'Now,' said Van der Bergh, briskly, 'you've got to find your way to your Government offices and interview somebody in authority. There's going to be hell in the world for the next five days. I hope your calculations are not wrong in that respect, Bevan!'

Hereford Bevan said nothing.

'It is very awkward!' It was Gold's quivering voice that spoke. 'But, of course, it'll be all right in a day or two.'

'I hope so,' said the professor's grim voice. 'If it's for five days little harm will be done, but – but if it's for ten days!'

Bevan's heart sank at the doubt in the old man's voice. 'If it's for ten days?' he repeated.

'The whole world will be dead,' said the professor, solemnly, and there was a deep silence.

'Dead?' whispered Gold and Van der Bergh swung round toward the voice.

'What's the matter with you?'

'Shell-shock,' muttered Bevan under his breath, and the old man's voice took on a softer note.

'Not all of us, perhaps,' he said, 'but the least intelligent. Don't you realise what has happened and what will happen? The world is going to starve. We are a blind world, and how shall we find food?'

A thrill of horror crept up Bevan's spine as he realised for the first time just what world-blindness meant.

'All the trains have stopped,' the professor went on; 'I've been figuring it out in my room this morning just what it means. There are blind men in the signal-boxes and blind men on the engines. All transport has come to a standstill. How are you going to get the food to the people? In a day's time the shops, if the people can reach them, will be sold out and it will be impossible to replenish the local stores. You can neither milk nor reap. All the great power-stations are at a standstill. There is no coal being got out of the mines. Wait, where is your telephone?'

Bevan fumbled for the instrument and passed it in the direction of the professor's voice. A pause, then: 'Take it back,' said the professor, 'of course, that will not be working. The exchange cannot see!'

Bevan heard a methodical puff-puff and the scent of tobacco came to him, and somehow this brought him comfort. The professor was smoking.

He rose unsteadily to his feet. 'Put your hand on my shoulder, professor, and, Gold, take hold of the professor's coat or something.'

'Where are you going?' asked Van der Bergh. 'To the kitchen,' said Bevan; 'there's some food there and I'm starving.' The meal consisted in the main of dry bread, biscuits, and cheese, washed down by water. Then Hereford Bevan began his remarkable pilgrimage.

He left the house, and keeping touch with the railings on his right, reached first Cockspur Street and then Whitehall. Halfway along the latter thoroughfare he thumped into a man and, putting out his hand, felt embossed buttons.

'Halloa,' he said, 'a policeman?'

'That's right, sir,' said a voice; 'I've been here since the morning. You're in Whitehall. What has happened, sir? Do you know?'

'It is a temporary blindness which has come upon everybody,' said Bevan, speaking quickly. 'I am a doctor. Now, constable, you are to tell your friends if you meet them and everybody you do meet that it is only temporary.'

'I'm not likely to meet anybody,' said the constable. 'I've been standing here hardly daring to move since it came.'

'What time did it happen?'

'About ten o'clock, as near as I can remember,' said the policeman.

'How far from here is Downing Street?'

The constable hesitated.

'I don't know where we are,' he said, 'but it can't be very far.' Two hours' diligent search, two hours of groping and of stumbling, two hours of discussing with frantic men and women whom he met on the way, brought him to Downing Street.

That journey along Whitehall would remain in his mind a horrible memory for all his days. He heard oaths and sobbings. He heard the wild jabberings of somebody – whether it was man or woman he could not say – who had gone mad under the stress of the calamity, and he came to Downing Street as the clock struck three.

He might have passed the Prime Minister's house but he heard voices and recognised one as that of Sexton.

The great man was moaning his trouble to somebody who spoke in a quiet unemotional voice. 'Halloa, Sexton!'

Bevan stumbled toward, and collided with the great physician. 'Who is it?' said Sexton.

'It is Hereford Bevan.'

'It's the man, Prime Minister, the doctor I spoke to you about.' A cool hand took Bevan's.

'Come this way,' said the voice; 'you had better stay, Sexton, you'll never find your way back.'

Bevan found himself led through what he judged to be a large hall and then suddenly his feet struck a heavy carpet.

'I think there's a chair behind you,' said the new voice, 'sit down and tell me all about it.' Dr Bevan spoke for ten minutes, his host merely interjecting a question here and there.

'It can only last for five days,' said the voice, with a quiver of emotion, 'and we can only last out that five days. You know, of course, that the food supply has stopped. There is no way of averting this terrible tragedy. Can you make a suggestion?'

'Yes, sir,' said Bevan. 'There are a number of blind institutes throughout the country. Get in touch with them and let their trained men organise the business of industry. I think it could be done.'

There was a pause.

'It might be done,' said the voice. 'Happily the telegraphs are working satisfactorily, as messages can be taken by sound. The wireless is also working and your suggestion shall be carried out.'

The days that followed were days of nightmare, days when men groped and stumbled in an unknown world, shrieking for food. On the evening of the second day the water supply failed. The pumping stations had ceased to work. Happily it rained and people were able to collect water in their mackintosh coats.

Dr Bevan made several excursions a day and in one of these he met another bold adventurer who told him that part of the Strand was on fire. Somebody had upset a lamp without noticing the fact. The doctor made his way toward the Strand but was forced to turn back by the clouds of pungent smoke which met him.

He and his informant (he was a butcher from Smithfield) locked arms and made their way back to the Institute. By some mischance they took a wrong turning and might have been irretrievably lost but they found a guardian angel in the shape of a woman against whom they blundered.

'The Jackson Institute?' she said. 'Oh yes, I can lead you there.'

She walked with unfaltering footsteps and with such decision that the doctor thought she had been spared the supreme affliction. He asked her this and she laughed.

'Oh, no,' she said, cheerfully. 'You see, I've been blind all my life. The Government has put us on point duty at various places to help people who have lost their way.'

She told them that, according to her information, big fires were raging in half a dozen parts of London. She had heard of no railway collisions and the Prime Minister told her –

'Told you?' said Bevan in surprise, and again she laughed. 'I've met him before, you see,' she said. 'I am Lord Selbury's daughter, Lillian Selbury.' Bevan remembered the name. It is curious that he had pictured her, for all the beauty of her voice, as a sad, middle-aged woman. She took his hand in hers and they walked slowly toward his house.

'You'll think I'm horrid if I say I am enjoying this,' she said, 'and yet I am. It's so lovely to be able to pity others! Of course, it is very dreadful and it is beginning to frighten me a little, and then there's nobody to tell me how pretty I am, because nobody can see. That is rather a drawback, isn't it?' and she laughed again.

'What does the Government think about this?'

'They are terribly upset,' she said, in a graver tone; 'you see, they cannot get at the people – they are so used to depending on the newspapers, but there are no newspapers now, and if there were nobody could read them. They have just stopped – You step down from the kerb here and walk twenty-five paces and step up again. We are crossing Whitehall Gardens. They have wonderful faith in this Dr Bevan.'

Hereford Bevan felt himself going red.

'I hope their faith is justified,' he said, grimly; 'I happen to be the wonderful doctor.' He felt her fingers grip him in an uncontrollable spasm of surprise.

'Are you really?' she said, with a new note of interest. 'Listen!'

They stopped, and he heard the tinkle of a bell.

'That is one of our people from St Mildreds,' she said; 'the Government is initiating a system of town-criers. It is the only way we can get news to the people.'

Bevan listened and heard the sing-song voice of the crier but could not distinguish what he said. The girl led him to his house and there left him. He felt her hand running down his right arm and wondered why until she took his hand and shook it.

Old Professor Van der Bergh roared a greeting as he came into the room.

'Is that you, Bevan?' he asked. 'I've got a knuckle of cold ham here, but be careful how you cut it, otherwise you're going to slice your fingers.'

He and Stuart Gold had spent the day feeding the

various specimens in the laboratory. The fourth day dawned and in the afternoon came a knock at the door. It was the girl.

'I've been ordered to place myself at your disposal, Dr Bevan,' she said; 'the Government may need you.'

He spent that day wandering through the deserted streets with the girl at his side and as the hundred and twentieth hour approached he found himself looking forward not so much to the end of the tragic experience which he shared with the world, but to seeing with his own eyes the face of this guide of his. He had slept the clock round and just before ten struck he made his way to the street. He heard Big Ben boom the hour and waited for light, but no light came. Another hour passed and yet another, and his soul was seized with blind panic. Suppose sight never returned, suppose his experiments were altogether wrong and that what happened in the case of the rabbits did not happen to Man! Suppose the blindness was permanent! He groaned at the thought.

The girl was with him, her arm in his, throughout that day. His nerves were breaking, and somehow she sensed this fact and comforted him as a mother might comfort a child. She led him into the park with sure footsteps and walked him up and down, trying to distract his mind from the horror with which it was oppressed.

In the afternoon he was sent for to the Cabinet Council and again told the story of his experiments.

'The hundred and twenty hours are passed, are they not, doctor?' said the Premier's voice.

'Yes, sir,' replied Bevan in a low voice, 'but it is humanly impossible to be sure that that is the exact time.'

No other question was asked him but the terror of his audience came back to him like an aura and shrivelled his very heart.

He did not lie down as was his wont that night, but wandered out alone into the streets of London. It must have been two o'clock in the morning when he came back to find the girl standing on the step talking with Van der Bergh.

She came toward him at the sound of his voice.

'There is another Cabinet meeting, doctor,' she said, 'will you come with me?'

'I hope I haven't kept you long,' he said, brokenly. His voice was husky and so unlike his own that she was startled.

'You're not to take this to heart, Dr Bevan,' she said, severely, as they began their pilgrimage to Whitehall. 'There's a terrible task waiting for the world which has to be faced.'

'Wait, wait!' he said, hoarsely, and gripped the rail with one hand and her arm with the other. Was it imagination? It was still dark, a fine drizzle of rain was falling, but the blackness was dappled with tones of less blackness. There was a dark, straight thing before him, something that seemed to hang in the centre of his eye, and a purple shape beyond, and he knew that he was looking at a London street, at a London lamp-post, with eyes that saw. Black London, London devoid of light, London whose streets were packed with motionless vehicles that stood just where they had stopped on the day the darkness fell, London with groping figures half mad with joy, shrieking and sobbing their relief – he drew a long breath.

'What is it? What is it?' said the girl in a frightened voice.

'I can see! I can see!' said Bevan in a whisper.

'Can you?' she said, wistfully. 'I – I am so glad. And now – '

He was near to tears and his arms went about her. He fumbled in his pocket for a match and struck a light. That blessed light he saw, and saw, too, the pale spiritual face turned up to his.

'I can see you,' he whispered again. 'My God! You're the most beautiful thing I have ever seen!'

London slept from sheer force of habit and woke with the grey dawn to see – to look out upon a world that had been lost for five and a half days, but in the night all the forces of the law and the Crown had been working at feverish pace, railways had dragged their drivers from their beds, carriers and stokers had been collected by the police, and slowly the wheels of life were turning again, and a humble world, grateful for the restoration of its greatest gift, hungered in patience and was happy.

The Bottle Imp

ROBERT LOUIS STEVENSON

There was a man of the Island of Hawaii, whom I shall call Keawe; for the truth is, he still lives, and his name must be kept secret; but the place of his birth was not far from Honaunau, where the bones of Keawe the Great lie hidden in a cave. This man was poor, brave, and active; he could read and write like a schoolmaster; he was a first-rate mariner besides, sailed for some time in the island steamers, and steered a whaleboat on the Hamakua coast. At length it came in Keawe's mind to have a sight of the great world and foreign cities, and he shipped on a vessel bound to San Francisco.

This is a fine town, with a fine harbour, and rich people uncountable; and in particular, there is one hill which is covered with palaces. Upon this hill Keawe was one day taking a walk with his pocket full of money, viewing the great houses upon either hand with pleasure. 'What fine houses these are!' he was thinking, 'and how happy must those people be who dwell in them, and take no care for the morrow!' The thought was in his mind when he came abreast of a house that was smaller than some others, but all finished and beautified like a toy; the steps of that house shone like silver, and the borders of the garden bloomed like garlands, and the windows were bright like diamonds; and Keawe stopped and wondered at the excellence of all he saw. So stopping, he was aware of a man that looked forth upon him through a window so clear that Keawe could see him as you see a fish in a pool upon the reef. The man was elderly, with a bald head and a black beard; and his face was heavy with sorrow, and he bitterly sighed. And the truth of it is, that as Keawe looked in upon the man, and the man looked out upon Keawe, each envied the other.

All of a sudden, the man smiled and nodded, and beckoned Keawe to enter, and met him at the door of the house.

'This is a fine house of mine,' said the man, and bitterly sighed. 'Would you not care to view the chambers?'

So he led Keawe all over it, from the cellar to the roof, and there was nothing there that was not perfect of its kind, and Keawe was astonished.

'Truly,' said Keawe, 'this is a beautiful house; if I lived in the like of it I should be laughing all day long. How comes it, then, that you should be sighing?'

'There is no reason,' said the man, 'why you should not have a house in all points similar to this, and finer, if you wish. You have some money, I suppose?'

'I have fifty dollars,' said Keawe; 'but a house like this will cost more than fifty dollars.'

The man made a computation. 'I am sorry you have no more,' said he, 'for it may raise you trouble in the future; but it shall be yours at fifty dollars.'

'The house?' asked Keawe.

'No, not the house,' replied the man; 'but the bottle. For, I must tell you, although I appear to you so rich and fortunate, all my fortune, and this house itself and its garden, came out of a bottle not much bigger than a pint. This is it.'

And he opened a lockfast place, and took out a round-bellied bottle with a long neck; the glass of it was white like milk, with changing rainbow colours in the grain. Withinsides something obscurely moved, like a shadow and a fire.

'This is the bottle,' said the man; and, when Keawe laughed, 'You do not believe me?' he added. 'Try, then, for yourself. See if you can break it.'

So Keawe took the bottle up and dashed it on the floor till he was weary; but it jumped on the floor like a child's ball, and was not injured.

'This is a strange thing,' said Keawe. 'For by the touch of it, as well as by the look, the bottle should be of glass.'

'Of glass it is,' replied the man, sighing more heavily than ever; 'but the glass of it was tempered in the flames of hell. An imp lives in it, and that is the shadow we behold there moving; or so I suppose. If any man buy this bottle the imp is at his command; all that he desires – love, fame, money, houses like this house, ay, or a city like this city – all are his at the word uttered. Napoleon had this bottle, and by it he grew to be the king of the world; but he sold it at the last, and fell. Captain Cook had this bottle, and by it he found his way to so many islands; but he, too sold it, and was slain upon Hawaii. For, once it is sold, the power goes and the protection; and unless a man remain content with what he has, ill will befall him.'

'And yet you talk of selling it yourself?' Keawe said.

'I have all I wish, and I am growing elderly,' replied the man. 'There is one thing the imp cannot do – he cannot prolong life; and, it would not be fair to conceal from you, there is a drawback to the bottle; for if a man die before he sells it, he must burn in hell for ever.'

'To be sure, that is a drawback and no mistake,' cried Keawe. 'I would not meddle with the thing. I can do without a house, thank God; but there is one thing I could not be doing with one particle, and that is to be damned.'

'Dear me, you must not run away with things,' returned the man. 'All you have to do is to use the power of the imp in moderation, and then sell it to someone else, as I do to you, and finish your life in comfort.'

'Well, I observe two things,' said Keawe. 'All the time you keep sighing like a maid in love, that is one; and, for the other, you sell this bottle very cheap.'

'I have told you already why I sigh,' said the man. 'It is because I fear my health is breaking up; and, as you said yourself, to die and go to the devil is a pity for anyone. As for why I sell so cheap, I must explain to you there is a peculiarity about the bottle. Long ago, when the devil brought it first upon earth, it was extremely expensive, and was sold first of all to Prester John for many millions of dollars; but it cannot be sold at all, unless sold at a loss. If you sell it for as much as you paid for it, back it comes to you again like a homing pigeon. It follows that the price has kept falling in these centuries, and the bottle is now remarkably cheap. I bought it myself from one of my great neighbours on this hill, and the price I paid was only ninety dollars. I could sell it for as high as eighty-nine dollars and ninety-nine cents, but not a penny dearer, or back the thing must come to me. Now, about this there are two bothers. First, when you offer a bottle so singular for eighty odd dollars, people suppose you to be jesting.

And second – but there is no hurry about that – and I need not go into it. Only remember it must be coined money that you sell it for.'

'How am I to know that this is all true?' asked Keawe.

'Some of it you can try at once,' replied the man. 'Give me your fifty dollars, take the bottle, and wish your fifty dollars back into your pocket. If that does not happen, I pledge you my honour I will cry off the bargain and restore your money.'

'You are not deceiving me?' said Keawe.

The man bound himself with a great oath.

'Well, I will risk that much,' said Keawe, 'for that can do no harm.' And he paid over his money to the man, and the man handed him the bottle.

'Imp of the bottle,' said Keawe, 'I want my fifty dollars back.' And sure enough he had scarce said the word before his pocket was as heavy as ever.

'To be sure this is a wonderful bottle,' said Keawe.

'And now, good-morning to you, my fine fellow, and the devil go with you for me!' said the man.

'Hold on,' said Keawe, 'I don't want any more of this fun. Here, take your bottle back.'

'You have bought it for less than I paid for it,' replied the man, rubbing his hands. 'It is yours now; and, for my part, I am only concerned to see the back of you.' And with that he rang for his Chinese servant, and had Keawe shown out of the house.

Now, when Keawe was in the street, with the bottle under his arm, he began to think. 'If all is true about this bottle, I may have made a losing bargain,' thinks he. 'But perhaps the man was only fooling me.' The first thing he did was to count his money; the sum was exact – forty-nine dollars American money, and one Chili piece. 'That looks like the truth,' said Keawe. 'Now I will try another part.'

The streets in that part of the city were as clean as a ship's decks, and though it was noon, there were no passengers. Keawe set the bottle in the gutter and walked away. Twice he looked back, and there was the milky, round-bellied bottle where he left it. A third time he looked back, and turned a corner; but he had scarce done so, when something knocked upon his elbow, and behold! it was the long neck sticking up; and as for the round belly, it was jammed into the pocket of his pilot-coat.

'And that looks like the truth,' said Keawe.

The next thing he did was to buy a corkscrew in a shop, and go apart into a secret place in the fields. And there he tried to draw the cork, but as often as he put the screw in, out it came again, and the cork as whole as ever.

'This is some new sort of cork,' said Keawe, and all at once he began to shake and sweat, for he was afraid of that bottle.

On his way back to the port-side, he saw a shop where a man sold shells and clubs from the wild islands, old heathen deities, old coined money, pictures from China and Japan, and all manner of things that sailors bring in their sea-chests. And here he had an idea. So he went in and offered the bottle for a hundred dollars. The man of the shop laughed at him at the first, and offered him five; but indeed, it was a curious bottle – such glass was never blown in any human glassworks, so prettily the colours shown under the milky white, and so strangely the shadow hovered in the midst; so, after he had disputed awhile after the manner of his kind, the shopman gave Keawe sixty silver dollars for the thing, and set it on a shelf in the midst of his window.

'Now,' said Keawe, 'I have sold that for sixty which I bought for fifty – so, to say truth, a little less, because one of my dollars was from Chili. Now I shall know the truth upon another point.'

So he went back on board his ship, and, when he opened his chest, there was the bottle, and had come more quickly than himself. Now Keawe had a mate on board whose name was Lopaka.

'What ails you?' said Lopaka, 'that you stare in your chest?'

They were alone in the ship's forecastle, and Keawe bound him to secrecy, and told all.

'This is a very strange affair,' said Lopaka; 'and I fear you will be in trouble about this bottle. But there is one point very clear – that you are sure of the trouble, and you had better have the profit in the bargain. Make up your mind what you want with it; give the order, and if it is done as you desire, I will buy the bottle myself; for I have an idea of my own to get a schooner, and go trading through the islands.'

'That is not my idea,' said Keawe; 'but to have a beautiful house and garden on the Kona Coast, where I was born, the sun shining in at the door, flowers in the garden, glass in the windows, pictures on the walls, and toys and fine carpets on the tables, for all the world like the house I was in this day – only a storey higher, and with balconies all about like the king's palace; and to live there without care and make merry with my friends and relatives.'

'Well,' said Lopaka, 'let us carry it back with us to Hawaii, and if all comes true, as you suppose, I will buy the bottle, as I said, and ask a schooner.'

Upon that they were agreed, and it was not long before the ship returned to Honolulu, carrying Keawe and Lopaka, and the bottle. They were scarce come ashore when they met a friend upon the beach, who began at once to condole with Keawe.

'I do not know what I am to be condoled about,' said Keawe.

'Is it possible you have not heard,' said the friend, 'your uncle – that good old man – is dead, and your cousin – that beautiful boy – was drowned at sea?'

Keawe was filled with sorrow, and, beginning to weep and to lament he forgot about the bottle. But Lopaka was thinking to himself, and presently, when Keawe's grief was a little abated, 'I have been thinking,' said Lopaka. 'Had not your uncle lands in Hawaii, in the district of Kau?'

'No,' said Keawe, 'not in Kau; they are on the mountain-side – a little way south of Hookena.'

'These lands will now be yours?' asked Lopaka.

'And so they will,' says Keawe, and began again to lament for his relatives.

'No,' said Lopaka, 'do not lament at present. I have a thought in my mind. How if this should be the doing of the bottle? For here is the place ready for your house.'

'If this be so,' cried Keawe, 'it is a very ill way to serve me by killing my relatives. But it may be, indeed; for it was in just such a station that I saw the house with my mind's eye.'

'The house, however, is not yet built,' said Lopaka.

'No, nor like to be!' said Keawe, 'for though my uncle has some coffee and ava and bananas, it will not be more than will keep me in comfort; and the rest of that land is the black lava.'

'Let us go to the lawyer,' said Lopaka; 'I have still this idea in my mind.'

Now, when they came to the lawyer's, it appeared Keawe's uncle had grown monstrous rich in the last days, and there was a fund of money.

'And here is the money for the house!' cried Lopaka.

'If you are thinking of a new house,' said the lawyer, 'here is the card of a new architect, of whom they tell me great things.'

'Better and better!' cried Lopaka. 'Here is all made plain for us. Let us continue to obey orders.'

So they went to the architect, and he had drawings of houses on his table.

'You want something out of the way,' said the architect. 'How do you like this?' and he handed a drawing to Keawe.

Now, when Keawe set eyes on the drawing, he cried out aloud, for it was the picture of his thought exactly drawn.

'I am for this house,' thought he. 'Little as I like the way it comes to me, I am in for it now, and I may as well take the good along with the evil.'

So he told the architect all that he wished, and how he would have that house furnished, and about the pictures on the wall and the knick-knacks on the tables; and he asked the man plainly for how much he would undertake the whole affair.

The architect put many questions, and took his pen and made a computation; and when he had done he named the very sum that Keawe had inherited.

Lopaka and Keawe looked at one another and nodded.

'It is quite clear,' thought Keawe, 'that I am to have

this house, whether or no. It comes from the devil, and I fear I will get little good by that; and of one thing I am sure, I will make no more wishes as long as I have this bottle. But with the house I am saddled, and I may as well take the good along with the evil.'

So he made his terms with the architect, and they signed a paper; and Keawe and Lopaka took ship again and sailed to Australia; for it was concluded between them they should not interfere at all, but leave the architect and the bottle imp to build and to adorn that house at their own pleasure.

The voyage was a good voyage, only all the time Keawe was holding in his breath, for he had sworn he would utter no more wishes, and take no more favours from the devil. The time was up when they go back. The architect told them that the house was ready, and Keawe and Lopaka took a passage in the *Hall*, and went down Kona way to view the house, and see if all had been done fitly according to the thought that was in Keawe's mind.

Now, the house stood on the mountain-side, visible to ships. Above, the forest ran up into the clouds of rain; below, the black lava fell in cliffs, where the kings of old lay buried. A garden bloomed about that house with every hue of flowers; and there was an orchard of papaia on the one hand and an orchard of breadfruit on the other, and right in front, toward the sea, a ship's mast had been rigged up and bore a flag. As for the house, it was three storeys high, with great chambers and broad balconies on each. The windows were of glass, so excellent that it was as clear as water and as bright as day. All manner of furniture adorned the chambers. Pictures hung upon the wall in golden frames: pictures of ships, and men fighting, and of the most beautiful women, and of singular places; nowhere in the world are there pictures of so bright a colour as those Keawe found hanging in his house. As for the knick-knacks, they were extraordinary fine; chiming clocks and musical boxes, little men with nodding heads, books filled with pictures, weapons of price from all quarters of the world, and the most elegant puzzles to entertain the leisure of a solitary man. And as no one would care to live in such chambers, only to walk through and view them, the balconies were made so broad that a whole town might have lived upon them in delight; and Keawe knew not which to prefer, whether the back porch, where you got the land breeze, and looked upon the orchards and the flowers, or the front balcony, where you could drink the wind of the sea, and look down the steep wall of the mountain and see the *Hall* going by once a week or so between Kookena and the hills of Pele, or the schooners plying up the coast for wood and ava and bananas.

When they had viewed all, Keawe and Lopaka sat on the porch.

'Well,' asked Lopaka, 'is it all as you designed?'

'Words cannot utter it,' said Keawe. 'It is better than I dreamed, and I am sick with satisfaction.'

'There is but one thing to consider,' said Lopaka; 'all this may be quite natural, and the bottle imp have nothing whatever to say to it. If I were to buy the bottle, and got no schooner after all, I should have put my hand in the fire for nothing. I gave you my word, I know; but yet I think you would not grudge me one more proof.'

'I have sworn I would take no more favours,' said Keawe. 'I have gone already deep enough.'

'This is no favour I am thinking of,' replied Lopaka. 'It is only to see the imp himself. There is nothing to be gained by that, and so nothing to be ashamed of; and yet, if I once saw him, I should be sure of the whole matter. So indulge me so far, and let me see the imp; and, after that, here is the money in my hand, and I will buy it.'

'There is only one thing I am afraid of,' said Keawe. 'The imp may be very ugly to view; and if you once set eyes upon him you might be very undesirous of the bottle.'

'I am a man of my word,' said Lopaka. 'And here is the money betwixt us.'

'Very well,' replied Keawe. 'I have a curiosity myself. So come, let us have one look at you, Mr Imp.'

Now as soon as that was said, the imp looked out of the bottle, and in again, swift as a lizard; and there sat Keawe and Lopaka turned to stone. The night had quite come, before either found a thought to say or voice to say it with; and then Lopaka pushed the money over and took the bottle.

'I am a man of my word,' said he, 'and had need to be so, or I would not touch this bottle with my foot. Well, I shall get my schooner and a dollar or two for my pocket; and then I will be rid of this devil as fast as I can. For to tell you the plain truth, the look of him has cast me down.'

'Lopaka,' said Keawe, 'do not you think any worse of me than you can help; I know it is night, and the roads bad, and the pass by the tombs an ill place to go by so late, but I declare since I have seen that little face, I cannot eat or sleep or pray till it is gone from me. I will give you a lantern, and a basket to put the bottle in, and any picture or fine thing in all my house that takes your fancy; and be gone at once, and go sleep at Hookena with Nahinu.'

'Keawe,' said Lopaka, 'many a man would take this ill; above all, when I am doing you a turn so friendly, as to keep my word and buy the bottle; and for that matter, the night and the dark, and the way by the tombs, must be all tenfold more dangerous to a man with such a sin upon his conscience, and such a bottle under his arm. But for my part, I am so extremely terrified myself, I have not the heart to blame you. Here I go then; and I pray God you may be happy in your house, and I fortunate with my schooner, and both get to heaven in the end in spite of the devil and his bottle.'

So Lopaka went down the mountain; and Keawe stood in his front balcony, and listened to the clink of the horse's shoes, and watched the lantern go shining down the path, and along the cliff of caves where the old dead are buried; and all the time he trembled and clasped his hands, and prayed for his friend, and gave glory to God that he himself had escaped out of that trouble.

But the next day came very brightly, and that new house of his was so delightful to behold that he forgot his terrors. One day followed another, and Keawe dwelt there in perpetual joy. He had his place on the back porch; it was there he ate and lived, and read the stories in the Honolulu newspapers; but when anyone came by they would go in and view the chambers and the pictures. And the fame of the house went far and wide; it was called Ka-Hale Nui – the Great House – in all Kona; and sometimes the Bright House, for Keawe kept a Chinaman, who was all day dusting and furbishing; and the glass and the gilt, and the fine stuffs, and the pictures, shown as bright as the morning. As for Keawe himself, he could not walk in the chambers without singing, his heart was so enlarged; and when ships sailed by upon the sea, he would fly his colours on the mast.

So time went by, until one day Keawe went upon a visit as far as Kailua to certain of his friends. There he was well feasted; and left as soon as he could the next morning, and rode hard, for he was impatient to behold his beautiful house; and, besides, the night then coming on was the night in which the dead of old days go abroad in the sides of Kona; and having already meddled with the devil, he was the more chary of meeting with the dead. A little beyond Honaunau, looking far ahead, he was aware of a woman bathing in the edge of the sea; and she seemed a well grown girl, but he thought no more of it. Then he saw her white shift flutter as she put it on, and then her red holoku; and by the time he came abreast of her she was done with her toilet, and had come up from the sea, and stood by the track-side in her red holoku, and she was all freshened with the bath, and her eyes shone and were kind. Now Keawe no sooner beheld her than he drew rein.

'I thought I knew everyone in this country,' said he. 'How comes it that I do not know you?'

'I am Kokua, daughter of Kiano,' said the girl, 'and I have just returned from Oahu. Who are you?'

'I will tell you who I am in a little,' said Keawe, dismounting from his horse, 'but not now. For I have a thought in my mind, and if you knew who I was, you might have heard of me, and would not give me a true answer. But tell me, first of all, one thing: Are you married?'

At this Kokua laughed out aloud. 'It is you who ask questions,' said she. 'Are you married yourself?'

'Indeed, Kokua, I am not,' repled Keawe, 'and never thought to be until this hour. But here is the plain truth. I have met you here at the roadside, and I saw your eyes, which are like the stars, and my heart went to you as swift as a bird. And so now, if you want none of me, say so, and I will go on to my own place; but if you think me no worse than any other young man, say so, too, and I will turn aside to your father's for the night, and tomorrow I will talk with the good man.'

Kokua said never a word, but she looked at the sea and laughed.

'Kokua,' said Keawe, 'if you say nothing, I will take that for the good answer; so let us be stepping to your father's door.'

She went on ahead of him, still without speech; only sometimes she glanced back and glanced away again, and she kept the string of her hat in her mouth.

Now, when they had come to the door, Kiano came out on his verandah, and cried out and welcomed Keawe by name. At that the girl looked over, for the fame of the great house had come to her ears; and, to be sure, it was a great temptation. All that evening they were very merry together; and the girl was as bold as brass under the eyes of her parents, and made a mock of Keawe, for she had a quick wit. The next day he had a word with Kiano, and found the girl alone.

'Kokua,' said he, 'you made a mock of me all the evening; and it is still time to bid me go. I would not tell you who I was, because I have so fine a house, and I feared you would think too much of that house and too little of the man that loves you. Now you know all, and if you wish to have seen the last of me, say so at once.'

'No,' said Kokua; but this time she did not laugh, nor did Keawe ask for more.

This was the wooing of Keawe; things had gone quickly; but so an arrow goes, and the ball of a rifle swifter still, and yet both may strike the target. Things had gone fast, but they had gone far also, and the thought of Keawe rang in the maiden's head; she heard his voice in the breach of the surf upon the lava, and for this young man that she had seen but twice she would have left father and mother and her native islands. As for Keawe himself, his horse flew up the path of the mountain under the cliff of tombs, and the sound of the hoofs, and the sound of Keawe singing to himself for pleasure echoed in the caverns of the dead. He came to the Bright House, and still he was singing. He sat and ate in the broad balcony, and the Chinaman wondered at his master, to hear how he sang between the mouthfuls. The sun went down into the sea, and the night came; and Keawe walked the balconies by lamplight, high on the mountains, and the voice of his singing startled men on ships.

'Here am I now upon my high place,' he said to himself. 'Life may be no better; this is the mountain top; and all shelves about me towards the worse. For the first time I will light up the chambers, and bathe in my fine bath with the hot water and the cold, and sleep alone in the bed of my bridal chamber.'

So the Chinaman had word, and he must rise from sleep and light the furnaces; and as he wrought below, beside the boilers, he heard his master singing and rejoicing above him in the lighted chambers. When the water began to be hot the Chinaman cried to his master; and Keawe went into the bathroom; and the Chinaman heard him sing as he filled the marble basin; and heard him sing, and the singing broken, as he undressed; until of a sudden, the song ceased. The Chinaman listened, and listened; he called up the house to Keawe to ask if all were well, and Keawe answered him 'Yes,' and bade him go to bed; but there was no more singing in the Bright House; and all night long, the Chinaman heard his master's feet go round and round the balconies without repose.

Now the truth of it was this: as Keawe undressed for his bath, he spied upon his flesh a patch like a patch of lichen on a rock, and it was then that he stopped singing. For he knew the likeness of that patch, and knew that he was fallen in the Chinese Evil. [Leprosy] Now, it is a sad thing for any man to fall into this sickness. And it would be a sad thing for anyone to leave a house so beautiful and so commodious, and depart from all his friends to the north coast of Molokai between the mighty cliff and the sea-breakers. But what was that to the case of the man Keawe, he who had met his love but yesterday, and won her but that morning, and now saw all his hopes break, in a moment, like a piece of glass?

Awhile he sat upon the edge of the bath; then sprang, with a cry, and ran outside; and to and fro, to and fro, along the balcony, like one despairing.

'Very willingly could I leave Hawaii, the home of my fathers,' Keawe was thinking. 'Very lightly could I leave my house, the high-placed, the many-windowed, here upon the mountains. Very bravely could I go to Molokai, to Kalaupapa by the cliffs, to live with the smitten and to sleep there, far from my fathers. But what wrong have I done, what sin lies upon my soul, that I should have encountered Kokua coming cool from the sea-water in the evening? Kokua, the soul ensnarer! Kokua, the light of my life! Her may I never wed, her may I look upon no longer, her may I no more handle with my living hand; and it is for this, it is for you, O Kokua! that I pour my lamentations!'

Now you are to observe what sort of a man Keawe was, for he might have dwelt there in the Bright House for years, and no one been the wiser of his sickness; but he reckoned nothing of that, if he must lose Kokua. And again, he might have wed Kokua even as he was; and so many would have done, because they have the souls of pigs; but Keawe loved the maid manfully, and he would do her no hurt and bring her in no danger.

A little beyond the midst of the night, there came in his mind the recollection of that bottle. He went round to the back porch, and called to memory the day when the devil had looked forth; and at the thought ice ran in his veins.

'A dreadful thing is the bottle,' thought Keawe, 'and dreadful is the imp, and it is a dreadful thing to risk the flames of hell. But what other hope have I to cure the sickness or to wed Kokua? What!' he thought, 'would I beard the devil once, only to get me a house, and not face him again to win Kokua?'

Thereupon he called to mind it was the next day the *Hall* went by on her return to Honolulu. 'There must I go first,' he thought, 'and see Lopaka. For the best hope that I have now is to find that same bottle I was so pleased to be rid of.'

Never a wink could he sleep; the food stuck in his throat; but he sent a letter to Kiano, and about the time when the steamer would be coming, rode down beside the cliff of the tombs. It rained; his horse went heavily; he looked up at the black mouths of the caves, and he envied the dead that slept there and were done with trouble; and called to mind how he had galloped by the day before, and was astonished. So he came down to Hookena, and there was all the country gathered for the steamer as usual. In the shed before the store they sat and jested and passed the news; but there was no matter of speech in Keawe's bosom, and he sat in their midst and looked without on the rain falling on the houses, and the surf beating among the rocks, and the sighs arose in his throat.

'Keawe of the Bright House is out of spirits,' said one to another. Indeed, and so he was, and little wonder.

Then the *Hall* came, and the whaleboat carried him on board. The after-part of the ship was full of Haoles (white men) who had been to visit the volcano, as their custom is; and the midst was crowded with Kanakas, and the forepart with wild bulls from Hilo and horses from Kau; but Keawe sat apart from all in his sorrow, and watched for the house of Kiano. There it sat, low upon the shore in the black rocks and shaded by the cocoa palms, and there by the door was a red holoku, no greater than a fly, and going to and fro with a fly's busyness.

'Ah, queen of my heart,' he cried, 'I'll venture my dear soul to win you!'

Soon after, darkness fell, and the cabins were lit up, and the Haoles sat and played at the cards and drank whisky as their custom is; but Keawe walked the deck all night; and all the next day, as they steamed under the lee of Maui or of Molokai, he was still pacing to and fro like a wild animal in a menagerie.

Towards evening they passed Diamond Head, and came to the pier of Honolulu. Keawe stepped out among the crowd and began to ask for Lopaka. It seemed he had become the owner of a schooner – none better in the islands – and was gone upon an adventure as far as Pola-Pola or Kahiki; so there was no help to be looked for from Lopaka. Keawe called to mind a friend of his, a lawyer in the town (I must not tell his name), and enquired of him. They said he was grown suddenly rich, and had a fine new house upon Waikiki shore; and this put a thought in Keawe's head, and he called a hack and drove to the lawyer's house.

The house was all brand new, and the trees in the garden no greater than walking-sticks, and the lawyer, when he came, had the air of a man well pleased.

'What can I do to serve you?' said the lawyer.

'You are a friend of Lopaka's,' replied Keawe, 'and Lopaka purchased from me a certain piece of goods that I thought you might enable me to trace.'

The lawyer's face became very dark. 'I do not profess to misunderstand you, Mr Keawe,' said he, 'though this is an ugly business to be stirring in. You may be sure I know nothing, but yet I have a guess, and if you would apply in a certain quarter I think you might have news.'

And he named the name of a man, which, again, I had better not repeat. So it was for days, and Keawe went from one to another, finding everywhere new clothes and carriages, and fine new houses and men everywhere in great contentment, although, to be sure, when he hinted at his business their faces would cloud over.

'No doubt I am upon the track,' thought Keawe.

'These new clothes and carriages are all the gifts of the little imp, and these glad faces are the faces of men who have taken their profit and got rid of the accursed thing in safety. When I see pale cheeks and hear sighing, I shall know that I am near the bottle.'

So it befell at last that he was recommended to a Haole in Beritania Street. When he came to the door, about the hour of the evening meal, there were the usual marks of the new house, and the young garden, and the electric light shining in the windows; but when the owner came, a shock of hope and fear ran through Keawe; for here was a young man, white as a corpse, and black about the eyes, the hair shedding from his head, and such a look in his countenance as a man may have when he is waiting for the gallows.

'Here it is, to be sure,' thought Keawe, and so with this man he no ways veiled his errand. 'I am come to buy the bottle,' said he.

At the word, the young Haole of Beritania Street reeled against the wall.

'The bottle!' he gasped. 'To buy the bottle!' Then he seemed to choke, and seizing Keawe by the arm carried him into a room and poured out wine in two glasses.

'Here is my respects,' said Keawe, who had been much about with Haoles in his time. 'Yes,' he added, 'I am come to buy the bottle. What is the price by now?'

At that word the young man let his glass slip through his fingers, and looked upon Keawe like a ghost.

'The price,' says he; 'the price! you do not know the price?'

'It is for that I am asking you,' returned Keawe.

'But why are you so much concerned? Is there anything wrong about the price?'

'It has dropped a great deal in value since your time, Mr Keawe,' said the young man, stammering.

'Well, well, I shall have the less to pay for it,' said Keawe. 'How much did it cost you?'

The young man was as white as a sheet. 'Two cents,' said he.

'What?' cried Keawe, 'two cents? Why, then, you can only sell it for one. And he who buys it – ' The words died upon Keawe's tongue; he who bought it could never sell it again, the bottle and the bottle imp must abide with him until he died, and when he died must carry him to the red end of hell.

The young man of Beritania Street fell upon his knees. 'For God's sake buy it!' he cried. 'You can have all my fortune in the bargain. I was mad when I bought it at that price. I had embezzled money at my store; I was lost else; I must have gone to jail.'

'Poor creature,' said Keawe, 'you would risk your soul upon so desperate an adventure, and to avoid the proper punishment of your own disgrace; and you think I could hesitate with love in front of me. Give me the bottle, and the change which I make sure you have all ready. Here is a five-cent piece.'

It was as Keawe supposed; the young man had the change ready in a drawer; the bottle changed hands, and Keawe's fingers were no sooner clasped upon the stalk than he had breathed his wish to be a clean man. And, sure enough, when he got home to his room and stripped himself before a glass, his flesh was whole like an infant's. And here was the strange thing: he had no sooner seen this miracle, than his mind was changed within him, and he cared naught for the Chinese Evil, and little enough for Kokua; and had but the one thought, that here he was bound to the bottle imp for time and for eternity, and had no better hope but to be a cinder for ever in the flames of hell. Away ahead of him he saw them blaze with his mind's eye, and his soul shrank, and darkness fell upon the light.

When Keawe came to himself a little, he was aware it was the night when the band played at the hotel. Thither he went, because he feared to be alone; and there, among happy faces, walked to and fro, and heard the tunes go up and down, and saw Berger beat the measure, and all the while he heard the flames crackle, and saw the red fire burning in the bottomless pit. Of a sudden the band played 'Hiki-au-ao'; that was a song that he had sung with Kokua, and at the strain courage returned to him.

'It is done now,' he thought, 'and once more let me take the good along with the evil.'

So it befell that he returned to Hawaii by the first steamer, and as soon as it could be managed he was wedded to Kokua, and carried her up the mountain-side to the Bright House.

Now it was so with these two, that when they were together, Keawe's heart was stilled; but so soon as he was alone he fell into a brooding horror, and heard the flames crackle, and saw the red fire burn in the bottomless pit. The girl, indeed, had come to him wholly; her heart leapt in her side at sight of him, her hand clung to his; and she was so fashioned from the hair upon her head to the nails upon her toes that none could see her without joy. She was pleasant in her nature. She had the good word always. Full of song she was, and went to and fro in the Bright House, the brightest thing in its three storeys, carolling like the birds. And Keawe beheld and heard her with delight, and then must shrink upon one side, and weep and groan to think upon the price that he had paid for her; and then he must dry his eyes, and wash his face, and go and sit with her on the broad balconies joining in her songs, and, with a sick spirit, answering her smiles.

There came a day when her feet began to be heavy and her songs more rare; and now it was not Keawe only that would weep apart, but each would sunder from the other and sit in opposite balconies with the whole width of the Bright House betwixt. Keawe was so sunk in his despair, he scarce observed the change, and was only glad he had more hours to sit alone and brood upon his destiny and was not so frequently condemned to pull a smiling face on a sick heart. But one day, coming softly through the house, he heard the sound of a child sobbing, and there was Kokua rolling her face upon the balcony floor, and weeping like the lost.

'You do well to weep in this house, Kokua,' he said. 'And yet I would give the head off my body that you (at least) might have been happy.'

'Happy!' she cried. 'Keawe, when you lived alone in your Bright House, you were the word of the island for a happy man; laughter and song were in your mouth, and your face was as bright as the sunrise. Then you wedded poor Kokua; and the good God knows what is amiss in her – but from that day you have not smiled. Ah!' she cried, 'what ails me? I thought I was pretty, and I knew I loved him. What ails me that I throw this cloud upon my husband?'

'Poor Kokua,' said Keawe. He sat down by her side, and sought to take her hand; but that she plucked away. 'Poor Kokua,' he said, again. 'My poor child – my pretty. And I thought all this while to spare you! Well, you shall know all. Then, at least, you will pity poor Keawe; then you will understand how much he loved you in the past – that he dared hell for your possession – and how much he loves you still (the poor condemned one), that he can yet call up a smile when he beholds you.'

With that, he told her all, even from the beginning.

'You have done this for me?' she cried. 'Ah, well, then what do I care!' – and she clasped and wept upon him.

'Ah, child!' said Keawe; 'and yet, when I consider of the fire of hell, I care a good deal!'

'Never tell me,' said she, 'no man can be lost because he loved Kokua, and no other fault. I tell you, Keawe, I shall save you with these hands, or perish in your company. What! you loved me, and gave your soul, and you think I will not die to save you in return?'

'Ah, my dear! you might die a hundred times, and what difference would that make?' he cried, 'except to leave me lonely till the time comes of my damnation?'

'You know nothing,' said she. 'I was educated in a school in Honolulu; I am no common girl. And I tell you, I shall save my lover. What is this you say about a cent? But all the world is not American. In England they have a piece they call a farthing, which is about half a cent. Ah! sorrow!' she cried, 'that makes it scarcely better, for the buyer must be lost, and we shall find none so brave as my Keawe! But, then, there is France; they have a small coin there which they call a centime, and these go five to the cent or thereabout. We could not do better. Come, Keawe, let us go to the French islands; let us go to Tahiti, as fast as ships can bear us. There we have four centimes, three centimes, two centimes, one centime; four possible sales to come and go on; and two of us to push the bargain. Come, my Keawe! kiss me, and banish care. Kokua will defend you.'

'Gift of God!' he cried. 'I cannot think that God will punish me for desiring aught so good! Be it as you will, then; take me where you please: I put my life and my salvation in your hands.'

Early the next day Kokua was about her preparations. She took Keawe's chest that he went with sailoring; and first she put the bottle in a corner; and then packed it with the richest of the clothes and the bravest of the knick-knacks in the house. 'For,' said she, 'we must seem to be rich folks, or who will believe in the bottle?' All the time of her preparation she was as gay as a bird; only when she looked upon Keawe, the tears would spring in her eye, and she must run and kiss him. As for Keawe, a weight was off his soul; now that he had his secret shared, and some hope in front of him, he seemed like a new man, his feet went lightly on the earth, and his breath was good to him again. Yet was terror still at his elbow; and ever and again, as the wind blows out a taper, hope died in him, and he saw the flames toss and the red fire burn in hell.

It was given out in the country they were gone pleasuring to the States, which was thought a strange thing, and yet not so strange as the truth, if any could have guessed it. So they went to Honolulu in the *Hall*, and thence in the *Umatilla* to San Francisco with a crowd of Haoles, and at San Francisco took their passage by the mail brigantine, the *Tropic Bird*, for Papeete, the chief place of the French in the south islands. Thither they came, after a pleasant voyage, on a fair day of the Trade Wind, and saw the reef with the surf breaking, and Motuiti with its palms, and the schooner riding withinside, and the white houses of the town low down along the shore among green trees, and overhead the mountains and the clouds of Tahiti, the wise island.

It was judged the most wise to hire a house, which they did accordingly, opposite the British Consul's, to make a great parade of money, and themselves conspicuous with carriages and horses. This it was very easy to do, so long as they had the bottle in their possession; for Kokua was more bold than Keawe, and whenever she had a mind, called on the imp for twenty or a hundred dollars. At this rate they soon grew to be remarked in the town; and the strangers from Hawaii, their riding and their driving, the fine holokus and the rich lace of Kokua, became the matter of much talk.

They got on well after the first with the Tahitian language, which is indeed like to the Hawaiian, with a change of certain letters; and as soon as they had any freedom of speech, began to push the bottle. You are to consider it was not an easy subject to introduce; it was not easy to persuade people you were in earnest, when you offered to sell them for four centimes the spring of health and riches inexhaustible. It was necessary besides to explain the dangers of the bottle; and either people disbelieved the whole thing and laughed or they thought the more of the darker part, became overcast with gravity, and drew away from Keawe and Kokua, as from persons who had dealings with the devil. So far from gaining ground, these two began to find they were avoided in the town; the children ran away from them screaming, a thing intolerable to Kokua; Catholics crossed themselves as they went by; and all persons began with one accord to disengage themselves from their advances.

Depression fell upon their spirits. They would sit at night in their new house, after a day's weariness, and not exchange one word, or the silence would be broken by Kokua bursting suddenly into sobs. Sometimes they would pray together; sometimes they would have the bottle out upon the floor, and sit all evening watching how the shadow hovered in the midst. At such times they would be afraid to go to rest. It was long ere slumber came to them, and if either dozed off, it would be to wake and find the other silently weeping in the dark, or perhaps, to wake alone, the other having fled from the house and the neighbourhood of that bottle, to pace under the bananas in the little garden, or to wander on the beach by moonlight.

One night it was so when Kokua awoke. Keawe was gone. She felt in the bed and his place was cold. Then fear fell upon her, and she sat up in bed. A little moonshine filtered through the shutters. The room was bright, and she could spy the bottle on the floor. Outside it blew high, the great trees of the avenue cried aloud, and the fallen leaves rattled in the verandah. In the midst of this Kokua was aware of another sound; whether of a beast or of a man she could scarce tell, but it was as sad as death, and cut her to the soul. Softly she arose, set the door ajar, and looked forth in the moonlit yard. There, under the bananas, lay Keawe, his mouth in the dust, and as he lay he moaned.

It was Kokua's first thought to run forward and

console him; her second potently withheld her. Keawe had borne himself before his wife like a brave man; it became her little in the hour of weakness to intrude upon his shame. With the thought she drew back into the house.

'Heavens!' she thought, 'how careless have I been – how weak! It is he, not I, that stands in this eternal peril; it was he, not I, that took the curse upon his soul. It is for my sake, and for the love of a creature of so little worth and such poor help, that he now beholds so close to him the flames of hell – ay, and smells the smoke of it, lying without there in the wind and moonlight. Am I so dull of spirit that never till now I have surmised my duty, or have I seen it before and turned aside? But now, at least, I take upon my soul in both the hands of my affection; now I say farewell to the white steps of heaven and the waiting faces of my friends. A love for a love, and let mine be equalled with Keawe's! A soul for a soul, and be it mine to perish!'

She was a deft woman with her hands, and was soon apparelled. She took in her hands the change – the precious centimes they kept ever at their side; for this coin is little used, and they had made provision at a Government office. When she was forth in the avenue clouds came on the wind, and the moon was blackened. The town slept, and she knew not whither to turn till she heard one coughing in the shadow of the trees.

'Old man,' said Kokua, 'what do you here abroad in the cold night?'

The old man could scarce express himself for coughing, but she made out that he was old and poor, and a stranger in the island.

'Will you do me a service?' said Kokua. 'As one stranger to another, and as an old man to a young woman, will you help a daughter of Hawaii?'

'Ah,' said the old man. 'So you are the witch from the eight islands, and even my old soul you seek to entangle. But I have heard of you, and defy your wickedness.'

'Sit down here,' said Kokua, 'and let me tell you a tale.' And she told him the story of Keawe from the beginning to the end.

'And now,' said she, 'I am his wife, whom he bought with his soul's welfare. And what should I do? If I went to him myself and offered to buy it, he would refuse. But if you go, he will sell it eagerly; I will await you here; you will buy it for four centimes, and I will buy it again for three. And the Lord strengthen a poor girl!'

'If you meant falsely,' said the old man, 'I think God would strike you dead.'

'He would!' cried Kokua. 'Be sure he would. I could not be so treacherous – God would not suffer it.'

'Give me the four centimes and await me here,' said the old man.

Now, when Kokua stood alone in the street, her spirit died. The wind roared in the trees, and it seemed to her the rushing of the flames of hell; the shadows tossed in the light of the street lamp, and they seemed to her the snatching hands of evil ones. If she had had the strength, she must have run away, and if she had had the breath she must have screamed aloud; but, in truth, she could do neither, and stood and trembled in the avenue, like an affrighted child.

Then she saw the old man returning, and he had the bottle in his hand.

'I have done your bidding,' said he. 'I left your husband weeping like a child; tonight he will sleep easy.' And he held the bottle forth.

'Before you give it me,' Kokua panted, 'take the good with the evil – ask to be delivered from your cough.'

'I am an old man,' replied the other, 'and too near the gate of the grave to take a favour from the devil. But what is this? Why do you not take the bottle? Do you hesitate?'

'Not hesitate!' cried Kokua. 'I am only weak. Give me a moment. It is my hand resists, my flesh shrinks back from the accursed thing. One moment only!'

The old man looked upon Kokua kindly. 'Poor child!' said he, 'you fear; your soul misgives you. Well, let me keep it. I am old and can never more be happy in this world, and as for the next – '

'Give it me!' gasped Kokua. 'There is your money. Do you think I am so base as that? Give me the bottle.'

'God bless you, child,' said the old man.

Kokua concealed the bottle under her holoku, said farewell to the old man, and walked off along the avenue, she cared not whither. For all roads were now the same to her, and led equally to hell. Sometimes she walked, and sometimes ran; sometimes she screamed out loud in the night, and sometimes lay by the wayside in the dust and wept. All that she had heard of hell came back to her; she saw the flames blaze, and she smelt the smoke, and her flesh withered on the coals.

Near the day she came to her mind again, and returned to the house. It was even as the old man said – Keawe slumbered like a child. Kokua stood and gazed upon his face.

'Now, my husband,' said she, 'it is your turn to sleep. When you wake it will be your turn to sing and laugh. But for poor Kokua, alas! that meant no evil – for poor Kokua no more sleep, no more singing, no more delight, whether in earth or heaven.'

With that she lay down in the bed by his side, and her misery was so extreme that she fell in a deep slumber instantly.

Late in the morning her husband woke her and gave her the good news. It seemed he was silly with delight, for he paid no heed to her distress, ill though she dissembled it. The words stuck in her mouth, it mattered not; Keawe did the speaking. She ate not a bite, but who was to observe it? For Keawe cleared the dish. Kokua saw and heard him, like some strange thing in a dream; there were times when she forgot or doubted, and put her hands to her brow; to know herself doomed and hear her husband babble, seemed so monstrous.

All the while Keawe was eating and talking, and planning the time of their return, and thanking her for saving him, and fondling her, and calling her the true helper after all. He laughed at the old man that was fool enough to buy that bottle.

'A worthy old man he seemed,' Keawe said. 'But no one can judge by appearances. For why did the old reprobate require the bottle?'

'My husband,' said Kokua, humbly, 'his purpose may have been good.'

Keawe laughed like an angry man.

'Fiddle-de-dee!' cried Keawe. 'An old rogue, I tell you; and an old ass to boot. For the bottle was hard enough to sell at four centimes; and at three it will be quite impossible. The margin is not broad enough, the thing begins to smell of scorching – brrr!' said he, and shuddered. 'It is true I bought it myself at a cent, when I knew not there were smaller coins. I was a fool for my pains; there will never be found another: and whoever has that bottle now will carry it to the pit.'

'O my husband!' said Kokua. 'Is it not a terrible thing to save oneself by the eternal ruin of another? It seems to me I could not laugh. I would be humbled. I would be filled with melancholy. I would pray for the poor holder.'

Then Keawe, because he felt the truth of what she said, grew the more angry. 'Heighty-teighty!' cried he. 'You may be filled with melancholy if you please. It is not the mind of a good wife. If you thought at all of me, you would sit shamed.'

Thereupon he went out, and Kokua was alone.

What chance had she to sell that bottle at two centimes? None, she perceived. And if she had any, here was her husband hurrying her away to a country where there was nothing lower than a cent. And here – on the morrow of her sacrifice – was her husband leaving her and blaming her.

She would not even try to profit by what time she had, but sat in the house, and now had the bottle out and viewed it with unutterable fear, and now, with loathing, hid it out of sight.

By and by, Keawe came back, and would have her take a drive.

'My husband, I am ill,' she said. 'I am out of heart. Excuse me, I can take no pleasure.'

Then was Keawe more wroth than ever. With her, because he thought she was brooding over the case of the old man; and with himself, because he thought she was right, and was ashamed to be so happy.

'This is your truth,' cried he, 'and this your affection! Your husband is just saved from eternal ruin, which he encountered for the love of you – and you take no pleasure! Kokua, you have a disloyal heart.'

He went forth again furious, and wandered in the town all day. He met friends, and drank with them; they hired a carriage and drove into the country, and there drank again. All the time Keawe was ill at ease, because he was taking this pastime while his wife was sad, and because he knew in his heart that she was more right than he; and the knowledge made him drink the deeper.

Now there was an old brutal Haole drinking with him, one that had been a boatswain of a whaler, a runaway, a digger in gold mines, a convict in prisons. He had a low mind and a foul mouth; he loved to drink and to see others drunken; and he pressed the glass upon Keawe. Soon there was no more money in the company.

'Here, you!' says the boatswain, 'you are rich, you have been always saying. You have a bottle or some foolishness.'

'Yes,' says Keawe, 'I am rich; I will go back and get some money from my wife, who keeps it.'

'That's a bad idea, mate,' said the boatswain. 'Never you trust a petticoat with dollars. They're all as false as water; you keep an eye on her.'

Now, this word struck in Keawe's mind; for he was muddled with what he had been drinking.

'I should not wonder but she was false, indeed,' thought he. 'Why else should she be so cast down at my release? But I will show her I am not the man to be fooled, I will catch her in the act.'

Accordingly, when they were back in town, Keawe

bade the boatswain wait for him at the corner, by the old calaboose, and went forward up the avenue alone to the door of his house. The night had come again; there was a light within, but never a sound; and Keawe crept about the corner, opened the back door softly, and looked in.

There was Kokua on the floor, the lamp at her side; before her was a milk-white bottle, with a round belly and a long neck; and as she viewed it, Kokua wrung her hands.

A long time Keawe stood and looked in the doorway. At first he was struck stupid; and then fear fell upon him that the bargain had been made amiss, and the bottle had come back to him as it came at San Francisco; and at that his knees were loosened, and the fumes of the wine departed from his head like mists off a river in the morning. And then he had another thought; and it was a strange one, that made his cheeks to burn.

'I must make sure of this,' thought he.

So he closed the door, and went softly round the corner again, and then came noisily in, as though he were but now returned. And, lo! by the time he opened the front door no bottle was to be seen; and Kokua sat in a chair and started up like one awakened out of sleep.

'I have been drinking all day and making merry,' said Keawe. 'I have been with good companions, and now I only come back for money, and return to drink and carouse with them again.'

Both his face and voice were as stern as judgment, but Kokua was too troubled to observe.

'You do well to use your own, my husband,' said she, and her words trembled.

'Oh, I do well in all things,' said Keawe, and he went straight to the chest and took out money. But he looked besides in the corner where they kept the bottle, and there was no bottle there.

At that the chest heaved upon the floor like a sea-billow, and the house span about him like a wreath of smoke, for he saw he was lost now, and there was no escape. 'It is what I feared,' he thought. 'It is she who bought it.'

And then he came to himself a little and rose up; but the sweat streamed on his face as thick as the rain and as cold as the well-water.

'Kokua,' said he, 'I said to you today what ill became me. Now I return to carouse with my jolly companions,' and at that he laughed a little quietly. 'I will take more pleasure in the cup if you forgive me.'

She clasped his knees in a moment; she kissed his knees with flowing tears.

'Oh,' she cried, 'I ask but a kind word!'

'Let us never one think hardly of the other,' said Keawe, and was gone out of the house.

Now, the money that Keawe had taken was only some of that store of centime pieces they had laid in at their arrival. It was very sure he had no mind to be drinking. His wife had given her soul for him, now he must give his for hers; no other thought was in the world with him.

At the corner, by the old calaboose, there was the boatswain waiting.

'My wife has the bottle,' said Keawe, 'and, unless you help me to recover it, there can be no more money and no more liquor tonight.'

'You do not mean to say you are serious about that bottle?' cried the boatswain.

'There is the lamp,' said Keawe. 'Do I look as if I was jesting?'

'That is so,' said the boatswain. 'You look as serious as a ghost.'

'Well, then,' said Keawe, 'here are two centimes; you must go to my wife in the house, and offer her these for the bottle, which (if I am not much mistaken) she will give you instantly. Bring it to me here, and I will buy it back from you for one; for that is the law with this bottle, that it still must be sold for a less sum. But whatever you do, never breathe a word to her that you have come from me.'

'Mate, I wonder are you making a fool of me?' asked the boatswain.

'It will do you no harm if I am,' returned Keawe.

'That is so, mate,' said the boatswain.

'And if you doubt me,' added Keawe, 'you can try. As soon as you are clear of the house, wish to have your pocket full of money, or a bottle of the best rum, or what you please, and you will see the virtue of the thing.'

'Very well, Kanaka,' says the boatswain. 'I will try; but if you are having your fun out of me, I will take my fun out of you with a belaying pin.'

So the whaler-man went off upon the avenue; and Keawe stood and waited. It was near the same spot where Kokua had waited the night before; but Keawe was more resolved, and never faltered in his purpose; only his soul was bitter with despair.

It seemed a long time he had to wait before he heard a voice singing in the darkness of the avenue. He knew the voice to be the boatswain's; but it was strange how drunken it appeared upon a sudden.

Next, the man himself came stumbling into the light

of the lamp. He had the devil's bottle buttoned in his coat; another bottle was in his hand; and even as he came in view he raised it to his mouth and drank.

'You have it,' said Keawe. 'I see that.'

'Hands off!' cried the boatswain, jumping back. 'Take a step near me, and I'll smash your mouth. You thought you could make a cat's-paw of me, did you?'

'What do you mean?' cried Keawe.

'Mean?' cried the boatswain. 'This is a pretty good bottle, this is; that's what I mean. How I got it for two centimes I can't make out; but I'm sure you shan't have it for one.'

'You mean you won't sell?' gasped Keawe.

'No, sir!' cried the boatswain. 'But I'll give you a drink of the rum, if you like.'

'I tell you,' said Keawe, 'the man who has that bottle goes to hell.'

'I reckon I'm going anyway,' returned the sailor; 'and this bottle's the best thing to go with I've struck yet. No, sir!' he cried again, 'this is my bottle now, and you can go and fish for another.'

'Can this be true?' Keawe cried. 'For your own sake, I beseech you, sell it me!'

'I don't value any of your talk,' replied the boatswain. 'You thought I was a flat; now you see I'm not; and there's an end. If you won't have a swallow of the rum, I'll have one myself. Here's your health, and good night to you!'

So off he went down the avenue towards town, and there goes the bottle out of the story.

But Keawe ran to Kokua light as the wind; and great was their joy that night; and great, since then, has been the peace of all their days in the Bright House.

A Pair of Hands

An Old Maid's Ghost Story

ARTHUR QUILLER-COUCH

'Yes,' said Miss Le Petyt, gazing into the deep fireplace and letting her hands and her knitting lie for the moment idle in her lap. 'Oh, yes, I have seen a ghost. In fact I have lived in a house with one for quite a long time.'

'How you *could* – ' began one of my host's daughters; and '*You*, Aunt Emily?' cried the other at the same moment.

Miss Le Petyt, gentle soul, withdrew her eyes from the fireplace and protested with a gay little smile. 'Well, my dears, I am not quite the coward you take me for. And, as it happens, mine was the most harmless ghost in the world. In fact' – and here she looked at the fire again – 'I was quite sorry to lose her.'

'It was a woman, then? Now *I* think,' said Miss Blanche, 'that female ghosts are the horridest of all. They wear little shoes with high red heels, and go about *tap, tap*, wringing their hands.'

'This one wrung her hands, certainly. But I don't know about the high red heels, for I never saw her feet. Perhaps she was like the Queen of Spain, and hadn't any. And as for the hands, it all depends *how* you wring them. There's an elderly shopwalker at Knightsbridge, for instance – '

'Don't be prosy, dear, when you know that we're just dying to hear the story.'

Miss Le Petyt turned to me with a small deprecating laugh. 'It's such a little one.'

'The story, or the ghost?'

'Both. It happened when I lived down in Cornwall, at Tresillack on the south coast. Tresillack was the name of the house, which stood quite alone at the head of a coombe, within sound of the sea but without sight of it; for though the coombe led down to a wide open beach, it wound and twisted half a dozen times on its way, and its overlapping sides closed the view from the house, which was advertised as "secluded". I was very poor in those days. Your father and all of us were poor then, as I trust, my dears, you will never be; but I was young enough to be romantic and wise enough to like independence, and this word "secluded" took my fancy.

'The misfortune was that it had taken the fancy, or just suited the requirements, of several previous tenants. You know, I dare say, the kind of person who rents a secluded house in the country? Well, yes, there are several kinds; but they seem to agree in being odious. No one knows where they come from, though they soon remove all doubt about where they're "going to", as the children say. "Shady" is the word, is it not? Well, the previous tenants of Tresillack (from first to last a bewildering series) had been shady with a vengeance.

'I knew nothing of this when I first made application to the landlord, a solid yeoman inhabiting a farm at the foot of the coombe, on a cliff overlooking the beach. To him I presented myself fearlessly as a spinster of decent family and small but assured income, intending a rural life of combined seemliness and economy. He met my advances politely enough, but with an air of suspicion which offended me. I began by disliking him for it: afterwards I set it down as an unpleasant feature in the local character. I was doubly mistaken. Farmer Hosking was slow-witted, but as honest a man as ever stood up against hard times; and a more open and hospitable race than the people on that coast I never wish to meet. It was the caution of a child who had burnt his fingers, not once but many times. Had I known what I afterwards learned of Farmer Hosking's tribulations as landlord of a "secluded country residence", I should have approached him with the bashfulness proper to my suit and faltered as I undertook to prove the bright exception in a long line of painful experiences. He had bought the Tresillack estate twenty years before – on mortgage, I fancy – because the land adjoined his own and would pay him for tillage. But the house was a nuisance, an incubus; and had been so from the beginning.

' "Well, miss," he said, "you're welcome to look over it; a pretty enough place, inside and out. There's no trouble about keys, because I've put in a housekeeper, a widow-woman, and she'll show you round. With your leave I'll step up the coombe so far with you, and put you in your way." As I thanked him he paused and rubbed his chin. "There's one thing I must tell you, though. Whoever takes the house must take Mrs Carkeek along with it."

' "Mrs Carkeek?" I echoed dolefully. "Is that the housekeeper?"

' "Yes: she was wife to my late hind. I'm sorry, miss," he added, my face telling him no doubt what sort of woman I expected Mrs Carkeek to be; "but I had to make it a rule after – after some things that happened. And I dare say you won't find her so bad. Mary Carkeek's a sensible comfortable woman, and knows the place. She was in service there to Squire Kendall when he sold up and went: her first place it was."

' "I may as well see the house, anyhow," said I dejectedly. So we started to walk up the coombe. The path, which ran beside a little chattering stream, was narrow for the most part, and Farmer Hosking, with an apology, strode on ahead to beat aside the brambles. But whenever its width allowed us to walk side by side I caught him from time to time stealing a shy inquisitive glance under his rough eyebrows. Courteously though he bore himself, it was clear that he could not sum me up to his satisfaction or bring me square with his notion of a tenant for his "secluded country residence".

'I don't know what foolish fancy prompted it, but about halfway up the coombe I stopped short and asked: "There are no ghosts, I suppose?"

'It struck me, a moment after I had uttered it, as a supremely silly question; but he took it quite seriously. "No; I never heard tell of any *ghosts*." He laid a queer sort of stress on the word. "There's always been trouble with servants, and maids' tongues will be runnin'. But Mary Carkeek lives up there alone, and she seems comfortable enough."

'We walked on. By and by he pointed with his stick. "It don't look like a place for ghosts, now, do it?"

'Certainly it did not. Above an untrimmed orchard rose a terrace of turf scattered with thorn bushes, and above this a terrace of stone, upon which stood the prettiest cottage I had ever seen. It was long and low and thatched; a deep verandah ran from end to end. Clematis, Banksia roses and honeysuckle climbed the posts of this verandah, and big blooms of the Maréchal Niel were clustered along its roof, beneath the lattices of the bedroom windows. The house was small enough to be called a cottage, and rare enough in features and in situation to confer distinction on any tenant. It suggested what in those days we should have called "elegant" living. And I could have clapped my hands for joy.

'My spirits mounted still higher when Mrs Carkeek opened the door to us. I had looked for a Mrs Gummidge, and I found a healthy middle-aged woman with a thoughtful but contented face, and a smile which, without a trace of obsequiousness, quite bore out the farmer's description of her. She was a comfortable woman; and while we walked through the rooms together (for Mr Hosking waited outside) I "took to" Mrs Carkeek. Her speech was direct and practical; the rooms, in spite of their faded furniture, were bright and exquisitely clean; and somehow the very atmosphere of the house gave me a sense of well-being, of feeling at home and cared for; yes, *of being loved*. Don't laugh, my dears; for when I've done you may not think this fancy altogether foolish.

'I stepped out into the verandah, and Farmer Hosking pocketed the pruning-knife which he had been using on a bush of jasmine.

' "This is better than anything I had dreamed of," said I.

' "Well, miss, that's not a wise way of beginning a bargain, if you'll excuse me."

'He took no advantage, however, of my admission;

and we struck the bargain as we returned down the coombe to his farm, where the hired chaise waited to convey me back to the market town. I had meant to engage a maid of my own, but now it occurred to me that I might do very well with Mrs Carkeek. This, too, was settled in the course of the next day or two, and within the week I had moved into my new home.

'I can hardly describe to you the happiness of my first month at Tresillack; because (as I now believe) if I take the reasons which I had for being happy, one by one, there remains over something which I cannot account for. I was moderately young, entirely healthy; I felt myself independent and adventurous; the season was high summer, the weather glorious, the garden in all the pomp of June, yet sufficiently unkempt to keep me busy, give me a sharp appetite for meals, and send me to bed in that drowsy stupor which comes of the odours of earth. I spent the most of my time out of doors, winding up the day's work as a rule with a walk down the cool valley, along the beach and back.

'I soon found that all housework could be safely left to Mrs Carkeek. She did not talk much; indeed her only fault (a rare one in housekeepers) was that she talked too little, and even when I addressed her seemed at times unable to give me her attention. It was as though her mind strayed off to some small job she had forgotten, and her eyes wore a listening look, as though she waited for the neglected task to speak and remind her. But as a matter of fact she forgot nothing. Indeed, my dears, I was never so well attended to in my life.

'Well, that is what I'm coming to. That, so to say, is just *it*. The woman not only had the rooms swept and dusted, and my meals prepared to the moment.

In a hundred odd little ways this orderliness, these preparations, seemed to read my desires. Did I wish the roses renewed in a bowl upon the dining-table, sure enough at the next meal they would be replaced by fresh ones. Mrs Carkeek (I told myself) must have surprised and interpreted a glance of mine. And yet I could not remember having glanced at the bowl in her presence. And how on earth had she guessed the very roses, the very shapes and colours I had lightly wished for? This is only an instance, you understand. Every day, and from morning to night, I happened on others, each slight enough, but all together bearing witness to a ministering intelligence as subtle as it was untiring.

'I am a light sleeper, as you know, with an uncomfortable knack of waking with the sun and roaming early. No matter how early I rose at Tresillack, Mrs Carkeek seemed to have prevented me. Finally I had to conclude that she arose and dusted and tidied as soon as she judged me safely a-bed. For once, finding the drawing-room (where I had been sitting late) 'redded up' at four in the morning, and no trace of a plate of raspberries which I had carried thither after dinner and left overnight, I determined to test her, and walked through to the kitchen, calling her by name. I found the kitchen as clean as a pin, and the fire laid, but no trace of Mrs Carkeek. I walked upstairs and knocked at her door. At the second knock a sleepy voice cried out, and presently the good woman stood before me in her nightgown, looking (I thought) very badly scared.

'"No," I said, "it's not a burglar. But I've found out what I wanted, that you do your morning's work over night. But you mustn't wait for me when I choose to sit up. And now go back to your bed like a good soul, whilst I take a run down to the beach."

'She stood blinking in the dawn. Her face was still white.

' "Oh, miss," she gasped, "I made sure you must have seen something!"

' "And so I have," I answered, "but it was neither burglars nor ghosts."

' "Thank God!" I heard her say as she turned her back to me in her grey bedroom – which faced the north. And I took this for a carelessly pious expression and ran downstairs, thinking no more of it.

'A few days later I began to understand.

'The plan of Tresillack house (I must explain) was simplicity itself. To the left of the hall as you entered was the dining-room; to the right the drawing-room, with a boudoir beyond. The foot of the stairs faced the front door, and beside it, passing a glazed inner door, you found two others right and left, the left opening on the kitchen, the right on a passage which ran by a store-cupboard under the bend of the stairs to a neat pantry with the usual shelves and linen-press, and under the window (which faced north) a porcelain basin and brass tap. On the first morning of my tenancy I had visited this pantry and turned the tap; but no water ran. I supposed this to be accidental. Mrs Carkeek had to wash up glass ware and crockery, and no doubt Mrs Carkeek would complain of any failure in the water supply.

'But the day after my surprise visit (as I called it) I had picked a basketful of roses, and carried them into the pantry as a handy place to arrange them in. I chose a china bowl and went to fill it at the tap. Again the water would not run.

'I called Mrs Carkeek. "What is wrong with this tap?" I asked. "The rest of the house is well enough supplied."

' "I don't know, miss. I never use it."

' "But there must be a reason; and you must find it a great nuisance washing up the plate and glasses in the kitchen. Come around to the back with me, and we'll have a look at the cisterns."

' "The cisterns'll be all right, miss. I assure you I don't find it a trouble."

'But I was not to be put off. The back of the house stood but ten feet from a wall which was really but a stone face built against the cliff cut away by the architect. Above the cliff rose the kitchen garden, and from its lower path we looked over the wall's parapet upon the cisterns. There were two – a very large one, supplying the kitchen and the bathroom above the kitchen; and a small one, obviously fed by the other, and as obviously leading, by a pipe which I could trace, to the pantry. Now the big cistern stood almost full, and yet the small one, though on a lower level, was empty.

' "It's as plain as daylight," said I. "The pipe between the two is choked." And I clambered on to the parapet.

' "I wouldn't, miss. The pantry tap is only cold water, and no use to me. From the kitchen boiler I gets it hot, you see."

' "But I want the pantry water for my flowers." I bent over and groped. "I thought as much!" said I, as I wrenched out a thick plug of cork and immediately the water began to flow. I turned triumphantly on Mrs Carkeek, who had grown suddenly red in the face. Her eyes were fixed on the cork in my hand. To keep it more firmly wedged in its place somebody had wrapped it round with a rag of calico print; and, discoloured though the rag was, I seemed to recall the pattern (a lilac sprig). Then, as our eyes met, it occurred to me that only two mornings before Mrs Carkeek had worn a print gown of that same sprigged pattern.

'I had the presence of mind to hide this very small discovery, sliding over it some quite trivial remark; and presently Mrs Carkeek regained her composure. But I own I felt disappointed in her. It seemed such a paltry thing to be disingenuous over. She had deliberately acted a fib before me; and why? Merely because she preferred the kitchen to the pantry tap. It was childish. "But servants are all the same," I told myself. "I must take Mrs Carkeek as she is; and, after all, she is a treasure."

'On the second night after this, and between eleven and twelve o'clock, I was lying in bed and reading myself sleepy over a novel of Lord Lytton's, when a small sound disturbed me. I listened. The sound was clearly that of water trickling; and I set it down to rain. A shower (I told myself) had filled the water-pipes which drained the roof. Somehow I could not fix the sound. There was a water-pipe against the wall just outside my window. I rose and drew up the blind.

'To my astonishment no rain was falling; no rain had fallen. I felt the slate window-sill; some dew had gathered there – no more. There was no wind, no cloud: only a still moon high over the eastern slope of the coombe, the distant plash of waves, and the fragrance of many roses. I went back to bed and listened again. Yes, the trickling sound continued, quite distinct in the silence of the house, not to be confused for a moment with the dull murmur of the beach. After a while it began to grate on my nerves. I caught up my candle, flung my dressing-gown about me, and stole softly downstairs.

'Then it was simple. I traced the sound to the pantry. "Mrs Carkeek has left the tap running," said I: and, sure enough, I found it so – a thin trickle steadily running to waste in the porcelain basin. I turned off the tap, went contentedly back to my bed, and slept.

' – for some hours. I opened my eyes in darkness, and at once knew what had awakened me. The tap was running again. Now it had shut easily in my hand, but not so easily that I could believe it had slipped open again of its own accord. "This is Mrs Carkeek's doing," said I; and am afraid I added "Bother Mrs Carkeek!"

'Well, there was no help for it: so I struck a light, looked at my watch, saw that the hour was just three o'clock, and descended the stairs again. At the pantry door I paused. I was not afraid – not one little bit. In fact the notion that anything might be wrong had never crossed my mind. But I remember thinking, with my hand on the door, that if Mrs Carkeek were in the pantry I might happen to give her a severe fright.

'I pushed the door open briskly. Mrs Carkeek was not there. But something *was* there, by the porcelain basin – something which might have sent me scurrying upstairs two steps at a time, but which as a matter of fact held me to the spot. My heart seemed to stand still – so still! And in the stillness I remember setting down the brass candlestick on a tall nest of drawers beside me.

'Over the porcelain basin and beneath the water trickling from the tap I saw two hands.

'That was all – two small hands, a child's hands. I cannot tell you how they ended.

'No: they were not cut off. I saw them quite distinctly: just a pair of small hands and the wrists, and after that – nothing. They were moving briskly – washing themselves clean. I saw the water trickle and splash over them – not *through* them – but just as it would on real hands. They were the hands of a little girl, too. Oh, yes, I was sure of that at once. Boys and girls wash their hands differently. I can't just tell you what the difference is, but it's unmistakable.

'I saw all this before my candle slipped and fell with a crash. I had set it down without looking – for my eyes were fixed on the basin – and had balanced it on the edge of the nest of drawers. After the crash, in the darkness there, with the water running, I suffered some bad moments. Oddly enough, the thought uppermost with me was that I *must* shut off that tap before escaping. I *had* to. And after a while I picked up all my courage, so to say, between my teeth, and with a little sob thrust out my hand and did it. Then I fled.

'The dawn was close upon me: and as soon as the sky reddened I took my bath, dressed and went downstairs. And there at the pantry door I found Mrs Carkeek, also dressed, with my candlestick in her hand.

' "Ah!" said I, "you picked it up."

'Our eyes met. Clearly Mrs Carkeek wished me to begin, and I determined at once to have it out with her.

' "And you knew all about it. That's what accounts for your plugging up the cistern."

' "You saw? . . . " she began.

' "Yes, yes. And you must tell me all about it – never mind how bad. Is – is it – murder?"

' "Law bless you, miss, whatever put such horrors in your head?"

' "She was washing her hands."

' "Ah, so she does, poor dear! But – murder! And dear little Miss Margaret, that wouldn't go to hurt a fly!"

' "Miss Margaret?"

' "Eh, she died at seven year. Squire Kendall's only daughter; and that's over twenty year ago. I was her nurse, miss, and I know – diphtheria it was; she took it down in the village."

' "But how do you know it is Margaret?"

' "Those hands – why, how could I mistake, that used to be her nurse?"

' "But why does she wash them?"

' "Well, miss, being always a dainty child – and the housework, you see – "

'I took a long breath. "Do you mean to tell me that all this tidying and dusting – " I broke off. "Is it *she* who has been taking this care of me?"

'Mrs Carkeek met my look steadily.

' "Who else, miss?"

' "Poor little soul!"

' "Well now" – Mrs Carkeek rubbed my candlestick with the edge of her apron – "I'm so glad you take it like this. For there isn't really nothing to be afraid of – is there?" She eyed me wistfully. "It's my belief she loves you, miss. But only to think what a time she must have had with the others!"

' "The others?" I echoed.

' "The other tenants, miss: the ones afore you."

' "Were they bad?"

' "They was awful. Didn't Farmer Hosking tell you? They carried on fearful – one after another, and each one worse than the last."

' "What was the matter with them? Drink?"

' "Drink, miss, with some of 'em. There was the Major – he used to go mad with it, and run about the coombe in his nightshirt. Oh, scandalous! And his wife drank too – that is, if she ever *was* his wife. Just think of that tender child washing up after their nasty doings!"

'I shivered.

' "But that wasn't the worst, miss – not by a long way. There was a pair here – from the colonies, or so they gave out – with two children, a boy and gel, the eldest scarce six. Poor mites!"

' "Why, what happened?"

' "They beat those children, miss – your blood would boil! – *and* starved, *and* tortured 'em, it's my belief. You could hear their screams, I've been told, away back in the highroad, and that's the best part of half a mile. Sometimes they was locked up without food for days together. But it's my belief that little Miss Margaret managed to feed them somehow. Oh, I can see her, creeping to the door and comforting!"

' "But perhaps she never showed herself when these awful people were here, but took to flight until they left."

' "You didn't never know her, miss. The brave she was! She'd have stood up to lions. She've been here all the while: and only to think what her innocent eyes and ears must have took in! There was another couple – " Mrs Carkeek sunk her voice.

' "Oh, hush!" said I, "if I'm to have any peace of mind in this house!"

' "But you won't go, miss? She loves you, I know she do. And think what you might be leaving her to – what sort of tenant might come next. For she can't go. She's been here ever since her father sold the place. He died soon after. You mustn't go!"

'Now I had resolved to go, but all of a sudden I felt how mean this resolution was.

' "After all," said I, "there's nothing to be afraid of."

' "That's it, miss; nothing at all. I don't even believe it's so very uncommon. Why, I've heard my mother tell of farmhouses where the rooms were swept every night as regular as clockwork, and the floors sanded, and the pots and pans scoured, and all while the maids slept. They put it down to the piskies; but we know better, miss, and now we've got the secret between us we can lie easy in our beds, and if we hear anything, say 'God bless the child!' and go to sleep."

' "Mrs Carkeek," said I, "there's only one condition I have to make."

' "What's that?"

' "Why, that you let me kiss you."

' "Oh, you dear!" said Mrs Carkeek as we embraced: and this was as close to familiarity as she allowed herself to go in the whole course of my acquaintance with her.

'I spent three years at Tresillack, and all that while Mrs Carkeek lived with me and shared the secret. Few women, I dare to say, were ever so completely wrapped around with love as we were during those three years. It ran through my waking life like a song: it smoothed my pillow, touched and made my table comely, in summer lifted the heads of the flowers as I passed, and in winter watched the fire with me and kept it bright.

' "Why did I ever leave Tresillack?" Because one day, at the end of five years, Farmer Hosking brought me word that he had sold the house – or was about to sell it; I forget which. There was no avoiding it, at any rate; the purchaser being a Colonel Kendall, a brother of the old Squire.'

' "A married man?" I asked.

' "Yes, miss; with a family of eight. As pretty children as ever you see, and the mother a good lady. It's the old home to Colonel Kendall."

' "I see. And that is why you feel bound to sell."

' "It's a good price, too, that he offers. You mustn't think but I'm sorry enough – "

' "To turn me out? I thank you, Mr Hosking; but you are doing the right thing."

'Since Mrs Carkeek was to stay, the arrangement lacked nothing of absolute perfection – except, perhaps, that it found no room for me.

' "*She* – Margaret – will be happy," I said; "with her cousins, you know."

' "Oh yes, miss, she will be happy, sure enough," Mrs Carkeek agreed.

'So when the time came I packed up my boxes, and tried to be cheerful. But on the last morning, when they stood corded in the hall, I sent Mrs Carkeek upstairs upon some poor excuse, and stepped alone into the pantry.

' "Margaret!" I whispered.

'There was no answer at all. I had scarcely dared to hope for one. Yet I tried again, and, shutting my eyes this time, stretched out both hands and whispered: "Margaret!"

'And I will swear to my dying day that two little hands stole and rested – for a moment only – in mine.'

The Facts in the Case of M. Valdemar

EDGAR ALLAN POE

Of course I shall not pretend to consider it any matter for wonder, that the extraordinary case of M. Valdemar has excited discussion. It would have been a miracle had it not – especially under the circumstances. Through the desire of all parties concerned, to keep the affair from the public, at least for the present, or until we had farther opportunities for investigation – through our endeavours to effect this – a garbled or exaggerated account made its way into society, and became the source of many unpleasant misrepresentations, and, very naturally, of a great deal of disbelief.

It is now rendered necessary that I give the *facts* – as far as I comprehend them myself. They are, succinctly, these.

My attention, for the last three years, had been repeatedly drawn to the subject of Mesmerism; and, about nine months ago it occurred to me, quite suddenly, that in the series of experiments made hitherto, there had been a very remarkable and most unaccountable omission: – no person had as yet been mesmerised *in articulo mortis*. It remained to be seen, first, whether, in such condition, there existed in the patient any susceptibility to the magnetic influence; secondly, whether, if any existed, it was impaired or increased by the condition; thirdly, to what extent, or for how long a period, the encroachments of Death might be arrested by the process. There were other points to be ascertained, but these most excited my curiosity – the last in especial, from the immensely important character of its consequences.

In looking around me for some subject by whose means I might test these particulars, I was brought to think of my friend, M. Ernest Valdemar, the well-known compiler of the *Bibliotheca Forensica*, and author (under the *nom de plume* of Issachar Marx) of the Polish versions of 'Wallenstein' and 'Gargantua'. M. Valdemar, who has resided principally at Harlem, NY, since the year 1839, is (or was) particularly noticeable for the extreme spareness of his person – his lower limbs much resembling those of John Randolph; and, also, for the whiteness of his whiskers, in violent contrast to the blackness of his hair – the latter, in consequence, being very generally mistaken for a wig. His temperament was markedly nervous, and rendered him a good subject for mesmeric experiment. On two or three occasions I had put him to sleep with little difficulty, but was disappointed in other results which his peculiar constitution had naturally led me to anticipate. His will was at no period positively, or thoroughly, under my control, and in regard to clairvoyance, I could accomplish with him nothing to be relied upon. I always attributed my failure at these points to the disordered state of his health. For some months previous to my becoming acquainted with him, his physicians had declared him in a confirmed phthisis. It was his custom, indeed, to speak calmly of his approaching dissolution, as of a matter neither to be avoided nor regretted.

When the ideas to which I have alluded first

occurred to me, it was of course very natural that I should think of M. Valdemar. I knew the steady philosophy of the man too well to apprehend any scruples from him; and he had no relatives in America who would be likely to interfere. I spoke to him frankly upon the subject; and, to my surprise, his interest seemed vividly excited. I say to my surprise, for, although he had always yielded his person freely to my experiments, he had never before given me any tokens of sympathy with what I did. His disease was of that character which would admit of exact calculation in respect to the epoch of its termination in death; and it was finally arranged between us that he would send for me about twenty-four hours before the period announced by his physicians as that of his decease.

It is now rather more than seven months since I received, from M. Valdemar himself, the subjoined note:

> MY DEAR P— You may as well come now. D— and F— are agreed that I cannot hold out beyond tomorrow midnight; and I think they have hit the time very nearly.
>
> VALDEMAR

I received this note within half an hour after it was written, and in fifteen minutes more I was in the dying man's chamber. I had not seen him for ten days, and was appalled by the fearful alteration which the brief interval had wrought in him. His face wore a leaden hue; the eyes were utterly lustreless; and the emaciation was so extreme that the skin had been broken through by the cheekbones. His expectoration was excessive. The pulse was barely perceptible. He retained, nevertheless, in a very remarkable manner, both his mental power and a certain degree of physical strength. He spoke with distinctness – took some palliative medicines without aid – and, when I entered the room, was occupied in pencilling memoranda in a pocketbook. He was propped up in the bed by pillows. Doctors D— and F— were in attendance.

After pressing Valdemar's hand, I took these gentlemen aside, and obtained from them a minute account of the patient's condition. The left lung had been for eighteen months in a semi-osseous or cartilaginous state, and was, of course, entirely useless for all purposes of vitality. The right, in its upper portion, was also partially, if not thoroughly, ossified, while the lower region was merely a mass of purulent tubercles, running one into another. Several extensive perforations existed; and, at one point, permanent adhesion to the ribs had taken place. These appearances in the right lobe were of comparatively recent date. The ossification had proceeded with very unusual rapidity; no sign of it had been discovered a month before, and the adhesion had only been observed during the three previous days. Independently of the phthisis, the patient was suspected of aneurism of the aorta; but on this point the osseous symptoms rendered an exact diagnosis impossible. It was the opinion of both physicians that M. Valdemar would die about midnight on the morrow (Sunday). It was then seven o'clock on Saturday evening.

On quitting the invalid's bedside to hold conversation with myself, Dr D— and Dr F— had bidden him a final farewell. It had not been their intention to return; but, at my request, they agreed to look in upon the patient about ten the next night.

When they had gone, I spoke freely with M. Valdemar on the subject of his approaching dissolution, as well as, more particularly, of the experiment proposed. He still professed himself quite willing and even anxious to have it made, and urged me to commence it at once. A male and a female nurse were in attendance; but I did not feel myself altogether at liberty to engage in a task of this character with no more reliable witnesses than these people, in case of sudden accident, might prove. I therefore postponed operations until about eight the next night, when the arrival of a medical student with whom I had some acquaintance, (Mr Theodore L—l), relieved me from farther embarrassment. It had been my design, originally, to wait for the physicians; but I was induced to proceed, first, by the urgent entreaties of M. Valdemar, and secondly, by my conviction that I had not a moment to lose, as he was evidently sinking fast.

Mr L—l was so kind as to accede to my desire that he would take notes of all that occurred, and it is from his memoranda that what I now have to relate is, for the most part, either condensed or copied verbatim.

It wanted about five minutes of eight when, taking the patient's hand, I begged him to state, as distinctly as he could, to Mr L—l, whether he (M. Valdemar) was entirely willing that I should make the experiment of mesmerising him in his then condition.

He replied feebly, yet quite audibly, 'Yes, I wish to be mesmerised' – adding immediately afterwards, 'I fear you have deferred it too long.'

While he spoke thus, I commenced the passes which I had already found most effectual in subduing him. He was evidently influenced with the first lateral stroke of my hand across his forehead; but although I exerted all my powers, no farther perceptible effect was induced until some minutes after ten o'clock, when Drs D— and F— called, according to appointment. I explained to them, in a few words, what I designed, and as they opposed no objection, saying that the patient was already in the death agony, I proceeded without hesitation – exchanging, however, the lateral passes for downward ones, and directing my gaze entirely into the right eye of the sufferer.

By this time his pulse was imperceptible and his breathing was stertorous, and at intervals of half a minute.

This condition was nearly unaltered for a quarter of an hour. At the expiration of this period, however, a natural although a very deep sigh escaped the bosom of the dying man, and the stertorous breathing ceased – that is to say, its stertorousness was no longer apparent; the intervals were undiminished. The patient's extremities were of an icy coldness.

At five minutes before eleven I perceived unequivocal signs of the mesmeric influence. The glassy roll of the eye was changed for that expression of uneasy *inward* examination which is never seen except in cases of sleep-waking, and which it is quite impossible to mistake. With a few rapid lateral passes I made the lids quiver, as in incipient sleep, and with a few more I closed them altogether. I was not satisfied, however, with this, but continued the manipulations vigorously, and with the fullest exertion of the will, until I had completely stiffened the limbs of the slumberer, after placing them in a seemingly easy position. The legs were at full length; the arms were nearly so, and reposed on the bed at a moderate distance from the loins. The head was very slightly elevated.

When I had accomplished this, it was fully midnight, and I requested the gentlemen present to examine M. Valdemar's condition. After a few experiments, they admitted him to be in an unusually perfect state of mesmeric trance. The curiosity of both the physicians was greatly excited. Dr D— resolved at once to remain with the patient all night, while Dr F— took leave with a promise to return at daybreak. Mr L—l and the nurses remained.

We left M. Valdemar entirely undisturbed until about three o'clock in the morning, when I approached him and found him in precisely the same condition as when Dr F— went away – that is to say, he lay in the same position; the pulse was imperceptible; the breathing was gentle (scarcely noticeable, unless through the application of a mirror to the lips); the eyes were closed naturally; and the limbs were as rigid and as cold as marble. Still, the general appearance was certainly not that of death.

As I approached M. Valdemar I made a kind of half effort to influence his right arm into pursuit of my own, as I passed the latter gently to and fro above his person. In such experiments with this patient I had never perfectly succeeded before, and assuredly I had little thought of succeeding now; but to my astonishment, his arm very readily, although feebly, followed every direction I assigned it with mine. I determined to hazard a few words of conversation.

'M. Valdemar,' I said, 'are you asleep?' He made no answer, but I perceived a tremor about the lips, and was thus induced to repeat the question, again and again. At its third repetition, his whole frame was agitated by a very slight shivering; the eyelids unclosed themselves so far as to display a white line of the ball; the lips moved sluggishly, and from between them, in a barely audible whisper, issued the words: 'Yes; – asleep now. Do not wake me! – let me die so!'

I here felt the limbs and found them as rigid as ever. The right arm, as before, obeyed the direction of my hand. I questioned the sleep-waker again: 'Do you still feel pain in the breast, M. Valdemar?'

The answer now was immediate, but even less audible than before: 'No pain – I am dying.'

I did not think it advisable to disturb him farther just then, and nothing more was said or done until the arrival of Dr F—, who came a little before sunrise, and expressed unbounded astonishment at finding the patient still alive. After feeling the pulse and applying a mirror to the lips, he requested me to speak to the sleep-waker again. I did so, saying: 'M. Valdemar, do you still sleep?'

As before, some minutes elapsed ere a reply was made; and during the interval the dying man seemed to be collecting his energies to speak. At my fourth repetition of the question, he said very faintly, almost inaudibly: 'Yes; still asleep – dying.'

It was now the opinion, or rather the wish, of the physicians, that M. Valdemar should be suffered to remain undisturbed in his present apparently tranquil condition, until death should supervene – and this, it was generally agreed, must now take place within a few minutes. I concluded, however, to speak to him once more, and merely repeated my previous question.

While I spoke, there came a marked change over the countenance of the sleep-waker. The eyes rolled themselves slowly open, the pupils disappearing upwardly; the skin generally assumed a cadaverous hue, resembling not so much parchment as white paper; and the circular hectic spots which, hitherto, had been strongly defined in the centre of each cheek, went out at once. I use this expression, because the suddenness of their departure put me in mind of nothing so much as the extinguishment of a candle by a puff of the breath. The upper lip, at the same time, writhed itself away from the teeth, which it had previously covered completely; while the lower jaw fell with an audible jerk, leaving the mouth widely extended, and disclosing in full view the swollen and blackened tongue. I presume that no member of the party then present had been unaccustomed to deathbed horrors; but so hideous beyond conception was the appearance of M. Valdemar at this moment, that there was a general shrinking back from the region of the bed.

I now feel that I have reached a point of this narrative at which every reader will be startled into positive disbelief. It is my business, however, simply to proceed.

There was no longer the faintest sign of vitality in M. Valdemar; and concluding him to be dead, we were consigning him to the charge of the nurses, when a strong vibratory motion was observable in the tongue. This continued for perhaps a minute. At the expiration of this period, there issued from the distended and motionless jaws a voice – such as it would be madness in me to attempt describing. There are, indeed, two or three epithets which might be considered as applicable to it in part; I might say, for example, that the sound was harsh, and broken and hollow; but the hideous whole is indescribable, for the simple reason that no similar sounds have ever jarred upon the ear of humanity. There were two particulars, nevertheless, which I thought then, and still think, might fairly be stated as characteristic of the intonation – as well adapted to convey some idea of its unearthly peculiarity. In the first place, the voice seemed to reach our ears – at least mine – from a vast distance, or from some deep cavern within the earth. In the second place, it impressed me (I fear, indeed, that it will be impossible to make myself comprehended) as gelatinous or glutinous matters impress the sense of touch.

I have spoken both of 'sound' and of 'voice'. I mean to say that the sound was one of distinct – of even wonderfully, thrillingly distinct – syllabification. M. Valdemar *spoke* – obviously in reply to the question I had propounded to him a few minutes before. I had asked him, it will be remembered, if he still slept. He now said: 'Yes; – no; – *I have been* sleeping – and now – now – *I am dead.*'

No person present even affected to deny, or attempted to repress, the unutterable, shuddering horror which these few words, thus uttered, were so well calculated to convey. Mr L—l (the student) swooned. The nurses immediately left the chamber, and could not be induced to return. My own impressions I would not pretend to render intelligible to the reader. For nearly an hour, we busied ourselves, silently – without the utterance of a word – in endeavours to revive Mr L—l. When he came to himself, we addressed ourselves again to an investigation of M. Valdemar's condition.

It remained in all respects as I have last described it, with the exception that the mirror no longer afforded evidence of respiration. An attempt to draw blood from the arm failed. I should mention, too, that this limb was no farther subject to my will. I endeavoured in vain to make it follow the direction of my hand. The only real indication, indeed, of the mesmeric influence, was now found in the vibratory movement of the tongue, whenever I addressed M. Valdemar a question. He seemed to be making an effort to reply, but had no longer sufficient volition. To queries put to him by any other person than myself he seemed utterly insensible – although I endeavoured to place each member of the company in mesmeric rapport with him. I believe that I have now related all that is necessary to an understanding of the sleep-waker's state at this epoch. Other nurses were procured; and at ten o'clock I left the house in company with the two physicians and Mr L—l.

In the afternoon we all called again to see the patient. His condition remained precisely the same. We had now some discussion as to the propriety and feasibility of awakening him; but we had little difficulty in agreeing that no good purpose would be served by so doing. It was evident that, so far, death (or what is usually termed death) had been arrested by the mesmeric process. It seemed clear to us all that to awaken M. Valdemar would be merely to insure his instant, or at least his speedy dissolution.

From this period until the close of last week – *an interval of nearly seven months* – we continued to make daily calls at M. Valdemar's house, accompanied, now and then, by medical and other friends. All this time the sleep-waker remained *exactly* as I have last described him. The nurses' attentions were continual.

It was on Friday last that we finally resolved to make the experiment of awakening or attempting to awaken him; and it is the (perhaps) unfortunate result of this latter experiment which has given rise to so much discussion in private circles – to so much of what I cannot help thinking unwarranted popular feeling.

For the purpose of relieving M. Valdemar from the mesmeric trance, I made use of the customary passes. These, for a time, were unsuccessful. The first indication of revival was afforded by a partial descent of the iris. It was observed, as especially remarkable, that this lowering of the pupil was accompanied by the profuse out-flowing of a yellowish ichor (from beneath the lids) of a pungent and highly offensive odour.

It was now suggested that I should attempt to influence the patient's arm, as heretofore. I made the attempt and failed. Dr F— then intimated a desire to have me put a question. I did so, as follows: 'M. Valdemar, can you explain to us what are your feelings or wishes now?'

There was an instant return of the hectic circles on the cheeks; the tongue quivered, or rather rolled violently in the mouth (although the jaws and lips remained rigid as before); and at length the same hideous voice which I have already described, broke forth: 'For God's sake! – quick! – quick! – put me to sleep – or, quick! – waken me! – quick! – *I say to you that I am dead!*'

I was thoroughly unnerved, and for an instant remained undecided what to do. At first I made an endeavour to re-compose the patient; but, failing in this through total abeyance of the will, I retraced my steps and as earnestly struggled to awaken him. In this attempt I soon saw that I should be successful – or at least I soon fancied that my success would be complete – and I am sure that all in the room were prepared to see the patient awaken.

For what really occurred, however, it is quite impossible that any human being could have been prepared.

As I rapidly made the mesmeric passes, amid ejaculations of 'dead! dead!' absolutely *bursting* from the tongue and not from the lips of the sufferer, his whole frame at once – within the space of a single minute, or even less, shrunk – crumbled – absolutely *rotted* away beneath my hands. Upon the bed, before that whole company, there lay a nearly liquid mass of loathsome – of detestable putridity.

The Beast with Five Fingers

W. F. HARVEY

The story, I suppose, begins with Adrian Borlsover, whom I met when I was a little boy and he an old man. My father had called to appeal for a subscription, and I was with him. Before we left, Mr Borlsover laid his right hand in blessing on my head. I shall never forget the awe in which I gazed up at his face and realised for the first time that eyes might be dark and beautiful and shining, and yet not able to see.

For Adrian Borlsover was blind.

He was an extraordinary man, who came of an eccentric stock. Borlsover sons for some reason always seemed to marry very ordinary women; which perhaps accounted for the fact that no Borlsover had been a genius, and only one Borlsover had been mad. But they were great champions of little causes, generous patrons of odd sciences, founders of querulous sects, trustworthy guides to the bypath meadows of erudition.

Adrian was an authority on the fertilisation of orchids. He had held at one time the family living at Borlsover Conyers, until a congenital weakness of the lungs obliged him to seek a less rigorous climate in the sunny south-coast watering-place where I had seen him. Occasionally he would relieve one or other of the local clergy. My father described him as a fine preacher, who gave long and inspiring sermons from what many men would have considered unprofitable texts. 'An excellent proof,' he would add, 'of the truth of the doctrine of direct verbal inspiration.'

Adrian Borlsover was exceedingly clever with his hands. His penmanship was exquisite. He illustrated all his scientific papers, made his own woodcuts, and carved the reredos that is at present the chief feature of interest in the church at Borlsover Conyers. He had an exceedingly clever knack in cutting silhouettes for young ladies and paper pigs and cows for little children, and made more than one complicated wind-instrument of his own devising

When he was fifty years old Adrian Borlsover lost his sight. In a wonderfully short time he adapted himself to the new conditions of life. He quickly learnt to read Braille. So marvellous indeed was his sense of touch that he was still able to maintain his interest in botany. The mere passing of his long supple fingers over a flower was sufficient means for its identification, though occasionally he would use his lips. I have found several letters of his among my father's correspondence; in no case was there anything to show that he was afflicted with blindness and this in spite of the fact that he exercised undue economy in the spacing of lines. Towards the close of his life Adrian Borlsover was credited with powers of touch that seemed almost uncanny. It has been said that he could tell at once the colour of a ribbon placed between his fingers. My father would neither confirm nor deny the story.

Adrian Borlsover was a bachelor. His elder brother, Charles, had married late in life, leaving one son, Eustace, who lived in the gloomy Georgian mansion at Borlsover Conyers, where he could work undisturbed in collecting material for his great book on heredity.

Like his uncle, he was a remarkable man. The Borlsovers had always been born naturalists, but Eustace possessed in a special degree the power of systematising his knowledge. He had received his university education in Germany; and then, after postgraduate work in Vienna and Naples, had travelled for four years in South America and the East, getting together a huge store of material for a new study into the processes of variation.

He lived alone at Borlsover Conyers with Saunders, his secretary, a man who bore a somewhat dubious reputation in the district, but whose powers as a mathematician, combined with his business abilities, were invaluable to Eustace.

Uncle and nephew saw little of each other. The visits of Eustace were confined to a week in the summer or autumn – tedious weeks, that dragged almost as slowly as the bath-chair in which the old man was drawn along the sunny seafront. In their way the two men were fond of each other, though their intimacy would, doubtless, have been greater, had they shared the same religious views. Adrian held to the old-fashioned evangelical dogmas of his early manhood; his nephew for many years had been thinking of embracing Buddhism. Both men possessed, too, the reticence the Borlsovers had always shown, and which their enemies sometimes called hypocrisy. With Adrian it was a reticence as to the things he had left undone; but with Eustace it seemed that the curtain which he was so careful to leave undrawn hid something more than a half-empty chamber.

Two years before his death, Adrian Borlsover developed, unknown to himself, the not uncommon power of automatic writing. Eustace made the discovery by accident. Adrian was sitting reading in bed, the forefinger of his left hand tracing the Braille characters, when his nephew noticed that a pencil the old man held in his right hand was moving slowly along the opposite page. He had left his seat in the window and sat down beside the bed. The right hand continued to move, and now he could see plainly that they were letters and words which it was forming.

'Adrian Borlsover,' wrote the hand, 'Eustace Borlsover, Charles Borlsover, Francis Borlsover, Sigismund Borlsover, Adrian Borlsover, Eustace Borlsover, Saville Borlsover. B for Borlsover. Honesty is the Best Policy Beautiful Belinda Borlsover.'

'What curious nonsense!' said Eustace to himself.

'King George ascended the throne in 1760,' wrote the hand. 'Crowd, a noun of multitude; a collection of individuals. Adrian Borlsover, Eustace Borlsover.'

'It seems to me,' said his uncle, closing the book, 'that you had much better make the most of the afternoon sunshine and take your walk now.'

'I think perhaps I will,' Eustace answered as he picked up the volume. 'I won't go far, and when I come back I can read to you those articles in *Nature* about which we were speaking.'

He went along the promenade, but stopped at the first shelter, and, seating himself in the corner best protected from the wind, he examined the book at leisure. Nearly every page was scored with a meaningless jumble of pencil-marks; rows of capital letters, short words, long words, complete sentences, copybook tags. The whole thing, in fact, had the appearance of a copybook, and, on a more careful scrutiny, Eustace thought that there was ample evidence to show that the handwriting at the beginning of the book, good though it was, was not nearly so good as the handwriting at the end.

He left his uncle at the end of October with a promise to return early in December. It seemed to him quite clear that the old man's power of automatic writing was developing rapidly, and for the first time he looked forward to a visit that would combine duty with interest.

But on his return he was at first disappointed. His uncle, he thought, looked older. He was listless, too, preferring others to read to him and dictating nearly all his letters. Not until the day before he left had Eustace an opportunity of observing Adrian Borlsover's new-found faculty.

The old man, propped up in bed with pillows, had sunk into a light sleep. His two hands lay on the coverlet, his left hand tightly clasping his right. Eustace took an empty manuscript book and placed a pencil within reach of the fingers of the right hand. They snatched at it eagerly, then dropped the pencil to loose the left hand from its restraining grasp.

'Perhaps to prevent interference I had better hold that hand,' said Eustace to himself, as he watched the pencil. Almost immediately it began to write.

'Blundering Borlsovers, unnecessarily unnatural, extraordinarily eccentric, culpably curious.'

'Who are you?' asked Eustace in a low voice.

'Never you mind,' wrote the hand of Adrian.

'Is it my uncle who is writing?'

'O my prophetic soul, mine uncle!'

'Is it anyone I know?'

'Silly Eustace, you'll see me very soon.'

'When shall I see you?'

'When poor old Adrian's dead.'

'Where shall I see you?'

'Where shall you not?'

Instead of speaking his next question, Eustace wrote it. 'What is the time?'

The fingers dropped the pencil and moved three or four times across the paper. Then, picking up the pencil, they wrote: 'Ten minutes before four. Put your book away, Eustace. Adrian mustn't find us working at this sort of thing. He doesn't know what to make of it, and I won't have poor old Adrian disturbed. *Au revoir!*'

Adrian Borlsover awoke with a start.

'I've been dreaming again,' he said; 'such queer dreams of leaguered cities and forgotten towns. You were mixed up in this one, Eustace, though I can't remember how. Eustace, I want to warn you. Don't walk in doubtful paths. Choose your friends well. Your poor grandfather . . . '

A fit of coughing put an end to what he was saying, but Eustace saw that the hand was still writing. He managed unnoticed to draw the book away. 'I'll light the gas,' he said, 'and ring for tea.' On the other side of the bedcurtain he saw the last sentence that had been written.

'It's too late, Adrian,' it said. 'We're friends already, aren't we, Eustace Borlsover?'

On the following day Eustace left. He thought his uncle looked ill when he said goodbye, and the old man spoke despondently of the failure his life had been.

'Nonsense, uncle,' said his nephew. 'You have got over your difficulties in a way not one in a hundred thousand would have done. Everyone marvels at your splendid perseverance in teaching your hand to take the place of your lost sight. To me it's been a revelation of the possibilities of education.'

'Education,' said his uncle dreamily, as if the word had started a new train of thought. 'Education is good so long as you know to whom and for what purpose you give it. But with the lower orders of men, the base and more sordid spirits, I have grave doubts as to its results. Well, goodbye, Eustace; I may not see you again. You are a true Borlsover, with all the Borlsover faults. Marry, Eustace. Marry some good, sensible girl. And if by any chance I don't see you again, my will is at my solicitors. I've not left you any legacy, because I know you're well provided for; but I thought you might like to have my books. Oh, and there's just another thing. You know, before the end, people often lose control over themselves and make absurd requests. Don't pay any attention to them, Eustace. Goodbye!' and he held out his hand. Eustace took it. It remained in his a fraction of a second longer than he had expected and gripped him with a virility that was surprising. There was, too, in its touch a subtle sense of intimacy.

'Why, uncle,' he said, 'I shall see you alive and well for many long years to come.'

* * *

Two months later Adrian Borlsover died.

Eustace Borlsover was in Naples at the time. He read the obituary notice in the *Morning Post* on the day announced for the funeral.

'Poor old fellow!' he said. 'I wonder whether I shall find room for all his books.'

The question occurred to him again with greater force when, three days later, he found himself standing in the library at Borlsover Conyers, a huge room built for use and not for beauty in the year of Waterloo by a Borlsover who was an ardent admirer of the great Napoleon. It was arranged on the plan of many college libraries, with tall projecting bookcases forming deep recesses of dusty silence, fit graves for the old hates of forgotten controversy, the dead passions of forgotten lives. At the end of the room, behind the bust of some unknown eighteenth-century divine, an ugly iron corkscrew stair led to a shelf-lined gallery. Nearly every shelf was full.

'I must talk to Saunders about it,' said Eustace. 'I suppose that we shall have to have the billiard-room fitted up with bookcases.'

The two men met for the first time after many weeks in the dining-room that evening.

'Hallo!' said Eustace, standing before the fire with his hands in his pockets. 'How goes the world, Saunders? Why these dress togs?'

He himself was wearing an old shooting-jacket. He did not believe in mourning, as he had told his uncle on his last visit; and, though he usually went in for quiet-coloured ties, he wore this evening one of an ugly red, in order to shock Morton the butler, and to make them thrash out the whole question of mourning for themselves in the servants' hall. Eustace was a true Borlsover.

'The world,' said Saunders, 'goes the same as usual, confoundedly slow. The dress togs are accounted for by an invitation from Captain Lockwood to bridge.'

'How are you getting there?'

'There's something the matter with the car, so I've told Jackson to drive me round in the dogcart. Any objection?'

'Oh dear me, no! We've had all things in common for far too many years for me to raise objections at this hour of the day.'

'You'll find your correspondence in the library,' went on Saunders. 'Most of it I've seen to. There are a few private letters I haven't opened. There's also a box with a rat or something inside it that came by the evening post. Very likely it's the six-toed beast Terry was sending us to cross with the four-toed albino. I didn't look because I didn't want to mess up my things; but I should gather from the way it's jumping about that it's pretty hungry.'

'Oh, I'll see to it,' said Eustace, 'while you and the captain earn an honest penny.'

Dinner over and Saunders gone, Eustace went into the library. Though the fire had been lit, the room was by no means cheerful.

'We'll have all the lights on, at any rate,' he said, as he turned the switches. 'And, Morton,' he added, when the butler brought the coffee, 'get me a screw-driver or something to undo this box. Whatever the animal is, he's kicking up the deuce of a row. What is it? Why are you dawdling?'

'If you please, sir, when the postman brought it, he told me that they'd bored the holes in the lid at the post office. There were no breathing holes in the lid, sir, and they didn't want the animal to die. That is all, sir.'

'It's culpably careless of the man, whoever he was,' said Eustace, as he removed the screws, 'packing an animal like this in a wooden box with no means of getting air. Confound it all! I meant to ask Morton to bring me a cage to put it in. Now I suppose I shall have to get one myself.'

He placed a heavy book on the lid from which the screws had been removed, and went into the billiard-room. As he came back into the library with an empty cage in his hand, he heard the sound of something falling, and then of something scuttling along the floor.

'Bother it! The beast's got out. How in the world am I to find it again in this library?'

To search for it did indeed seem hopeless. He tried to follow the sound of the scuttling in one of the recesses, where the animal seemed to be running behind the books in the shelves; but it was impossible to locate it. Eustace resolved to go on quietly reading. Very likely the animal might gain confidence and show itself. Saunders seemed to have dealt in his usual methodical manner with most of the correspondence. There were still the private letters.

What was that? Two sharp clicks and the lights in the hideous candelabras that hung from the ceiling suddenly went out.

'I wonder if something has gone wrong with the fuse,' said Eustace, as he went to the switches by the door. Then he stopped. There was a noise at the other end of the room, as if something was crawling up the iron corkscrew stair. 'If it's gone into the gallery,' he said, 'well and good.' He hastily turned on the lights, crossed the room, and climbed up the stair. But he could see nothing. His grandfather had placed a little gate at the top of the stair, so that children could run and romp in the gallery without fear of accident. This Eustace closed, and, having considerably narrowed the circle of his search, returned to his desk by the fire.

How gloomy the library was! There was no sense

of intimacy about the room. The few busts that an eighteenth-century Borlsover had brought back from the Grand Tour might have been in keeping in the old library. Here they seemed out of place. They made the room feel cold in spite of the heavy red damask curtains and great gilt cornices.

With a crash two heavy books fell from the gallery to the floor; then, as Borlsover looked, another and yet another.

'Very well. You'll starve for this, my beauty!' he said. 'We'll do some little experiments on the metabolism of rats deprived of water. Go on! Chuck them down! I think I've got the upper hand.' He turned once more to his correspondence. One letter was from the family solicitor. It spoke of his uncle's death, and of the valuable collection of books that had been left to him in the will.

> There was one request [he read] which certainly came as a surprise to me. As you know, Mr Adrian Borlsover had left instructions that his body was to be buried in as simple a manner as possible at Eastbourne. He expressed a desire that there should be neither wreaths nor flowers of any kind, and hoped that his friends and relatives would not consider it necessary to wear mourning. The day before his death we received a letter cancelling these instructions. He wished the body to be embalmed (he gave us the address of the man we were to employ – Pennifer, Ludgate Hill), with orders that his right hand should be sent to you, stating that it was at your special request. The other arrangements about the funeral remained unaltered.

'Good Lord,' said Eustace, 'what in the world was

the old boy driving at? And what in the name of all that's holy is that?'

Someone was in the gallery. Someone had pulled the cord attached to one of the blinds, and it had rolled up with a snap. Someone must be in the gallery, for a second blind did the same. Someone must be walking round the gallery, for one after the other the blinds sprang up, letting in the moonlight.

'I haven't got to the bottom of this yet,' said Eustace, 'but I will do, before the night is very much older,' and he hurried up the corkscrew stair. He had just got to the top, when the lights went out a second time, and he heard again the scuttling along the floor. Quickly he stole on tiptoe in the dim moonshine in the direction of the noise, feeling, as he went, for one of the switches. His fingers touched the metal knob at last. He turned on the electric light.

About ten yards in front of him, crawling along the floor, was a man's hand. Eustace stared at it in utter amazement. It was moving quickly in the manner of a geometer caterpillar, the fingers humped up one moment, flattened out the next; the thumb appeared to give a crablike motion to the whole. While he was looking, too surprised to stir, the hand disappeared round the corner.

Eustace ran forward. He no longer saw it, but he could hear it as it squeezed its way behind the books on one of the shelves. A heavy volume had been displaced. There was a gap in the row of books, where it had got in. In his fear lest it should escape him again, he seized the first book that came to his hand and plugged it into the hole. Then, emptying two shelves of their contents, he took the wooden boards and propped them up in front to make his barrier doubly sure.

'I wish Saunders was back,' he said; 'one can't tackle this sort of thing alone.' It was after eleven, and there seemed little likelihood of Saunders returning before twelve. He did not dare to leave the shelf unwatched even to run downstairs to ring the bell. Morton, the butler, often used to come round about eleven to see that the windows were fastened, but he might not come tonight. Eustace was thoroughly unstrung. At last he heard steps down below.

'Morton!' he shouted. 'Morton!'

'Sir?'

'Has Mr Saunders got back yet?'

'Not yet, sir.'

'Well, bring me some brandy, and hurry up about it. I'm up in the gallery, you duffer.'

Morton fetched the brandy.

'Thanks,' said Eustace, as he emptied the glass. 'Don't go to bed yet, Morton. There are a lot of books that have fallen down by accident. Bring them up and put them back in their shelves.'

Morton had never seen Borlsover in so talkative a mood as on that night. 'Here,' said Eustace, when the books had been put back and dusted, 'you might hold up these boards for me, Morton. That beast in the box got out, and I've been chasing it all over the place.'

'I think I can hear it clawing at the books, sir. They're not valuable, I hope? I think that's the carriage, sir; I'll go and call Mr Saunders.'

It seemed to Eustace that he was away for five minutes but it could hardly have been more than one when he returned with Saunders. 'All right, Morton, you can go now. I'm up here, Saunders.'

'What's all the row?' asked Saunders, as he lounged forward with his hands in his pockets. The luck had been with him all the evening. He was completely satisfied, both with himself and with Captain Lockwood's taste in wines. 'What's the matter? You look to me to be in an absolutely blue funk.'

'That old devil of an uncle of mine,' began Eustace – 'Oh, I can't explain it all. It's his hand that's been playing Old Harry all the evening. But I've got it cornered behind these books. You've got to help me to catch it.'

'What's up with you, Eustace? What's the game?'

'It's no game, you silly idiot! If you don't believe me, take out one of those books and put your hand in and feel.'

'All right,' said Saunders; 'but wait till I've rolled up my sleeve. The accumulated dust of centuries, eh?' He took off his coat, knelt down, and thrust his arm along the shelf.

'There's something there right enough,' he said. 'It's got a funny, stumpy end to it, whatever it is, and nips like a crab. Ah! no, you don't!' He pulled his hand out in a flash. 'Shove in a book quickly. Now it can't get out.'

'What was it?' asked Eustace.

'Something that wanted very much to get hold of me. I felt what seemed like a thumb and forefinger. Give me some brandy.'

'How are we to get it out of there? What about a landing-net?'

'No good. It would be too smart for us. I tell you, Saunders, it can cover the ground far faster than I can walk. But I think I see how we can manage it. The two books at the end of the shelf are big ones that go right back against the wall. The others are very thin. I'll take out one at a time, and you slide the rest along, until we have it squashed between the end two.'

It certainly seemed to be the best plan. One by one as they took out the books, the space behind grew smaller and smaller. There was something in it that was certainly very much alive. Once they caught sight of fingers feeling for a way of escape. At last they had it pressed between the two big books.

'There's muscle there, if there isn't warm flesh and blood,' said Saunders, as he held them together. 'It seems to be a hand right enough, too. I suppose this is a sort of infectious hallucination. I've read about such cases before.'

'Infectious fiddlesticks!' said Eustace, his face white with anger; 'bring the thing downstairs. We'll get it back into the box.'

It was not altogether easy, but they were successful at last. 'Drive in the screws,' said Eustace, 'we won't run any risks. Put the box in this old desk of mine. There's nothing in it that I want. Here's the key. Thank goodness there's nothing wrong with the lock.'

'Quite a lively evening,' said Saunders. 'Now let's hear more about your uncle.'

They sat up together until early morning. Saunders had no desire for sleep. Eustace was trying to explain and forget; to conceal from himself a fear that he had never felt before – the fear of walking alone down the long corridor to his bedroom.

* * *

'Whatever it was,' said Eustace to Saunders on the following morning, 'I propose that we drop the subject. There's nothing to keep us here for the next ten days. We'll motor up to the Lakes and get some climbing.'

'And see nobody all day, and sit bored to death with each other every night. Not for me, thanks. Why not run up to town? Run's the exact word in this case, isn't it? We're both in such a blessed funk. Pull yourself together, Eustace, and let's have another look at the hand.'

'As you like,' said Eustace; 'there's the key.'

They went into the library and opened the desk. The box was as they had left it on the previous night.

'What are you waiting for?' asked Eustace.

'I am waiting for you to volunteer to open the lid. However, since you seem to funk it, allow me. There doesn't seem to be the likelihood of any rumpus this morning at all events.' He opened the lid and picked out the hand.

'Cold?' asked Eustace.

'Tepid. A bit below blood heat by the feel. Soft and supple too. If it's the embalming, it's a sort of embalming I've never seen before. Is it your uncle's hand?'

'Oh, yes, it's his all right,' said Eustace. 'I should know those long thin fingers anywhere. Put it back in the box, Saunders. Never mind about the screws. I'll lock the desk, so that there'll be no chance of its getting out. We'll compromise by motoring up to town for a week. If we can get off soon after lunch, we ought to be at Grantham or Stamford by night.'

'Right,' said Saunders, 'and tomorrow – oh, well, by tomorrow we shall have forgotten all about this beastly thing.'

If, when the morrow came, they had not forgotten, it was certainly true that at the end of the week they were able to tell a very vivid ghost-story at the little supper Eustace gave on Hallowe'en.

'You don't want us to believe that it's true, Mr Borlsover? How perfectly awful!'

'I'll take my oath on it, and so would Saunders here, wouldn't you, old chap?'

'Any number of oaths,' said Saunders. 'It was a long, thin hand, you know, and it gripped me just like that.'

'Don't, Mr Saunders! Don't! How perfectly horrid! Now tell us another one, do! Only a really creepy one, please.'

'Here's a pretty mess!' said Eustace on the following day, as he threw a letter across the table to Saunders. 'It's your affair, though. Mrs Merritt, if I understand it, gives a month's notice.'

'Oh, that's quite absurd on Mrs Merritt's part,' replied Saunders. 'She doesn't know what she's talking about. Let's see what she says.

'DEAR SIR – This is to let you know that I must give you a month's notice as from Tuesday, the 13th. For a long time I've felt the place too big for me; but when Jane Parfit and Emma Laidlaw go off with scarcely as much as an "If you please," after frightening the wits out of the other girls, so that they can't turn out a room by themselves or walk alone down the stairs for fear of treading on half-frozen toads or hearing it run along the passages at night, all I can say is that it's no place for me. So I must ask you, Mr Borlsover, sir, to find a new housekeeper, that has no objection to large and lonely houses, which some people do say – not that I believe them for a minute, my poor mother always having been a Wesleyan – are haunted.

'Yours faithfully, ELIZABETH MERRITT

'PS – I should be obliged if you would give my respects to Mr Saunders. I hope that he won't run any risks with his cold.'

'Saunders,' said Eustace, 'you've always had a wonderful way with you in dealing with servants. You mustn't let poor old Merritt go.'

'Of course she shan't go,' said Saunders. 'She's probably only angling for a rise in salary. I'll write to her this morning.'

'No. There's nothing like a personal interview. We've had enough of town. We'll go back tomorrow, and you must work your cold for all it's worth. Don't forget that it's got on to the chest, and will require weeks of feeding up and nursing.'

'All right; I think I can manage Mrs Merritt.'

But Mrs Merritt was more obstinate than he had thought. She was very sorry to hear of Mr Saunders's cold, and how he lay awake all night in London coughing; very sorry indeed. She'd change his room for him gladly and get the south room aired, and wouldn't he have a hot basin of bread and milk last thing at night? But she was afraid that she would have to leave at the end of the month.

'Try her with an increase of salary,' was the advice of Eustace.

It was no use. Mrs Merritt was obdurate, though she knew of a Mrs Goddard, who had been housekeeper to Lord Gargrave, who might be glad to come at the salary mentioned.

'What's the matter with the servants, Morton?'

asked Eustace that evening, when he brought the coffee into the library. 'What's all this about Mrs Merritt wanting to leave?'

'If you please, sir, I was going to mention it myself. I have a confession to make, sir. When I found your note, asking me to open that desk and take out the box with the rat, I broke the lock, as you told me, and was glad to do it, because I could hear the animal in the box making a great noise, and I thought it wanted food. So I took out the box, sir, and got a cage, and was going to transfer it, when the animal got away.'

'What in the world are you talking about? I never wrote any such note.'

'Excuse me, sir; it was the note I picked up here on the floor the day you and Mr Saunders left. I have it in my pocket now.'

It certainly seemed to be in Eustace's handwriting. It was written in pencil and began somewhat abruptly.

'Get a hammer, Morton,' he read, 'or some tool and break open the lock in the old desk in the library. Take out the box that is inside. You need not do anything else. The lid is already open. Eustace Borlsover.'

'And you opened the desk?'

'Yes, sir; and, as I was getting the cage ready, the animal hopped out.'

'What animal?'

'The animal inside the box, sir.'

'What did it look like?'

'Well, sir, I couldn't tell you,' said Morton, nervously. 'My back was turned, and it was halfway down the room when I looked up.'

'What was its colour?' asked Saunders. 'Black?'

'Oh, no, sir; a greyish white. It crept along in a very funny way, sir. I don't think it had a tail.'

'What did you do then?'

'I tried to catch it; but it was no use. So I set the rat-traps and kept the library shut. Then that girl, Emma Laidlaw, left the door open when she was cleaning, and I think it must have escaped.'

'And you think it is the animal that's been frightening the maids?'

'Well, no, sir, not quite. They said it was – you'll excuse me, sir – a hand that they saw. Emma trod on it once at the bottom of the stairs. She thought then it was a half-frozen toad, only white. And then Parfit was washing up the dishes in the scullery. She wasn't thinking about anything in particular. It was close on dusk. She took her hands out of the water and was drying them absent-minded-like on the roller towel, when she found she was drying someone else's hand as well, only colder than hers.'

'What nonsense!' exclaimed Saunders.

'Exactly, sir; that's what I told her, but we couldn't get her to stop.'

'You don't believe all this?' said Eustace, turning suddenly towards the butler.

'Me, sir? Oh, no, sir! I've not seen anything.'

'Nor heard anything?'

'Well, sir, if you must know the bells do ring at odd times, and there's nobody there when we go; and when we go round to draw the blinds of a night, as often as not somebody's been there before us. But, as I says to Mrs Merritt, a young monkey might do wonderful things, and we all know that Mr Borlsover has had some strange animals about the place.'

'Very well, Morton, that will do.'

'What do you make of it?' asked Saunders, when they were alone. 'I mean of the letter he said you wrote.'

'Oh, that's simple enough,' said Eustace. 'See the paper it's written on? I stopped using that paper years ago, but there were a few odd sheets and envelopes left in the old desk. We never fastened up the lid of the box before locking it in. The hand got out, found a pencil, wrote this note, and shoved it through the crack on to the floor, where Morton found it. That's plain as daylight.'

'But the hand couldn't write!'

'Couldn't it? You've not seen it do the things I've seen.' And he told Saunders more of what had happened at Eastbourne.

'Well,' said Saunders, 'in that case we have at least an explanation of the legacy. It was the hand which wrote, unknown to your uncle, that letter to your solicitor bequeathing itself to you. Your uncle had no more to do with that request than I. In fact, it would seem that he had some idea of this automatic writing and feared it.'

'Then if it's not my uncle, what is it?'

'I suppose some people might say that a disembodied spirit had got your uncle to educate and prepare a little body for it. Now it's got into that little body and is off on its own.'

'Well, what are we to do?'

'We'll keep our eyes open,' said Saunders, 'and try to catch it. If we can't do that, we shall have to wait till the bally clockwork runs down. After all, if it's flesh and blood, it can't live for ever.'

For two days nothing happened. Then Saunders saw it sliding down the banister in the hall. He was taken unawares and lost a full second before he started in pursuit, only to find that the thing had escaped him. Three days later, Eustace, writing alone in the library at night, saw it sitting on an open book at the other end of the room. The fingers crept over the page, as if it were reading, but before he had time to get up from his seat, it had taken the alarm, and was pulling itself up the curtains. Eustace watched it grimly, as it hung on to the cornice with three fingers and flicked thumb and forefinger at him in an expression of scornful derision.

'I know what I'll do,' he said. 'If I only get it into the open, I'll set the dogs on to it.'

He spoke to Saunders of the suggestion.

'It's a jolly good idea,' he said; 'only we won't wait till we find it out of doors. We'll get the dogs. There are the two terriers and the under-keeper's Irish mongrel that's on to rats like a flash. Your spaniel has not got spirit enough for this sort of game.'

They brought the dogs into the house, and the keeper's Irish mongrel chewed up the slippers, and the terriers tripped up Morton, as he waited at table; but all three were welcome. Even false security is better than no security at all.

For a fortnight nothing happened. Then the hand was caught, not by the dogs, but by Mrs Merritt's grey parrot. The bird was in the habit of periodically removing the pins that kept his seed- and water-tins in place, and then escaping through the holes in the side of his cage. When once at liberty, Peter would show no inclination to return, and would often be about the house for days. Now, after six consecutive weeks of captivity, Peter had again discovered a new way of unloosing his bolts and was at large, exploring the tapestried forests of the curtains and singing songs in praise of liberty from cornice and picture-rail.

'It's no use your trying to catch him,' said Eustace

to Mrs Merritt, as she came into the study one afternoon towards dusk with a stepladder. 'You'd much better leave Peter alone. Starve him into surrender, Mrs Merritt: and don't leave bananas and seed about for him to peck at when he fancies he's hungry. You're far too soft-hearted.'

'Well, sir, I see he's right out of reach now on that picture-rail; so, if you wouldn't mind closing the door, sir, when you leave the room, I'll bring his cage in tonight and put some meat inside it. He's that fond of meat, though it does make him pull out his feathers to suck the quills. They say that if you cook – '

'Never mind, Mrs Merritt,' said Eustace, who was busy writing; 'that will do; I'll keep an eye on the bird.'

For a short time there was silence in the room.

'Scratch poor Peter,' said the bird. 'Scratch poor old Peter!'

'Be quiet, you beastly bird!'

'Poor old Peter! Scratch poor Peter; do!'

'I'm more likely to wring your neck, if I get hold of you.' He looked up at the picture-rail, and there was the hand, holding on to a hook with three fingers, and slowly scratching the head of the parrot with the fourth. Eustace ran to the bell and pressed it hard; then across to the window, which he closed with a bang. Frightened by the noise, the parrot shook its wings preparatory to flight, and, as it did so, the fingers of the hand got hold of it by the throat. There was a shrill scream from Peter, as he fluttered across the room, wheeling round in circles that ever descended, borne down under the weight that clung to him. The bird dropped at last quite suddenly, and Eustace saw fingers and feathers rolled into an inextricable mass on the floor. The struggle abruptly ceased, as finger and thumb squeezed the neck; the bird's eyes rolled up to show the whites, and there was a faint, half-choked gurgle. But, before the fingers had time to loose their hold, Eustace had them in his own.

'Send Mr Saunders here at once,' he said to the maid who came in answer to the bell. 'Tell him I want him immediately.'

Then he went with the hand to the fire. There was a ragged gash across the back, where the bird's beak had torn it, but no blood oozed from the wound. He noted with disgust that the nails had grown long and discoloured.

'I'll burn the beastly thing,' he said. But he could not burn it. He tried to throw it into the flames, but his own hands, as if impelled by some old primitive feeling, would not let him. And so Saunders found him, pale and irresolute, with the hand still clasped tightly in his fingers.

'I've got it at last,' he said, in a tone of triumph.

'Good, let's have a look at it.'

'Not when it's loose. Get me some nails and a hammer and a board of some sort.'

'Can you hold it all right?'

'Yes, the thing's quite limp; tired out with throttling poor old Peter, I should say.'

'And now,' said Saunders, when he returned with the things, 'what are we going to do?'

'Drive a nail through it first, so that it can't get away. Then we can take our time over examining it.'

'Do it yourself,' said Saunders. 'I don't mind helping you with guinea-pigs occasionally, when there's something to be learned, partly because I don't fear a guinea-pig's revenge. This thing's different.'

'Oh, my aunt!' Eustace giggled hysterically, 'look

at it now.' For the hand was writhing in agonised contortions, squirming and wriggling upon the nail like a worm upon the hook.

'Well,' said Saunders, 'you've done it now. I'll leave you to examine it.'

'Don't go, in heaven's name! Cover it up, man; cover it up! Shove a cloth over it! Here!' and he pulled off the antimacassar from the back of a chair and wrapped the board in it. 'Now get the keys from my pocket and open the safe. Chuck the other things out. Oh, Lord, it's getting itself into frightful knots! Open it quick!' He threw the thing in and banged the door.

'We'll keep it there till it dies,' he said. 'May I burn in hell, if I ever open the door of that safe again.'

* * *

Mrs Merritt departed at the end of the month. Her successor, Mrs Handyside, certainly was more successful in the management of the servants. Early in her rule she declared that she would stand no nonsense, and gossip soon withered and died.

'I shouldn't be surprised if Eustace married one of these days,' said Saunders. 'Well, I'm in no hurry for such an event. I know him far too well for the future Mrs Borlsover to like me. It will be the same old story again; a long friendship slowly made – marriage – and a long friendship quickly forgotten.'

But Eustace did not follow the advice of his uncle and marry. Old habits crept over and covered his new experience. He was, if anything, less morose, and showed a greater inclination to take his natural part in country society.

Then came the burglary. The men, it was said, broke into the house by way of the conservatory. It was really little more than an attempt, for they only succeeded in carrying away a few pieces of plate from the pantry. The safe in the study was certainly found open and empty, but, as Mr Borlsover informed the police inspector, he had kept nothing of value in it during the last six months.

'Then you're lucky in getting off so easily, sir,' the man replied. 'By the way they have gone about their business, I should say they were experienced cracksmen. They must have caught the alarm when they were just beginning their evening's work.'

'Yes,' said Eustace, 'I suppose I am lucky.'

'I've no doubt,' said the inspector, 'that we shall be able to trace the men. I've said that they must have been old hands at the game. The way they got in and opened the safe shows that. But there's one little thing that puzzles me. One of them was careless enough not to wear gloves, and I'm bothered if I know what he was trying to do. I've traced his fingermarks on the new varnish on the window-sashes in every one of the downstairs rooms. They are very distinctive ones too.'

'Right or left hand, or both?' asked Eustace.

'Oh, right every time. That's the funny thing. He must have been a foolhardy fellow, and I rather think it was him that wrote that.' He took out a slip of paper from his pocket. 'That's what he wrote, sir: *I've got out, Eustace Borlsover, but I'll be back before long.* Some jailbird just escaped, I suppose. It will make it all the easier for us to trace him. Do you know the writing, sir?'

'No,' said Eustace. 'It's not the writing of anyone I know.'

'I'm not going to stay here any longer,' said Eustace

to Saunders at luncheon. 'I've got on far better during the last six months than I expected, but I'm not going to run the risk of seeing that thing again. I shall go up to town this afternoon. Get Morton to put my things together, and join me with the car at Brighton on the day after tomorrow. And bring the proofs of those two papers with you. We'll run over them together.'

'How long are you going to be away?'

'I can't say for certain, but be prepared to stay for some time. We've stuck to work pretty closely through the summer, and I for one need a holiday. I'll engage the rooms at Brighton. You'll find it best to break the journey at Hitchin. I'll wire to you there at the Crown to tell you the Brighton address.'

The house he chose at Brighton was in a terrace. He had been there before. It was kept by his old college gyp, a man of discreet silence, who was admirably partnered by an excellent cook. The rooms were on the first floor; the two bedrooms were at the back, and opened out of each other. 'Mr Saunders can have the smaller one, though it is the only one with a fireplace,' he said. 'I'll stick to the larger of the two, since it's got a bathroom adjoining. I wonder what time he'll arrive with the car.'

Saunders came about seven, cold and cross and dirty. 'We'll light the fire in the dining-room,' said Eustace, 'and get Prince to unpack some of the things while we are at dinner. What were the roads like?'

'Rotten. Swimming with mud, and a beastly cold wind against us all day. And this is July. Dear old England!'

'Yes,' said Eustace, 'I think we might do worse than leave old England for a few months.'

They turned in soon after twelve.

'You oughtn't to feel cold, Saunders,' said Eustace, 'when you can afford to sport a great fur-lined coat like this. You do yourself very well, all things considered. Look at those gloves, for instance. Who could possibly feel cold when wearing them?'

'They are far too clumsy, though, for driving. Try them on and see' – and he tossed them through the door on to Eustace's bed and went on with his unpacking. A minute later he heard a shrill cry of terror. 'Oh, Lord,' he heard, 'it's in the glove! Quick, Saunders, quick!' Then came a smacking thud. Eustace had thrown it from him. 'I've chucked it into the bathroom,' he gasped; 'it's hit the wall and fallen into the bath. Come now, if you want to help.' Saunders, with a lighted candle in his hand, looked over the edge of the bath. There it was, old and maimed, dumb and blind, with a ragged hole in the middle, crawling, staggering, trying to creep up the slippery sides, only to fall back helpless.

'Stay there,' said Saunders. 'I'll empty a collar-box or something, and we'll jam it in. It can't get out while I'm away.'

'Yes, it can,' shouted Eustace. 'It's getting out now; it's climbing up the plug-chain. No, you brute, you filthy brute, you don't! Come back, Saunders; it's getting away from me. I can't hold it; it's all slippery. Curse its claws! Shut the window, you idiot! It's got out.' There was the sound of something dropping on to the hard flagstones below, and Eustace fell back fainting.

* * *

For a fortnight he was ill.

'I don't know what to make of it,' the doctor said to Saunders. 'I can only suppose that Mr Borlsover has suffered some great emotional shock. You had better let me send someone to help you nurse him. And by all means indulge that whim of his never to be left alone in the dark. I would keep a light burning all night, if I were you. But he must have more fresh air. It's perfectly absurd, this hatred of open windows.'

Eustace would have no one with him but Saunders.

'I don't want the other man,' he said. 'They'd smuggle it in somehow. I know they would.'

'Don't worry about it, old chap. This sort of thing can't go on indefinitely. You know I saw it this time as well as you. It wasn't half so active. It won't go on living much longer, especially after that fall. I heard it hit the flags myself. As soon as you're a bit stronger, we'll leave this place, not bag and baggage, but with only the clothes on our backs, so that it won't be able to hide anywhere. We'll escape it that way. We won't give any address, and we won't have any parcels sent after us. Cheer up, Eustace! You'll be well enough to leave in a day or two. The doctor says I can take you out in a chair tomorrow.'

'What have I done?' asked Eustace. 'Why does it come after me? I'm no worse than other men. I'm no worse than you, Saunders; you know I'm not. It was you who was at the bottom of that dirty business in San Diego, and that was fifteen years ago.'

'It's not that, of course,' said Saunders. 'We are in the twentieth century, and even the parsons have dropped the idea of your old sins finding you out. Before you caught the hand in the library, it was filled with pure malevolence – to you and all mankind. After you spiked it through with that nail, it naturally forgot about other people and concentrated its attention on you. It was shut up in that safe, you know, for nearly six months. That gives plenty of time for thinking of revenge.'

Eustace Borlsover would not leave his room, but he thought there might be something in Saunders's suggestion of a sudden departure from Brighton. He began rapidly to regain his strength.

'We'll go on the 1st of September,' he said.

* * *

The evening of the 31st of August was oppressively warm. Though at midday the windows had been wide open, they had been shut an hour or so before dusk. Mrs Prince had long since ceased to wonder at the strange habits of the gentlemen on the first floor. Soon after their arrival she had been told to take down the heavy window curtains in the two bedrooms, and day by day the rooms had seemed to grow more bare. Nothing was left lying about.

'Mr Borlsover doesn't like to have any place where dirt can collect,' Saunders had said as an excuse. 'He likes to see into all the corners of the room.'

'Couldn't I open the window just a little?' he said to Eustace that evening. 'We're simply roasting in here, you know.'

'No, leave well alone. We're not a couple of boarding-school misses fresh from a course of hygiene lectures. Get the chessboard out.'

They sat down and played. At ten o'clock Mrs Prince came to the door with a note. 'I am sorry I didn't bring it before,' she said, 'but it was left in the letterbox.'

'Open it, Saunders, and see if it wants answering.'

It was very brief. There was neither address nor signature. *Will eleven o'clock tonight be suitable for our last appointment?*

'Who is it from?' asked Borlsover.

'It was meant for me,' said Saunders. 'There's no answer, Mrs Prince,' and he put the paper into his pocket. 'A dunning letter from a tailor; I suppose he must have got wind of our leaving.'

It was a clever lie, and Eustace asked no more questions. They went on with their game.

On the landing outside Saunders could hear the grandfather clock whispering the seconds, blurting out the quarter-hours.

'Check,' said Eustace. The clock struck eleven. At the same time there was a gentle knocking on the door; it seemed to come from the bottom panel.

'Who's there?' asked Eustace.

There was no answer.

'Mrs Prince, is that you?'

'She is up above,' said Saunders; 'I can hear her walking about the room.'

'Then lock the door; bolt it too. Your move, Saunders.'

While Saunders sat with his eyes on the chessboard, Eustace walked over to the window and examined the fastenings. He did the same in Saunders's room and the bathroom. There were no doors between the three rooms, or he would have shut and locked them too.

'Now, Saunders,' he said, 'don't stay all night over your move. I've had time to smoke one cigarette already. It's bad to keep an invalid waiting. There's only one possible thing for you to do. What was that?'

'The ivy blowing against the window. There, it's your move now, Eustace.'

'It wasn't the ivy, you idiot! It was someone tapping at the window,' and he pulled up the blind. On the outer side of the window, clinging to the sash, was the hand.

'What is that it's holding?'

'It's a pocketknife. It's going to try to open the window by pushing back the fastener with the blade.'

'Well, let it try,' said Eustace. 'Those fasteners screw down; they can't be opened that way. Anyhow, we'll close the shutters. It's your move, Saunders. I've played.'

But Saunders found it impossible to fix his attention on the game. He could not understand Eustace, who seemed all at once to have lost his fear. 'What do you say to some wine?' he asked. 'You seem to be taking things coolly, but I don't mind confessing that I'm in a blessed funk.'

'You've no need to be. There's nothing supernatural about that hand, Saunders. I mean, it seems to be governed by the laws of time and space. It's not the sort of thing that vanishes into thin air or slides through oaken doors. And since that's so, I defy it to get in here. We'll leave the place in the morning. I for one have bottomed the depths of fear. Fill your glass, man! The windows are all shuttered; the door is locked and bolted. Pledge me my Uncle Adrian! Drink, man! What are you waiting for?'

Saunders was standing with his glass half raised. 'It can get in,' he said hoarsely; 'it can get in! We've forgotten. There's the fireplace in my bedroom. It will come down the chimney.'

'Quick!' said Eustace, as he rushed into the other room; 'we haven't a minute to lose. What can we do? Light the fire, Saunders. Give me a match, quick!'

'They must be all in the other room. I'll get them.'

'Hurry, man, for goodness' sake! Look in the bookcase! Look in the bathroom! Here, come and stand here; I'll look.'

'Be quick!' shouted Saunders. 'I can hear something!'

'Then plug a sheet from your bed up the chimney. No, here's a match!' He had found one, at last, that had slipped into a crack in the floor.

'Is the fire laid? Good, but it may not burn. I know – the oil from that old reading-lamp and this cotton-wool. Now the match, quick! Pull the sheet away, you fool! We don't want it now.'

There was a great roar from the grate, as the flames shot up. Saunders had been a fraction of a second too late with the sheet. The oil had fallen on to it. It, too, was burning.

'The whole place will be on fire!' cried Eustace, as he tried to beat out the flames with a blanket. 'It's no good! I can't manage it. You must open the door, Saunders, and get help.'

Saunders ran to the door and fumbled with the bolts. The key was stiff in the lock. 'Hurry,' shouted Eustace, 'or the heat will be too much for me.' The key turned in the lock at last. For half a second Saunders stopped to look back. Afterwards he could never be quite sure as to what he had seen, but at the time he thought that something black and charred was creeping slowly, very slowly, from the mass of flames towards Eustace Borlsover. For a moment he thought of returning to his friend; but the noise and the smell of the burning sent him running down the passage, crying: 'Fire! Fire!' He rushed to the telephone to summon help, and then back to the bathroom – he should have thought of that before – for water. As he burst into the bedroom there came a scream of terror which ended suddenly, and then the sound of a heavy fall.

* * *

This is the story which I heard on successive Saturday evenings from the senior mathematical master at a second-rate suburban school. For Saunders has had to earn a living in a way which other men might reckon less congenial than his old manner of life. I had mentioned by chance the name of Adrian Borlsover, and wondered at the time why he changed the conversation with such unusual abruptness. A week later Saunders began to tell me something of his own history; sordid enough, though shielded with a reserve I could well understand, for it had to cover not only his failings, but those of a dead friend. Of the final tragedy he was at first especially loath to speak; and it was only gradually that I was able to piece together the narrative of the preceding pages. Saunders was reluctant to draw any conclusions. At one time he thought that the fingered beast had been animated by the spirit of Sigismund Borlsover, a sinister eighteenth-century ancestor, who, according to legend, built and worshipped in the ugly pagan temple that overlooked the lake. At another time, Saunders believed the spirit to belong to a man whom Eustace had once employed as a laboratory assistant – 'A black-haired, spiteful little brute,' he said, 'who died cursing his doctor because the fellow couldn't help him to live to settle some paltry score with Borlsover.'

From the point of view of direct contemporary

evidence, Saunders's story is practically uncorroborated. All the letters mentioned in the narrative were destroyed, with the exception of the last note which Eustace received, or rather, which he would have received, had not Saunders intercepted it. That I have seen myself. The handwriting was thin and shaky, the handwriting of an old man. I remember the Greek 'e' was used in 'appointment'. A little thing that amused me at the time was that Saunders seemed to keep the note pressed between the pages of his Bible.

I had seen Adrian Borlsover once. Saunders I learnt to know well. It was by chance, however, and not by design, that I met a third person of the story – Morton, the butler. Saunders and I were walking in the Zoological Gardens one Sunday afternoon, when he called my attention to an old man who was standing before the door of the Reptile House.

'Why, Morton,' he said, clapping him on the back, 'how is the world treating you?'

'Poorly, Mr Saunders,' said the old fellow, though his face lighted up at the greeting. 'The winters drag terribly nowadays. There don't seem to be no summers or springs.'

'You haven't found what you were looking for, I suppose?'

'No, sir, not yet; but I shall some day. I always told them that Mr Borlsover kept some queer animals.'

'And what is he looking for?' I asked, when we had parted from him.

'A beast with five fingers,' said Saunders. 'This afternoon, since he has been in the Reptile House, I suppose it will be a reptile with a hand. Next week it will be a monkey with practically no body. The poor old chap is a born materialist.'

Thurnley Abbey

PERCEVAL LANDON

Three years ago I was on my way out to the East, and as an extra day in London was of some importance, I took the Friday evening mail-train to Brindisi instead of the usual Thursday morning Marseilles express. Many people shrink from the long forty-eight-hour train journey through Europe, and the subsequent rush across the Mediterranean on the nineteen-knot *Isis* or *Osiris*; but there is really very little discomfort on either the train or the mail-boat, and unless there is actually nothing for me to do, I always like to save the extra day and a half in London before I say goodbye to her for one of my longer tramps. This time – it was early, I remember, in the shipping season, probably about the beginning of September – there were few passengers, and I had a compartment in the P&O Indian express to myself all the way from Calais. All Sunday I watched the blue waves dimpling the Adriatic, and the pale rosemary along the cuttings; the plain white towns, with their flat roofs and their bold 'duomos', and the grey-green gnarled olive orchards of Apulia. The journey was just like any other. We ate in the dining-car as often and as long as we decently could. We slept after luncheon; we dawdled the afternoon away with yellow-backed novels; sometimes we exchanged platitudes in the smoking-room, and it was there that I met Alastair Colvin.

Colvin was a man of middle height, with a resolute, well-cut jaw; his hair was turning grey; his moustache was sun-whitened, otherwise he was clean-shaven – obviously a gentleman, and obviously also a preoccupied man. He had no great wit. When spoken to, he made the usual remarks in the right way, and I dare say he refrained from banalities only because he spoke less than the rest of us; most of the time he buried himself in the Wagon-lit Company's timetable, but seemed unable to concentrate his attention on any one page of it. He found that I had been over the Siberian railway, and for a quarter of an hour he discussed it with me. Then he lost interest in it, and rose to go to his compartment. But he came back again very soon, and seemed glad to pick up the conversation again.

Of course this did not seem to me to be of any importance. Most travellers by train become a trifle infirm of purpose after thirty-six hours' rattling. But Colvin's restless way I noticed in somewhat marked contrast with the man's personal importance and dignity; especially ill suited was it to his finely made large hand with strong, broad, regular nails and its few lines. As I looked at his hand I noticed a long, deep, and recent scar of ragged shape. However, it is absurd to pretend that I thought anything was unusual. I went off at five o'clock on Sunday afternoon to sleep away the hour or two that had still to be got through before we arrived at Brindisi.

Once there, we few passengers transshipped our hand baggage, verified our berths – there were only a score of us in all – and then, after an aimless ramble of half an hour in Brindisi, we returned to dinner at the Hotel International, not wholly surprised that the town had been the death of Virgil. If I remember rightly, there is a gaily painted hall at the International – I do not wish to advertise anything, but there is no other place in Brindisi at which to await the coming of the mails – and after dinner I was looking with awe at a trellis overgrown with blue vines, when Colvin moved across the room to my table. He picked up *Il Secolo*, but almost immediately gave up the pretence of reading it. He turned squarely to me and said: 'Would you do me a favour?'

One doesn't do favours to stray acquaintances on Continental expresses without knowing something more of them than I knew of Colvin. But I smiled in a noncommittal way, and asked him what he wanted. I wasn't wrong in part of my estimate of him; he said bluntly: 'Will you let me sleep in your cabin on the *Osiris*?' And he coloured a little as he said it.

Now, there is nothing more tiresome than having to put up with a stable-companion at sea, and I asked him rather pointedly: 'Surely there is room for all of us?' I thought that perhaps he had been partnered off with some mangy Levantine, and wanted to escape from him at all hazards.

Colvin, still somewhat confused, said: 'Yes; I am in a cabin by myself. But you would do me the greatest favour if you would allow me to share yours.'

This was all very well, but, besides the fact that I always sleep better when alone, there had been some recent thefts on board English liners, and I hesitated, frank and honest and self-conscious as Colvin was. Just then the mail-train came in with a clatter and a rush of escaping steam, and I asked him to see me again about it on the boat when we started. He answered me curtly – I suppose he saw the mistrust in my manner –

'I am a member of White's.' I smiled to myself as he said it, but I remembered in a moment that the man – if he were really what he claimed to be, and I make no doubt that he was – must have been sorely put to it before he urged the fact as a guarantee of his respectability to a total stranger at a Brindisi hotel.

That evening, as we cleared the red and green harbour-lights of Brindisi, Colvin explained. This is his story in his own words.

* * *

'When I was travelling in India some years ago, I made the acquaintance of a youngish man in the Woods and Forests. We camped out together for a week, and I found him a pleasant companion. John Broughton was a light-hearted soul when off duty, but a steady and capable man in any of the small emergencies that continually arise in that department. He was liked and trusted by the natives, and though a trifle over-pleased with himself when he escaped to civilisation at Simla or Calcutta, Broughton's future was well assured in Government service, when a fair-sized estate was unexpectedly left to him, and he joyfully shook the dust of the Indian plains from his feet and returned to England. For five years he drifted about London. I saw him now and then. We dined together about every eighteen months, and I could trace pretty exactly the gradual sickening of Broughton with a merely idle life. He then set out on a couple of long voyages, returned as restless as before, and at last told me that he had decided to marry and settle down at his place, Thurnley Abbey, which had long been empty. He spoke about looking after the property and standing for his constituency in the usual way. Vivien

Wilde, his *fiancée*, had, I suppose, begun to take him in hand. She was a pretty girl with a deal of fair hair and rather an exclusive manner; deeply religious in a narrow school, she was still kindly and high-spirited, and I thought that Broughton was in luck. He was quite happy and full of information about his future.

'Among other things, I asked him about Thurnley Abbey. He confessed that he hardly knew the place. The last tenant, a man called Clarke, had lived in one wing for fifteen years and seen no one. He had been a miser and a hermit. It was the rarest thing for a light to be seen at the Abbey after dark. Only the barest necessities of life were ordered, and the tenant himself received them at the side-door. His one half-caste manservant, after a month's stay in the house, had abruptly left without warning, and had returned to the Southern States. One thing Broughton complained bitterly about: Clarke had wilfully spread the rumour among the villagers that the Abbey was haunted, and had even condescended to play childish tricks with spirit-lamps and salt in order to scare trespassers away at night. He had been detected in the act of this tomfoolery, but the story spread, and no one, said Broughton, would venture near the house except in broad daylight. The hauntedness of Thurnley Abbey was now, he said with a grin, part of the gospel of the countryside, but he and his young wife were going to change all that. Would I propose myself any time I liked? I, of course, said I would, and equally, of course, intended to do nothing of the sort without a definite invitation.

'The house was put in thorough repair, though not a stick of the old furniture and tapestry were removed. Floors and ceilings were relaid: the roof was made watertight again, and the dust of half a century was scoured out. He showed me some photographs of the place. It was called an Abbey, though as a matter of fact it had been only the infirmary of the long-vanished Abbey of Clouster some five miles away. The larger part of the building remained as it had been in pre-Reformation days, but a wing had been added in Jacobean times, and that part of the house had been kept in something like repair by Mr Clarke. He had in both the ground and first floors set a heavy timber door, strongly barred with iron, in the passage between the earlier and the Jacobean parts of the house, and had entirely neglected the former. So there had been a good deal of work to be done.

'Broughton, whom I saw in London two or three times about this period, made a deal of fun over the positive refusal of the workmen to remain after sun-down. Even after the electric light had been put into every room, nothing would induce them to remain, though, as Broughton observed, electric light was death on ghosts. The legend of the Abbey's ghosts had gone far and wide, and the men would take no risks. They went home in batches of five and six, and even during the daylight hours there was an inordinate amount of talking between one and another, if either happened to be out of sight of his companion. On the whole, though nothing of any sort or kind had been conjured up even by their heated imaginations during their five months' work upon the Abbey, the belief in the ghosts was rather strengthened than otherwise in Thurnley because of the men's confessed nervous-ness, and local tradition declared itself in favour of the ghost of an immured nun.

' "Good old nun!" said Broughton.

'I asked him whether in general he believed in the possibility of ghosts, and, rather to my surprise, he said that he couldn't say he entirely disbelieved in them. A man in India had told him one morning in camp that he believed that his mother was dead in England, as her vision had come to his tent the night before. He had not been alarmed, but had said nothing, and the figure vanished again. As a matter of fact, the next possible dak-walla brought on a telegram announcing the mother's death. "There the thing was," said Broughton. But at Thurnley he was practical enough. He roundly cursed the idiotic selfishness of Clarke, whose silly antics had caused all the inconvenience. At the same time, he couldn't refuse to sympathise to some extent with the ignorant workmen. "My own idea," said he, "is that if a ghost ever does come in one's way, one ought to speak to it."

'I agreed. Little as I knew of the ghost world and its conventions, I had always remembered that a spook was in honour bound to wait to be spoken to. It didn't seem much to do, and I felt that the sound of one's own voice would at any rate reassure oneself as to one's wakefulness. But there are few ghosts outside Europe – few, that is, that a white man can see – and I had never been troubled with any. However, as I have said, I told Broughton that I agreed.

'So the wedding took place, and I went to it in a tall hat which I bought for the occasion, and the new Mrs Broughton smiled very nicely at me afterwards. As it had to happen, I took the Orient Express that evening and was not in England again for nearly six months. Just before I came back I got a letter from Broughton. He asked if I could see him in London or come to Thurnley, as he thought I should be better able to help him than anyone else he knew. His wife sent a nice message to me at the end, so I was reassured about at least one thing. I wrote from Budapest that I would come and see him at Thurnley two days after my arrival in London, and as I sauntered out of the Pannonia into the Kerepesi Utcza to post my letters, I wondered of what earthly service I could be to Broughton. I had been out with him after tiger on foot, and I could imagine few men better able at a pinch to manage their own business. However, I had nothing to do, so after dealing with some small accumulations of business during my absence, I packed a kitbag and departed to Euston.

'I was met by Broughton's great limousine at Thurnley Road station, and after a drive of nearly seven miles we echoed through the sleepy streets of Thurnley village, into which the main gates of the park thrust themselves, splendid with pillars and spread-eagles and tomcats rampant atop of them. I never was a herald, but I know that the Broughtons have the right to supporters – Heaven knows why! From the gates a quadruple avenue of beech trees led inwards for a quarter of a mile. Beneath them a neat strip of fine turf edged the road and ran back until the the poison of the dead beech-leaves killed it under the trees. There were many wheel-tracks on the road, and a comfortable little pony trap jogged past me laden with a country parson and his wife and daughter. Evidently there was some garden party going on at the Abbey. The road dropped away to the right at the end of the avenue, and I could see the Abbey across a wide pasturage and a broad lawn thickly dotted with guests.

'The end of the building was plain. It must have been almost mercilessly austere when it was first built, but time had crumbled the edges and toned the stone down to an orange-lichened grey wherever it showed behind its curtain of magnolia, jasmine, and ivy. Farther on was the three-storeyed Jacobean house, tall and handsome. There had not been the slightest attempt to adapt the one to the other, but the kindly ivy had glossed over the touching-point. There was a tall flinche in the middle of the building, surmounting a small bell tower. Behind the house there rose the mountainous verdure of Spanish chestnuts all the way up the hill.

'Broughton had seen me coming from afar, and walked across from his other guests to welcome me before turning me over to the butler's care. This man was sandy-haired and rather inclined to be talkative. He could, however, answer hardly any questions about the house; he had, he said, only been there three weeks. Mindful of what Broughton had told me, I made no enquiries about ghosts, though the room into which I was shown might have justified anything. It was a very large low room with oak beams projecting from the white ceiling. Every inch of the walls, including the doors, was covered with tapestry, and a remarkably fine Italian four-post bedstead, heavily draped, added to the darkness and dignity of the place. All the furniture was old, well made, and dark. Underfoot there was a plain green pile carpet, the only new thing about the room except the electric light fittings and the jugs and basins. Even the looking-glass on the dressing-table was an old pyramidal Venetian glass set in heavy *repoussé* frame of tarnished silver.

'After a few minutes' cleaning up, I went downstairs and out upon the lawn, where I greeted my hostess. The people gathered there were of the usual country type, all anxious to be pleased and roundly curious as to the new master of the Abbey. Rather to my surprise, and quite to my pleasure, I rediscovered Glenham, whom I had known well in old days in Barotseland: he lived quite close, as, he remarked with a grin, I ought to have known. "But," he added, "I don't live in a place like this." He swept his hand to the long, low lines of the Abbey in obvious admiration, and then, to my intense interest, muttered beneath his breath, "Thank God!" He saw that I had overheard him, and turning to me said decidedly, "Yes, 'thank God', I said, and I meant it. I wouldn't live at the Abbey for all Broughton's money."

' "But surely," I demurred, "you know that old Clarke was discovered in the very act of setting light on his bug-a-boos?"

'Glenham shrugged his shoulders. "Yes, I know about that. But there is something wrong with the place still. All I can say is that Broughton is a different man since he has lived there. I don't believe that he will remain much longer. But – you're staying here? – well, you'll hear all about it tonight. There's a big dinner, I understand." The conversation turned off to old reminiscences, and Glenham soon after had to go.

'Before I went to dress that evening I had twenty minutes' talk with Broughton in his library. There was no doubt that the man was altered, gravely altered. He was nervous and fidgety, and I found him looking at me only when my eye was off him. I naturally asked him what he wanted of me. I told him I would do anything I could, but that I couldn't conceive what he lacked that I could provide. He said with a lustreless smile that there was, however, something, and that he would tell me the following morning. It struck me that he was somehow ashamed of himself, and perhaps ashamed of the part he was asking me to play. However, I dismissed the subject from my mind and went up to dress in my palatial room. As I shut the door a draught blew out the Queen of Sheba from the wall, and I noticed that the tapestries were not fastened to the wall at the bottom. I have always held very practical views about spooks, and it has often seemed to me that the slow waving in firelight of loose tapestry upon a wall would account for ninety-nine per cent of the stories one hears. Certainly the dignified undulation of this lady with her attendants and huntsmen – one of whom was untidily cutting the throat of a fallow deer upon the very steps on which King Solomon, a grey-faced Flemish nobleman with the order of the Golden Fleece, awaited his fair visitor – gave colour to my hypothesis.

'Nothing much happened at dinner. The people were very much like those of the garden party. A young woman next me seemed anxious to know what was being read in London. As she was far more familiar than I with the most recent magazines and literary supplements, I found salvation in being myself instructed in the tendencies of modern fiction. All true art, she said, was shot through and through with melancholy. How vulgar were the attempts at wit that marked so many modern books! From the beginning of literature it had always been tragedy that embodied the highest attainment of every age. To call such works morbid merely begged the question. No man – she looked sternly at me through the steel rim of her glasses – could fail to agree with me. Of course, as one would, I immediately and properly said that I slept with Pett Ridge and Jacobs under my pillow at night, and that if *Jorrocks* weren't quite so large and cornery, I would add him to the company. She hadn't read any of them, so I was saved – for a time. But I remember grimly that she said that the dearest wish of her life was to be in some awful and soul-freezing situation of horror, and I remember that she dealt hardly with the hero of Nat Paynter's vampire story, between nibbles at her brown-bread ice. She was a cheerless soul, and I couldn't help thinking that if there were many such in the neighbourhood, it was not surprising that old Glenham had been stuffed with some nonsense or other about the Abbey. Yet nothing could well have been less creepy than the glitter of silver and glass, and the subdued lights and cackle of conversation all round the dinner-table.

'After the ladies had gone I found myself talking to the rural dean. He was a thin, earnest man, who at once turned the conversation to old Clarke's buffooneries. But, he said, Mr Broughton had introduced such a new and cheerful spirit, not only into the Abbey, but, he might say, into the whole neighbourhood, that he had great hopes that the ignorant superstitions of the past were from henceforth destined to oblivion. Thereupon his other neighbour, a portly gentleman of independent means and position, audibly remarked "Amen," which damped the rural dean, and we talked to partridges past, partridges present, and pheasants to come. At the other end of the table Broughton sat with a couple of his friends, red-faced hunting men. Once I noticed that they were discussing me, but I paid no attention to it at the time. I remembered it a few hours later.

'By eleven all the guests were gone, and Broughton, his wife, and I were alone together under the fine plaster ceiling of the Jacobean drawing-room. Mrs Broughton talked about one or two of the neighbours, and then, with a smile, said that she knew I would excuse her, shook hands with me, and went off to bed. I am not very good at analysing things, but I felt that she talked a little uncomfortably and with a suspicion of effort, smiled rather conventionally, and was obviously glad to go. These things seem trifling enough to repeat, but I had throughout the faint feeling that everything was not quite square. Under the circumstances, this was enough to set me wondering what on earth the service could be that I was to render – wondering also whether the whole business were not some ill-advised jest in order to make me come down from London for a mere shooting-party.

'Broughton said little after she had gone. But he was evidently labouring to bring the conversation round to the so-called haunting of the Abbey. As soon as I saw this, of course I asked him directly about it. He then seemed at once to lose interest in the matter. There was no doubt about it: Broughton was somehow a changed man, and to my mind he had changed in no way for the better. Mrs Broughton seemed no sufficient cause. He was clearly very fond of her, and she of him. I reminded him that he was going to tell me what I could do for him in the morning, pleaded my journey, lighted a candle, and went upstairs with him. At the end of the passage leading into the old house he grinned weakly and said, "Mind, if you see a ghost, do talk to it; you said you would." He stood irresolutely a moment and then turned away. At the door of his dressing-room he paused once more: "I'm here," he called out, "if you should want anything. Good-night," and he shut the door.

'I went along the passage to my room, undressed, switched on a lamp beside my bed, read a few pages of *The Jungle Book*, and then, more than ready for sleep, turned the light off and went fast asleep.

* * *

'Three hours later I woke up. There was not a breath of wind outside. There was not even a flicker of light from the fireplace. As I lay there, an ash tinkled slightly as it cooled, but there was hardly a gleam of the dullest red in the grate. An owl cried among the silent Spanish chestnuts on the slope outside. I idly reviewed the events of the day, hoping that I should fall off to sleep again before I reached dinner. But at the end I seemed as wakeful as ever. There was no help for it. I must read my *Jungle Book* again till I felt ready to go off, so I fumbled for the pear at the end of the cord that hung down inside the bed, and I switched on the bedside lamp. The sudden glory dazzled me for a moment. I felt under my pillow for my book with half-shut eyes. Then, growing used to the light, I happened to look down to the foot of my bed.

'I can never tell you really what happened then. Nothing I could ever confess in the most abject words could even faintly picture to you what I felt. I know that my heart stopped dead, and my throat shut automatically. In one instinctive movement I crouched back up against the headboards of the bed, staring at the horror. The movement set my heart going again, and the sweat dripped from every pore. I am not a particularly religious man, but I had always believed that God would never allow any supernatural appearance to present itself to man in such a guise and in such circumstances that harm, either bodily or mental, could result to him. I can only tell you that at the moment both my life and my reason rocked unsteadily on their seats.'

* * *

The other *Osiris* passengers had gone to bed. Only he and I remained leaning over the starboard railing, which rattled uneasily now and then under the fierce vibration of the over-engined mail-boat. Far over, there were the lights of a few fishing-smacks riding out the night, and a great rush of white combing and seething water fell out and away from us overside.

At last Colvin went on: 'Leaning over the foot of my bed, looking at me, was a figure swathed in a rotten and tattered veiling. This shroud passed over the head, but left both eyes and the right side of the face bare. It then followed the line of the arm down to where the hand grasped the bed-end. The face was not entirely that of a skull, though the eyes and the flesh of the face were totally gone. There was a thin, dry skin drawn tightly over the features, and there was some skin left on the hand. One wisp of hair crossed the forehead. It was perfectly still. I looked at it, and it looked at me, and my brains turned dry and hot in my head. I had still got the pear of the electric lamp in my hand, and I played idly with it; only I dared not turn the light out again. I shut my eyes, only to open them in a hideous terror the same second. The thing had not moved. My heart was thumping, and the sweat cooled me as it evaporated. Another cinder tinkled in the grate, and a panel creaked in the wall.

'My reason failed me. For twenty minutes, or twenty seconds, I was able to think of nothing else but this awful figure, till there came, hurtling through the empty channels of my senses, the remembrances that Broughton and his friends had discussed me furtively at dinner. The dim possibility of its being a hoax stole gratefully into my unhappy mind, and once there, one's pluck came creeping back along a thousand tiny veins. My first sensation was one of blind unreasoning thankfulness that my brain was going to stand the trial. I am not a timid man, but the best of us needs some human handle to steady him in time of extremity, and in this faint but growing hope that after all it might be only a brutal hoax, I found the fulcrum that I needed. At last I moved.

'How I managed to do it I cannot tell you, but with one spring towards the foot of the bed I got within arm's-length and struck out one fearful blow with my fist at the thing. It crumbled under it, and my hand was cut to the bone. With a sickening revulsion after my terror, I dropped half-fainting across the end of the bed. So it was merely a foul trick after all. No doubt the trick had been played many a time before: no doubt Broughton and his friends had had some large bet among themselves as to what I should do when I discovered the gruesome thing. From my state of abject terror I found myself transported into an insensate anger. I shouted curses upon Broughton. I dived rather than climbed over the bed-end of the sofa. I tore at the robed skeleton – how well the whole thing had been carried out, I thought – I broke the skull against the floor, and stamped upon its dry bones. I flung the head away under the bed, and rent the brittle bones of the trunk in pieces. I snapped the thin thighbones across my knee, and flung them in different directions. The shinbones I set up against a stool and broke with my heel. I raged like a Berserker against the loathly thing, and stripped the ribs from the backbone and slung the breastbone against the cupboard. My fury increased as the work of destruction went on. I tore the frail rotten veil into twenty pieces, and the dust went up over everything, over the clean blotting-paper and the silver inkstand. At last my work was done. There was but a raffle of broken bones and strips of parchment and crumbling wool. Then, picking up a piece of the skull – it was the cheek and temple bone of the right side, I remember – I opened the door and went down the passage to Broughton's dressing-room. I remember still how my sweat-dripping pyjamas clung to me as I walked. At the door I kicked and entered.

'Broughton was in bed. He had already turned the light on and seemed shrunken and horrified. For a moment he could hardly pull himself together. Then I spoke. I don't know what I said. Only I know that from a heart full and over-full with hatred and contempt, spurred on by shame of my own recent cowardice, I let my tongue run on. He answered nothing. I was amazed at my own fluency. My hair still clung lankly to my wet temples, my hand was bleeding profusely, and I must have looked a strange sight. Broughton huddled himself up at the head of the bed just as I had. Still he made no answer, no defence. He seemed preoccupied with something besides my reproaches, and once or twice moistened his lips with his tongue. But he could say nothing though he moved his hands now and then, just as a baby who cannot speak moves its hands.

'At last the door into Mrs Broughton's rooms opened and she came in, white and terrified. "What is it? What is it? Oh, in God's name! what is it?" she cried again and again, and then she went up to her husband and sat on the bed in her nightdress, and the two faced me. I told her what the matter was. I spared her husband not a word for her presence there. Yet he seemed hardly to understand. I told the pair that I had spoiled their cowardly joke for them. Broughton looked up.

' "I have smashed the foul thing into a hundred pieces," I said. Broughton licked his lips again and his mouth worked. "By God!" I shouted, "it would serve you right if I thrashed you within an inch of your life. I will take care that not a decent man or woman of my acquaintance ever speaks to you again. And there," I added, throwing the broken piece of the skull upon the floor beside his bed, "there is a souvenir for you, of your damned work tonight!"

'Broughton saw the bone, and in a moment it was his turn to frighten me. He squealed like a hare caught in a trap. He screamed and screamed till Mrs Broughton, almost as bewildered as myself, held on to him and coaxed him like a child to be quiet. But Broughton – and as he moved I thought that ten minutes ago I perhaps looked as terribly ill as he did – thrust her from him, and scrambled out of bed on to the floor, and still screaming put out his hand to the bone. It had blood on it from my hand. He paid no attention to me whatever. In truth I said nothing. This was a new turn indeed to the horrors of the evening. He rose from the floor with the bone in his hand and stood silent. He seemed to be listening. "Time, time, perhaps," he muttered, and almost at the same moment fell at full length on the carpet, cutting his head against the fender. The bone flew from his hand and came to rest near the door. I picked Broughton up, haggard and broken, with blood over his face. He whispered hoarsely and quickly, "Listen, listen!" We listened.

'After ten seconds' utter quiet, I seemed to hear something. I could not be sure, but at last there was no doubt. There was a quiet sound as one moving along the passage. Little regular steps came towards us over the hard oak flooring. Broughton moved to where his wife sat, white and speechless, on the bed, and pressed her face into his shoulder.

'Then, the last thing that I could see as he turned the light out, he fell forward with his own head pressed into the pillow of the bed. Something in their company, something in their cowardice, helped me, and I faced the open doorway of the room, which was outlined fairly clearly against the dimly lighted passage. I put out one hand and touched Mrs Broughton's shoulder in the darkness. But at the last moment I too failed. I sank on my knees and put my face in the bed. Only we all heard. The footsteps came to the door and there they stopped. The piece of bone was lying a yard inside the door. There was a rustle of moving stuff, and the thing was in the room. Mrs Broughton was silent: I could hear Broughton's voice praying, muffled in the pillow: I was cursing my own cowardice. Then the steps moved out again on the oak boards of the passage, and I heard the sounds dying away. In a flash of remorse I went to the door and looked out. At the end of the corridor I thought I saw something that moved away. A moment later the passage was empty. I stood with my forehead against the jamb of the door almost physically sick.

' "You can turn the light on," I said, and there was an answering flare. There was no bone at my feet. Mrs Broughton had fainted. Broughton was almost useless, and it took me ten minutes to bring her to. Broughton only said one thing worth remembering. For the most part he went on muttering prayers. But I was glad afterwards to recollect that he had said that thing. He said in a colourless voice, half as a question, half as a reproach, "You didn't speak to her."

'We spent the remainder of the night together. Mrs Broughton actually fell off into a kind of sleep before dawn, but she suffered so horribly in her dreams that I shook her into consciousness again. Never was dawn so long in coming. Three or four times Broughton spoke to himself. Mrs Broughton would then just tighten her hold on his arm, but she could say nothing. As for me, I can honestly say that I grew worse as the hours passed and the light strengthened. The two violent reactions had battered down my steadiness of view, and I felt that the foundations of my life had been built upon the sand. I said nothing, and after binding up my hand with a towel, I did not move. It was better so. They helped me and I helped them, and we all three knew that our reason had gone very near to ruin that night. At last, when the light came in pretty strongly, and the birds outside were chattering and singing, we felt that we must do something. Yet we never moved. You might have thought that we should particularly dislike being found as we were by the servants: yet nothing of that kind mattered a straw, and an overpowering listlessness bound us as we sat, until Chapman, Broughton's man, actually knocked and opened the door. None of us moved. Broughton, speaking hardly and stiffly, said, "Chapman, you can come back in five minutes." Chapman was a discreet man, but it would have made no difference to us if he had carried his news to the "room" at once.

'We looked at each other and I said I must go back. I meant to wait outside till Chapman returned. I simply dared not re-enter my bedroom alone. Broughton roused himself and said that he would come with me. Mrs Broughton agreed to remain in her own room for five minutes if the blinds were drawn up and all the doors left open.

'So Broughton and I, leaning stiffly one against the other, went down to my room. By the morning light that filtered past the blinds we could see our way, and I released the blinds. There was nothing wrong with the room from end to end, except smears of my own blood on the end of the bed, on the sofa, and on the carpet where I had torn the thing to pieces.'

* * *

Colvin had finished his story. There was nothing to say. Seven bells stuttered out from the fo'c'sle, and the answering cry wailed through the darkness. I took him downstairs.

'Of course I am much better now, but it is a kindness of you to let me sleep in your cabin.'

A Terribly Strange Bed

WILKIE COLLINS

Shortly after my education at college was finished, I happened to be staying at Paris with an English friend. We were both young men then, and lived, I am afraid, rather a wild life, in the delightful city of our sojourn. One night we were idling about the neighbourhood of the Palais Royal, doubtful to what amusement we should next betake ourselves. My friend proposed a visit to Frascati's, but his suggestion was not to my taste. I knew Frascati's, as the French saying is, by heart; had lost and won plenty of five-franc pieces there, merely for amusement's sake, until it was amusement no longer; and was thoroughly tired, in fact, of all the ghastly respectabilities of such a social anomaly as a respectable gambling-house. 'For heaven's sake,' said I to my friend, 'let us go somewhere where we can see a little genuine, blackguard, poverty-stricken gaming, with no false gingerbread glitter thrown over it all. Let us get away from fashionable Frascati's to a house where they don't mind letting in a man with a ragged coat, or a man with no coat, ragged or otherwise.' 'Very well,' said my friend, 'we needn't go out of the Palais Royal to find the sort of company you want. Here's the place just before us, as blackguard a place, by all report, as you could possibly wish to see.' In another minute we arrived at the door, and entered the house.

When we got upstairs, and had left our hats and sticks with the doorkeeper, we were admitted into the chief gambling-room. We did not find many people assembled there. But, few as the men were who looked up at us on our entrance, they were all types – lamentably true types – of their respective classes.

We had come to see blackguards, but these men were something worse. There is a comic side, more or less appreciable, in all blackguardism – here there was nothing but tragedy – mute, weird tragedy. The quiet in the room was horrible. The thin, haggard, long-haired young man, whose sunken eyes fiercely watched the turning of the cards, never spoke; the flabby, fat-faced, pimply player, who pricked his piece of pasteboard perseveringly, to register how often black won, and how often red – never spoke; the dirty wrinkled old man, with the vulture eyes and the darned greatcoat, who had lost his last sou, and still looked on desperately, after he could play no longer – never spoke. Even the voice of the croupier sounded as if it were strangely dulled and thickened in the atmosphere of the room. I had entered the place to laugh, but the spectacle before me was something to weep over. I soon found it necessary to take refuge in excitement from the depression of spirits which was fast stealing on me. Unfortunately I sought the nearest excitement, by going to the table and beginning to play. Still more unfortunately, as the event will show, I won – won prodigiously, won incredibly, won at such a rate that the regular players at the table crowded round me and, staring at my stakes with hungry, superstitious eyes, whispered to one another that the English stranger was going to break the bank.

The game was Rouge et Noir. I had played at it in every city in Europe, without, however, the care or the wish to study the Theory of Chances – that philosopher's stone of all gamblers! And a gambler, in the strict sense of the word, I had never been. I was heart-whole from the corroding passion for play. My gaming was a mere idle amusement. I never resorted to it by necessity, because I never knew what it was to want money. I never practised it so incessantly as to lose more than I could afford, or to gain more than I could coolly pocket without being thrown off my balance by good luck. In short, I had hitherto frequented gambling-tables – just as I frequented ballrooms and opera-houses – because they amused me, and because I had nothing better to do with my leisure hours.

But on this occasion it was very different – now, for the first time in my life, I felt what the passion for play really was. My success first bewildered, and then, in the most literal meaning of the word, intoxicated me. Incredible as it may appear, it is nevertheless true, that I only lost when I attempted to estimate chances, and played according to previous calculation. If I left everything to luck, and staked without any care or consideration, I was sure to win – to win in the face of every recognised probability in favour of the bank. At first, some of the men present ventured their money safely enough on my colour, but I speedily increased my stakes to sums which they dared not risk. One after another they left off playing, and breathlessly looked on at my game.

Still, time after time, I staked higher and higher, and still won. The excitement in the room rose to fever pitch. The silence was interrupted by a deep-muttered chorus of oaths and exclamations, in different languages, every time the gold was shovelled across to my side of the table – even the imperturbable croupier dashed his rake on the floor in a (French) fury of astonishment at my success. But one man present preserved his self-possession, and that man was my friend. He came to my side, and whispering in English, begged me to leave the place, satisfied with what I had already gained. I must do to him the justice to say that he repeated his warnings and entreaties several times, and only left me and went away after I had rejected his advice (I was to all intents and purposes gambling drunk) in terms which rendered it impossible for him to address me again that night.

Shortly after he had gone, a hoarse voice behind me cried: 'Permit me, my dear sir! – permit me to restore to their proper place two Napoleons which you have dropped. Wonderful luck, sir! I pledge you my word of honour, as an old soldier, in the course of my long experience in this sort of thing, I never saw such luck as yours! – never! Go on, sir – *Sacré mille bombes!* Go on boldly, and break the bank!'

I turned round and saw, nodding and smiling at me with inveterate civility, a tall man, dressed in a frogged and braided surtout.

If I had been in my senses, I should have considered him, personally, as being rather a suspicious specimen of an old soldier. He had goggling bloodshot eyes, mangy mustachios and a broken nose. His voice betrayed a barrack-room intonation of the worst order, and he had the dirtiest pair of hands I ever saw – even in France. These little personal peculiarities exercised, however, no repelling influence on me. In the mad excitement, the reckless triumph of that moment, I was ready to 'fraternise' with anybody who encouraged me in my game. I accepted the old soldier's offered pinch of snuff, clapped him on the back and swore he was the honestest fellow in the world – the most glorious relic of the Grand Army that I had ever met with. 'Go on!' cried my military friend, snapping his fingers in ecstasy – 'Go on, and win! Break the bank – *Mille tonnerres!* my gallant English comrade, break the bank!'

And I *did* go on – went on at such a rate that in another quarter of an hour the croupier called out: 'Gentlemen! the bank has discontinued for tonight.' All the notes and all the gold in that 'bank' now lay in a heap under my hands, the whole floating capital of the gambling-house was waiting to pour into my pockets!

'Tie up the money in your pocket-handkerchief, my worthy sir,' said the old soldier, as I wildly plunged my hands into my heap of gold. 'Tie it up, as we used to tie up a bit of dinner in the Grand Army; your winnings are too heavy for any breeches pockets that ever were sewed. There! that's it! – shovel them in, notes and all! *Crediê!* what luck! – Stop! another Napoleon on the floor! Ah! *sacré petit polisson de Napoléon!* have I found thee at last? Now then, sir – two tight double knots each way with your honourable permission, and the money's safe. Feel it! feel it, fortunate sir! hard and round as a cannon ball – Ah, bah! if they had only fired such cannon balls at us at Austerlitz – *nom d'une pipe!* if they only had! And now, as an ancient grenadier, as an ex-brave of the French army, what remains for me to do? I ask what? Simply this, to entreat my valued English friend to drink a bottle of champagne with me, and toast the goddess Fortune in foaming goblets before we part!'

Excellent ex-brave! Convivial ancient gambler! Champagne by all means! An English cheer for an old soldier! Hurrah! hurrah! Another English cheer for the goddess Fortune! Hurrah! hurrah! hurrah!

'Bravo! the Englishman, the amiable, gracious Englishman, in whose veins circulates the vivacious blood of France! Another glass? Ah, bah! – the bottle is empty! Never mind! *Vive le vin!* I, the old soldier, order another bottle, and half a pound of *bonbons* with it!'

'No, no, ex-brave; never – ancient grenadier! *Your* bottle last time, *my* bottle this. Behold it! Toast away! The French Army! – the great Napoleon! – the present company! the croupier! the honest croupier's wife and daughters – if he has any! the ladies generally! Everybody in the world!'

By the time the second bottle of champagne was emptied, I felt as if I had been drinking liquid fire – my brain seemed all aflame. No excess in wine had ever had this effect on me before in my life. Was it the result of a stimulant acting upon my system when I was in a highly excited state? Was my stomach in a particularly disordered condition? Or was the champagne amazingly strong?

'Ex-brave of the French Army!' cried I, in a mad state of exhilaration, '*I* am on fire! how are *you*? You have set me on fire! Do you hear, my hero of Austerlitz? Let us have a third bottle of champagne to put the flame out!'

The old soldier wagged his head, rolled his goggle eyes, until I expected to see them slip out of their sockets, placed his dirty forefinger by the side of his dirty broken nose, solemnly ejaculated 'Coffee!' and immediately ran off into an inner room.

The word pronounced by the eccentric veteran seemed to have a magical effect on the rest of the company present. With one accord they all rose to depart. Probably they had expected to profit by my intoxication, but, finding that my new friend was benevolently bent on preventing me from getting dead drunk, had now abandoned all hope of thriving pleasantly on my winnings. Whatever their motive might be, at any rate they went away in a body. When the old soldier returned and sat down again opposite me at the table, we had the room to ourselves. I could see the croupier, in a sort of vestibule which opened out of it, eating his supper in solitude. The silence was now deeper than ever.

A sudden change, too, had come over the 'ex-brave'. He assumed a portentously solemn look and when he spoke to me again his speech was ornamented by no oaths, enforced by no finger-snapping, enlivened by no apostrophes or exclamations.

'Listen, my dear sir,' said he, in mysteriously confidential tones, 'listen to an old soldier's advice. I have been to the mistress of the house (a very charming woman, with a genius for cookery!) to impress on her the necessity of making us some particularly strong and good coffee. You must drink this coffee in order to get rid of your little amiable exaltation of spirits before you think of going home – you *must*, my good and gracious friend! With all that money to take home tonight, it is a sacred duty to yourself to have your wits about you. You are known to be a winner to an enormous extent by several gentlemen present tonight, who, in a certain point of view, are very worthy and excellent fellows, but they are mortal men, my dear sir, and they have their amiable weaknesses! Need I say more? Ah, no, no! you understand me! Now, this is what you must do – send for a cabriolet when you feel quite well again – draw up all the windows when you get into it – and tell the driver to take you home only through the large and well-lighted thoroughfares. Do this, and you and your money will be safe. Do this, and tomorrow you will thank an old soldier for giving you a word of honest advice.'

Just as the ex-brave ended his oration in very lachrymose tones, the coffee came in, ready poured out in two cups. My attentive friend handed me one of the cups with a bow. I was parched with thirst, and drank it off at a draught. Almost instantly afterwards, I was seized with a fit of giddiness, and felt more completely intoxicated than ever. The room whirled round and round furiously, the old soldier seemed to be regularly bobbing up and down before me like the piston of a steam-engine. I was half deafened by a violent singing in my ears; a feeling of utter bewilderment, helplessness, idiocy, overcame me. I rose from my chair, holding on by the table to keep my balance, and stammered out that I felt dreadfully unwell – so unwell that I did not know how I was to get home.

'My dear friend,' answered the old soldier – and even his voice seemed to be bobbing up and down as he spoke – 'my dear friend, it would be madness to go home in *your* state; you would be sure to lose your money; you might be robbed and murdered with the greatest ease. *I* am going to sleep here; do *you* sleep here, too – they make up capital beds in this house –

take one, sleep off the effects of the wine, and go home safely with your winnings tomorrow – tomorrow, in broad daylight.'

I had but two ideas left – one, that I must never let go hold of my handkerchief full of money, the other, that I must lie down somewhere immediately, and fall off into a comfortable sleep. So I agreed to the proposal about the bed, and took the offered arm of the old soldier, carrying my money with my disengaged hand. Preceded by the croupier, we passed along some passages and up a flight of stairs into the bedroom which I was to occupy. The ex-brave shook me warmly by the hand, proposed that we should breakfast together, and then, followed by the croupier, left me for the night.

I ran to the wash-hand stand; drank some of the water in my jug; poured the rest out, and plunged my face into it; then sat down in a chair and tried to compose myself. I soon felt better. The change for my lungs from the fetid atmosphere of the gambling-room to the cool air of the apartment I now occupied, the almost equally refreshing change for my eyes from the glaring lights of the 'salon' to the dim, quiet flicker of one bedroom candle, both aided wonderfully the restorative effects of cold water. The giddiness left me, and I began to feel a little like a reasonable being again. My first thought was of the risk of sleeping all night in a gambling-house; my second, of the still greater risk of trying to get out after the house was closed, and of going home alone at night, through the streets of Paris, with a large sum of money about me. I had slept in worse places than this on my travels; so I determined to lock, bolt and barricade my door and take my chance till the next morning.

Accordingly, I secured myself against all intrusion; looked under the bed, and into the cupboard; tried the fastening of the window; and then, satisfied that I had taken every proper precaution, pulled off my upper clothing, put my light, which was a dim one, on the hearth among a feathery litter of wood ashes, and got into bed, with the handkerchief full of money under my pillow.

I soon felt that I could not go to sleep – that I could not even close my eyes. I was wide awake, and in a high fever. Every nerve in my body trembled – every one of my senses seemed to be preternaturally sharpened. I tossed and rolled, and tried every kind of position, and perseveringly sought out the cold corners of the bed, and all to no purpose. Now, I thrust my arms over the clothes; now, I violently shot my legs straight out down to the bottom of the bed; now, I convulsively coiled them up as near my chin as they would go; now, I shook out my crumpled pillow, changed it to the cool side, patted it flat, and lay down quietly on my back: now, I fiercely doubled it in two, set it up on end, thrust it against the board of the bed, and tried a sitting posture. Every effort was in vain; I groaned in vexation, as I felt that I was in for a sleepless night.

What could I do? I had no book to read. And yet, unless I found out some method of diverting my mind, I felt certain that I was in the condition to imagine all sorts of horrors; to rack my brain with forebodings of every possible and impossible danger; in short, to pass the night in suffering all conceivable varieties of nervous terror.

I raised myself on my elbow, and looked about the room – which was brightened by a lovely moonlight pouring straight through the window – to see if it contained any pictures or ornaments that I could at all clearly distinguish. While my eyes wandered from wall to wall, a remembrance of Le Maistre's delightful little book, *Voyage autour de ma Chambre*, occurred to me. I resolved to imitate the French author, and find occupation and amusement enough to relieve the tedium of my wakefulness by making a mental inventory of every article of furniture I could see, and by following up to their sources the multitude associations which even a chair, a table or a wash-hand stand may be made to call forth.

In the nervous unsettled state of my mind at that moment, I found it much easier to make my inventory than to make my reflections, and thereupon soon gave up all hope of thinking in Le Maistre's fanciful track – or, indeed, of thinking at all. I looked about the room at different articles of furniture; and did nothing more.

There was, first, the bed I was lying in; a four-post bed, of all things in the world to meet with in Paris! – yes, a thorough clumsy British four-poster, with the regular top lined with chintz – the regular fringed valance all round – the regular stifling unwholesome curtains, which I remembered having mechanically drawn back against the posts without particularly noticing the bed when I first got into the room. Then there was the marble-topped wash-hand stand, from which the water I had spilt, in my hurry to pour it out, was still dripping, slowly and more slowly, on to the brick floor. Then two small chairs, with my coat, waistcoat and trousers flung on them. Then a large elbow-chair, covered with dirty-white dimity, with my cravat and shirt collar thrown over the back. Then a chest of drawers with two of the brass handles off, and a tawdry, broken china inkstand placed on it by way of ornament for the top. Then the dressing-table, adorned by a very small looking-glass and a very large pincushion. Then the window – an unusually large window. Then a dark old picture, which the feeble candle dimly showed me. It was the picture of a fellow in a high Spanish hat, crowned with a plume of towering feathers. A swarthy sinister ruffian, looking upward, shading his eyes with his hand and looking intently upward – it might be at some tall gallows on which he was going to be hanged. At any rate, he had the appearance of thoroughly deserving it.

This picture put a kind of constraint upon me to look upward too – at the top of the bed. It was a gloomy and not an interesting object, and I looked back at the picture. I counted the feathers in the man's hat – they stood out in relief – three white, two green. I observed the crown of his hat, which was of a conical shape, according to the fashion supposed to have been favoured by Guido Fawkes. I wondered what he was looking up at. It couldn't be at the stars; such a desperado was neither astrologer nor astronomer. It must be the high gallows, and he was going to be hanged presently. Would the executioner come into possession of his conical-crowned hat and plume of feathers? I counted the feathers again – three white, two green.

While I still lingered over this very improving and intellectual employment, my thoughts insensibly began to wander. The moonlight shining into the room reminded me of a certain moonlight night in England – the night after a picnic party in a Welsh valley. Every incident of the drive homeward, through lovely scenery, which the moonlight made lovelier than ever, came back to my remembrance, though I had never given the picnic a thought for years – though, if I had *tried* to recollect it, I could certainly have recalled little or nothing of that scene long past. Of all the wonderful faculties that help to tell us we are immortal, which speaks the sublime truth more eloquently than memory? Here was I, in a strange house of the most suspicious character, in a situation of uncertainty and even of peril, which might seem to make the cool exercise of my recollection almost out of the question, nevertheless, remembering, quite involuntarily, places, people, conversations, minute circumstances of every kind, which I had thought forgotten for ever; which I could not possibly have recalled at will, even under the most favourable auspices. And what cause had produced in a moment the whole of this strange, complicated, mysterious effect? Nothing but some rays of moonlight shining in at my bedroom window.

I was still thinking of that picnic – of our merriment on the drive home – of the sentimental young lady who *would* quote *Childe Harold* because it was moonlight. I was absorbed by these past scenes and past amusements, when, in an instant, the thread on which my memories hung snapped asunder, my attention immediately came back to present things more vividly than ever and I found myself, I neither knew why nor wherefore, looking hard at the picture again.

Looking for what?

Good God! the man had pulled his hat down on his brows! – No! the hat itself was gone! Where was the conical crown? Where were the feathers – three white, two green? Not there? In place of the hat and feathers, what dusky object was it that now hid his forehead, his eyes, his shading hand?

Was the bed moving?

I turned on my back and looked up. Was I mad? – drunk? – dreaming? – giddy again? – or was the top of the bed really moving down – sinking slowly, regularly, silently, horribly, right down throughout the whole of its length and breadth – right down upon me, as I lay underneath?

My blood seemed to stand still. A deadly paralysing coldness stole all over me as I turned my head round on the pillow, and determined to test whether the bed-top was really moving or not by keeping my eye on the man in the picture.

The next look in that direction was enough. The dull, black, frowsy outline of the valance above me was within an inch of being parallel with his waist. I still looked breathlessly. And steadily, and slowly – very slowly – I saw the figure, and the line of frame below the figure, vanish, as the valance moved down before it.

I am, constitutionally, anything but timid. I have been on more than one occasion in peril of my life, and have not lost my self-possession for an instant, but when the conviction first settled on my mind that the bed-top was really moving, was steadily and continuously sinking down upon me, I looked up shuddering, helpless, panic-stricken, beneath the hideous machinery for murder which was advancing closer and closer to suffocate me where I lay.

I looked up, motionless, speechless, breathless. The candle, fully spent, went out, but the moonlight still brightened the room. Down and down, without pausing and without sounding, came the bed-top, and still my panic terror seemed to bind me faster and faster to the mattress on which I lay – down and down it sank, till the dusty odour from the lining of the canopy came stealing into my nostrils.

At that final moment the instinct of self-preservation startled me out of my trance, and I moved at last. There was just room for me to roll myself sideways off the bed. As I dropped noiselessly to the floor, the edge of the murderous canopy touched me on the shoulder.

Without stopping to draw my breath, without wiping the cold sweat from my face, I rose instantly on my knees to watch the bed-top. I was literally spellbound by it. If I had heard footsteps behind me, I could not have turned round; if a means of escape had been miraculously provided for me, I could not have moved to take advantage of it. The whole life in me was, at that moment, concentrated in my eyes.

It descended – the whole canopy, with the fringe round it, came down – down – close down, so close that there was not room now to squeeze my finger between the bed-top and the bed. I felt at the sides, and discovered that what had appeared to me from beneath to be the ordinary light canopy of a four-poster bed, was in reality a thick, broad mattress, the substance of which was concealed by the valance and its fringe. I looked up and saw the four posts rising hideously bare. In the middle of the bed-top was a huge wooden screw that had evidently worked it down through a hole in the ceiling, just as ordinary presses are worked down on the substance selected for compression. The frightful apparatus moved without making the faintest noise. There had been no creaking as it came down; there was not the faintest sound from the room above. Amid a dead and awful silence I beheld before me – in the nineteenth century, and in the civilised capital of France – such a machine for secret murder by suffocation as might have existed in the worst days of the Inquisition, in the lonely inns among the Hartz Mountains, in the mysterious tribunals of Westphalia! Still, as I looked on it, I could not move, I could hardly breathe, but I began to recover the power of thinking, and in a moment I discovered the murderous conspiracy framed against me in all its horror.

My cup of coffee had been drugged, and drugged too strongly. I had been saved from being smothered by having taken an overdose of some narcotic. How I had chafed and fretted at the fever-fit which had preserved my life by keeping me awake! How recklessly I had confided myself to the two wretches who had led me into this room, determined, for the sake of my winnings, to kill me in my sleep by the surest and most horrible contrivance for secretly accomplishing my destruction! How many men, winners like me, had slept, as I had proposed to sleep, in that bed, and had never been seen or heard of more? I shuddered at the bare idea of it.

But, ere long, all thought was again suspended by the sight of the murderous canopy moving once more. After it had remained on the bed – as nearly as I could guess – about ten minutes, it began to move up again. The villains who worked it from above evidently believed that their purpose was now accomplished. Slowly and silently, as it descended, that horrible bed-top rose towards its former place. When it reached the upper extremities of the four posts, it reached the ceiling too. Neither hole nor screw could be seen; the bed became in appearance an ordinary bed again – the canopy an ordinary canopy – even to the most suspicious eyes.

Now, for the first time, I was able to move – to rise from my knees – to dress myself in my upper clothing – and to consider of how I should escape. If I betrayed, by the smallest noise, that the attempt to suffocate me had failed, I was certain to be murdered. Had I made any noise already? I listened intently, looking towards the door.

No! no footsteps in the passage outside – no sound of a tread, light or heavy, in the room above – absolute silence everywhere. Besides locking and bolting my door, I had moved an old wooden chest against it, which I had found under the bed. To remove this chest (my blood ran cold as I thought of what its contents *might* be!) without making some disturbance was impossible, and, moreover, to think of escaping through the house, now barred up for the night, was sheer insanity. Only one chance was left me – the window. I stole to it on tiptoe.

My bedroom was on the first floor, above an *entresol*, and looked into a back street. I raised my hand to open the window, knowing that on that action hung, by the merest hair's breadth, my chance of safety. They keep vigilant watch in a House of Murder. If any part of the frame cracked, if the hinge creaked, I was a lost man! It must have occupied me at least five minutes, reckoning by time – five *hours*, reckoning by suspense – to open that window. I succeeded in doing it silently – in doing it with all the dexterity of a housebreaker – and then looked down into the street. To leap the distance beneath me would be almost certain destruction! Next, I looked round at the sides of the house. Down the left side ran a thick water-pipe – it passed close by the outer edge of the window. The moment I saw the pipe, I knew I must be saved. My breath came and went freely for the first time since I had seen the canopy of the bed moving down upon me!

To some men the means of escape which I had discovered might have seemed difficult and dangerous enough – to *me* the prospect of slipping down the pipe into the street did not suggest even a thought of peril. I had always been accustomed, by the practice of gymnastics, to keep up my schoolboy powers as a daring and expert climber, and knew that my head, hands and feet would serve me faithfully in any hazards of ascent or descent. I had already got one leg over the window-sill when I remembered the handkerchief filled with money under my pillow. I could have well afforded to leave it behind me, but I was revengefully determined that the miscreants of the gambling-house should miss their plunder as well as their victim. So I went back to the bed and tied the heavy handkerchief at my back by my cravat.

Just as I had made it tight and fixed it in a comfortable place, I thought I heard a sound of breathing outside the door. The chill feeling of horror ran through me again as I listened. No! dead silence still in the passage – I had only heard the night air blowing softly into the room. The next moment I was on the window-sill – and the next I had a firm grip on the water-pipe with my hands and knees.

I slid down into the street easily and quietly, as I thought I should, and immediately set off at the top of my speed to a branch prefecture of police, which I knew was situated in the immediate neighbourhood. A sub-prefect, and several picked men among his subordinates, happened to be up, maturing, I believe, some scheme for discovering the perpetrator of a mysterious murder which all Paris was talking of just then. When I began my story, in a breathless hurry and in very bad French, I could see that the sub-prefect suspected me of being a drunken Englishman who had robbed somebody, but he soon altered his opinion as I went on, and before I had anything like concluded, he shoved all the papers before him into a drawer, put on his hat, supplied me with another (for I was bareheaded), ordered a file of soldiers, desired his expert followers to get ready all sorts of tools for breaking open doors and ripping up brick-flooring, and took my arm, in the most friendly and familiar manner possible, to lead me with him out of the house. I will venture to say that when the sub-prefect was a little boy, and was taken for the first time to the play, he was not half as much pleased as he was now at the job in prospect for him at the gambling-house!

Away we went through the streets, the sub-prefect cross-examining and congratulating me in the same breath as we marched at the head of our formidable *posse comitatus.* Sentinels were placed at the back and front of the house the moment we got to it and a tremendous battery of knocks was directed against the door; a light appeared at a window; I was told to conceal myself behind the police; then came more knocks, and a cry of, 'Open in the name of the law!' At that terrible summons bolts and locks gave way before an invisible hand, and the moment after the sub-prefect was in the passage, confronting a waiter half dressed and ghastly pale. This was the short dialogue which immediately took place: 'We want to see the Englishman who is sleeping in this house.'

'He went away hours ago.'

'He did no such thing. His friend went away, *he* remained. Show us to his bedroom!'

'I swear to you, *Monsieur le Sous-préfet*, he is not here! He – '

'I swear to you, *Monsieur le Garçon*, he is. He slept here – he didn't find your bed comfortable – he came to us to complain of it – here he is among my men – and here am I ready to look for a flea or two in his bedstead. Renaudin!' (calling to one of the subordinates, and pointing to the waiter) 'collar that man, and tie his hands behind him. Now then, gentlemen, let us walk upstairs!'

Every man and woman in the house was secured – the 'old soldier' the first. Then I identified the bed in which I had slept, and then we went into the room above.

No object that was at all extraordinary appeared in any part of it. The sub-prefect looked round the place, commanded everybody to be silent, stamped twice on the floor, called for a candle, looked attentively at the spot he had stamped on, and ordered the flooring there to be carefully taken up. This was done in no time. Lights were produced, and we saw a deep raftered cavity between the floor of this room and the ceiling of the room beneath. Through this cavity there ran perpendicularly a sort of case of iron thickly greased, and inside the case appeared the screw, which communicated with the bed-top below. Extra lengths of screws, freshly oiled, levers covered with felt, all the complete upper works of a heavy press –

constructed with infernal ingenuity so as to join the fixtures below, and when taken to pieces again to go into the smallest possible compass – were next discovered and pulled out on the floor. After some little difficulty, the sub-prefect succeeded in putting the machinery together and, leaving his men to work it, descended with me to the bedroom. The smothering canopy was then lowered, but not so noiselessly as I had seen it lowered. When I mentioned this to the sub-prefect, his answer, simple as it was, had a terrible significance. 'My men,' said he, 'are working down the bed-top for the first time – the men whose money you won were in better practice.'

We left the house in the sole possession of two police agents – every one of the inmates being removed to prison on the spot. The sub-prefect, after taking down my *procès verbal* in his office, returned with me to my hotel to get my passport. 'Do you think,' I asked, as I gave it to him, 'that any men have really been smothered in that bed, as they tried to smother me?'

'I have seen dozens of drowned men laid out at the morgue,' answered the sub-prefect, 'in whose pocketbooks were found letters stating that they had committed suicide in the Seine, because they had lost everything at the gaming-table. Do I know how many of those men entered the same gambling-house that you entered? – won as *you* won? – took that bed as you took it? – slept in it? – were smothered in it? – and were privately thrown into the river, with a letter of explanation written by the murderers and placed in their pocketbooks? No man can say how many or how few have suffered the fate from which you have escaped. The people of the gambling-house kept their bedstead machinery a secret from *us* – even from the police! The dead kept the rest of the secret for them. Good-night, or rather good-morning, Monsieur Faulkner! Be at my office again at nine o'clock – in the meantime, *au revoir*!'

The rest of my story is soon told. I was examined and re-examined, the gambling-house was strictly searched all through from top to bottom, the prisoners were separately interrogated and two of the less guilty among them made a confession. I discovered that the old soldier was the master of the gambling-house – justice discovered that he had been drummed out of the army as a vagabond years ago, that he had been guilty of all sorts of villainies since, that he was in possession of stolen property, which the owners identified, and that he, the croupier, another accomplice, and the woman who had made my cup of coffee, were all in the secret of the bedstead. There appeared some reason to doubt whether the inferior persons attached to the house knew anything of the suffocating machinery, and they received the benefit of that doubt by being treated simply as thieves and vagabonds. As for the old soldier and his two head-myrmidons, they went to the galleys; the woman who had drugged my coffee was imprisoned for I forget how many years, the regular attendants at the gambling-house were considered 'suspicious', and placed under 'surveillance', and I became, for one whole week (which is a long time), the head 'lion' in Parisian society. My adventure was dramatised by three illustrious play-makers, but never saw theatrical daylight, for the censorship forbade the introduction on the stage of a correct copy of the gambling-house bedstead.

One good result was produced by my adventure,

which any censorship must have approved – it cured me of ever again trying Rouge et Noir as an amusement. The sight of a green cloth with packs of cards and heaps of money on it will henceforth be for ever associated in my mind with the sight of a bed-canopy descending to suffocate me in the silence and darkness of the night.

The Yellow Wallpaper

CHARLOTTE PERKINS GILMAN

It is very seldom that mere ordinary people like John and myself secure ancestral halls for the summer.

A colonial mansion, a hereditary estate, I would say a haunted house, and reach the height of romantic felicity – but that would be asking too much of fate!

Still I will proudly declare that there is something queer about it.

Else, why should it be let so cheaply? And why have stood so long untenanted?

John laughs at me, of course, but one expects that in marriage.

John is practical in the extreme. He has no patience with faith, an intense horror of superstition, and he scoffs openly at any talk of things not to be felt and seen and put down in figures.

John is a physician, and *perhaps* – (I would not say it to a living soul, of course, but this is dead paper and a great relief to my mind) – *perhaps* that is one reason I do not get well faster.

You see he does not believe I am sick!

And what can one do?

If a physician of high standing, and one's own husband, assures friends and relatives that there is really nothing the matter with one but temporary nervous depression – a slight hysterical tendency – what is one to do?

My brother is also a physician, and also of high standing, and he says the same thing.

So I take phosphates or phosphites – whichever it is, and tonics, and journeys, and air, and exercise, and am absolutely forbidden to 'work' until I am well again.

Personally, I disagree with their ideas.

Personally, I believe that congenial work, with excitement and change, would do me good.

But what is one to do?

I did write for a while in spite of them; but it *does* exhaust me a good deal – having to be so sly about it, or else meet with heavy opposition.

I sometimes fancy that my condition if I had less opposition and more society and stimulus – but John says the very worst thing I can do is to think about my condition, and I confess it always makes me feel bad.

So I will let it alone and talk about the house.

The most beautiful place! It is quite alone, standing well back from the road, quite three miles from the village. It makes me think of English places that you read about, for there are hedges and walls and gates that lock, and lots of separate little houses for the gardeners and people.

There is a *delicious* garden! I never saw such a garden – large and shady, full of box-bordered paths, and lined with long grape-covered arbours with seats under them.

There were greenhouses, too, but they are all broken now.

There was some legal trouble, I believe, something about the heirs and co-heirs; anyhow, the place has been empty for years.

That spoils my ghostliness, I am afraid, but I don't

care – there is something strange about the house – I can feel it.

I even said so to John one moonlight evening, but he said what I felt was a *draught*, and shut the window.

I get unreasonably angry with John sometimes. I'm sure I never used to be so sensitive. I think it is due to this nervous condition.

But John says if I feel so, I shall neglect proper self-control; so I take pains to control myself – before him, at least, and that makes me very tired.

I don't like our room a bit. I wanted one downstairs that opened on the piazza and had roses all over the window, and such pretty old-fashioned chintz hangings! but John would not hear of it.

He said there was only one window and not room for two beds, and no near room for him if he took another.

He is very careful and loving, and hardly lets me stir without special direction.

I have a schedule prescription for each hour in the day; he takes all care from me, and so I feel basely ungrateful not to value it more.

He said we came here solely on my account, that I was to have perfect rest and all the air I could get. 'Your exercise depends on your strength, my dear,' said he, 'and your food somewhat on your appetite; but air you can absorb all the time.' So we took the nursery at the top of the house.

It is a big, airy room, the whole floor nearly, with windows that look all ways, and air and sunshine galore. It was nursery first and then playroom and gymnasium, I should judge; for the windows are barred for little children, and there are rings and things in the walls.

The paint and paper look as if a boys' school had used it. It is stripped off – the paper – in great patches all around the head of my bed, about as far as I can reach, and in a great place on the other side of the room low down. I never saw a worse paper in my life.

One of those sprawling flamboyant patterns committing every artistic sin.

It is dull enough to confuse the eye in following, pronounced enough to constantly irritate and provoke study, and when you follow the lame uncertain curves for a little distance they suddenly commit suicide – plunge off at outrageous angles, destroy themselves in unheard of contradictions.

The colour is repellent, almost revolting; a smouldering unclean yellow, strangely faded by the slow-turning sunlight.

It is a dull yet lurid orange in some places, a sickly sulphur tint in others.

No wonder the children hated it! I should hate it myself if I had to live in this room long.

There comes John, and I must put this away – he hates to have me write a word.

We have been here two weeks, and I haven't felt like writing before, since that first day.

I am sitting by the window now, up in this atrocious nursery, and there is nothing to hinder my writing as much as I please, save lack of strength.

John is away all day, and even some nights when his cases are serious.

I am glad my case is not serious!

But these nervous troubles are dreadfully depressing.

John does not know how much I really suffer. He knows there is no *reason* to suffer, and that satisfies him.

Of course it is only nervousness. It does weigh on me so not to do my duty in any way!

I meant to be such a help to John, such a real rest and comfort, and here I am a comparative burden already!

Nobody would believe what an effort it is to do what little I am able – to dress and entertain, and other things.

It is fortunate Mary is so good with the baby. Such a dear baby!

And yet I *cannot* be with him, it makes me so nervous.

I suppose John never was nervous in his life. He laughs at me so about this wallpaper!

At first he meant to re-paper the room, but afterwards he said that I was letting it get the better of me, and that nothing was worse for a nervous patient than to give way to such fancies.

He said that after the wallpaper was changed it would be the heavy bedstead, and then the barred windows, and then that gate at the head of the stairs, and so on.

'You know the place is doing you good,' he said, 'and really, dear, I don't care to renovate the house just for a three months' rental.'

'Then do let us go downstairs,' I said, 'there are such pretty rooms there.'

Then he took me in his arms and called me a blessed little goose, and said he would go down to the cellar, if I wished, and have it whitewashed into the bargain.

But he is right enough about the beds and windows and things.

It is an airy and comfortable room as any one need

wish, and, of course, I would not be so silly as to make him uncomfortable just for a whim.

I'm really getting quite fond of the big room, all but that horrid paper.

Out of one window I can see the garden, those mysterious deep shaded arbours, the riotous old-fashioned flowers, and bushes and gnarly trees.

Out of another I get a lovely view of the bay and a little private wharf belonging to the estate. There is a beautiful shaded lane that runs down there from the house. I always fancy I see people walking in these numerous paths and arbours, but John has cautioned me not to give way to fancy in the least. He says that with my imaginative power and habit of story-making, a nervous weakness like mine is sure to lead to all manner of excited fancies, and that I ought to use my will and good sense to check the tendency. So I try.

I think sometimes that if I were only well enough to write a little it would relieve the press of ideas and rest me.

But I find I get pretty tired when I try.

It is so discouraging not to have any advice and companionship about my work. When I get really well, John says we will ask Cousin Henry and Julia down for a long visit; but he says he would as soon put fireworks in my pillowcase as to let me have those stimulating people about now.

I wish I could get well faster.

But I must not think about that. This paper looks to me as if it *knew* what a vicious influence it had!

There is a recurrent spot where the pattern lolls like a broken neck and two bulbous eyes stare at you upside down.

I get positively angry with the impertinence of it and the everlastingness. Up and down and sideways they crawl, and those absurd, unblinking eyes are everywhere. There is one place where two breadths didn't match, and the eyes go all up and down the line, one a little higher than the other.

I never saw so much expression in an inanimate thing before, and we all know how much expression they have! I used to lie awake as a child and get more entertainment and terror out of blank walls and plain furniture than most children could find in a toy store.

I remember what a kindly wink the knobs of our big, old bureau used to have, and there was one chair that always seemed like a strong friend.

I used to feel that if any of the other things looked too fierce I could always hop into that chair and be safe.

The furniture in this room is no worse than inharmonious, however, for we had to bring it all from downstairs. I suppose when this was used as a playroom they had to take the nursery things out, and no wonder! I never saw such ravages as the children have made here.

The wallpaper, as I said before, is torn off in spots, and it sticketh closer than a brother – they must have had perseverance as well as hatred.

Then the floor is scratched and gouged and splintered, the plaster itself is dug out here and there, and this great heavy bed, which is all we found in the room, looks as if it had been through the wars.

But I don't mind it a bit – only the paper.

There comes John's sister. Such a dear girl as she is, and so careful of me! I must not let her find me writing.

She is a perfect and enthusiastic housekeeper, and hopes for no better profession. I verily believe she thinks it is the writing which made me sick!

But I can write when she is out, and see her a long way off from these windows.

There is one that commands the road, a lovely shaded winding road, and one that just looks off over the country. A lovely country, too, full of great elms and velvet meadows.

This wallpaper has a kind of sub-pattern in a different shade, a particularly irritating one, for you can only see it in certain lights, and not clearly then.

But in the places where it isn't faded and where the sun is just so – I can see a strange, provoking, formless sort of figure, that seems to skulk about behind that silly and conspicuous front design.

There's sister on the stairs!

Well, the Fourth of July is over! The people are gone and I am tired out. John thought it might do me good to see a little company, so we just had mother and Nellie and the children down for a week.

Of course I didn't do a thing. Jennie sees to everything now.

But it tired me all the same.

John says if I don't pick up faster he shall send me to Weir Mitchell in the fall.

But I don't want to go there at all. I had a friend who was in his hands once, and she says he is just like John and my brother, only more so!

Besides, it is such an undertaking to go so far.

I don't feel as if it was worth while to turn my hand over for anything, and I'm getting dreadfully fretful and querulous.

I cry at nothing, and cry most of the time.

Of course I don't when John is here, or anybody else, but when I am alone.

And I am alone a good deal just now. John is kept in town very often by serious cases, and Jennie is good and lets me alone when I want her to.

So I walk a little in the garden or down that lovely lane, sit on the porch under the roses, and lie down up here a good deal.

I'm getting really fond of the room in spite of the wallpaper. Perhaps *because* of the wallpaper.

It dwells in my mind so!

I lie here on this great immovable bed – it is nailed down, I believe – and follow that pattern about by the hour. It is as good as gymnastics, I assure you. I start, we'll say, at the bottom, down in the corner over there where it has not been touched, and I determine for the thousandth time that I *will* follow that pointless pattern to some sort of a conclusion.

I know a little of the principle of design, and I know this thing was not arranged on any laws of radiation, or alternation, or repetition, or symmetry, or anything else that I ever heard of.

It is repeated, of course, by the breadths, but not otherwise.

Looked at in one way each breadth stands alone, the bloated curves and flourishes – a kind of 'debased Romanesque' with *delirium tremens* – go waddling up and down in isolated columns of fatuity.

But, on the other hand, they connect diagonally, and the sprawling outlines run off in great slanting waves of optic horror, like a lot of wallowing seaweeds in full chase.

The whole thing goes horizontally, too, at least it

seems so, and I exhaust myself in trying to distinguish the order of its going in that direction.

They have used a horizontal breadth for a frieze, and that adds wonderfully to the confusion.

There is one end of the room where it is almost intact, and there, when the cross lights fade and the low sun shines directly upon it, I can almost fancy radiation after all – the interminable grotesques seem to form around a common centre and rush off in headlong plunges of equal distraction.

It makes me tired to follow it. I'll take a nap I guess.

I don't know why I should write this.

I don't want to.

I don't feel able.

And I know John would think it absurd. But I *must say* what I feel and think in some way – it is such a relief!

But the effort is getting to be greater than the relief.

Half the time now I am awfully lazy, and lie down ever so much.

John says I mustn't lose my strength, and has me take cod liver oil and lots of tonics and things, to say nothing of ale and wine and rare meat.

Dear John! He loves me very dearly, and hates to have me sick. I tried to have a real earnest reasonable talk with him the other day, and tell him how I wish he would let me go and make a visit to Cousin Henry and Julia.

But he said I wasn't able to go, nor able to stand it after I got there; and I did not make out a very good case for myself, for I was crying before I had finished.

It is getting to be a great effort for me to think straight. Just this nervous weakness I suppose.

And dear John gathered me up in his arms, and just

carried me upstairs and laid me on the bed, and sat by me and read to me till it tired my head.

He said I was his darling and his comfort and all he had, and that I must take care of myself for his sake, and keep well.

He says no one but myself can help me out of it, that I must use my will and self-control and not let any silly fancies run away with me.

There's one comfort, the baby is well and happy, and does not have to occupy this nursery with the horrid wallpaper.

If we had not used it, that blessed child would have! What a fortunate escape! Why, I wouldn't have a child of mine, an impressionable little thing, live in such a room for worlds.

I never thought of it before, but it is lucky that John kept me here after all, I can stand it so much easier than a baby, you see.

Of course I never mention it to them any more – I am too wise – but I keep watch of it all the same.

There are things in that paper that nobody knows but me, or ever will.

Behind that outside pattern the dim shapes get clearer every day.

It is always the same shape, only very numerous.

And it is like a woman stooping down and creeping about behind that pattern. I don't like it a bit. I wonder – I begin to think – I wish John would take me away from here!

It is so hard to talk with John about my case, because he is so wise, and because he loves me so.

But I tried it last night.

It was moonlight. The moon shines in all around just as the sun does.

I hate to see it sometimes, it creeps so slowly, and always comes in by one window or another.

John was asleep and I hated to waken him, so I kept still and watched the moonlight on that undulating wallpaper till I felt creepy.

The faint figure behind seemed to shake the pattern, just as if she wanted to get out.

I got up softly and went to feel and see if the paper *did* move, and when I came back John was awake.

'What is it, little girl?' he said. 'Don't go walking about like that – you'll get cold.'

I thought it was a good time to talk, so I told him that I really was not gaining here, and that I wished he would take me away.

'Why darling!' said he, 'our lease will be up in three weeks, and I can't see how to leave before.

'The repairs are not done at home, and I cannot possibly leave town just now. Of course if you were in any danger, I could and would, but you really are better, dear, whether you can see it or not. I am a doctor, dear, and I know. You are gaining flesh and colour, your appetite is better, I feel really much easier about you.'

'I don't weigh a bit more,' said I, 'nor as much; and my appetite may be better in the evening when you are here, but it is worse in the morning when you are away!'

'Bless her little heart!' said he with a big hug, 'she shall be as sick as she pleases! But now let's improve the shining hours by going to sleep, and talk about it in the morning!'

'And you won't go away?' I asked gloomily.

'Why, how can I, dear? It is only three weeks more and then we will take a nice little trip of a few days while Jennie is getting the house ready. Really dear you are better!'

'Better in body perhaps – ' I began, and stopped short, for he sat up straight and looked at me with such a stern, reproachful look that I could not say another word.

'My darling,' said he, 'I beg of you, for my sake and for our child's sake, as well as for your own, that you will never for one instant let that idea enter your mind! There is nothing so dangerous, so fascinating, to a temperament like yours. It is a false and foolish fancy. Can you not trust me as a physician when I tell you so?'

So of course I said no more on that score, and we went to sleep before long. He thought I was asleep first, but I wasn't, and lay there for hours trying to decide whether that front pattern and the back pattern really did move together or separately.

On a pattern like this, by daylight, there is a lack of sequence, a defiance of law, that is a constant irritant to a normal mind.

The colour is hideous enough, and unreliable enough, and infuriating enough, but the pattern is torturing.

You think you have mastered it, but just as you get well underway in following, it turns a back-somersault and there you are. It slaps you in the face, knocks you down, and tramples upon you. It is like a bad dream.

The outside pattern is a florid arabesque, reminding one of a fungus. If you can imagine a toadstool in joints, an interminable string of toadstools, budding and sprouting in endless convolutions – why, that is something like it.

That is, sometimes!

There is one marked peculiarity about this paper, a thing nobody seems to notice but myself, and that is that it changes as the light changes.

When the sun shoots in through the east window – I always watch for that first long, straight ray – it changes so quickly that I never can quite believe it.

That is why I watch it always.

By moonlight – the moon shines in all night when there is a moon – I wouldn't know it was the same paper.

At night in any kind of light, in twilight, candle light, lamplight, and worst of all by moonlight, it becomes bars! The outside pattern I mean, and the woman behind it is as plain as can be.

I didn't realise for a long time what the thing was that showed behind, that dim sub-pattern, but now I am quite sure it is a woman.

By daylight she is subdued, quiet. I fancy it is the pattern that keeps her so still. It is so puzzling. It keeps me quiet by the hour.

I lie down ever so much now. John says it is good for me, and to sleep all I can.

Indeed he started the habit by making me lie down for an hour after each meal.

It is a very bad habit, I am convinced, for you see I don't sleep.

And that cultivates deceit, for I don't tell them I'm awake – Oh no!

The fact is I am getting a little afraid of John.

He seems very queer sometimes, and even Jennie has an inexplicable look.

It strikes me occasionally, just as a scientific hypothesis, that perhaps it is the paper!

I have watched John when he did not know I was looking, and come into the room suddenly on the most innocent excuses, and I've caught him several times *looking at the paper*! And Jennie too. I caught Jennie with her hand on it once.

She didn't know I was in the room, and when I asked her in a quiet, a very quiet voice, with the most restrained manner possible, what she was doing with the paper – she turned around as if she had been caught stealing, and looked quite angry – asked me why I should frighten her so!

Then she said that the paper stained everything it touched, that she had found yellow smooches on all my clothes and John's, and she wished we would be more careful!

Did not that sound innocent? But I know she was studying that pattern, and I am determined that nobody shall find it out but myself!

Life is very much more exciting now than it used to be. You see I have something more to expect, to look forward to, to watch. I really do eat better, and am more quiet than I was.

John is so pleased to see me improve! He laughed a little the other day, and said I seemed to be flourishing in spite of my wallpaper.

I turned it off with a laugh. I had no intention of telling him it was *because* of the wallpaper – he would make fun of me. He might even want to take me away.

I don't want to leave now until I have found it out. There is a week more, and I think that will be enough.

I'm feeling ever so much better! I don't sleep much at night, for it is so interesting to watch developments; but I sleep a good deal in the daytime.

In the daytime it is tiresome and perplexing.

There are always new shoots on the fungus, and new shades of yellow all over it. I cannot keep count of them, though I have tried conscientiously.

It is the strangest yellow, that wallpaper! It makes me think of all the yellow things I ever saw – not beautiful ones like buttercups, but old foul, bad yellow things.

But there is something else about that paper – the smell! I noticed it the moment we came into the room, but with so much air and sun it was not bad. Now we have had a week of fog and rain, and whether the windows are open or not, the smell is here.

It creeps all over the house.

I find it hovering in the dining-room, skulking in the parlour, hiding in the hall, lying in wait for me on the stairs.

It gets into my hair.

Even when I go to ride, if I turn my head suddenly and surprise it – there is that smell!

Such a peculiar odour, too! I have spent hours in trying to analyse it, to find what it smelled like.

It is not bad – at first, and very gentle, but quite the subtlest, most enduring odour I ever met.

In this damp weather it is awful, I wake up in the night and find it hanging over me.

It used to disturb me at first. I thought seriously of burning the house – to reach the smell.

But now I am used to it. The only thing I can think of that it is like is the *colour* of the paper! A yellow smell.

There is a very funny mark on this wall, low down, near the mop-board. A streak that runs round the room. It goes behind every piece of furniture, except the bed, a long, straight, even *smooch*, as if it had been rubbed over and over.

I wonder how it was done and who did it, and what they did it for. Round and round and round – round and round and round – it makes me dizzy!

I really have discovered something at last.

Through watching so much at night, when it changes so, I have finally found out.

The front pattern *does* move – and no wonder! The woman behind shakes it!

Sometimes I think there are a great many women behind, and sometimes only one, and she crawls around fast, and her crawling shakes it all over.

Then in the very bright spots she keeps still, and in the very shady spots she just takes hold of the bars and shakes them hard.

And she is all the time trying to climb through. But nobody could climb through that pattern – it strangles so; I think that is why it has so many heads.

They get through, and then the pattern strangles them off and turns them upside down, and makes their eyes white!

If those heads were covered or taken off it would not be half so bad.

I think that woman gets out in the daytime!

And I'll tell you why – privately – I've seen her!

I can see her out of every one of my windows!

It is the same woman, I know, for she is always creeping, and most women do not creep by daylight.

I see her on that long road under the trees, creeping along, and when a carriage comes she hides under the blackberry vines.

I don't blame her a bit. It must be very humiliating to be caught creeping by daylight!

I always lock the door when I creep by daylight. I can't do it at night, for I know John would suspect something at once.

And John is so queer now, that I don't want to irritate him. I wish he would take another room! Besides, I don't want anybody to get that woman out at night but myself.

I often wonder if I could see her out of all the windows at once.

But, turn as fast as I can, I can only see out of one at a time.

And though I always see her, she *may* be able to creep faster than I can turn!

I have watched her sometimes away off in the open country, creeping as fast as a cloud shadow in a high wind.

If only that top pattern could be gotten off from the under one! I mean to try it, little by little.

I have found out another funny thing, but I shan't tell it this time! It does not do to trust people too much.

There are only two more days to get this paper off, and I believe John is beginning to notice. I don't like the look in his eyes.

And I heard him ask Jennie a lot of professional questions about me. She had a very good report to give. She said I slept a good deal in the daytime.

John knows I don't sleep very well at night, for all I'm so quiet!

He asked me all sorts of questions, too, and pretended to be very loving and kind.

As if I couldn't see through him!

Still, I don't wonder he acts so, sleeping under this paper for three months.

It only interests me, but I feel sure John and Jennie are secretly affected by it.

Hurrah! This is the last day, but it is enough. John is to stay in town over night, and won't be out until this evening.

Jennie wanted to sleep with me – the sly thing! but I told her I should undoubtedly rest better for a night all alone.

That was clever, for really I wasn't alone a bit! As soon as it was moonlight and that poor thing began to crawl and shake the pattern, I got up and ran to help her.

I pulled and she shook, I shook and she pulled, and before morning we had peeled off yards of that paper.

A strip about as high as my head and half around the room.

And then when the sun came and that awful pattern began to laugh at me, I declared I would finish it today!

We go away tomorrow, and they are moving all my furniture down again to leave things as they were before.

Jennie looked at the wall in amazement, but I told her merrily that I did it out of pure spite at the vicious thing.

She laughed and said she wouldn't mind doing it herself, but I must not get tired.

How she betrayed herself that time!

But I am here, and no person touches this paper but me – not *alive*!

She tried to get me out of the room – it was too patent! But I said it was so quiet and empty and clean now that I believed I would lie down again and sleep all I could; and not to wake me even for dinner – I would call when I woke.

So now she is gone, and the servants are gone, and the things are gone, and there is nothing left but that great bedstead nailed down, with the canvas mattress we found on it.

We shall sleep downstairs tonight, and take the boat home tomorrow.

I quite enjoy the room, now it is bare again.

How those children did tear about here!

This bedstead is fairly gnawed!

But I must get to work.

I have locked the door and thrown the key down into the front path.

I don't want to go out, and I don't want to have anybody come in, till John comes.

I want to astonish him.

I've got a rope up here that even Jennie did not find. If that woman does get out, and tries to get away, I can tie her!

But I forgot I could not reach far without anything to stand on!

This bed will *not* move!

I tried to lift and push it until I was lame, and then I got so angry I bit off a little piece at one corner – but it hurt my teeth.

Then I peeled off all the paper I could reach standing on the floor. It sticks horribly and the pattern just enjoys it! All those strangled heads and bulbous eyes and waddling fungus growths just shriek with derision!

I am getting angry enough to do something desperate. To jump out of the window would be admirable exercise, but the bars are too strong even to try.

Besides I wouldn't do it. Of course not. I know well enough that a step like that is improper and might be misconstrued.

I don't like to *look* out of the windows even – there are so many of those creeping women, and they creep so fast.

I wonder if they all come out of that wallpaper as I did?

But I am securely fastened now by my well-hidden rope – you don't get *me* out in the road there!

I suppose I shall have to get back behind the pattern when it comes night, and that is hard!

It is so pleasant to be out in this great room and creep around as I please!

I don't want to go outside. I won't, even if Jennie asks me to.

For outside you have to creep on the ground, and everything is green instead of yellow.

But here I can creep smoothly on the floor, and my shoulder just fits in that long smooch around the wall, so I cannot lose my way.

Why there's John at the door!

It is no use, young man, you can't open it!

How he does call and pound!

Now he's crying for an axe.

It would be a shame to break down that beautiful door!

'John dear!' said I in the gentlest voice, 'the key is down by the front steps, under a plantain leaf!'

That silenced him for a few moments.

Then he said – very quietly indeed, 'Open the door, my darling!'

'I can't,' said I. 'The key is down by the front door under a plantain leaf!'

And then I said it again, several times, very gently and slowly, and said it so often that he had to go and see, and he got it of course, and came in. He stopped short by the door.

'What is the matter?' he cried. 'For God's sake, what are you doing!'

I kept on creeping just the same, but I looked at him over my shoulder.

'I've got out at last,' said I, 'in spite of you and Jane. And I've pulled off most of the paper, so you can't put me back!'

Now why should that man have fainted? But he did, and right across my path by the wall, so that I had to creep over him every time!

The Monkey's Paw

W. W. JACOBS

I

Without, the night was cold and wet, but in the small parlour of Lakesnam Villa the blinds were drawn and the fire burned brightly. Father and son were at chess, the former, who possessed ideas about the game involving radical changes, putting his king into such sharp and unnecessary perils that it even provoked comment from the white-haired old lady knitting placidly by the fire.

'Hark at the wind,' said Mr White, who, having seen a fatal mistake after it was too late, was amiably desirous of preventing his son from seeing it.

'I'm listening,' said the latter, grimly surveying the board as he stretched out his hand. 'Check.'

'I should hardly think that he'd come tonight,' said his father, with his hand poised over the board.

'Mate,' replied the son.

'That's the worst of living so far out,' bawled Mr White, with sudden and unlooked-for violence; 'of all the beastly, slushy, out-of-the-way places to live in, this is the worst. Pathway's a bog and the road's a torrent. I don't know what people are thinking about. I suppose because only two houses on the road are let, they think it doesn't matter.'

'Never mind, dear,' said his wife soothingly; 'perhaps you'll win the next one.'

Mr White looked up sharply, just in time to intercept a knowing glance between mother and son. The words died away on his lips, and he hid a guilty grin in his thin grey beard.

'There he is,' said Herbert White, as the gate banged to loudly and heavy footsteps came towards the door.

The old man rose with hospitable haste, and opening the door, was heard condoling with the new arrival. The new arrival also condoled with himself, so that Mrs White said, 'Tut, tut!' and coughed gently as her husband entered the room, followed by a tall burly man, beady of eye and rubicund of visage.

'Sergeant-Major Morris,' he said, introducing him.

The sergeant-major shook hands, and taking the proffered seat by the fire, watched contentedly while his host got out whisky and tumblers and stood a small copper kettle on the fire.

At the third glass his eyes got brighter, and he began to talk, the little family circle regarding with eager interest this visitor from distant parts, as he squared his broad shoulders in the chair and spoke of strange scenes and doughty deeds, of wars and plagues and strange peoples.

'Twenty-one years of it,' said Mr White, nodding at his wife and son. 'When he went away he was a slip of a youth in the warehouse. Now look at him.'

'He don't look to have taken much harm,' said Mrs White politely.

'I'd like to go to India myself,' said the old man, 'just to look round a bit, you know.'

'Better where you are,' said the sergeant-major, shaking his head. He put down the empty glass, and sighing softly, shook it again.

'I should like to see those old temples and fakirs and jugglers,' said the old man. 'What was that you started telling me the other day about a monkey's paw or something, Morris?'

'Nothing,' said the soldier hastily. 'Leastways, nothing worth hearing.'

'Monkey's paw?' said Mrs White curiously.

'Well, it's just a bit of what you might call magic, perhaps,' said the sergeant-major off-handedly.

His three listeners leaned forward eagerly. The visitor absent-mindedly put his empty glass to his lips and then set it down again. His host filled it for him.

'To look at,' said the sergeant-major, fumbling in his pocket, 'it's just an ordinary little paw, dried to a mummy.'

He took something out of his pocket and proffered it. Mrs White drew back with a grimace, but her son, taking it, examined it curiously.

'And what is there special about it?' enquired Mr White, as he took it from his son, and having examined it, placed it upon the table.

'It had a spell put on it by an old fakir,' said the sergeant-major, 'a very holy man. He wanted to show that fate ruled people's lives, and that those who interfered with it did so to their sorrow. He put a spell on it so that three separate men could each have three wishes from it.'

His manner was so impressive that his hearers were conscious that their light laughter jarred somewhat.

'Well, why don't you have three, sir?' said Herbert White cleverly.

The soldier regarded him in the way that middle age is wont to regard presumptuous youth. 'I have,' he said quietly, and his blotchy face whitened.

'And did you really have the three wishes granted?' asked Mrs White.

'I did,' said the sergeant-major, and his glass tapped against his strong teeth.

'And has anybody else wished?' enquired the old lady.

'The first man had his three wishes, yes,' was the reply. 'I don't know what the first two were, but the third was for death. That's how I got the paw.'

His tones were so grave that a hush fell upon the group.

'If you've had your three wishes, it's no good to you now, then, Morris,' said the old man at last. 'What do you keep it for?'

The soldier shook his head. 'Fancy, I suppose,' he said slowly. 'I did have some idea of selling it, but I don't think I will. It has caused enough mischief already. Besides, people won't buy. They think it's a fairy tale, some of them, and those who do think anything of it want to try it first and pay me afterwards.'

'If you could have another three wishes,' said the old man, eyeing him keenly, 'would you have them?'

'I don't know,' said the other. 'I don't know.'

He took the paw, and dangling it between his front finger and thumb, suddenly threw it upon the fire. White, with a slight cry, stooped down and snatched it off.

'Better let it burn,' said the soldier solemnly.

'If you don't want it, Morris,' said the old man, 'give it to me.'

'I won't,' said his friend doggedly. 'I threw it on the fire. If you keep it, don't blame me for what happens. Pitch it on the fire again, like a sensible man.'

The other shook his head and examined his new possession closely. 'How do you do it?' he enquired.

'Hold it up in your right hand and wish aloud,' said the sergeant-major, 'but I warn you of the consequences.'

'Sounds like *The Arabian Nights*,' said Mrs White, as she rose and began to set the supper. 'Don't you think you might wish for four pairs of hands for me?'

Her husband drew the talisman from his pocket, and then all three burst into laughter as the sergeant-major, with a look of alarm on his face, caught him by the arm.

'If you must wish,' he said gruffly, 'wish for something sensible.'

Mr White dropped it back into his pocket, and placing chairs, motioned his friend to the table. In the business of supper the talisman was partly forgotten, and afterwards the three sat listening in an enthralled fashion to a second instalment of the soldier's adventures in India.

'If the tale about the monkey paw is not more truthful than those he has been telling us,' said Herbert, as the door closed behind their guest, just in time for him to catch the last train, 'we shan't make much out of it.'

'Did you give him anything for it, father?' enquired Mrs White, regarding her husband closely.

'A trifle,' said he, colouring slightly. 'He didn't want it, but I made him take it. And he pressed me again to throw it away.'

'Likely,' said Herbert, with pretended horror. 'Why, we're going to be rich, and famous, and happy. Wish to be an emperor, father, to begin with; then you can't be henpecked.'

He darted round the table, pursued by the maligned Mrs White armed with an antimacassar.

Mr White took the paw from his pocket and eyed it dubiously. 'I don't know what to wish for, and that's a fact,' he said slowly. 'It seems to me I've got all I want.'

'If you only cleared the house, you'd be quite happy, wouldn't you?' said Herbert, with his hand on his shoulder. 'Well, wish for two hundred pounds, then; that'll just do it.'

His father, smiling shamefacedly at his own credulity, held up the talisman, as his son, with a solemn face somewhat marred by a wink at his mother, sat down at the piano and struck a few impressive chords.

'I wish for two hundred pounds!' said the old man distinctly.

A fine crash from the piano greeted the words, interrupted by a shuddering cry from the old man. His wife and son ran to him.

'It moved,' he cried, with a glance of disgust at the object as it lay on the floor. 'As I wished, it twisted in my hands like a snake.'

'Well, I don't see the money,' said his son, as he picked it up and placed it on the table, 'and I bet I never shall.'

'It must have been your fancy, father,' said his wife, regarding him anxiously.

He shook his head. 'Never mind, though; there's no harm done, but it gave me a shock all the same.'

They sat down by the fire again while the two men finished their pipes. Outside, the wind was higher than ever, and the old man started nervously at the sound of a door banging upstairs. A silence unusual and depressing settled upon all three, which lasted until the old couple rose to retire for the night.

'I expect you'll find the cash tied up in a big bag in the middle of your bed,' said Herbert, as he bade them good-night, 'and something horrible squatting up on top of the wardrobe watching you as you pocket your ill-gotten gains.'

2

In the brightness of the wintry sun next morning as it streamed over the breakfast table Herbert laughed at his fears. There was an air of prosaic wholesomeness about the room which it had lacked on the previous night, and the dirty, shrivelled little paw was pitched on the sideboard with a carelessness which betokened no great belief in its virtues.

'I suppose all old soldiers are the same,' said Mrs White. 'The idea of our listening to such nonsense! How could wishes be granted in these days? And if they could, how could two hundred pounds hurt you, father?'

'Might drop on his head from the sky,' said the frivolous Herbert.

'Morris said the things happened so naturally,' said his father, 'that you might if you so wished attribute it to coincidence.'

'Well, don't break into the money before I come back,' said Herbert, as he rose from the table. 'I'm afraid it'll turn you into a mean, avaricious man, and we shall have to disown you.'

His mother laughed, and following him to the door, watched him down the road, and returning to the breakfast table, was very happy at the expense of her husband's credulity. All of which did not prevent her from scurrying to the door at the postman's knock, nor prevent her from referring somewhat shortly to retired sergeant-majors of bibulous habits when she found that the post brought a tailor's bill.

'Herbert will have some more of his funny remarks, I expect, when he comes home,' she said, as they sat at dinner.

'I dare say,' said Mr White, pouring himself out some beer; 'but for all that, the thing moved in my hand; that I'll swear to.'

'You thought it did,' said the old lady soothingly.

'I say it did,' replied the other. 'There was no thought about it; I had just – What's the matter?'

His wife made no reply. She was watching the mysterious movements of a man outside, who, peering in an undecided fashion at the house, appeared to be trying to make up his mind to enter. In mental connection with the two hundred pounds, she noticed that the stranger was well dressed and wore a silk hat of glossy newness. Three times he paused at the gate, and then walked on again. The fourth time he stood with his hand upon it, and then with sudden resolution flung it open and walked up the path. Mrs White at the same moment placed her hands behind her, and hurriedly unfastening the strings of her apron, put that useful article of apparel beneath the cushion of her chair.

She brought the stranger, who seemed ill at ease, into the room. He gazed furtively at Mrs White, and listened in a preoccupied fashion as the old lady apologised for the appearance of the room, and her husband's coat, a garment which he usually reserved for the garden. She then waited as patiently as her sex would permit for him to broach his business, but he was at first strangely silent.

'I – was asked to call,' he said at last, and stooped and picked a piece of cotton from his trousers. 'I come from Maw and Meggins.'

The old lady started. 'Is anything the matter?' she asked breathlessly. 'Has anything happened to Herbert? What is it? What is it?'

Her husband interposed. 'There, there, mother,' he said hastily. 'Sit down, and don't jump to conclusions. You've not brought bad news, I'm sure, sir,' and he eyed the other wistfully.

'I'm sorry – ' began the visitor.

'Is he hurt?' demanded the mother.

The visitor bowed in assent. 'Badly hurt,' he said quietly, 'but he is not in any pain.'

'Oh, thank God!' said the old woman, clasping her hands. 'Thank God for that! Thank – '

She broke off suddenly as the sinister meaning of the assurance dawned upon her and she saw the awful confirmation of her fears in the other's averted face. She caught her breath, and turning to her slower-witted husband, laid her trembling old hand upon his. There was a long silence.

'He was caught in the machinery,' said the visitor at length, in a low voice.

'Caught in the machinery,' repeated Mr White, in a dazed fashion, 'yes.'

He sat staring blankly out at the window, and taking his wife's hand between his own, pressed it as he had been wont to do in their old courting days nearly forty years before.

'He was the only one left to us,' he said, turning gently to the visitor. 'It is hard.'

The other coughed, and rising, walked slowly to the window. 'The firm wished me to convey their sincere sympathy with you in your great loss,' he said, without looking round. 'I beg that you will understand I am only their servant and merely obeying orders.'

There was no reply; the old woman's face was white, her eyes staring, and her breath inaudible; on the husband's face was a look such as his friend the sergeant might have carried into his first action.

'I was to say that Maw and Meggins disclaim all responsibility,' continued the other. 'They admit no liability at all, but in consideration of your son's services they wish to present you with a certain sum as compensation.'

Mr White dropped his wife's hand, and rising to his feet, gazed with a look of horror at his visitor. His dry lips shaped the words, 'How much?'

'Two hundred pounds,' was the answer.

Unconscious of his wife's shriek, the old man smiled faintly, put out his hands like a sightless man, and dropped, a senseless heap, to the floor.

3

In the huge new cemetery, some two miles distant, the old people buried their dead, and came back to a house steeped in shadow and silence. It was all over so quickly that at first they could hardly realise it, and remained in a state of expectation as though of something else to happen – something else which was to lighten this load, too heavy for old hearts to bear.

But the days passed, and expectation gave place to resignation – the hopeless resignation of the old, sometimes miscalled apathy. Sometimes they hardly exchanged a word, for now they had nothing to talk about, and their days were long to weariness.

It was about a week after that that the old man, waking suddenly in the night, stretched out his hand and found himself alone. The room was in darkness, and the sound of subdued weeping came from the window. He raised himself in bed and listened.

'Come back,' he said tenderly. 'You will be cold.'

'It is colder for my son,' said the old woman, and wept afresh.

The sound of her sobs died away on his ears. The bed was warm, and his eyes heavy with sleep. He dozed fitfully, and then slept until a sudden wild cry from his wife awoke him with a start.

'The monkey's paw!' she cried wildly. 'The monkey's paw!'

He started up in alarm. 'Where? Where is it? What's the matter?'

She came stumbling across the room towards him. 'I want it,' she said quietly. 'You've not destroyed it?'

'It's in the parlour, on the bracket,' he replied, marvelling. 'Why?'

She cried and laughed together, and bending over, kissed his cheek.

'I only just thought of it,' she said hysterically. 'Why didn't I think of it before? Why didn't you think of it?'

'Think of what?' he questioned.

'The other two wishes,' she replied rapidly. 'We've only had one.'

'Was not that enough?' he demanded fiercely.

'No,' she cried triumphantly; 'we'll have one more. Go down and get it quickly, and wish our boy alive again.'

The man sat up in bed and flung the bedclothes

from his quaking limbs. 'Good God, you are mad!' he cried, aghast.

'Get it,' she panted; 'get it quickly, and wish – Oh, my boy, my boy!'

Her husband struck a match and lit the candle. 'Get back to bed,' he said unsteadily. 'You don't know what you are saying.'

'We had the first wish granted,' said the old woman feverishly; 'why not the second?'

'A coincidence,' stammered the old man.

'Go and get it and wish,' cried the old woman, and dragged him towards the door.

He went down in the darkness, and felt his way to the parlour, and then to the mantelpiece. The talisman was in its place, and a horrible fear that the unspoken wish might bring his mutilated son before him ere he could escape from the room seized upon him, and he caught his breath as he found that he had lost the direction of the door. His brow cold with sweat, he felt his way round the table, and groped along the wall until he found himself in the small passage with the unwholesome thing in his hand.

Even his wife's face seemed changed as he entered the room. It was white and expectant, and to his fears seemed to have an unnatural look upon it. He was afraid of her.

'Wish!' she cried, in a strong voice.

'It is foolish and wicked,' he faltered.

'Wish!' repeated his wife.

He raised his hand. 'I wish my son alive again.'

The talisman fell to the floor, and he regarded it shudderingly. Then he sank trembling into a chair as the old woman, with burning eyes, walked to the window and raised the blind.

He sat until he was chilled with the cold, glancing occasionally at the figure of the old woman peering through the window. The candle end, which had burnt below the rim of the china candlestick, was throwing pulsating shadows on the ceiling and walls, until, with a flicker larger than the rest, it expired. The old man, with an unspeakable sense of relief at the failure of the talisman, crept back to his bed, and a minute or two afterwards the old woman came silently and apathetically beside him.

Neither spoke, but both lay silently listening to the ticking of the clock. A stair creaked, and a squeaky mouse scurried noisily through the wall. The darkness was oppressive, and after lying for some time screwing up his courage, the husband took the box of matches, and striking one, went downstairs for a candle.

At the foot of the stairs the match went out, and he paused to strike another, and at the same moment a knock, so quiet and stealthy as to be scarcely audible, sounded on the front door.

The matches fell from his hand. He stood motionless, his breath suspended until the knock was repeated. Then he turned and fled swiftly back to the bedroom, and closed the door behind him. A third knock sounded through the house.

'*What's that?*' cried the old woman, starting up.

'A rat,' said the old man, in shaking tones – 'a rat. It passed me on the stairs.'

His wife sat up in bed listening. A loud knock resounded through the house.

'It's Herbert!' she screamed. 'It's Herbert!'

She ran to the door, but her husband was before her, and catching her by the arm, held her tightly.

'What are you going to do?' he whispered hoarsely.

'It's my boy; it's Herbert!' she cried, struggling mechanically. 'I forgot it was two miles away. What are you holding me for? Let go. I must open the door.'

'For God's sake, don't let it in,' cried the old man, trembling.

'You're afraid of your own son,' she cried, struggling. 'Let me go. I'm coming, Herbert; I'm coming.'

There was another knock, and another. The old woman with a sudden wrench broke free and ran from the room. Her husband followed to the landing, and called after her appealingly as she hurried downstairs. He heard the chain rattle back and the bottom bolt drawn slowly and stiffly from the socket. Then the old woman's voice, strained and panting.

'The top bolt,' she cried loudly. 'Come down. I can't reach it.'

But her husband was on his hands and knees groping wildly on the floor in search of the paw. If he could only find it before the thing outside got in. A perfect fusillade of knocks reverberated through the house, and he heard the scraping of a chair as his wife put it down in the passage against the door. He heard the creaking of the bolt as it came slowly back, and at the same moment he found the monkey's paw, and frantically breathed his third and last wish.

The knocking ceased suddenly, although the echoes of it were still in the house. He heard the chair drawn back and the door opened. A cold wind rushed up the staircase, and a long loud wail of disappointment and misery from his wife gave him courage to run down to her side, and then to the gate beyond. The street lamp flickering opposite shone on a quiet and deserted road.

The Damned Thing

AMBROSE BIERCE

I

One Does Not Always Eat What is on the Table

By the light of a tallow candle which had been placed on one end of a rough table a man was reading something written in a book. It was an old account book, greatly worn; and the writing was not, apparently, very legible, for the man sometimes held the page close to the flame of the candle to get a stronger light on it. The shadow of the book would then throw into obscurity a half of the room, darkening a number of faces and figures; for besides the reader, eight other men were present. Seven of them sat against the rough log walls, silent, motionless, and the room being small, not very far from the table. By extending an arm any one of them could have touched the eighth man, who lay on the table, face upward, partly covered by a sheet, his arms at his sides. He was dead.

The man with the book was not reading aloud, and no one spoke; all seemed to be waiting for something to occur; the dead man only was without expectation. From the blank darkness outside came in, through the aperture that served for a window, all the ever unfamiliar noises of night in the wilderness – the long nameless note of a distant coyote; the stilly pulsing thrill of tireless insects in trees; strange cries of night birds, so different from those of the birds of day; the drone of great blundering beetles, and all that mysterious chorus of small sounds that seem always to have been but half heard when they have suddenly ceased, as if conscious of an indiscretion. But nothing of all this was noted in that company; its members were not overmuch addicted to idle interest in matters of no practical importance; that was obvious in every line of their rugged faces – obvious even in the dim light of the single candle. They were evidently men of the vicinity – farmers and woodsmen.

The person reading was a trifle different; one would have said of him that he was of the world, worldly, albeit there was that in his attire which attested a certain fellowship with the organisms of his environment. His coat would hardly have passed muster in San Francisco; his footgear was not of urban origin, and the hat that lay by him on the floor (he was the only one uncovered) was such that if one had considered it as an article of mere personal adornment one would have missed its meaning. In countenance the man was rather prepossessing, with just a hint of sternness; though that he may have assumed or cultivated, as appropriate to one in authority. For he was a coroner. It was by virtue of his office that he had possession of the book in which he was reading; it had been found among the dead man's effects – in his cabin, where the inquest was now taking place.

When the coroner had finished reading he put the book into his breast pocket. At that moment the door was pushed open and a young man entered. He, clearly, was not of mountain birth and breeding: he was clad as those who dwell in cities. His clothing was dusty, however, as from travel. He had, in fact, been riding hard to attend the inquest.

The coroner nodded; no one else greeted him.

'We have waited for you,' said the coroner. 'It is necessary to have done with this business tonight.'

The young man smiled. 'I am sorry to have kept you,' he said. 'I went away, not to evade your summons, but to post to my newspaper an account of what I suppose I am called back to relate.'

The coroner smiled.

'The account that you posted to your newspaper,' he said, 'differs, probably, from that which you will give here under oath.'

'That,' replied the other, rather hotly and with a visible flush, 'is as you please. I used manifold paper and have a copy of what I sent. It was not written as news, for it is incredible, but as fiction. It may go as a part of my testimony under oath.'

'But you say it is incredible.'

'That is nothing to you, sir, if I also swear that it is true.'

The coroner was silent for a time, his eyes upon the floor. The men about the sides of the cabin talked in whispers, but seldom withdrew their gaze from the face of the corpse. Presently the coroner lifted his eyes and said: 'We will resume the inquest.'

The men removed their hats. The witness was sworn.

'What is your name?' the coroner asked.

'William Harker.'

'Age?'

'Twenty-seven.'

'You knew the deceased, Hugh Morgan?'

'Yes.'

'You were with him when he died?'

'Near him.'

'How did that happen – your presence, I mean?'

'I was visiting him at this place to shoot and fish. A part of my purpose, however, was to study him and his odd, solitary way of life. He seemed a good model for a character in fiction. I sometimes write stories.'

'I sometimes read them.'

'Thank you.'

'Stories in general – not yours.'

Some of the jurors laughed. Against a sombre background humour shows high lights. Soldiers in the intervals of battle laugh easily, and a jest in the death chamber conquers by surprise.

'Relate the circumstances of this man's death,' said the coroner. 'You may use any notes or memoranda that you please.'

The witness understood. Pulling a manuscript from his breast pocket he held it near the candle and turning the leaves until he found the passage that he wanted began to read.

2

What May Happen in a Field of Wild Oats

'. . . The sun had hardly risen when we left the house. We were looking for quail, each with a shotgun, but we had only one dog. Morgan said that our best ground was beyond a certain ridge that he pointed out, and we crossed it by a trail through the *chaparral.* On the other side was comparatively level ground, thickly covered with wild oats. As we emerged from the *chaparral* Morgan was but a few yards in advance. Suddenly we heard, at a little distance to our right and partly in front, a noise as of some animal thrashing about in the bushes, which we could see were violently agitated.

' "We've started a deer," I said. "I wish we had brought a rifle."

'Morgan, who had stopped and was intently watching the agitated *chaparral*, said nothing, but had cocked both barrels of his gun and was holding it in readiness to aim. I thought him a trifle excited, which surprised me, for he had a reputation for exceptional coolness, even in moments of sudden and imminent peril.

' "Oh, come," I said. "You are not going to fill up a deer with quail-shot, are you?"

'Still he did not reply; but catching a sight of his face as he turned it slightly toward me I was struck by the intensity of his look. Then I understood that we had serious business in hand, and my first conjecture was that we had "jumped" a grizzly. I advanced to Morgan's side, cocking my piece as I moved.

'The bushes were now quiet and the sounds had ceased, but Morgan was as attentive to the place as before.

' "What is it? What the devil is it?" I asked.

' "That Damned Thing!" he replied, without turning his head. His voice was husky and unnatural. He trembled visibly.

'I was about to speak further, when I observed the wild oats near the place of the disturbance moving – in the most inexplicable way. I can hardly describe it. They seemed as if stirred by a streak of wind, which not only bent them, but pressed them down – crushed them so that they did not rise; and this movement was slowly prolonging itself directly towards us.

'Nothing that I had ever seen had affected me so strangely as this unfamiliar and unaccountable phenomenon, yet I am unable to recall any sense of fear. I remember – and tell it here because, singularly enough, I recollected it then – that once in looking carelessly out of an open window I momentarily mistook a small tree close at hand for one of a group of larger trees at a little distance away. It looked the same size as the others, but being more distinctly and sharply defined in mass and detail seemed out of harmony with them. It was a mere falsification of the law of aerial perspective, but it startled, almost terrified me. We so rely upon the orderly operation of familiar natural laws that any seeming suspension of them is noted as a menace to our safety, a warning of unthinkable calamity. So now the apparently causeless movement of the herbage and the slow, undeviating approach of the line of disturbance were distinctly disquieting. My companion appeared actually frightened, and I could hardly credit my senses when I saw him suddenly throw his gun to his shoulder and fire both barrels at the agitated grain! Before the smoke of the discharge had cleared away I heard a loud savage cry – a scream like that of a wild animal – and flinging his gun upon the ground Morgan sprang away and ran swiftly from the spot. At the same instant I was thrown violently to the ground by the impact of something unseen in the smoke – some soft, heavy substance that seemed thrown against me with great force.

'Before I could get upon my feet and recover my

gun, which seemed to have been struck from my hands, I heard Morgan crying out as if in mortal agony, and mingling with his cries were such hoarse, savage sounds as one hears from fighting dogs. Inexpressibly terrified, I struggled to my feet and looked in the direction of Morgan's retreat; and may heaven in mercy spare me from another sight like that! At a distance of less than thirty yards was my friend, down upon one knee, his head thrown back at a frightful angle, hatless, his long hair in disorder and his whole body in violent movement from side to side, backwards and forwards. His right arm was lifted and seemed to lack the hand – at least, I could see none. The other arm was invisible. At times, as my memory now reports this extraordinary scene, I could discern but a part of his body; it was as if he had been partly blotted out – I cannot otherwise express it – then a shifting of his position would bring it all into view again.

'All this must have occurred within a few seconds, yet in that time Morgan assumed all the postures of a determined wrestler vanquished by superior weight and strength. I saw nothing but him, and him not always distinctly. During the entire incident his shouts and curses were heard, as if through an enveloping uproar of such sounds of rage and fury as I had never heard from the throat of man or brute!

'For a moment only I stood irresolute, then throwing down my gun I ran forward to my friend's assistance. I had a vague belief that he was suffering from a fit, or some form of convulsion. Before I could reach his side he was down and quiet. All sounds had ceased, but with a feeling of such terror as even these awful events had not inspired I now saw again the mysterious movement of the wild oats, prolonging itself from the trampled area about the prostrate man towards the edge of a wood. It was only when it had reached the wood that I was able to withdraw my eyes and look at my companion. He was dead.'

3

A Man Though Naked May be in Rags

The coroner rose from his seat and stood beside the dead man. Lifting an edge of the sheet he pulled it away, exposing the entire body, altogether naked and showing in the candlelight a claylike yellow. It had, however, broad maculations of bluish black, obviously caused by extravasated blood from contusions. The chest and sides looked as if they had been beaten with a bludgeon. There were dreadful lacerations; the skin was torn in strips and shreds.

The coroner moved round to the end of the table and undid a silk handkerchief which had been passed under the chin and knotted on the top of the head. When the handkerchief was drawn away it exposed what had been the throat. Some of the jurors who had risen to get a better view repented their curiosity and turned away their faces. Witness Harker went to the open window and leaned out across the sill, faint and sick. Dropping the handkerchief upon the dead man's neck the coroner stepped to an angle of the room and from a pile of clothing produced one garment after another, each of which he held up a moment for inspection. All were torn, and stiff with blood. The jurors did not make a closer inspection. They seemed rather uninterested. They had, in truth, seen all this before, the only thing that was new to them being Harker's testimony.

'Gentlemen,' the coroner said, 'we have no more evidence, I think. Your duty has been already explained to you; if there is nothing you wish to ask you may go outside and consider your verdict.'

The foreman rose – a tall, bearded man of sixty, coarsely clad.

'I should like to ask one question, Mr Coroner,' he said. 'What asylum did this yer last witness escape from?'

'Mr Harker,' said the coroner gravely and tranquilly, 'from what asylum did you last escape?'

Harker flushed crimson again, but said nothing, and the seven jurors rose and solemnly filed out of the cabin.

'If you have done insulting me, sir,' said Harker, as soon as he and thc officer were left alone with the dead man, 'I suppose I am at liberty to go?'

'Yes.'

Harker started to leave, but paused, with his hand on the door latch. The habit of his profession was strong in him – stronger than his sense of personal dignity. He turned about and said: 'The book that you have there – I recognise it as Morgan's diary. You seemed greatly interested in it; you read in it while I was testifying. May I see it? The public would like – '

'The book will cut no figure in this matter,' replied the official, slipping it into his coat pocket; 'all the entries in it were made before the writer's death.'

As Harker passed out of the house the jury re-entered and stood about the table, on which the now covered corpse showed under the sheet with sharp definition. The foreman seated himself near the candle, produced from his breast pocket a pencil and scrap of paper and wrote rather laboriously the following verdict, which with various degrees of effort all signed: 'We, the jury, do find that the remains come to their death at the hands of a mountain lion, but some of us thinks, all the same, they had fits.'

4

An Explanation from the Tomb

In the diary of the late Hugh Morgan are certain interesting entries having, possibly, a scientific value as suggestions. At the inquest upon his body the book was not put in evidence; possibly the coroner thought it not worthwhile to confuse the jury. The date of the first of the entries mentioned cannot be ascertained; the upper part of the leaf is torn away; the part of the entry remaining follows:

. . . would run in a half-circle, keeping his head turned always towards the centre, and again he would stand still, barking furiously. At last he ran away into the brush as fast as he could go. I thought at first that he had gone mad, but on returning to the house found no other alteration in his manner than what was obviously due to fear of punishment.

Can a dog see with his nose? Do odours impress some cerebral centre with images of the thing that emitted them? . . .

September 2 – Looking at the stars last night as they rose above the crest of the ridge east of the house, I observed them successively disappear – from left to right. Each was eclipsed but an instant, and only a few at the same time, but along the entire length of the ridge all that were within a degree or two of the crest were blotted out. It was as if something had passed along between me and them; but I could not see it, and the stars were not thick enough to define its outline. Ugh! don't like this . . .

Several weeks' entries are missing, three leaves being torn from the book.

September 27 – It has been about here again – I find evidences of its presence every day. I watched again all last night in the same cover, gun in hand, double-charged with buckshot. In the morning the fresh foot-prints were there, as before. Yet I would have sworn that I did not sleep – indeed, I hardly sleep at all. It is terrible, insupportable! If these amazing experiences are real I shall go mad; if they are fanciful I am mad already.

October 3 – I shall not go – it shall not drive me away. No, this is *my* house, *my* land. God hates a coward . . .

October 5 – I can stand it no longer; I have invited Harker to pass a few weeks with me – he has a level head. I can judge from his manner if he thinks me mad.

October 7 – I have the solution of the mystery; it came to me last night – suddenly, as by revelation. How simple – how terribly simple!

There are sounds that we cannot hear. At either end of the scale are notes that stir no chord of that imperfect instrument, the human ear. They are too high or too grave. I have observed a flock of blackbirds occupying an entire tree top – the tops of several trees – and all in full song. Suddenly – in a moment – at absolutely the same instant – all sprang into the air and flew away. How? They could not all see one another – whole tree tops intervened. At no point could a leader have been visible to all. There must have been a signal of warning or command, high and shrill above the din, but by me unheard. I have observed, too, the same simultaneous flight when all were silent, among not only blackbirds, but other birds – quail, for example, widely separated by bushes – even on opposite sides of a hill.

It is known to seamen that a school of whales basking or sporting on the surface of the ocean, miles apart, with the convexity of the earth between, will sometimes dive at the same instant – all gone out of sight in a moment. The signal has been sounded – too grave for the ear of the sailor at the masthead and his comrades on the deck – who nevertheless feel its vibrations in the ship as the stones of a cathedral are stirred by the bass of the organ.

As with sounds, so with colours. At each end of the solar spectrum the chemist can detect the presence of what are known as 'actinic' rays. They represent colours – integral colours in the composition of light – which we are unable to discern. The human eye is an imperfect instrument; its range is but a few octaves of the real 'chromatic scale'. I am not mad; there are colours that we cannot see.

And, God help me! the Damned Thing is of such a colour!

The Squaw

BRAM STOKER

Nürnberg at the time was not so much exploited as it has been since then. Irving had not been playing *Faust*, and the very name of the old town was hardly known to the great bulk of the travelling public. My wife and I being in the second week of our honeymoon, naturally wanted someone else to join our party, so that when the cheery stranger, Elias P. Hutcheson, hailing from Isthmian City, Bleeding Gulch, Maple Tree County, Nebraska turned up at the station at Frankfort, and casually remarked that he was going on to see the most all-fired old Methuselah of a town in Yurrup, and that he guessed that so much travelling alone was enough to send an intelligent, active citizen into the melancholy ward of a daft house, we took the pretty broad hint and suggested that we should join forces. We found, on comparing notes afterwards, that we had each intended to speak with some diffidence or hesitation so as not to appear too eager, such not being a good compliment to the success of our married life; but the effect was entirely marred by our both beginning to speak at the same instant – stopping simultaneously and then going on together again. Anyhow, no matter how, it was done; and Elias P. Hutcheson became one of our party. Straightway Amelia and I found the pleasant benefit; instead of quarrelling, as we had been doing, we found that the restraining influence of a third party was such that we now took every opportunity of spooning in odd corners. Amelia declares that ever since she has, as the result of that experience, advised all her friends to take a friend on the honeymoon. Well, we 'did' Nürnberg together, and much enjoyed the racy remarks of our Trans-atlantic friend, who, from his quaint speech and his wonderful stock of adventures, might have stepped out of a novel. We kept for the last object of interest in the city to be visited the Burg, and on the day appointed for the visit strolled round the outer wall of the city by the eastern side.

The Burg is seated on a rock dominating the town and an immensely deep fosse guards it on the northern side. Nürnberg has been happy in that it was never sacked; had it been it would certainly not be so spick and span perfect as it is at present. The ditch has not been used for centuries, and now its base is spread with tea-gardens and orchards, of which some of the trees are of quite respectable growth. As we wandered round the wall, dawdling in the hot July sunshine, we often paused to admire the views spread before us, and in especial the great plain covered with towns and villages and bounded with a blue line of hills, like a landscape of Claude Lorraine. From this we always turned with new delight to the city itself, with its myriad of quaint old gables and acre-wide red roofs dotted with dormer windows, tier upon tier. A little to our right rose the towers of the Burg, and nearer still, standing grim, the Torture Tower, which was, and is, perhaps, the most interesting place in the city. For centuries the tradition of the Iron Virgin of Nürnberg has been handed down as an instance of the horrors of cruelty of which man is capable; we had long looked forward to seeing it; and here at last was its home.

In one of our pauses we leaned over the wall of the moat and looked down. The garden seemed quite fifty or sixty feet below us, and the sun pouring into it with an intense, moveless heat like that of an oven. Beyond rose the grey, grim wall seemingly of endless height, and losing itself right and left in the angles of bastion and counterscarp. Trees and bushes crowned the wall, and above again towered the lofty houses on whose massive beauty Time has only set the hand of approval. The sun was hot and we were lazy; time was our own, and we lingered, leaning on the wall. Just below us was a pretty sight – a great black cat lying stretched in the sun, whilst round her gambolled prettily a tiny black kitten. The mother would wave her tail for the kitten to play with, or would raise her feet and push away the little one as an encouragement to further play. They were just at the foot of the wall, and Elias P. Hutcheson, in order to help the play, stooped and took from the walk a moderate-sized pebble.

'See!' he said, 'I will drop it near the kitten, and they will both wonder where it came from.'

'Oh, be careful,' said my wife; 'you might hit the dear little thing!'

'Not me, ma'am,' said Elias P. 'Why, I'm as tender as a Maine cherry tree. Lor' bless ye. I wouldn't hurt the poor pooty little critter more'n I'd scalp a baby. An' you may bet your variegated socks on that! See, I'll drop it fur away on the outside so's not to go near her!' Thus saying, he leaned over and held his arm out at full length and dropped the stone. It may be that there is some attractive force which draws lesser matters to greater; or more probably that the wall was not plump but sloped to its base – we not noticing the inclination from above; but the stone fell with a sickening thud that came up to us through the hot air, right on the kitten's head, and shattered out its little brains then and there. The black cat cast a swift upward glance, and we saw her eyes like green fire fixed an instant on Elias P. Hutcheson; and then her attention was given to the kitten, which lay still with just a quiver of her tiny limbs, whilst a thin red stream trickled from a gaping wound. With a muffled cry, such as a human being might give, she bent over the kitten licking its wounds and moaning. Suddenly she seemed to realise that it was dead, and again threw her eyes up at us. I shall never forget the sight, for she looked the perfect incarnation of hate. Her green eyes blazed with lurid fire, and the white, sharp teeth seemed to almost shine through the blood which dabbled her mouth and whiskers. She gnashed her teeth, and her claws stood out stark and at full length on every paw. Then she made a wild rush up the wall as if to reach us, but when the momentum ended fell back, and further added to her horrible appearance for she fell on the kitten, and rose with her black fur smeared with its brains and blood. Amelia turned quite faint, and I had to lift her back from the wall. There was a seat close by in shade of a spreading plane tree, and here I placed her whilst she composed herself. Then I went back to Hutcheson, who stood without moving, looking down on the angry cat below.

As I joined him, he said: 'Wall, I guess that air the savagest beast I ever see – 'cept once when an Apache squaw had an edge on a half-breed what they nicknamed "Splinters" 'cos of the way he fixed up her papoose which he stole on a raid just to show that he appreciated the way they had given his mother the fire torture. She got that kinder look so set on her face that it jest seemed to grow there. She followed Splinters mor'n three year till at last the braves got him and handed him over to her. They did say that no man, white or Injun, had ever been so long a-dying under the tortures of the Apaches. The only time I ever see her smile was when I wiped her out. I kem on the camp just in time to see Splinters pass in his checks, and he wasn't sorry to go either. He was a hard citizen, and though I never could shake with him after that papoose business – for it was bitter bad, and he should have been a white man, for he looked like one – I see he had got paid out in full. Durn me, but I took a piece of his hide from one of his skinnin' posts an' had it made into a pocketbook. It's here now!' and he slapped the breast pocket of his coat.

Whilst he was speaking the cat was continuing her frantic efforts to get up the wall. She would take a run back and then charge up, sometimes reaching an incredible height. She did not seem to mind the heavy fall which she got each time but started with renewed vigour; and at every tumble her appearance became more horrible. Hutcheson was a kind-hearted man – my wife and I had both noticed little acts of kindness to animals as well as to persons – and he seemed concerned at the state of fury to which the cat had wrought herself.

'Wall, now!' he said, 'I du declare that that poor critter seems quite desperate. There! there! poor thing, it was all an accident – though that won't bring back your little one to you. Say! I wouldn't have had such a thing happen for a thousand! Just shows what a clumsy fool of a man can do when he tries to play! Seems I'm too darned slipper-handed to even play with a cat. Say Colonel!' it was a pleasant way he had to bestow titles freely – 'I hope your wife don't hold no grudge against me on account of this unpleasantness? Why, I wouldn't have had it occur on no account.'

He came over to Amelia and apologised profusely, and she with her usual kindness of heart hastened to assure him that she quite understood that it was an accident. Then we all went again to the wall and looked over.

The cat missing Hutcheson's face had drawn back across the moat, and was sitting on her haunches as though ready to spring. Indeed, the very instant she saw him she did spring, and with a blind unreasoning fury, which would have been grotesque, only that it was so frightfully real. She did not try to run up the wall, but simply launched herself at him as though hate and fury could lend her wings to pass straight through the great distance between them. Amelia, womanlike, got quite concerned, and said to Elias P. in a warning voice: 'Oh! you must be very careful. That animal would try to kill you if she were here; her eyes look like positive murder.'

He laughed out jovially. 'Excuse me, ma'am,' he said, 'but I can't help laughin'. Fancy a man that has fought grizzlies an' Injuns bein' careful of bein' murdered by a cat!'

When the cat heard him laugh, her whole demeanour seemed to change. She no longer tried to jump or run up the wall, but went quietly over, and sitting again beside the dead kitten began to lick and fondle it as though it were alive.

'See!' said I, 'the effect of a really strong man. Even that animal in the midst of her fury recognises the voice of a master, and bows to him!'

'Like a squaw!' was the only comment of Elias P. Hutcheson, as we moved on our way round the city fosse. Every now and then we looked over the wall and each time saw the cat following us. At first she had kept going back to the dead kitten, and then as the distance grew greater took it in her mouth and so followed. After a while, however, she abandoned this, for we saw her following all alone; she had evidently hidden the body somewhere. Amelia's alarm grew at the cat's persistence, and more than once she repeated her warning; but the American always laughed with amusement, till finally, seeing that she was beginning to be worried, he said: 'I say, ma'am, you needn't be skeered over that cat. I go heeled, I du!' Here he slapped his pistol pocket at the back of his lumbar region. 'Why sooner'n have you worried, I'll shoot the critter, right here, an' risk the police interferin' with a citizen of the United States for carryin' arms contrairy to reg'lations!' As he spoke he looked over the wall, but the cat, on seeing him, retreated, with a growl, into a bed of tall flowers, and was hidden. He went on: 'Blest if that ar critter ain't got more sense of what's good for her than most Christians. I guess we've seen the last of her! You bet, she'll go back now to that busted kitten and have a private funeral of it, all to herself!'

Amelia did not like to say more, lest he might, in mistaken kindness to her, fulfil his threat of shooting the cat: and so we went on and crossed the little wooden bridge leading to the gateway whence ran the steep paved roadway between the Burg and the pentagonal Torture Tower. As we crossed the bridge we saw the cat again down below us. When she saw us her fury seemed to return, and she made frantic efforts to get up the steep wall. Hutcheson laughed as he looked down at her, and said: 'Goodbye, old girl. Sorry I injured your feelin's, but you'll get over it in time! So long!' And then we passed through the long, dim archway and came to the gate of the Burg.

When we came out again after our survey of this most beautiful old place which not even the well-intentioned efforts of the Gothic restorers of forty years ago have been able to spoil – though their restoration was then glaring white – we seemed to have quite forgotten the unpleasant episode of the morning. The old lime tree with its great trunk gnarled with the passing of nearly nine centuries, the deep well cut through the heart of the rock by those captives of old, and the lovely view from the city wall whence we heard, spread over almost a full quarter of an hour, the multitudinous chimes of the city, had all helped to wipe out from our minds the incident of the slain kitten.

We were the only visitors who had entered the Torture Tower that morning – so at least said the old custodian – and as we had the place all to ourselves were able to make a minute and more satisfactory survey than would have otherwise been possible. The custodian, looking to us as the sole source of his gains for the day, was willing to meet our wishes in any way. The Torture Tower is truly a grim place, even now when many thousands of visitors have sent a stream of life, and the joy that follows life, into the place; but at the time I mention it wore its grimmest and most gruesome aspect. The dust of ages seemed to have settled on it, and the darkness and the horror of its memories seem to have become sentient in a way that would have satisfied the Pantheistic souls of Philo or Spinoza. The lower chamber where we entered was seemingly, in its normal state, filled with incarnate darkness; even the hot sunlight streaming in through the door seemed to be lost in the vast thickness of the walls, and only showed the masonry rough as when the builder's scaffolding had come down, but coated with dust and marked here and there with patches of dark stain which, if walls could speak, could have given their own dread memories of fear and pain. We were glad to pass up the dusty wooden staircase, the custodian leaving the outer door open to light us somewhat on our way; for to our eyes the one long-wick'd, evil-smelling candle stuck in a sconce on the wall gave an inadequate light. When we came up through the open trap in the corner of the chamber overhead, Amelia held on to me so tightly that I could actually feel her heart beat. I must say for my own part that I was not surprised at her fear, for this room was even more gruesome than that below. Here there was certainly more light, but only just sufficient to realise the horrible surroundings of the place. The builders of the tower had evidently intended that only they who should gain the top should have any of the joys of light and prospect. There, as we had noticed from below, were ranges of windows, albeit of mediaeval smallness, but elsewhere in the tower were only a very few narrow slits such as were habitual in places of mediaeval defence. A few of these only lit the chamber, and these so high up in the wall that from no part could the sky be seen through the thickness of the walls. In racks, and leaning in disorder against the walls, were a number of headsmen's swords, great double-handed weapons with broad blade and keen edge. Hard by were several blocks whereon the necks of the victims had lain, with here and there deep notches where the steel had bitten through the guard of flesh and shored into the wood. Round the chamber, placed in all sorts of irregular ways, were many implements of torture which made one's heart ache to see – chairs full of spikes which gave instant and excruciating pain; chairs and couches with dull knobs whose torture was seemingly less, but which, though slower, were equally efficacious; racks, belts, boots, gloves, collars, all made for compressing at will; steel baskets in which the head could be slowly crushed into a pulp if necessary; watchmen's hooks with long handle and knife that cut at resistance – this a speciality of the old Nürnberg police system; and many, many other devices for man's injury to man. Amelia grew quite pale with the horror of the things, but fortunately did not faint, for being a little overcome she sat down on a torture chair, but jumped up again with a shriek, all tendency to faint gone. We both pretended that it was the injury done to her dress by the dust of the chair, and the rusty spikes which had upset her, and Mr Hutcheson acquiesced in accepting the explanation with a kind-hearted laugh.

But the central object in the whole of this chamber of horrors was the engine known as the Iron Virgin, which stood near the centre of the room. It was a rudely-shaped figure of a woman, something of the bell order, or, to make a closer comparison, of the figure of Mrs Noah in the children's Ark, but without that slimness of waist and perfect *rondeur* of hip which marks the aesthetic type of the Noah family. One would hardly have recognised it as intended for a human figure at all had not the founder shaped on the forehead a rude semblance of a woman's face. This machine was coated with rust without, and covered with dust; a rope was fastened to a ring in the front of the figure, about where the waist should have been, and was drawn through a pulley, fastened on the wooden pillar which sustained the flooring above. The custodian pulling this rope showed that a section of the front was hinged like a door at one side; we then saw that the engine was of considerable thickness, leaving just room enough inside for a man to be placed. The door was of equal thickness and of great weight, for it took the custodian all his strength, aided though he was by the contrivance of the pulley, to open it. This weight was partly due to the fact that the door was of manifest purpose hung so as to throw its weight downwards, so that it might shut of its own accord when the strain was released. The inside was honeycombed with rust – nay more, the rust alone that comes through time would hardly have eaten so deep into the iron walls; the rust of the cruel stains was deep indeed! It was only, however, when we came to look at the inside of the door that the diabolical intention was manifest to the full. Here were several long spikes, square and massive, broad at the base and sharp at the points, placed in such a position that when the door should close the upper ones would pierce the eyes of the victim, and the lower ones his heart and vitals. The sight was too much for poor Amelia, and this time she fainted dead off, and I had to carry her down the stairs, and place her on a bench outside till she recovered. That she felt it to the quick was afterwards shown by the fact that my eldest son bears to this day a rude birthmark on his breast, which has, by family consent, been accepted as representing the Nürnberg Virgin.

When we got back to the chamber we found Hutcheson still opposite the Iron Virgin; he had been evidently philosophising, and now gave us the benefit of his thought in the shape of a sort of exordium.

'Wall, I guess I've been learnin' somethin' here while madam has been gettin' over her faint. 'Pears to me that we're a long way behind the times on our side of the big drink. We uster think out on the plains that the Injun could give us points in tryin' to make a man uncomfortable; but I guess your old mediaeval law-and-order party could raise him every time. Splinters was pretty good in his bluff on the squaw, but this here young miss held a straight flush all high on him. The points of them spikes air sharp enough still, though even the edges air eaten out by what uster be on them. It'd be a good thing for our Indian section to get some specimens of this here play-toy to send round to the Reservations jest to knock the stuffin' out of the bucks, and the squaws too, by showing them as how old civilisation lays over them at their best. Guess but I'll get in that box a minute jest to see how it feels!'

'Oh no! no!' said Amelia. 'It is too terrible!'

'Guess, ma'am, nothin's too terrible to the explorin' mind. I've been in some queer places in my time. Spent a night inside a dead horse while a prairie fire swept over me in Montana Territory – an' another time slept inside a dead buffler when the Comanches was on the war path an' I didn't keer to leave my kyard on them. I've been two days in a caved-in tunnel in the Billy Broncho gold mine in New Mexico, an' was one of the four shut up for three parts of a day in the caisson what slid over on her side when we was settin' the foundations of the Buffalo Bridge. I've not funked an odd experience yet, an' I don't propose to begin now!'

We saw that he was set on the experiment, so I said: 'Well, hurry up, old man, and get through it quick!'

'All right, General,' said he, 'but I calculate we ain't quite ready yet. The gentlemen, my predecessors, what stood in that thar canister, didn't volunteer for the office – not much! And I guess there was some ornamental tyin' up before the big stroke was made. I want to go into this thing fair and square, so I must get fixed up proper first. I dare say this old galoot can rise some string and tie me up accordin' to sample?'

This was said interrogatively to the old custodian, but the latter, who understood the drift of his speech, though perhaps not appreciating to the full the niceties of dialect and imagery, shook his head. His protest was, however, only formal and made to be overcome. The American thrust a gold piece into his hand, saying: 'Take it, pard! it's your pot; and don't be skeer'd. This ain't no necktie party that you're asked to assist in!' He produced some thin frayed rope and proceeded to bind our companion with sufficient strictness for the purpose. When the upper part of his body was bound, Hutcheson said: 'Hold on a moment, Judge. Guess I'm too heavy for you to tote into the canister. You jest let me walk in, and then you can wash up regardin' my legs!'

Whilst speaking he had backed himself into the opening which was just enough to hold him. It was a close fit and no mistake. Amelia looked on with fear in her eyes, but she evidently did not like to say anything. Then the custodian completed his task by tying the American's feet together so that he was now absolutely helpless and fixed in his voluntary prison. He seemed to really enjoy it, and the incipient smile which was habitual to his face blossomed into actuality as he said: 'Guess this here Eve was made out of the rib of a dwarf! There ain't much room for a full-grown citizen of the United States to hustle. We uster make our coffins more roomier in Idaho Territory. Now, Judge, you jest begin to let this door down, slow, on to me. I want to feel the same pleasure as the other jays had when those spikes began to move toward their eyes!'

'Oh no! no! no!' broke in Amelia hysterically. 'It is too terrible! I can't bear to see it! – I can't! I can't!' But the American was obdurate. 'Say, Colonel,' said he, 'why not take Madame for a little promenade? I wouldn't hurt her feelin's for the world; but now that I am here, havin' kem eight thousand miles, wouldn't it be too hard to give up the very experience I've been pinin' an' pantin' fur? A man can't get to feel like canned goods every time! Me and the Judge here'll fix up this thing in no time, an' then you'll come back, an' we'll all laugh together!'

Once more the resolution that is born of curiosity triumphed, and Amelia stayed holding tight to my arm and shivering whilst the custodian began to slacken slowly inch by inch the rope that held back the iron door. Hutcheson's face was positively radiant as his eyes followed the first movement of the spikes.

'Wall!' he said, 'I guess I've not had enjoyment like this since I left Noo York. Bar a scrap with a French sailor at Wapping – an' that warn't much of a picnic neither – I've not had a show fur real pleasure in this dod-rotted Continent, where there ain't no b'ars nor no Injuns, an' wheer nary man goes heeled. Slow there, Judge! Don't you rush this business! I want a show for my money this game – I du!'

The custodian must have had in him some of the blood of his predecessors in that ghastly tower, for he worked the engine with a deliberate and excruciating slowness which after five minutes, in which the outer edge of the door had not moved half as many inches, began to overcome Amelia. I saw her lips whiten, and felt her hold upon my arm relax. I looked around an instant for a place whereon to lay her, and when I looked at her again found that her eye had become fixed on the side of the Virgin. Following its direction I saw the black cat crouching out of sight. Her green eyes shone like danger lamps in the gloom of the place, and their colour was heightened by the blood which still smeared her coat and reddened her mouth. I cried out: 'The cat! look out for the cat!' for even then she sprang out before the engine. At this moment she looked like a triumphant demon. Her eyes blazed with ferocity, her hair bristled out till she seemed twice her normal size, and her tail lashed about as does a tiger's when the quarry is before it. Elias P. Hutcheson when he saw her was amused, and his eyes positively sparkled with fun as he said: 'Darned if the squaw hain't got on all her war paint! Jest give her a shove off if she comes any of her tricks on me, for I'm so fixed everlastingly by the boss, that durn my skin if I can keep my eyes from her if she wants them! Easy there, Judge! don't you slack that ar rope or I'm euchered!'

At this moment Amelia completed her faint, and I had to clutch hold of her round the waist or she would have fallen to the floor. Whilst attending to her I saw the black cat crouching for a spring, and jumped up to turn the creature out.

But at that instant, with a sort of hellish scream, she hurled herself, not as we expected at Hutcheson, but straight at the face of the custodian. Her claws seemed to be tearing wildly as one sees in the Chinese drawings of the dragon rampant, and as I looked I saw one of them light on the poor man's eye, and actually tear through it and down his cheek, leaving a wide band of red where the blood seemed to spurt from every vein.

With a yell of sheer terror which came quicker than even his sense of pain, the man leaped back, dropping as he did so the rope which held back the iron door. I jumped for it, but was too late, for the cord ran like lightning through the pulley-block, and the heavy mass fell forward from its own weight.

As the door closed I caught a glimpse of our poor companion's face. He seemed frozen with terror. His eyes stared with a horrible anguish as if dazed, and no sound came from his lips.

And then the spikes did their work. Happily the end was quick, for when I wrenched open the door they had pierced so deep that they had locked in the bones of the skull through which they had crushed, and actually tore him – it – out of his iron prison till, bound as he was, he fell at full length with a sickly thud upon the floor, the face turning upward as he fell.

I rushed to my wife, lifted her up and carried her out, for I feared for her very reason if she should wake from her faint to such a scene. I laid her on the bench outside and ran back. Leaning against the wooden column was the custodian moaning in pain whilst he held his reddening handkerchief to his eyes. And sitting on the head of the poor American was the cat, purring loudly as she licked the blood which trickled through the gashed socket of his eyes.

I think no one will call me cruel because I seized one of the old executioner's swords and shore her in two as she sat.

The Horror in the Museum

H. P. LOVECRAFT

It was languid curiosity which first brought Stephen Jones to Rogers' Museum. Someone had told him about the queer underground place in Southwark Street across the river, where waxen things so much more horrible than the worst effigies at Madame Tussaud's were shown, and he had strolled in one April day to see how disappointing he would find it. Oddly, he was not disappointed. There was something different and distinctive here, after all. Of course, the usual gory commonplaces were present – Landru, Dr Crippen, Madame Demers, Rizzio, Lady Jane Grey, endless maimed victims of war and revolution, and monsters like Gilles de Rais and Marquis de Sade – but there were other things which had made him breathe faster and stay till the ringing of the closing bell. The man who had fashioned this collection could be no ordinary mountebank. There was imagination – even a kind of diseased genius – in some of this stuff.

Later he had learned about George Rogers. The man had been on the Tussaud staff, but some trouble had developed which led to his discharge. There were aspersions on his sanity and tales of his crazy forms of secret worship – though latterly his success with his own basement museum had dulled the edge of some criticisms while sharpening the insidious point of others. Teratology and the iconography of nightmare were his hobbies, and even he had had the prudence to screen off some of his worst effigies in a special alcove for adults only. It was this alcove which had fascinated Jones so much. There were lumpish hybrid things which only fantasy could spawn, moulded with devilish skill, and coloured in a horribly lifelike fashion.

Some were the figures of well-known myth – gorgons, chimaeras, dragons, cyclops, and all their shuddersome congeners. Others were drawn from darker and more furtively whispered cycles of subterranean legend – black, formless Tsathoggua, many-tentacled Cthulhu, proboscidian Chaugnar Faugn, and other rumoured blasphemies from forbidden books like the *Necronomicon*, the *Book of Eibon*, or the *Unaussprechlichen Kulten* of von Junzt. But the worst were wholly original with Rogers, and represented shapes which no tale of antiquity had ever dared to suggest. Several were hideous parodies on forms of organic life we know, while others seemed taken from feverish dreams of other planets and other galaxies. The wilder paintings of Clark Ashton Smith might suggest a few – but nothing could suggest the effect of poignant, loathsome terror created by their great size and fiendishly cunning workmanship, and by the diabolically clever lighting conditions under which they were exhibited.

Stephen Jones, as a leisurely connoisseur of the bizarre in art, had sought out Rogers himself in the dingy office and workroom behind the vaulted museum chamber – an evil-looking crypt lighted dimly by dusty windows set slit-like and horizontal in the brick wall on a level with the ancient cobblestones of a hidden courtyard. It was here that the images were repaired – here, too, where some of them had been made. Waxen arms, legs, heads, and torsos lay in grotesque array on various benches, while on high tiers of shelves matted wigs, ravenous-looking teeth, and glassy, staring eyes were indiscriminately scattered. Costumes of all sorts hung from hooks, and in one alcove were great piles of flesh-coloured wax-cakes and shelves filled with paint-cans and brushes of every description. In the centre of the room was a large melting-furnace used to prepare the wax for moulding, its firebox topped by a huge iron container on hinges, with a spout which permitted the pouring of melted wax with the merest touch of a finger.

Other things in the dismal crypt were less describable – isolated parts of problematical entities whose assembled forms were the phantoms of delirium. At one end was a door of heavy plank, fastened by an unusually large padlock and with a very peculiar symbol painted over it. Jones, who had once had access to the dreaded *Necronomicon*, shivered involuntarily as he recognised that symbol. This showman, he reflected, must indeed be a person of disconcertingly wide scholarship in dark and dubious fields.

Nor did the conversation of Rogers disappoint him. The man was tall, lean, and rather unkempt, with large black eyes which gazed combustively from a pallid and usually stubble-covered face. He did not resent Jones's intrusion, but seemed to welcome the chance of unburdening himself to an interested person. His voice was of singular depth and resonance, and harboured a sort of repressed intensity bordering on the feverish. Jones did not wonder that many had thought him mad.

With every successive call – and such calls became a habit as the weeks went by – Jones had found Rogers more communicative and confidential. From the first there had been hints of strange faiths and practices on the showman's part, and later on these hints expanded into tales – despite a few odd corroborative photographs – whose extravagance was almost comic. It was some time in June, on a night when Jones had brought a bottle of good whiskey and plied his host somewhat freely, that the really demented talk first appeared. Before that there had been wild enough stories – accounts of mysterious trips to Thibet, the African interior, the Arabian desert, the Amazon valley, Alaska, and certain little-known islands of the South Pacific, plus claims of having read such monstrous and half-fabulous books as the prehistoric Pnakotic fragments and the Dhol chants attributed to malign and non-human Leng – but nothing in all this had been so unmistakably insane as what had cropped out that June evening under the spell of the whiskey.

To be plain, Rogers began making vague boasts of having found certain things in Nature that no one had found before, and of having brought back tangible evidences of such discoveries. According to his bibulous harangue, he had gone farther than anyone else in interpreting the obscure and primal books he studied, and had been directed by them to certain remote places where strange survivals are hidden – survivals of aeons and life-cycles earlier than mankind, and in some cases connected with other dimensions and other worlds, communication with which was frequent in the forgotten pre-human days. Jones marvelled at the fancy which could conjure up such notions, and wondered just what Rogers's mental history had been. Had his work amidst the morbid grotesqueries of Madame Tussaud's been the start of his imaginative flights, or was the tendency innate, so that his choice of occupation was merely one of its manifestations? At any rate, the man's work was very closely linked with his notions. Even now there was no mistaking the trend of his blackest hints about the nightmare monstrosities in the screened-off 'Adults only' alcove. Heedless of ridicule, he was trying to imply that not all of these daemoniac abnormalities were artificial.

It was Jones's frank scepticism and amusement at these irresponsible claims which broke up the growing cordiality. Rogers, it was clear, took himself very seriously; for he now became morose and resentful, continuing to tolerate Jones only through a dogged urge to break down his wall of urbane and complacent incredulity. Wild tales and suggestions of rites and sacrifices to nameless elder gods continued, and now and then Rogers would lead his guest to one of the hideous blasphemies in the screened-off alcove and point out features difficult to reconcile with even the finest human craftsmanship. Jones continued his visits through sheer fascination, though he knew he had forfeited his host's regard. At times he would try to humour Rogers with pretended assent to some mad hint or assertion, but the gaunt showman was seldom to be deceived by such tactics.

The tension came to a head later in September. Jones had casually dropped into the museum one afternoon, and was wandering through the dim corridors whose horrors were now so familiar, when he heard a very peculiar sound from the general direction of Rogers' workroom. Others heard it, too, and started nervously as the echoes reverberated through the great vaulted basement. The three attendants exchanged odd glances; and one of them, a dark, taciturn, foreign-looking fellow who always served Rogers as a repairer and assistant designer, smiled in a way which seemed to puzzle his colleagues and which grated very harshly on some facet of Jones's sensibilities. It was the yelp or scream of a dog, and was such a sound as could be made only under conditions of the utmost fright and agony combined. Its stark, anguished frenzy was appalling to hear, and in this setting of grotesque abnormality it held a double hideousness. Jones remembered that no dogs were allowed in the museum.

He was about to go to the door leading into the workroom, when the dark attendant stopped him with a word and a gesture. Mr Rogers, the man said in a soft, somewhat accented voice at once apologetic and vaguely sardonic, was out, and there were standing orders to admit no one to the workroom during his absence. As for that yelp, it was undoubtedly something out in the courtyard behind the museum. This neighbourhood was full of stray mongrels, and their fights were sometimes shockingly noisy. There were no dogs in any part of the museum. But if Mr Jones wished to see Mr Rogers he might find him just before closing-time.

After this Jones climbed the old stone steps to the street outside and examined the squalid neighbourhood curiously. The leaning, decrepit buildings – once dwellings but now largely shops and warehouses –

were very ancient indeed. Some of them were of a gabled type seeming to go back to Tudor times, and a faint miasmatic stench hung subtly about the whole region. Beside the dingy house whose basement held the museum was a low archway pierced by a dark cobbled alley, and this Jones entered in a vague wish to find the courtyard behind the workroom and settle the affair of the dog more comfortably in his mind. The courtyard was dim in the late afternoon light, hemmed in by rear walls even uglier and more intangibly menacing than the crumbling street façades of the evil old houses. Not a dog was in sight, and Jones wondered how the aftermath of such a frantic turmoil could have completely vanished so soon.

Despite the assistant's statement that no dog had been in the museum, Jones glanced nervously at the three small windows of the basement workroom – narrow, horizontal rectangles close to the grass-grown pavement, with grimy panes that stared repulsively and incuriously like the eyes of dead fish. To their left a worn flight of steps led to an opaque and heavily bolted door. Some impulse urged him to crouch low on the damp, broken cobblestones and peer in, on the chance that the thick green shades, worked by long cords that hung down to a reachable level, might not be drawn. The outer surfaces were thick with dirt, but as he rubbed them with his handkerchief he saw there was no obscuring curtain in the way of his vision.

So shadowed was the cellar from the inside that not much could be made out, but the grotesque working paraphernalia now and then loomed up spectrally as Jones tried each of the windows in turn. It seemed evident at first that no one was within; yet when he peered through the extreme right-hand window – the one nearest the entrance alley – he saw a glow of light at the farther end of the apartment which made him pause in bewilderment. There was no reason why any light should be there. It was an inner side of the room, and he could not recall any gas or electric fixture near that point. Another look defined the glow as a large vertical rectangle, and a thought occurred to him. It was in that direction that he had always noticed the heavy plank door with the abnormally large padlock – the door which was never opened, and above which was crudely smeared that hideous cryptic symbol from the fragmentary records of forbidden elder magic. It must be open now – and there was a light inside. All his former speculations as to where that door led, and as to what lay behind it, were now renewed with trebly disquieting force.

Jones wandered aimlessly around the dismal locality till close to six o'clock, when he returned to the museum to make the call on Rogers. He could hardly tell why he wished so especially to see the man just then, but there must have been some subconscious misgivings about that terribly unplaceable canine scream of the afternoon, and about the glow of light in that disturbing and usually unopened inner doorway with the heavy padlock. The attendants were leaving as he arrived, and he thought that Orabona – the dark foreign-looking assistant – eyed him with something like sly, repressed amusement. He did not relish that look – even though he had seen the fellow turn it on his employer many times.

The vaulted exhibition room was ghoulish in its desertion, but he strode quickly through it and rapped at the door of the office and workroom. Response was slow in coming, though there were footsteps inside. Finally, in response to a second knock, the lock rattled, and the ancient six-panelled portal creaked reluctantly open to reveal the slouching, feverish-eyed form of George Rogers. From the first it was clear that the showman was in an unusual mood. There was a curious mixture of reluctance and actual gloating in his welcome, and his talk at once veered to extravagances of the most hideous and incredible sort.

Surviving elder gods – nameless sacrifices – the other than artificial nature of some of the alcove horrors – all the usual boasts, but uttered in a tone of peculiarly increasing confidence. Obviously, Jones reflected, the poor fellow's madness was gaining on him. From time to time Rogers would send furtive glances toward the heavy, padlocked inner door at the end of the room, or toward a piece of coarse burlap on the floor not far from it, beneath which some small object appeared to be lying. Jones grew more nervous as the moments passed, and began to feel as hesitant about mentioning the afternoon's oddities as he had formerly been anxious to do so.

Rogers' sepulchrally resonant bass almost cracked under the excitement of his fevered rambling.

'Do you remember,' he shouted, 'what I told you about that ruined city in Indo-China where the Tcho-Tchos lived? You had to admit I'd been there when you saw the photographs, even if you did think I made that oblong swimmer in darkness out of wax. If you'd seen it writhing in the underground pools as I did. . . .

'Well, this is bigger still. I never told you about this, because I wanted to work out the later parts before making any claim. When you see the snapshots you'll know the geography couldn't have been faked, and I fancy I have another way of proving that *It* isn't any waxed concoction of mine. You've never seen it, for the experiments wouldn't let me keep It on exhibition.'

The showman glanced queerly at the padlocked door.

'It all comes from that long ritual in the eighth Pnakotic fragment. When I got it figured out I saw it could have only one meaning. There were things in the north before the land of Lomar – before mankind existed – and this was one of them. It took us all the way to Alaska, and up the Noatak from Fort Morton, but the thing was there as we knew it would be. Great Cyclopean ruins, acres of them. There was less left than we had hoped for, but after three million years what could one expect? And weren't the Esquimau legends all in the right direction? We couldn't get one of the beggars to go with us, and had to sledge all the way back to Nome for Americans. Orabona was no good up in that climate – it made him sullen and hateful.

'I'll tell you later how we found It. When we got the ice blasted out of the pylons of the central ruin the stairway was just as we knew it would be. Some carvings still there, and it was no trouble keeping the Yankees from following us in. Orabona shivered like a leaf – you'd never think it from the damned insolent way he struts around here. He knew enough of the Elder Lore to be properly afraid. The eternal light was gone, but our torches shewed enough. We saw the bones of others who had been before us – aeons ago, when the climate was warm. Some of these bones were of things you couldn't even imagine. At the third level down we found the ivory throne the fragments said so much about – and I may as well tell you it wasn't empty.

'The thing on that throne didn't move – and we knew then that It needed the nourishment of sacrifice. But we didn't want to wake It then. Better to get It to London first. Orabona and I went to the surface for the big box, but when we had packed it we couldn't get It up the three flights of steps. These steps weren't made for human beings, and their size bothered us. Anyway, it was devilish heavy. We had to have the Americans down to get It out. They weren't anxious to go into the place, but of course the worst thing was safely inside the box. We told them it was a batch of ivory carvings – archaeological stuff; and after seeing the carved throne they probably believed us. It's a wonder they didn't suspect hidden treasure and demand a share. They must have told queer tales around Nome later on; though I doubt if they ever went back to those ruins, even for the ivory throne.'

Rogers paused, felt around in his desk, and produced an envelope of good-sized photographic prints. Extracting one and laying it face down before him, he handed the rest to Jones. The set was certainly an odd one: ice-clad hills, dog sledges, men in furs, and vast tumbled ruins against a background of snow – ruins whose bizarre outlines and enormous stone blocks could hardly be accounted for. One flashlight view shewed an incredible interior chamber with wild carvings and a curious throne whose proportion could not have been designed for a human occupant. The carvings on the gigantic masonry – high walls and peculiar vaulting overhead – were mainly symbolic, and involved both wholly unknown designs and certain hieroglyphs darkly cited in obscene legends. Over the throne loomed the same dreadful symbol which was now painted on the workroom wall above the padlocked plank door. Jones darted a nervous glance at the closed portal. Assuredly, Rogers had been to strange places and had seen strange things. Yet this mad interior picture might easily be a fraud – taken from a very clever stage setting. One must not be too credulous. But Rogers was continuing: 'Well, we shipped the box from Nome and got to London without any trouble. That was the first time we'd ever brought back anything that had a chance of coming alive. I didn't put It on display, because there were more important things to do for It. It needed the nourishment of sacrifice, for It was a god. Of course I couldn't get It the sort of sacrifices which It used to have in Its day, for such things don't exist now. But there were other things which might do. The blood is the life, you know. Even the lemurs and elementals that are older than the earth will come when the blood of men or beasts is offered under the right conditions.'

The expression on the narrator's face was growing very alarming and repulsive, so that Jones fidgeted involuntarily in his chair. Rogers seemed to notice his guest's nervousness, and continued with a distinctly evil smile.

'It was last year that I got It, and ever since then I've been trying rites and sacrifices. Orabona hasn't been much help, for he was always against the idea of waking It. He hates It – probably because he's afraid of what It will come to mean. He carries a pistol all the time to protect himself – fool, as if there were human protection against It! If I ever see him draw that pistol, I'll strangle him. He wanted me to kill It and make an effigy of It. But I've stuck by my plans, and I'm coming out on top in spite of all the cowards like Orabona and damned sniggering sceptics like you, Jones! I've chanted the rites and made certain sacrifices, *and last week the transition came.* The sacrifice was – received and enjoyed!'

Rogers actually licked his lips, while Jones held himself uneasily rigid. The showman paused and rose, crossing the room to the piece of burlap at which he had glanced so often. Bending down, he took hold of one corner as he spoke again.

'You've laughed enough at my work – now it's time for you to get some facts. Orabona tells me you heard a dog screaming around here this afternoon. *Do you know what that meant?*'

Jones started. For all his curiosity he would have been glad to get out without further light on the point which had so puzzled him. But Rogers was inexorable, and began to lift the square of burlap. Beneath it lay a crushed, almost shapeless mass which Jones was slow to classify. Was it a once-living thing which some agency had flattened, sucked dry of blood, punctured in a thousand places, and wrung into a limp, broken-boned heap of grotesqueness? After a moment Jones realised what it must be. It was what was left of a dog – a dog, perhaps of considerable size and whitish colour. Its breed was past recognition, for distortion had come in nameless and hideous ways. Most of the hair was burned off as by some pungent acid, and the exposed, bloodless skin was riddled by innumerable circular wounds or incisions. The form of torture necessary to cause such results was past imagining.

Electrified with a pure loathing which conquered his mounting disgust, Jones sprang up with a cry.

'You damned sadist – you madman – you do a thing like this and dare to speak to a decent man!'

Rogers dropped the burlap with a malignant sneer and faced his oncoming guest. His words held an unnatural calm.

'Why, you fool, do you think *I* did this? Let us admit that the results are unbeautiful from our limited human standpoint. What of it? It is not human and does not pretend to be. To sacrifice is merely to offer. I gave the dog to *It*. What happened is Its work, not mine. It needed the nourishment of the offering, and took it in Its own way. But let me shew you what It looks like.'

As Jones stood hesitating, the speaker returned to his desk and took up the photograph he had laid face down without showing. Now he extended it with a curious look. Jones took it and glanced at it in an almost mechanical way. After a moment the visitor's glance became sharper and more absorbed, for the utterly satanic force of the object depicted had an almost hypnotic effect. Certainly, Rogers had outdone himself in modelling the eldritch nightmare which the camera had caught. The thing was a work of sheer, infernal genius, and Jones wondered how the public would react when it was placed on exhibition. So hideous a thing had no right to exist – probably the mere contemplation of it, after it was done, had completed the unhinging of its maker's mind and led him to worship it with brutal sacrifices. Only a stout sanity could resist the insidious suggestion that the blasphemy was – or had once been – some morbid and exotic form of actual life.

The thing in the picture squatted or was balanced on what appeared to be a clever reproduction of the monstrously carved throne in the other curious photograph. To describe it with any ordinary vocabulary would be impossible, for nothing even roughly corresponding to it has ever come within the imagination of sane mankind. It represented something meant perhaps to be roughly connected with the vertebrates of this planet – though one could not be too sure of that. Its bulk was Cyclopean, for even squatted it towered to almost twice the height of Orabona, who was shown beside it. Looking sharply, one might trace its approximations toward the bodily features of the higher vertebrates.

There was an almost globular torso, with six long, sinuous limbs terminating in crablike claws. From the upper end a subsidiary globe bulged forward bubblelike; its triangle of three staring, fishy eyes, its foot-long and evidently flexible proboscis, and a distended lateral system analogous to gills, suggesting that it was a head. Most of the body was covered with what at first appeared to be fur, but which on closer examination proved to be a dense growth of dark, slender tentacles or sucking filaments, each tipped with a mouth suggesting the head of an asp. On the head and below the proboscis the tentacles tended to be longer and thicker, and marked with spiral stripes – suggesting the traditional serpent-locks of Medusa. To say that such a thing could have an *expression* seems paradoxical; yet Jones felt that that triangle of bulging fish-eyes and that obliquely poised proboscis all bespoke a blend of hate, greed, and sheer cruelty incomprehensible to mankind because mixed with other emotions not of the world or this solar system. Into this bestial abnormality, he reflected, Rogers must have poured at once all his malignant insanity and all his uncanny sculptural genius. The thing was incredible – and yet the photograph proved that it existed.

Rogers interrupted his reveries.

'Well – what do you think of It? Now do you wonder what crushed the dog and sucked it dry with a million mouths? It needed nourishment – and It will need more. It is a god, and I am the first priest of Its latter-day hierarchy. Iä! Shub-Niggurath! The Goat with a Thousand Young!'

Jones lowered the photograph in disgust and pity.

'See here, Rogers, this won't do. There are limits, you know. It's a great piece of work, and all that, but it isn't good for you. Better not see it any more – let Orabona break it up, and try to forget about it. And let me tear this beastly picture up, too.'

With a snarl, Rogers snatched the photograph and returned it to the desk.

'Idiot – you – and you still think It's all a fraud! You still think I made It, and you still think my figures are nothing but lifeless wax! Why, damn you, you're a worse clod than a wax image yourself! But I've got proof this time, and you're going to know! Not just now, for It is resting after the sacrifice – but later. Oh, yes – you will not doubt the power of It then.'

As Rogers glanced toward the padlocked inner door Jones retrieved his hat and stick from a nearby bench.

'Very well, Rogers, let it be later. I must be going now, but I'll call around tomorrow afternoon. Think my advice over and see if it doesn't sound sensible. Ask Orabona what he thinks, too.'

Rogers actually bared his teeth in wild-beast fashion.

'Must be going now, eh? Afraid, after all! Afraid, for all your bold talk! You say the effigies are only wax, and yet you run away when I begin to prove that they aren't. You're like the fellows who take my standing bet that they daren't spend the night in the museum – they come boldly enough, but after an hour they shriek and hammer to get out! Want me to ask Orabona, eh? You two – always against me! You want to break down the coming earthly reign of It!'

Jones preserved his calm.

'No, Rogers – there's nobody against you. And I'm not afraid of your figures, either, much as I admire your skill. But we're both a bit nervous tonight, and I fancy some rest will do us good.'

Again Rogers checked his guest's departure.

'Not afraid, eh? – then why are you so anxious to go? Look here – do you or don't you dare to stay alone here in the dark? What's your hurry if you don't believe in It?'

Some new idea seemed to have struck Rogers, and Jones eyed him closely.

'Why, I've no special hurry – but what would be gained by my staying here alone? What would it prove? My only objection is that it isn't very comfortable for sleeping. What good would it do either of us?'

This time it was Jones who was struck with an idea. He continued in a tone of conciliation.

'See here, Rogers – I've just asked you what it would prove if I stayed, when we both know. It would prove that your effigies are just effigies, and that you oughtn't to let your imagination go the way it's been going lately. Suppose I *do* stay. If I stick it out till morning, will you agree to take a new view of things – go on a vacation for three months or so and let Orabona destroy that new thing of yours? Come, now – isn't that fair?'

The expression on the showman's face was hard to read. It was obvious that he was thinking quickly, and that of sundry conflicting emotions, malign triumph was getting the upper hand. His voice held a choking quality as he replied.

'Fair enough! *If you do stick it out*, I'll take your advice. But stick you must. We'll go out for dinner and come back. I'll lock you in the display room and go home. In the morning I'll come down ahead of Orabona – he comes half an hour before the rest – and see how you are. But don't try it unless you are *very* sure of your scepticism. Others have backed out – you have that chance. And I suppose a pounding on the outer door would always bring a constable. You may not like it so well after a while – you'll be in the same building, though not in the same room with It.'

As they left the rear door into the dingy courtyard, Rogers took with him the piece of burlap – weighted with a gruesome burden. Near the centre of the court was a manhole, whose cover the showman lifted quietly, and with a shuddersome suggestion of familiarity. Burlap and all, the burden went down to the oblivion of a cloacal labyrinth. Jones shuddered, and almost shrank from the gaunt figure at his side as they emerged into the street.

By unspoken mutual consent, they did not dine together, but agreed to meet in front of the museum at eleven.

Jones hailed a cab, and breathed more freely when he had crossed Waterloo Bridge and was approaching the brilliantly lighted Strand. He dined at a quiet café, and subsequently went to his home in Portland Place to bathe and get a few things. Idly he wondered what Rogers was doing. He had heard that the man had a vast, dismal house in the Walworth Road, full of obscure and forbidden books, occult paraphernalia, and wax images which he did not choose to place on exhibition. Orabona, he understood, lived in separate quarters in the same house.

At eleven Jones found Rogers waiting by the basement door in Southwark Street. Their words were few, but each seemed taut with a menacing tension. They agreed that the vaulted exhibition room alone should form the scene of the vigil, and Rogers did not insist that the watcher sit in the special adult alcove of supreme horrors. The showman, having extinguished all the lights with switches in the workroom, locked the door of that crypt with one of the keys on his crowded ring. Without shaking hands he passed out the street door, locked it after him, and stamped up the worn steps to the sidewalk outside. As his tread receded, Jones realised that the long, tedious vigil had commenced.

2

Later, in the utter blackness of the great arched cellar, Jones cursed the childish naïveté which had brought him there. For the first half-hour he had kept flashing on his pocket-light at intervals, but now just sitting in the dark on one of the visitors' benches had become a more nerve-racking thing. Every time the beam shot out it lighted up some morbid, grotesque object – a guillotine, a nameless hybrid monster, a pasty-bearded face crafty with evil, a body with red torrents streaming from a severed throat. Jones knew that no sinister reality was attached to these things, but after that first half-hour he preferred not to see them.

Why he had bothered to humour that madman he could scarcely imagine. It would have been much simpler merely to have let him alone, or to have called in a mental specialist. Probably, he reflected, it was the fellow-feeling of one artist for another. There was so much genius in Rogers that he deserved every possible chance to be helped quietly out of his growing mania. Any man who could imagine and construct the incredibly lifelike things that he had produced was surely not far from actual greatness. He had the fancy of a Sime or a Doré joined to the minute, scientific craftsmanship of a Blatschka. Indeed, he had done for the world of nightmare what the Blatschkas with their marvellously accurate plant models of finely wrought and coloured glass had done for the world of botany.

At midnight the strokes of a distant clock filtered through the darkness, and Jones felt cheered by the message from a still-surviving outside world. The vaulted museum chamber was like a tomb – ghastly in its utter solitude. Even a mouse would be cheering company; yet Rogers had once boasted that – for 'certain reasons', as he said – no mice or even insects ever came near the place. That was very curious, yet it seemed to be true. The deadness and silence were virtually complete. If only something would make a sound! He shuffled his feet, and the echoes came spectrally out of the absolute stillness. He coughed, but there was something mocking in the staccato reverberations. He could not, he vowed, begin talking to himself. That meant nervous disintegration. Time seemed to pass with abnormal and disconcerting slowness. He could have sworn that hours had elapsed since he last flashed the light on his watch, yet here was only the stroke of midnight.

He wished that his senses were not so preternaturally keen. Something in the darkness and stillness seemed to have sharpened them, so that they responded to faint intimations hardly strong enough to be called true impressions. His ears seemed at times to catch a faint, elusive susurrus which could not *quite* be identified with the nocturnal hum of the squalid streets outside, and he thought of vague, irrelevant things like the music of the spheres and the unknown, inaccessible life of alien dimensions pressing on our own. Rogers often speculated about such things.

The floating specks of light in his blackness-drowned eyes seemed inclined to take on curious symmetries of pattern and motion. He had often wondered about those strange rays from the unplumbed abyss which scintillate before us in the absence of all earthly illumination, but he had never known any that behaved just as these were behaving. They lacked the restful aimlessness of ordinary light-specks – suggesting some will and purpose remote from any terrestrial conception.

Then there was that suggestion of odd stirrings. Nothing was open, yet in spite of the general draughtlessness Jones felt that the air was not uniformly quiet. There were intangible variations in pressure – not quite decided enough to suggest the loathsome pawings of unseen elementals. It was abnormally chilly, too. He did not like any of this. The air tasted salty, as if it were mixed with the brine of dark subterrene waters, and there was a bare hint of some odour of ineffable mustiness. In the daytime he had never noticed that the waxen figures had an odour. Even now that half-received hint was not the way wax figures ought to smell. It was more like the faint smell of specimens in a natural-history museum. Curious, in view of Rogers' claims that his figures were not all artificial – indeed, it was probably that claim which made one's imagination conjure up the olfactory suspicion. One must guard against excesses of the imagination – had not such things driven poor Rogers mad?

But the utter loneliness of this place was frightful. Even the distant chimes seemed to come from across cosmic gulfs. It made Jones think of that insane picture which Rogers had shewed him – the wildly carved chamber with the cryptic throne which the fellow had claimed was part of a three-million-year-old ruin in the shunned and inaccessible solitudes of the Arctic. Perhaps Rogers had been to Alaska, but that picture was certainly nothing but stage scenery. It couldn't normally be otherwise, with all that carving and those terrible symbols. And that monstrous shape supposed to have been found on that throne – what a flight of diseased fancy! Jones wondered just how far he actually was from the insane masterpiece in wax – probably it was kept behind that heavy, padlocked plank door leading somewhere out of the workroom. But it would never do to brood about a waxen image. Was not the present room full of such things, some of them scarcely less horrible than the dreadful '*it*'? And beyond a thin canvas screen on the left was the 'Adults only' alcove with its nameless phantoms of delirium.

The proximity of the numberless waxen shapes began to get on Jones's nerves more and more as the quarter-hours wore on. He knew the museum so well that he could not get rid of their usual images even in the total darkness. Indeed, the darkness had the effect of adding to the remembered images certain very disturbing imaginative overtones. The guillotine seemed to creak, and the bearded face of Landru – slayer of his fifty wives – twisted itself into expressions of monstrous menace. From the severed throat of Madame Demers a hideous bubbling sound seemed to emanate, while the headless, legless victim of a trunk murder tried to edge closer and closer on its gory stumps. Jones began shutting his eyes to see if that would dim the images, but found it was useless. Besides, when he shut his eyes the strange, purposeful patterns of light-specks became more disturbingly pronounced.

Then suddenly he began trying to keep the hideous images he had formerly been trying to banish. He tried to keep them because they were giving place to still more hideous ones. In spite of himself his memory began reconstructing the utterly non-human blasphemies that lurked in the obscurer corners, and these lumpish hybrid growths oozed and wriggled toward him as though hunting him down in a circle. Black Tsathoggua moulded itself from a toad-like gargoyle to a long, sinuous line with hundreds of rudimentary feet, and a lean, rubbery night-gaunt spread its wings as if to advance and smother the watcher. Jones braced himself to keep from screaming. He knew he was reverting to the traditional terrors of his childhood, and resolved to use his adult reason to keep the phantoms at bay. It helped a bit, he found, to flash the light again. Frightful as were the images it shewed, these were not as bad as what his fancy called out of the utter blackness.

But there were drawbacks. Even in the light of his torch he could not help suspecting a slight, furtive trembling on the part of the canvas partition screening off the terrible 'Adults only' alcove. He knew what lay beyond, and shivered. Imagination called up the shocking form of fabulous Yog-Sothoth – only a congeries of iridescent globes, yet stupendous in its malign suggestiveness. What was this accursed mass slowly floating toward him and bumping on the partition that stood in the way? A small bulge in the canvas far to the right suggested the sharp horn of Gnoph-keh, the hairy myth-thing of the Greenland ice, that walked sometimes on two legs, sometimes on four, and sometimes on six. To get this stuff out of his head Jones walked boldly toward the hellish alcove with torch burning steadily. Of course, none of his fears was true. Yet were not the long, facial tentacles of great Cthulhu actually swaying, slowly and insidiously? He knew they were flexible, but he had not realised that the draught caused by his advance was enough to set them in motion.

Returning to his former seat outside the alcove, he shut his eyes and let the symmetrical light-specks do their worst. The distant clock boomed a single stroke. Could it be only one? He flashed the light on his watch and saw that it was precisely that hour. It would be hard indeed waiting for morning. Rogers would be down at about eight o'clock, ahead of even Orabona. It would be light outside in the main basement long before that, but none of it could penetrate here. All the windows in this basement had been bricked up but the three small ones facing the court. A pretty bad wait, all told.

His ears were getting most of the hallucinations now – for he could swear he heard stealthy, plodding footsteps in the workroom beyond the closed and locked door. He had no business thinking of that unexhibited horror which Rogers called 'It'. The thing was a contamination – it had driven its maker mad, and now even its picture was calling up imaginative terrors. It could not be in the workroom – it was very obviously beyond that padlocked door of heavy planking. Those steps were certainly pure imagination.

Then he thought he heard the key turn in the workroom door. Flashing on his torch, he saw nothing but the ancient six-panelled portal in its proper position. Again he tried darkness and closed eyes, but there followed a harrowing illusion of creaking – not the guillotine this time, but the slow, furtive opening of the workroom door. He would not scream. Once he screamed, he would be lost. There was a sort of padding or shuffling audible now, and it was slowly advancing toward him. He must retain command of himself. Had he not done so when the nameless brain-shapes tried to close in on him? The shuffling crept nearer, and his resolution failed. He did not scream but merely gulped out a challenge.

'Who goes there? Who are you? What do you want?'

There was no answer, but the shuffling kept on. Jones did not know which he feared most to do – turn on his flashlight or stay in the dark while the thing crept upon him. This thing was different, he felt profoundly, from the other terrors of the evening. His fingers and throat worked spasmodically. Silence was impossible, and the suspense of utter blackness was beginning to be the most intolerable of all conditions. Again he cried out hysterically – 'Halt! Who goes there?' – as he switched on the revealing beams of his torch. Then, paralysed by what he saw, he dropped the flashlight and screamed – not once but many times.

Shuffling toward him in the darkness was the gigantic, blasphemous form of a black thing not wholly ape and not wholly insect. Its hide hung loosely upon its frame, and its rugose, dead-eyed rudiment of a head swayed drunkenly from side to side. Its fore paws were extended, with talons spread wide, and its whole body was taut with murderous malignity despite its utter lack of facial expression. After the screams and the final coming of darkness it leaped, and in a moment had Jones pinned to the floor. There was no struggle, for the watcher had fainted.

Jones's fainting spell could not have lasted more than a moment, for the nameless thing was apishly dragging him through the darkness when he began recovering consciousness. What started him fully awake were the sounds which the thing was making – or rather, the voice with which it was making them. That voice was human, and it was familiar. Only one living being could be behind the hoarse, feverish accents which were chanting to an unknown horror.

'Iä! Iä!' it was howling. 'I am coming, O Rhan-Tegoth, coming with the nourishment. You have waited long and fed ill, but now you shall have what was promised. That and more, for instead of Orabona it will be one of high degree who had doubted you. You shall crush and drain him, with all his doubts, and grow strong thereby. And ever after among men he shall be shown as a monument to your glory. Rhan-Tegoth, infinite and invincible, I am your slave and high-priest. You are hungry, and I provide. I read the sign and have led you forth. I shall feed you with blood, and you shall feed me with power. Iä! Shub-Niggurath! The Goat with a Thousand Young!'

In an instant all the terrors of the night dropped from Jones like a discarded cloak. He was again master of his mind, for he knew the very earthly and material peril he had to deal with. This was no monster of fable, but a dangerous madman. It was Rogers, dressed in some nightmare covering of his own insane designing, and about to make a frightful sacrifice to the devil-god he had fashioned out of wax. Clearly, he must have entered the workroom from the rear courtyard, donned his disguise, and then advanced to seize his neatly trapped and fear-broken victim. His strength was prodigious, and if he was to be thwarted, one must act quickly. Counting on the madman's confidence in his unconsciousness he determined to take him by surprise, while his grasp was relatively lax. The feel of a threshold told him he was crossing into the pitch-black workroom.

With the strength of mortal fear Jones made a sudden spring from the half-recumbent posture in which he was being dragged. For an instant he was free of the astonished maniac's hands, and in another instant a lucky lunge in the dark had put his own hands at his captor's weirdly concealed throat. Simultaneously Rogers gripped him again, and without further preliminaries the two were locked in a desperate struggle of life and death. Jones's athletic training, without doubt, was his sole salvation; for his mad assailant, freed from every inhibition of fair play, decency, or even self-preservation, was an engine of savage destruction as formidable as a wolf or panther.

Guttural cries sometimes punctured the hideous tussle in the dark. Blood spurted, clothing ripped, and Jones at last felt the actual throat of the maniac, shorn of its spectral mask. He spoke not a word, but put every ounce of energy into the defence of his life. Rogers kicked, gouged, butted, bit, clawed, and spat – yet found strength to yelp out actual sentences at times. Most of his speech was in a ritualistic jargon full of references to 'It' or 'Rhan-Tegoth', and to Jones's overwrought nerves it seemed as if the cries echoed from an infinite distance of daemonic snortings and bayings. Toward the last they were rolling on the floor, overturning benches or striking against the walls and the brick foundations of the central melting-furnace. Up to the very end Jones could not be certain of saving himself, but chance finally intervened in his favour. A jab of his knee against Rogers' chest produced a general relaxation, and a moment later he knew he had won.

Though hardly able to hold himself up, Jones rose and stumbled about the walls seeking the light-switch – for his flashlight was gone, together with most of his clothing. As he lurched along he dragged his limp opponent with him, fearing a sudden attack when the madman came to. Finding the switch-box, he fumbled till he had the right handle. Then, as the wildly disordered workroom burst into sudden radiance, he set about binding Rogers with such cords and belts as he could easily find. The fellow's disguise – or what was left of it – seemed to be made of a puzzlingly queer sort of leather. For some reason it made Jones's flesh crawl to touch it, and there seemed to be an alien, rusty odour about it. In the normal clothes beneath it was Rogers' key-ring, and this the exhausted victor seized as his final passport to freedom. The shades at the small, slit-like windows were all securely drawn, and he let them remain so.

Washing off the blood of battle at a convenient sink, Jones donned the most ordinary-looking and least ill-fitting clothes he could find on the costume hooks. Testing the door to the courtyard, he found it fastened with a spring-lock which did not require a key from the inside. He kept the key-ring, however, to admit him on his return with aid – for plainly, the thing to do was to call in an alienist. There was no telephone in the museum, but it would not take long to find an all-night restaurant or chemist's shop where one could be had. He had almost opened the door to go when a torrent of hideous abuse from across the room told him that Rogers – whose visible injuries were confined to a long, deep scratch down the left cheek – had regained consciousness.

'Fool! Spawn of Noth-Yidik and effluvium of K'thun! Son of the dogs that howl in the maelstrom of Azathoth! You would have been sacred and immortal, and now you are betraying It and Its priest! Beware – for It is hungry! It would have been Orabona – that damned treacherous dog ready to turn against me and It – but I give you the first honour instead. Now you must both beware, for It is not gentle without Its priest.

'Iä! Iä! Vengeance is at hand! Do you know you would have been immortal? Look at the furnace! There is a fire ready to light, and there is wax in the kettle. I would have done with you as I have done with other once-living forms. Hei! You, who have vowed all my effigies are waxen, would have become a waxen effigy yourself! The furnace was all ready! When It had had Its fill, and you were like that dog I shewed you, I would have made your flattened, punctured fragments immortal! Wax would have done it. Haven't you said I'm a great artist? Wax in every pore – wax over every square inch of you – Iä! Iä! And ever after the world would have looked at your mangled carcass and wondered how I ever imagined and made such a thing! Hei! And Orabona would have come next, and others after him – and thus would my waxen family have grown!

'Dog – do you still think I *made* all my effigies? Why not say *preserved*? You know by this time the strange places I've been to, and the strange things I've brought back. Coward – you could never face the dimensional shambler whose hide I put on to scare you – the mere sight of it alive, or even the full-fledged thought of it, would kill you instantly with fright! Iä! Iä! It waits hungry for the blood that is the life!'

Rogers, propped against the wall, swayed to and fro in his bonds.

'See here, Jones – if I let you go will you let me go? It must be taken care of by Its high-priest. Orabona will be enough to keep It alive – and when he is finished I will make his fragments immortal in wax for the world to see. It could have been you, but you have rejected the honour. I won't bother you again. Let me go, and I will share with you the power that It will bring me. Iä! Iä! Great is Rhan-Tegoth! Let me go! Let me go! It is starving down there beyond that door, and if It dies the Old Ones can never come back. Hei! Hei! Let me go!'

Jones merely shook his head, though the hideousness of the showman's imaginings revolted him. Rogers, now staring wildly at the padlocked plank door, thumped his head again and again against the brick wall and kicked with his tightly bound ankles. Jones was afraid he would injure himself, and advanced to bind him more firmly to some stationary object. Writhing, Rogers edged away from him and set up a series of frenetic ululations whose utter, monstrous unhumanness was appalling, and whose sheer volume was almost incredible. It seemed impossible that any human throat could produce noises so loud and piercing, and Jones felt that if this continued there would be no need to telephone for aid. It could not be long before a constable would investigate, even granting that there were no listening neighbours in this deserted warehouse district.

'Wza-y'ei! Wza-y'ei!' howled the madman. *'Y'kaa haa bho – ii, Rhan-Tegoth – Cthulhu fhtagn – Ei! Ei! Ei! Ei! – Rhan-Tegoth, Rhan-Tegoth, Rhan-Tegoth!'*

The tautly trussed creature, who had started squirming his way across the littered floor, now reached the padlocked plank door and commenced knocking his head thunderously against it. Jones dreaded the task of binding him further, and wished he were not so exhausted from the previous struggle. This violent aftermath was getting hideously on his nerves, and he began to feel a return of the nameless qualms he had felt in the dark. Everything about Rogers and his museum was so hellishly morbid and suggestive of black vistas beyond life! It was loathsome to think of the waxen masterpiece of abnormal genius which must at this very moment be lurking close at hand in the blackness beyond the heavy, padlocked door.

And now something happened which sent an additional chill down Jones's spine, and caused every hair – even the tiny growth on the backs of his hands – to bristle with a vague fright beyond classification.

Rogers had suddenly stopped screaming and beating his head against the stout plank door, and was straining up to a sitting posture, head cocked on one side as if listening intently for something. All at once a smile of devilish triumph overspread his face, and he began speaking intelligibly again – this time in a hoarse whisper contrasting oddly with his former stentorian howling.

'Listen, fool! Listen hard! *It* has heard me, and is coming. Can't you hear It splashing out of Its tank down there at the end of the runway? I dug it deep, because there was nothing too good for It. It is amphibious, you know – you saw the gills in the picture. It came to the earth from lead-grey Yuggoth, where the cities are under the warm deep sea. It can't stand up in there – too tall – has to sit or crouch. Let me get my keys – we must let It out and kneel down before It. Then we will go out and find a dog or cat – or perhaps a drunken man – to give It the nourishment It needs.'

It was not what the madman said, but the way he said it, that disorganised Jones so badly. The utter, insane confidence and sincerity in that crazed whisper were damnably contagious. Imagination, with such a stimulus, could find an active menace in the devilish wax figure that lurked unseen just beyond the heavy planking. Eyeing the door in unholy fascination, Jones noticed that it bore several distinct cracks, though no marks of violent treatment were visible on this side. He wondered how large a room or closet lay behind it, and how the waxen figure was arranged. The maniac's idea of a tank and runway was as clever as all his other imaginings.

Then, in one terrible instant, Jones completely lost

the power to draw a breath. The leather belt he had seized for Rogers' further strapping fell from his limp hands, and a spasm of shivering convulsed him from head to foot. He might have known the place would drive him mad as it had driven Rogers – and now he *was* mad. He was mad, for he now harboured hallucinations more weird than any which had assailed him earlier that night. The madman was bidding him hear the splashing of a mythical monster in a tank beyond the door – and now, God help him, *he did hear it!*

Rogers saw the spasm of horror reach Jones's face and transform it to a staring mask of fear. He cackled.

'At last, fool, you believe! At last you know! You hear It and It comes! Get me my keys, fool – we must do homage and serve It!'

But Jones was past paying attention to any human words, mad or sane. Phobic paralysis held him immobile and half-conscious, with wild images racing phantasmagorically through his helpless imagination. There *was* a splashing. There *was* a padding or shuffling, as of great wet paws on a solid surface. Something *was* approaching. Into his nostrils, from the cracks in that nightmare plank door, poured a noisome animal stench like and yet unlike that of the mammal cages at the zoological gardens in Regent's Park.

He did not know now whether Rogers was talking or not. Everything real had faded away, and he was a statue obsessed with dreams and hallucinations so unnatural that they became almost objective and remote from him. He thought he heard a sniffing or snorting from the unknown gulf beyond the door, and when a sudden baying, trumpeting noise assailed his ears he could not feel sure that it came from the tightly bound maniac whose image swam uncertainly in his shaken vision. The photograph of that accursed, unseen wax thing persisted in floating through his consciousness. Such a thing had no right to exist. Had it not driven him mad?

Even as he reflected, a fresh evidence of madness beset him. Something, he thought, was fumbling with the latch of the heavy padlocked door. It was patting and pawing and pushing at the planks. There was a thudding on the stout wood, which grew louder and louder. The stench was horrible. And now the assault on that door from the inside was a malign, determined pounding like the strokes of a battering-ram. There was an ominous cracking – a splintering – a welling foetor – a falling plank – *a black paw ending in a crablike claw. . . .*

'Help! Help! God help me! . . . Aaaaaaa! . . .'

With intense effort Jones is today able to recall a sudden bursting of his fear-paralysis into the liberation of frenzied automatic flight. What he evidently did must have paralleled curiously the wild, plunging flights of maddest nightmares; for he seems to have leaped across the disordered crypt at almost a single bound, yanked open the outside door, which closed and locked itself after him with a clatter, sprung up the worn stone steps three at a time, and raced frantically and aimlessly out of that dank cobblestoned court and through the squalid streets of Southwark.

Here the memory ends. Jones does not know how he got home, and there is no evidence of his having hired a cab. Probably he raced all the way by blind instinct – over Waterloo Bridge, along the Strand and Charing Cross, and up Haymarket and Regent Street to his own neighbourhood. He still had on the queer mélange of museum costumes when he grew conscious enough to call the doctor.

A week later the nerve specialists allowed him to leave his bed and walk in the open air.

But he had not told the specialists much. Over his whole experience hung a pall of madness and nightmare, and he felt that silence was the only course. When he was up, he scanned intently all the papers which had accumulated since that hideous night, but found no reference to anything queer at the museum. How much, after all, had been reality? Where did reality end and morbid dream begin? Had his mind gone wholly to pieces in that dark exhibition chamber, and had the whole fight with Rogers been a phantasm of fever? It would help to put him on his feet if he could settle some of these maddening points. He *must* have seen that damnable photograph of the wax image called 'It', for no brain but Rogers' could ever have conceived such a blasphemy.

It was a fortnight before he dared to enter Southwark Street again. He went in the middle of the morning, when there was the greatest amount of sane, wholesome activity around the ancient, crumbling shops and warehouses. The museum's sign was still there, and as he approached he saw that the place was open. The gateman nodded in a pleasant recognition as he summoned up the courage to enter, and in the vaulted chamber below an attendant touched his cap cheerfully. Perhaps everything had been a dream. Would he dare to knock at the door of the workroom and look for Rogers?

Then Orabona advanced to greet him. His dark, sleek face was a trifle sardonic, but Jones felt that he was not unfriendly. He spoke with a trace of accent.

'Good-morning, Mr Jones. It is some time since we have seen you here. Did you wish Mr Rogers? I'm sorry, but he is away. He had word of business in America, and had to go. Yes, it was very sudden. I am in charge now – here, and at the house. I try to maintain Mr Rogers' high standard – till he is back.'

The foreigner smiled – perhaps from affability alone. Jones scarcely knew how to reply, but managed to mumble out a few enquiries about the day after his last visit. Orabona seemed greatly amused by the questions, and took considerable care in framing his replies.

'Oh, yes, Mr Jones – the twenty-eighth of last month. I remember it for many reasons. In the morning – before Mr Rogers got here, you understand – I found the workroom in quite a mess. There was a great deal of – cleaning up – to do. There had been – late work, you see. Important new specimen given its secondary baking process. I took complete charge when I came.

'It was a hard specimen to prepare – but of course Mr Rogers has taught me a great deal. He is, as you know, a very great artist. When he came he helped me complete the specimen – helped very materially, I assure you – but he left soon without even greeting the men. As I tell you, he was called away suddenly. There were important chemical reactions involved. They made loud noises – in fact, some teamsters in the court outside fancy they heard several pistol shots – very amusing idea!

'As for the new specimen – that matter is very unfortunate. It is a great masterpiece – designed and made, you understand, by Mr Rogers. He will see about it when he gets back.'

Again Orabona smiled.

'The police, you know. We put it on display a week ago, and there were two or three faintings. One poor fellow had an epileptic fit in front of it. You see, it is a trifle – stronger – than the rest. Larger, for one thing. Of course, it was in the adult alcove. The next day a couple of men from Scotland Yard looked it over and said it was too morbid to be shown. Said we'd have to remove it. It was a tremendous shame – such a masterpiece of art – but I didn't feel justified in appealing to the courts in Mr Rogers' absence. He would not like so much publicity with the police now – but when he gets back – when he gets back – '

For some reason or other Jones felt a mounting tide of uneasiness and repulsion. But Orabona was continuing.

'You are a connoisseur, Mr Jones. I am sure I violate no law in offering you a private view. It may be – subject, of course, to Mr Rogers' wishes – that we shall destroy the specimen some day – but that would be a crime.'

Jones had a powerful impulse to refuse the sight and flee precipitately, but Orabona was leading him forward by the arm with an artist's enthusiasm. The adult alcove, crowded with nameless horrors, held no visitors. In the farther corner a large niche had been curtained off, and to this the smiling assistant advanced.

'You must know, Mr Jones, that the title of this specimen is "The Sacrifice to Rhan-Tegoth".'

Jones started violently, but Orabona appeared not to notice.

'The shapeless, colossal god is a feature in certain obscure legends which Mr Rogers has studied. All nonsense, of course, as you've so often assured Mr Rogers. It is supposed to have come from outer space, and to have lived in the Arctic three million years ago. It treated its sacrifices rather peculiarly and horribly, as you shall see. Mr Rogers had made it fiendishly lifelike – even to the face of the victim.'

Now trembling violently, Jones clung to the brass railing in front of the curtained niche. He almost reached out to stop Orabona when he saw the curtain beginning to swing aside, but some conflicting impulse held him back. The foreigner smiled triumphantly.

'Behold!'

Jones reeled in spite of his grip on the railing.

'God! – great God!'

Fully ten feet high despite a shambling, crouching attitude expressive of infinite cosmic malignancy, a monstrosity of unbelievable horror was shown starting forward from a Cyclopean ivory throne covered with grotesque carvings. In the central pair of its six legs it bore a crushed, flattened, distorted, bloodless thing, riddled with a million punctures, and in places seared as with some pungent acid. Only the mangled head of the victim, lolling upside down at one side, revealed that it represented something once human.

The monster itself needed no title for one who had seen a certain hellish photograph. That damnable print had been all too faithful; yet it could not carry the full horror which lay in the gigantic actuality. The globular torso – the bubblelike suggestion of a head – the three fishy eyes – the foot-long proboscis – the bulging gills – the monstrous capillation of asp-like suckers – the six sinuous limbs with their black paws and crablike claws – God! the familiarity of that black paw ending in a crablike claw! . . .

Orabona's smile was utterly damnable. Jones choked, and stared at the hideous exhibit with a mounting fascination which perplexed and disturbed him. What half-revealed horror was holding and forcing him to look longer and search out details? This had driven Rogers mad . . . Rogers, supreme artist . . . said they weren't artificial. . . .

Then he localised the thing that held him. It was the crushed waxen victim's lolling head, and something that it implied. This head was not entirely devoid of a face, and that face was familiar. It was like the mad face of poor Rogers. Jones peered closer, hardly knowing why he was driven to do so. Wasn't it natural for a mad egotist to mould his own features into his masterpiece? Was there anything more that subconscious vision had seized on and suppressed in sheer terror?

The wax of the mangled face had been handled with boundless dexterity. Those punctures – how perfectly they reproduced the myriad wounds somehow inflicted on that poor dog! But there was something more. On the left cheek one could trace an irregularity which seemed outside the general scheme – as if the sculptor had sought to cover up a defect of his first modelling. The more Jones looked at it, the more mysteriously it horrified him – and then, suddenly, he remembered a circumstance which brought his horror to a head. That night of hideousness – the tussle – the bound madman – *and the long, deep scratch down the left cheek of the actual living Rogers* . . .

Jones, releasing his desperate clutch on the railing, sank in a total faint.

Orabona continued to smile.

The Mark of the Beast

RUDYARD KIPLING

Your Gods and my Gods – do you or I
know which are the stronger?

NATIVE PROVERB

East of Suez, some hold, the direct control of Providence ceases; Man being there handed over to the power of the Gods and Devils of Asia, and the Church of England Providence only exercising an occasional and modified supervision in the case of Englishmen.

This theory accounts for some of the more unnecessary horrors of life in India: it may be stretched to explain my story.

My friend Strickland of the Police, who knows as much of natives of India as is good for any man, can bear witness to the facts of the case. Dumoise, our doctor, also saw what Strickland and I saw. The inference which he drew from the evidence was entirely incorrect. He is dead now; he died, in a rather curious manner, which has been elsewhere described.

When Fleete came to India he owned a little money and some land in the Himalayas, near a place called Dharmsala. Both properties had been left him by an uncle, and he came out to finance them. He was a big, heavy, genial, and inoffensive man. His knowledge of natives was, of course, limited, and he complained of the difficulties of the language.

He rode in from his place in the hills to spend New Year in the station, and he stayed with Strickland. On New Year's Eve there was a big dinner at the club, and the night was excusably wet. When men foregather from the uttermost ends of the Empire, they have a right to be riotous. The Frontier had sent down a contingent o' Catch-'em-Alive-O's who had not seen twenty white faces for a year, and were used to ride fifteen miles to dinner at the next Fort at the risk of a Khyberee bullet where their drinks should lie. They profited by their new security, for they tried to play pool with a curled-up hedgehog found in the garden, and one of them carried the marker round the room in his teeth. Half a dozen planters had come in from the south and were talking 'horse' to the Biggest Liar in Asia, who was trying to cap all their stories at once. Everybody was there, and there was a general closing up of ranks and taking stock of our losses in dead or disabled that had fallen during the past year. It was a very wet night, and I remember that we sang 'Auld Lang Syne' with our feet in the Polo Championship Cup, and our heads among the stars, and swore that we were all dear friends. Then some of us went away and annexed Burma, and some tried to open up the Soudan and were opened up by Fuzzies in that cruel scrub outside Suakim, and some found stars and medals, and some were married, which was bad, and some did other things which were worse, and the others of us stayed in our chains and strove to make money on insufficient experiences.

Fleete began the night with sherry and bitters, drank champagne steadily up to dessert, then raw, rasping Capri with all the strength of whisky, took

Benedictine with his coffee, four or five whiskies and sodas to improve his pool strokes, beer and bones at half-past two, winding up with old brandy. Consequently, when he came out, at half-past three in the morning, into fourteen degrees of frost, he was very angry with his horse for coughing, and tried to leap-frog into the saddle. The horse broke away and went to his stables; so Strickland and I formed a Guard of Dishonour to take Fleete home.

Our road lay through the bazaar, close to a little temple of Hanuman, the Monkey-god, who is a leading divinity worthy of respect. All gods have good points, just as have all priests. Personally, I attach much importance to Hanuman, and am kind to his people – the great grey apes of the hills. One never knows when one may want a friend.

There was a light in the temple, and as we passed, we could hear voices of men chanting hymns. In a native temple, the priests rise at all hours of the night to do honour to their god. Before we could stop him, Fleete dashed up the steps, patted two priests on the back, and was gravely grinding the ashes of his cigar-butt into the forehead of the red stone image of Hanuman. Strickland tried to drag him out, but he sat down and said solemnly: 'Shee that? Mark of the B-beasht! *I* made it. Ishn't it fine?'

In half a minute the temple was alive and noisy, and Strickland, who knew what came of polluting gods, said that things might occur. He, by virtue of his official position, long residence in the country, and weakness for going among the natives, was known to the priests and he felt unhappy. Fleete sat on the ground and refused to move. He said that 'good old Hanuman' made a very soft pillow.

Then, without any warning, a Silver Man came out of a recess behind the image of the god. He was perfectly naked in that bitter, bitter cold, and his body shone like frosted silver, for he was what the Bible calls 'a leper as white as snow'. Also he had no face, because he was a leper of some years' standing and his disease was heavy upon him. We two stooped to haul Fleete up, and the temple was filling and filling with folk who seemed to spring from the earth, when the Silver Man ran in under our arms, making a noise exactly like the mewing of an otter, caught Fleete round the body and dropped his head on Fleete's breast before we could wrench him away. Then he retired to a corner and sat mewing while the crowd blocked all the doors.

The priests were very angry until the Silver Man touched Fleete. That nuzzling seemed to sober them.

At the end of a few minutes' silence one of the priests came to Strickland and said, in perfect English, 'Take your friend away. He has done with Hanuman, but Hanuman has not done with him.' The crowd gave room and we carried Fleete into the road.

Strickland was very angry. He said that we might all three have been knifed, and that Fleete should thank his stars that he had escaped without injury.

Fleete thanked no one. He said that he wanted to go to bed. He was gorgeously drunk.

We moved on, Strickland silent and wrathful, until Fleete was taken with violent shivering fits and sweating. He said that the smells of the bazaar were overpowering, and he wondered why slaughterhouses were permitted so near English residences. 'Can't you smell the blood?' said Fleete.

We put him to bed at last, just as the dawn was

breaking, and Strickland invited me to have another whisky and soda. While we were drinking he talked of the trouble in the temple, and admitted that it baffled him completely. Strickland hates being mystified by natives, because his business in life is to over match them with their own weapons. He has not yet succeeded in doing this, but in fifteen or twenty years he will have made some small progress.

'They should have mauled us,' he said, 'instead of mewing at us. I wonder what they meant. I don't like it one little bit.'

I said that the Managing Committee of the temple would in all probability bring a criminal action against us for insulting their religion. There was a section of the Indian Penal Code which exactly met Fleete's offence. Strickland said he only hoped and prayed that they would do this. Before I left I looked into Fleete's room, and saw him lying on his right side, scratching his left breast. Then, I went to bed cold, depressed, and unhappy, at seven o'clock in the morning.

At one o'clock I rode over to Strickland's house to enquire after Fleete's head. I imagined that it would be a sore one. Fleete was breakfasting and seemed unwell. His temper was gone, for he was abusing the cook for not supplying him with an underdone chop. A man who can eat raw meat after a wet night is a curiosity. I told Fleete this and he laughed.

'You breed queer mosquitoes in these parts,' he said. 'I've been bitten to pieces, but only in one place.'

'Let's have a look at the bite,' said Strickland. 'It may have gone down since this morning.'

While the chops were being cooked, Fleete opened his shirt and showed us, just over his left breast, a mark, the perfect double of the black rosettes – the five or six irregular blotches arranged in a circle – on a leopard's hide. Strickland looked and said, 'It was only pink this morning. It's grown black now.'

Fleete ran to a glass.

'By Jove!' he said, 'this is nasty. What is it?'

We could not answer. Here the chops came in, all red and juicy, and Fleete bolted three in a most offensive manner. He ate on his right grinders only, and threw his head over his right shoulder as he snapped the meat. When he had finished, it struck him that he had been behaving strangely, for he said apologetically, 'I don't think I ever felt so hungry in my life. I've bolted like an ostrich.'

After breakfast Strickland said to me, 'Don't go. Stay here, and stay for the night.'

Seeing that my house was not three miles from Strickland's, this request was absurd. But Strickland insisted, and was going to say something when Fleete interrupted by declaring in a shamefaced way that he felt hungry again. Strickland sent a man to my house to fetch over my bedding and a horse, and we three went down to Strickland's stables to pass the hours until it was time to go out for a ride. The man who has a weakness for horses never wearies of inspecting them; and when two men are killing time in this way they gather knowledge and lies the one from the other.

There were five horses in the stables, and I shall never forget the scene as we tried to look them over. They seemed to have gone mad. They reared and screamed and nearly tore up their pickets; they sweated and shivered and lathered and were distraught with fear. Strickland's horses used to know him as well as his dogs; which made the matter more curious. We left the stable for fear of the brutes throwing themselves in their panic. Then Strickland turned back and called me. The horses were still frightened, but they let us 'gentle' and make much of them, and put their heads in our bosoms.

'They aren't afraid of *us*,' said Strickland. 'D'you know, I'd give three months' pay if Outrage here could talk.'

But Outrage was dumb, and could only cuddle up to his master and blow out his nostrils, as is the custom of horses when they wish to explain things but can't. Fleete came up when we were in the stalls, and as soon as the horses saw him, their fright broke out afresh. It was all that we could do to escape from the place unkicked. Strickland said, 'They don't seem to love you, Fleete.'

'Nonsense,' said Fleete; 'my mare will follow me like a dog.' He went to her; she was in a loosebox; but as he slipped the bars she plunged, knocked him down, and broke away into the garden. I laughed, but Strickland was not amused. He took his moustache in both fists and pulled at it till it nearly came out. Fleete, instead of going off to chase his property, yawned, saying that he felt sleepy. He went to the house to lie down, which was a foolish way of spending New Year's Day.

Strickland sat with me in the stables and asked if I had noticed anything peculiar in Fleete's manner. I said that he ate his food like a beast; but that this might have been the result of living alone in the hills out of the reach of society as refined and elevating as ours for instance. Strickland was not amused. I do not think that he listened to me, for his next sentence referred to the mark on Fleete's breast, and I said that it might have been caused by blister-flies, or that it was possibly a birthmark newly born and now visible for the first time. We both agreed that it was unpleasant to look at, and Strickland found occasion to say that I was a fool.

'I can't tell you what I think now,' said he, 'because you would call me a madman; but you must stay with me for the next few days, if you can. I want you to watch Fleete, but don't tell me what you think till I have made up my mind.'

'But I am dining out tonight,' I said. 'So am I,' said Strickland, 'and so is Fleete. At least if he doesn't change his mind.'

We walked about the garden smoking, but saying nothing – because we were friends, and talking spoils good tobacco – till our pipes were out. Then we went to wake up Fleete. He was wide awake and fidgeting about his room.

'I say, I want some more chops,' he said. 'Can I get them?'

We laughed and said, 'Go and change. The ponies will be round in a minute.'

'All right,' said Fleete. 'I'll go when I get the chops – underdone ones, mind.'

He seemed to be quite in earnest. It was four o'clock, and we had had breakfast at one; still, for a long time, he demanded those underdone chops. Then he changed into riding clothes and went out into the verandah. His pony – the mare had not been caught – would not let him come near. All three horses were unmanageable – mad with fear – and finally Fleete said that he would stay at home and get something to eat. Strickland and I rode out wondering. As we passed the temple of Hanuman, the Silver Man came out and mewed at us.

'He is not one of the regular priests of the temple,' said Strickland. 'I think I should peculiarly like to lay my hands on him.'

There was no spring in our gallop on the racecourse that evening. The horses were stale, and moved as though they had been ridden out.

'The fright after breakfast has been too much for them,' said Strickland.

That was the only remark he made through the remainder of the ride. Once or twice I think he swore to himself; but that did not count.

We came back in the dark at seven o'clock, and saw that there were no lights in the bungalow. 'Careless ruffians my servants are!' said Strickland.

My horse reared at something on the carriage drive, and Fleete stood up under its nose.

'What are you doing, grovelling about the garden?' said Strickland.

But both horses bolted and nearly threw us. We dismounted by the stables and returned to Fleete, who was on his hands and knees under the orange-bushes.

'What the devil's wrong with you?' said Strickland.

'Nothing, nothing in the world,' said Fleete, speaking very quickly and thickly. 'I've been gardening – botanising you know. The smell of the earth is delightful. I think I'm going for a walk – a long walk-all night.'

Then I saw that there was something excessively out of order somewhere, and I said to Strickland, 'I am not dining out.'

'Bless you!' said Strickland. 'Here, Fleete, get up. You'll catch fever there. Come in to dinner and let's have the lamps lit. We'll all dine at home.'

Fleete stood up unwillingly, and said, 'No lamps – no lamps. It's much nicer here. Let's dine outside and have some more chops – lots of 'em and underdone – bloody ones with gristle.'

Now a December evening in Northern India is bitterly cold, and Fleete's suggestion was that of a maniac.

'Come in,' said Strickland sternly. 'Come in at once.'

Fleete came, and when the lamps were brought, we saw that he was literally plastered with dirt from head to foot. He must have been rolling in the garden. He shrank from the light and went to his room. His eyes were horrible to look at. There was a green light behind them, not in them, if you understand, and the man's lower lip hung down.

Strickland said, 'There is going to be trouble – big trouble – tonight. Don't you change your riding-things.'

We waited and waited for Fleete's reappearance, and ordered dinner in the meantime. We could hear him moving about his own room, but there was no light there. Presently from the room came the long-drawn howl of a wolf.

People write and talk lightly of blood running cold and hair standing up and things of that kind. Both sensations are too horrible to be trifled with. My heart stopped as though a knife had been driven through it, and Strickland turned as white as the tablecloth.

The howl was repeated, and was answered by another howl far across the fields.

That set the gilded roof on the horror. Strickland dashed into Fleete's room. I followed, and we saw Fleete getting out of the window. He made beast-noises in the back of his throat. He could not answer us when we shouted at him. He spat.

I don't quite remember what followed, but I think that Strickland must have stunned him with the long boot-jack or else I should never have been able to sit on his chest. Fleete could not speak, he could only snarl, and his snarls were those of a wolf, not of a man. The human spirit must have been giving way all day and have died out with the twilight. We were dealing with a beast that had once been Fleete.

The affair was beyond any human and rational experience. I tried to say 'Hydrophobia', but the word wouldn't come, because I knew that I was lying.

We bound this beast with leather thongs of the punkah-rope, and tied its thumbs and big toes together, and gagged it with a shoehorn, which makes a very efficient gag if you know how to arrange it. Then we carried it into the dining-room, and sent a man to Dumoise, the doctor, telling him to come over at once. After we had despatched the messenger and were drawing breath, Strickland said, 'It's no good. This isn't any doctor's work.' I, also, knew that he spoke the truth.

The beast's head was free, and it threw it about from side to side. Any one entering the room would have believed that we were curing a wolf's pelt. That was the most loathsome accessory of all.

Strickland sat with his chin in the heel of his fist, watching the beast as it wriggled on the ground, but saying nothing. The shirt had been torn open in the scuffle and showed the black rosette mark on the left breast. It stood out like a blister.

In the silence of the watching we heard something without mewing like a she-otter. We both rose to our feet, and, I answer for myself, not Strickland, felt sick – actually and physically sick. We told each other, as did the men in *Pinafore*, that it was the cat.

Dumoise arrived, and I never saw a little man so unprofessionally shocked. He said that it was a heart-rending case of hydrophobia, and that nothing could be done. At least any palliative measures would only prolong the agony. The beast was foaming at the mouth. Fleete, as we told Dumoise, had been bitten by dogs once or twice. Any man who keeps half a dozen terriers must expect a nip now and again. Dumoise could offer no help. He could only certify that Fleete was dying of hydrophobia. The beast was then howling, for it had managed to spit out the shoehorn. Dumoise said that he would be ready to certify to the cause of death, and that the end was certain. He was a good little man, and he offered to remain with us; but Strickland refused the kindness. He did not wish to poison Dumoise's New Year. He would only ask him not to give the real cause of Fleete's death to the public.

So Dumoise left, deeply agitated; and as soon as the noise of the cart-wheels had died away, Strickland told me, in a whisper, his suspicions. They were so wildly improbable that he dared not say them out aloud; and I, who entertained all Strickland's beliefs, was so ashamed of owning to them that I pretended to disbelieve.

'Even if the Silver Man had bewitched Fleete for polluting the image of Hanuman, the punishment could not have fallen so quickly.'

As I was whispering this the cry outside the house rose again, and the beast fell into a fresh paroxysm of struggling till we were afraid that the thongs that held it would give way.

'Watch!' said Strickland. 'If this happens six times I shall take the law into my own hands. I order you to help me.'

He went into his room and came out in a few minutes with the barrels of an old shotgun, a piece of fishing-line, some thick cord, and his heavy wooden bedstead. I reported that the convulsions had followed the cry by two seconds in each case, and the beast seemed perceptibly weaker.

Strickland muttered, 'But he can't take away the life! He can't take away the life!'

I said, though I knew that I was arguing against myself, 'It may be a cat. It must be a cat. If the Silver Man is responsible, why does he dare to come here?'

Strickland arranged the wood on the hearth, put the gun-barrels into the glow of the fire, spread the twine on the table and broke a walking stick in two. There was one yard of fishing-line, gut, lapped with wire, such as is used for mahseer-fishing, and he tied the two ends together in a loop.

Then he said, 'How can we catch him? He must be taken alive and unhurt.'

I said that we must trust in Providence, and go out softly with polo-sticks into the shrubbery at the front of the house. The man or animal that made the cry was evidently moving round the house as regularly as a night-watchman. We could wait in the bushes till he came by and knock him over.

Strickland accepted this suggestion, and we slipped out from a bathroom window into the front verandah and then across the carriage drive into the bushes.

In the moonlight we could see the leper coming round the corner of the house. He was perfectly naked, and from time to time he mewed and stopped to dance with his shadow. It was an unattractive sight, and thinking of poor Fleete, brought to such degradation by so foul a creature, I put away all my doubts and resolved to help Strickland from the heated gun-barrels to the loop of twine – from the loins to the head and back again – with all tortures that might be needful.

The leper halted in the front porch for a moment and we jumped out on him with the sticks. He was wonderfully strong, and we were afraid that he might escape or be fatally injured before we caught him. We had an idea that lepers were frail creatures, but this proved to be incorrect. Strickland knocked his legs from under him and I put my foot on his neck. He mewed hideously, and even through my riding-boots I could feel that his flesh was not the flesh of a clean man.

He struck at us with his hand and feet-stumps. We looped the lash of a dog-whip round him, under the armpits, and dragged him backwards into the hall and so into the dining-room where the beast lay. There we tied him with trunk-straps. He made no attempt to escape, but mewed.

When we confronted him with the beast the scene was beyond description. The beast doubled backwards into a bow as though he had been poisoned with strychnine, and moaned in the most pitiable fashion. Several other things happened also, but they cannot be put down here.

'I think I was right,' said Strickland. 'Now we will ask him to cure this case.'

But the leper only mewed. Strickland wrapped a towel round his hand and took the gun-barrels out of the fire. I put the half of the broken walking stick through the loop of fishing-line and buckled the leper comfortably to Strickland's bedstead. I understood then how men and women and little children can endure to see a witch burnt alive; for the beast was moaning on the floor, and though the Silver Man had no face, you could see horrible feelings passing through the slab that took its place, exactly as waves of heat play across red-hot iron – gun-barrels for instance.

Strickland shaded his eyes with his hands for a moment and we got to work. This part is not to be printed.

The dawn was beginning to break when the leper spoke. His mewings had not been satisfactory up to that point. The beast had fainted from exhaustion and the house was very still. We unstrapped the leper and told him to take away the evil spirit. He crawled to the beast and laid his hand upon the left breast. That was all. Then he fell face down and whined, drawing in his breath as he did so.

We watched the face of the beast, and saw the soul of Fleete coming back into the eyes. Then a sweat broke out on the forehead and the eyes – they were human eyes – closed. We waited for an hour but Fleete still slept. We carried him to his room and bade the leper go, giving him the bedstead, and the sheet on the bedstead to cover his nakedness, the gloves and the towels with which we had touched him, and the whip that had been hooked round his body. He put the sheet about him and went out into the early morning without speaking or mewing.

Strickland wiped his face and sat down. A night-gong, far away in the city, made seven o'clock.

'Exactly four-and-twenty hours!' said Strickland.

'And I've done enough to ensure my dismissal from the service, besides permanent quarters in a lunatic asylum. Do you believe that we are awake?'

The red-hot gun-barrel had fallen on the floor and was singeing the carpet. The smell was entirely real.

That morning at eleven we two together went to wake up Fleete. We looked and saw that the black leopard-rosette on his chest had disappeared. He was very drowsy and tired, but as soon as he saw us, he said, 'Oh! Confound you fellows. Happy New Year to you. Never mix your liquors. I'm nearly dead.'

'Thanks for your kindness, but you're over time,' said Strickland. 'Today is the morning of the second. You've slept the clock round with a vengeance.'

The door opened, and little Dumoise put his head in. He had come on foot, and fancied that we were laying out Fleete.

'I've brought a nurse,' said Dumoise. 'I suppose that she can come in for . . . what is necessary.'

'By all means,' said Fleete cheerily, sitting up in bed. 'Bring on your nurses.'

Dumoise was dumb. Strickland led him out and explained that there must have been a mistake in the diagnosis. Dumoise remained dumb and left the house hastily. He considered that his professional reputation had been injured, and was inclined to make a personal matter of the recovery. Strickland went out too. When he came back, he said that he had been to call on the Temple of Hanuman to offer redress for the pollution of the god, and had been solemnly assured that no white man had ever touched the idol and that he was an incarnation of all the virtues labouring under a delusion.

'What do you think?' said Strickland.

I said, ' "There are more things . . . " '

But Strickland hates that quotation. He says that I have worn it threadbare.

One other curious thing happened which frightened me as much as anything in all the night's work. When Fleete was dressed he came into the dining-room and sniffed. He had a quaint trick of moving his nose when he sniffed. 'Horrid doggy smell, here,' said he. 'You should really keep those terriers of yours in better order. Try sulphur, Strick.'

But Strickland did not answer. He caught hold of the back of a chair, and, without warning, went into an amazing fit of hysterics. It is terrible to see a strong man overtaken with hysteria. Then it struck me that we had fought for Fleete's soul with the Silver Man in that room, and had disgraced ourselves as Englishmen for ever, and I laughed and gasped and gurgled just as shamefully as Strickland, while Fleete thought that we had both gone mad. We never told him what we had done.

Some years later, when Strickland had married and was a church-going member of society for his wife's sake, we reviewed the incident dispassionately, and Strickland suggested that I should put it before the public.

I cannot myself see that this step is likely to clear up the mystery; because, in the first place, no one will believe a rather unpleasant story, and, in the second, it is well known to every right-minded man that the gods of the heathen are stone and brass, and any attempt to deal with them otherwise is justly condemned.

The Undying Thing

BARRY PAIN

I

Up and down the oak-panelled dining-hall of Mansteth the master of the house walked restlessly. At formal intervals down the long severe table were placed four silver candlesticks, but the light from these did not serve to illuminate the whole of the surroundings. It just touched the portrait of a fair-haired boy with a sad and wistful expression that hung at one end of the room; it sparkled on the lid of a silver tankard. As Sir Edric passed to and fro it lit up his face and figure. It was a bold and resolute face with a firm chin and passionate, dominant eyes. A bad past was written in the lines of it. And yet every now and then there came over it a strange look of very anxious gentleness that gave it some resemblance to the portrait of the fair-haired boy. Sir Edric paused a moment before the portrait and surveyed it carefully, his strong brown hands locked behind him, his gigantic shoulders thrust a little forward.

'Ah, what I was!' he murmured to himself – 'what I was!'

Once more he commenced pacing up and down. The candles, mirrored in the polished wood of the table, had burnt low. For hours Sir Edric had been waiting, listening intently for some sound from the room above or from the broad staircase outside. There had been sounds – the wailing of a woman, a quick abrupt voice, the moving of rapid feet. But for the last hour he had heard nothing. Quite suddenly he stopped and dropped on his knees against the table: 'God, I have never thought of Thee. Thou knowest that – Thou knowest that by my devilish behaviour and cruelty I did veritably murder Alice, my first wife, albeit the physicians did maintain that she died of a decline – a wasting sickness. Thou knowest that all here in Mansteth do hate me, and that rightly. They say, too, that I am mad; but that they say not rightly, seeing that I know how wicked I am. I always knew it, but I never cared until I loved – Oh, God, I never cared!'

His fierce eyes opened for a minute, glared round the room, and closed again tightly. He went on: 'God, for myself I ask nothing; I make no bargaining with Thee. Whatsoever punishment Thou givest me to bear I will bear it; whatsoever Thou givest me to do I will do it. Whether Thou killest Eve or whether Thou keepest her in life – and never have I loved but her – I will from this night be good. In due penitence will I receive the holy Sacrament of Thy Body and Blood. And my son, the one child that I had by Alice, I will fetch back again from Challonsea, where I kept him in order that I might not look upon him, and I will be to him a father in deed and very truth. And in all things, so far as in me lieth, I will make restitution and atonement. Whether Thou hearest me or whether Thou hearest me not, these things shall be. And for my prayer, it is but this: of Thy loving-kindness, most merciful God, be Thou with Eve and make her happy;

and after these great pains and perils of childbirth send her Thy peace. Of Thy loving-kindness, Thy merciful loving-kindness, O God!'

Perhaps the prayer that is offered when the time for praying is over is more terribly pathetic than any other. Yet one might hesitate to say that this prayer was unanswered.

Sir Edric rose to his feet. Once more he paced the room. There was a strange simplicity about him, the simplicity that scorns an incongruity. He felt that his lips and throat were parched and dry. He lifted the heavy silver tankard from the table and raised the lid; there was still a good draught of mulled wine in it with the burnt toast, cut heart-shaped, floating on the top.

'To the health of Eve and her child,' he said aloud, and drained it to the last drop.

Click, click! As he put the tankard down he heard distinctly two doors opened and shut quickly, one after the other. And then slowly down the stairs came a hesitating step. Sir Edric could bear the suspense no longer. He opened the dining-room door, and the dim light strayed out into the dark hall beyond.

'Dennison,' he said, in a low, sharp whisper, 'is that you?'

'Yes, yes. I am coming, Sir Edric.'

A moment afterwards Dr Dennison entered the room. He was very pale; perspiration streamed from his forehead; his cravat was disarranged. He was an old man, thin, with the air of proud humility. Sir Edric watched him narrowly.

'Then she is dead,' he said, with a quiet that Dr Dennison had not expected.

'Twenty physicians – a hundred physicians could

not have saved her, Sir Edric. She was . . . ' He gave some details of medical interest.

'Dennison,' said Sir Edric, still speaking with calm and restraint, 'why do you seem thus indisposed and panic-stricken? You are a physician; have you never looked upon the face of death before? The soul of my wife is with God – '

'Yes,' murmured Dennison, 'a good woman, a perfect, saintly woman.'

'And,' Sir Edric went on, raising his eyes to the ceiling as though he could see through it, 'her body lies in great dignity and beauty upon the bed, and there is no horror in it. Why are you afraid?'

'I do not fear death, Sir Edric.'

'But your hands – they are not steady. You are evidently overcome. Does the child live?'

'Yes, it lives.'

'Another boy – a brother for young Edric, the child that Alice bore me?'

'There – there is something wrong. I do not know what to do. I want you to come upstairs. And, Sir Edric, I must tell you, you will need your self-command.'

'Dennison, the hand of God is heavy upon me; but from this time forth until the day of my death I am submissive to it, and God send that that day may come quickly! I will follow you and I will endure.'

He took one of the high silver candlesticks from the table and stepped towards the door. He strode quickly up the staircase, Dr Dennison following a little way behind him.

As Sir Edric waited at the top of the staircase he heard suddenly from the room before him a low cry. He put down the candlestick on the floor and leaned back against the wall listening. The cry came again, a vibrating monotone ending in a growl.

'Dennison, Dennison!'

His voice choked; he could not go on.

'Yes,' said the doctor, 'it is in there. I had the two women out of the room, and got it here. No one but myself has seen it. But you must see it, too.'

He raised the candle and the two men entered the room – one of the spare bedrooms. On the bed there was something moving under cover of a blanket. Dr Dennison paused for a moment and then flung the blanket partially back.

They did not remain in the room for more than a few seconds. The moment they got outside, Dr Dennison began to speak.

'Sir Edric, I would fain suggest somewhat to you. There is no evil, as Sophocles hath it in his *Antigone*, for which man hath not found a remedy, except it be death, and here – '

Sir Edric interrupted him in a husky voice.

'Downstairs, Dennison. This is too near.'

It was, indeed, passing strange. When once the novelty of this – this occurrence had worn off, Dr Dennison seemed no longer frightened. He was calm, academic, interested in an unusual phenomenon. But Sir Edric, who was said in the village to fear nothing in earth or heaven, or hell, was obviously much moved.

When they had got back to the dining-room, Sir Edric motioned the doctor to a seat.

'Now, then,' he said, 'I will hear you. Something must be done – and tonight.'

'Exceptional cases,' said Dr Dennison, 'demand

exceptional remedies. Well, it lies there upstairs and is at our mercy. We can let it live or, placing one hand over the mouth and nostrils, we can – '

'Stop,' said Sir Edric. 'This thing has so crushed and humiliated me that I can scarcely think. But I recall that while I waited for you I fell upon my knees and prayed that God would save Eve. And as I confessed unto Him more than I will ever confess unto man, it seemed to me that it were ignoble to offer a price for His favour. And I said that whatsoever punishment I had to bear, I would bear it; and whatsoever He called upon me to do, I would do it; and I made no conditions.'

'Well?'

'Now my punishment is of two kinds. Firstly my wife, Eve, is dead. And this I bear more easily because I know that she is numbered with the company of God's saints, and with them her pure spirit finds happier communion than with me; I was not worthy of her. And yet she would call my roughness by gentle, pretty names. She gloried, Dennison, in the mere strength of my body, and in the greatness of my stature. And I am thankful that she never saw this – this shame that has come upon the house. For she was a proud woman, with all her gentleness, even as I was proud and bad until it pleased God this night to break me even to the dust. And for my second punishment, that, too, I must bear. This thing that lies upstairs, I will take and rear; it is bone of my bone and flesh of my flesh; only, if it be possible, I will hide my shame so that no man but you shall know of it.'

'This is not possible. You cannot keep a living being in this house unless it be known. Will not these women say, "Where is the child?" '

Sir Edric stood upright, his powerful hands linked before him, his face working in agony; but he was still resolute.

'Then if it must be known, it shall be known. The fault is mine. If I had but done sooner what Eve asked, this would not have happened. I will bear it.'

'Sir Edric, do not be angry with me, for if I did not say this, then I should be but an ill counsellor. And, firstly, do not use the word shame. The ways of nature are past all explaining; if a woman be frail and easily impressed, and other circumstances concur, then in some few rare cases a thing of this sort does happen. If there be shame, it is not upon you but upon nature – to whom one would not lightly impute shame. Yet it is true that common and uninformed people might think that this shame was yours. And herein lies the great trouble – the shame would rest also on her memory.'

'Then,' said Sir Edric, in a low, unfaltering voice, 'this night for the sake of Eve I will break my word, and lose my own soul eternally.'

About an hour afterwards Sir Edric and Dr Dennison left the house together. The doctor carried a stable lantern in his hand. Sir Edric bore in his arms something wrapped in a blanket. They went through the long garden, out into the orchard that skirts the north side of the park, and then across a field to a small dark plantation known as Hal's Planting. In the very heart of Hal's Planting there are some curious caves: access to the innermost chamber of them is exceedingly difficult and dangerous, and only possible to a climber of exceptional skill and courage. As they returned from these caves, Sir Edric no longer carried his burden. The dawn was breaking and the birds began to sing.

'Could not they be quiet just for this morning?' said Sir Edric wearily.

There were but few people who were asked to attend the funeral of Lady Vanquerest and of the baby which, it was said, had only survived her by a few hours. There were but three people who knew that only one body – the body of Lady Vanquerest – was really interred on that occasion. These three were Sir Edric Vanquerest, Dr Dennison, and a nurse whom it had been found expedient to take into their confidence.

During the next six years Sir Edric lived, almost in solitude, a life of great sanctity, devoting much of his time to the education of the younger Edric, the child that he had by his first wife. In the course of this time some strange stories began to be told and believed in the neighbourhood with reference to Hal's Planting, and the place was generally avoided.

When Sir Edric lay on his deathbed the windows of the chamber were open, and suddenly through them came a low cry. The doctor in attendance hardly regarded it, supposing that it came from one of the owls in the trees outside. But Sir Edric, at the sound of it, rose right up in bed before anyone could stay him, and flinging up his arms cried, 'Wolves! wolves! wolves!' Then he fell forward on his face, dead.

And four generations passed away.

2

Towards the latter end of the nineteenth century, John Marsh, who was the oldest man in the village of Mansteth, could be prevailed upon to state what he recollected. His two sons supported him in his old age; he never felt the pinch of poverty, and he always had money in his pocket; but it was a settled principle with him that he would not pay for the pint of beer which he drank occasionally in the parlour of The Stag. Sometimes Farmer Wynthwaite paid for the beer; sometimes it was Mr Spicer from the post office; sometimes the landlord of The Stag himself would finance the old man's evening dissipation. In return, John Marsh was prevailed upon to state what he recollected; this he would do with great heartiness and strict impartiality, recalling the intemperance of a former Wynthwaite and the dishonesty of some ancestral Spicer, while he drank the beer of their direct descendants. He would tell you, with two tough old fingers crooked round the handle of the pewter that you had provided, how your grandfather was a poor thing, 'fit for nowt but to breok stones by ta roadside'. He was so disrespectful that it was believed that he spoke truth. He was particularly disrespectful when he spoke of that most devilish family, the Vanquerests; and he never tired of recounting the stories that from generation to generation had grown up about them. It would be objected, sometimes, that the present Sir Edric, the last surviving member of the race, was a pleasant-spoken young man, with none of the family wildness and hot temper. It was for no sin of his that Hal's Planting was haunted – a thing which everyone in Mansteth, and many beyond it, most devoutly believed. John Marsh would hear no apology for him, nor for any of his ancestors; he recounted the prophecy that an old mad woman had made of the family before her strange death, and hoped, fervently, that he might live to see it fulfilled.

The third baronet, as has already been told, had

lived the latter part of his life, after his second wife's death, in peace and quietness. Of him John Marsh remembered nothing, of course, and could only recall the few fragments of information that had been handed down to him. He had been told that this Sir Edric, who had travelled a good deal, at one time kept wolves, intending to train them to serve as dogs; these wolves were not kept under proper restraint, and became a kind of terror to the neighbourhood. Lady Vanquerest, his second wife, had asked him frequently to destroy these beasts, but Sir Edric, although it was said that he loved his second wife even more than he hated the first, was obstinate when any of his whims were crossed, and put her off with promises. Then one day Lady Vanquerest herself was attacked by the wolves; she was not bitten, but she was badly frightened. That filled Sir Edric with remorse, and, when it was too late, he went out into the yard where the wolves were kept and shot them all. A few months afterwards Lady Vanquerest died in childbirth. It was a queer thing, John Marsh noted, that it was just at this time that Hal's Planting began to get such a bad name. The fourth baronet was, John Marsh considered, the worst of the race; it was to him that the old mad woman had made her prophecy, an incident that Marsh himself had witnessed in his childhood and still vividly remembered.

The baronet, in his old age, had been cast up by his vices on the shores of melancholy; heavy-eyed, grey-haired, bent, he seemed to pass through life as in a dream. Every day he would go out on horseback, always at a walking pace, as though he were following the funeral of his past self. One night he was riding up the village street as this old woman came down it. Her name was Ann Ruthers; she had a kind of reputation in the village, and although all said that she was mad, many of her utterances were remembered, and she was treated with respect. It was growing dark, and the village street was almost empty; but just at the lower end was the usual group of men by the door of The Stag, dimly illuminated by the light that came through the quaint windows of the old inn. They glanced at Sir Edric as he rode slowly past them, taking no notice of their respectful salutes. At the upper end of the street there were two persons. One was Ann Ruthers, a tall, gaunt old woman, her head wrapped in a shawl; the other was John Marsh. He was then a boy of eight, and he was feeling somewhat frightened. He had been on an expedition to a distant and foetid pond, and in the black mud and clay about its borders he had discovered live newts; he had three of them in his pocket, and this was to some extent a joy to him, but his joy was damped by his knowledge that he was coming home much too late, and would probably be chastised in consequence. He was unable to walk fast or to run, because Ann Ruthers was immediately in front of him, and he dared not pass her, especially at night. She walked on until she met Sir Edric, and then, standing still, she called him by name. He pulled in his horse and raised his heavy eyes to look at her. Then in loud clear tones she spoke to him, and John Marsh heard and remembered every word that she said; it was her prophecy of the end of the Vanquerests. Sir Edric never answered a word. When she had finished, he rode on, while she remained standing there, her eyes fixed on the stars above her. John Marsh dared not pass the mad woman; he turned round and walked back, keeping close to Sir Edric's horse. Quite suddenly, without a word of warning, as if in a moment of ungovernable irritation, Sir Edric wheeled his horse round and struck the boy across the face with his switch.

On the following morning John Marsh – or rather, his parents – received a handsome solatium in coin of the realm; but sixty-five years afterwards he had not forgiven that blow, and still spoke of the Vanquerests as a most devilish family, still hoped and prayed that he might see the prophecy fulfilled. He would relate, too, the death of Ann Ruthers, which occurred either later on the night of her prophecy or early on the following day. She would often roam about the country all night, and on this particular night she left the main road to wander over the Vanquerest lands, where trespassers, especially at night, were not welcomed. But no one saw her, and it seemed that she had made her way to a part where no one was likely to see her; for none of the keepers would have entered Hal's Planting by night. Her body was found there at noon on the following day, lying under the tall bracken, dead, but without any mark of violence upon it. It was considered that she had died in a fit. This naturally added to the ill-repute of Hal's Planting. The woman's death caused considerable sensation in the village. Sir Edric sent a messenger to the married sister with whom she had lived, saying that he wished to pay all the funeral expenses. This offer, as John Marsh recalled with satisfaction, was refused.

Of the last two baronets he had but little to tell. The fifth baronet was credited with the family temper, but he conducted himself in a perfectly conventional way, and did not seem in the least to belong to romance.

He was a good man of business, and devoted himself to making up, as far as he could, for the very extravagant expenditure of his predecessors. His son, the present Sir Edric, was a fine young fellow and popular in the village. Even John Marsh could find nothing to say against him; other people in the village were interested in him. It was said that he had chosen a wife in London – a Miss Guerdon – and would shortly be back to see that Mansteth Hall was put in proper order for her before his marriage at the close of the season. Modernity kills ghostly romance. It was difficult to associate this modern and handsome Sir Edric, bright and spirited, a good sportsman and a good fellow, with the doom that had been foretold for the Vanquerest family. He himself knew the tradition and laughed at it. He wore clothes made by a London tailor, looked healthy, smiled cheerfully, and, in a vain attempt to shame his own head keeper, had himself spent a night alone in Hal's Planting. This last was used by Mr Spicer in argument, who would ask John Marsh what he made of it. John Marsh replied, contemptuously, that it was 'nowt'. It was not so that the Vanquerest family was to end; but when the thing, whatever it was, that lived in Hal's Planting, left it and came up to the house, to Mansteth Hall itself, then one would see the end of the Vanquerests. So Ann Ruthers had prophesied. Sometimes Mr Spicer would ask the pertinent question, how did John Marsh know that there really was anything in Hal's Planting? This he asked, less because he disbelieved, than because he wished to draw forth an account of John's personal experiences. These were given in great detail, but they did not amount to very much. One night John Marsh had been taken by business – Sir Edric's keepers would have called the business by hard names – into the neighbourhood of Hal's Planting. He had been suddenly startled by a cry, and had run away as though he were running for his life. That was all he could tell about the cry – it was the kind of cry to make a man lose his head and run. And then it always happened that John Marsh was urged by his companions to enter Hal's Planting himself, and discover what was there. John pursed his thin lips together, and hinted that that also might be done one of these days. Whereupon Mr Spicer looked across his pipe to Farmer Wynthwaite, and smiled significantly.

Shortly before Sir Edric's return from London, the attention of Mansteth was once more directed to Hal's Planting, but not by any supernatural occurrence. Quite suddenly, on a calm day, two trees there fell with a crash; there were caves in the centre of the plantation, and it seemed as if the roof of some big chamber in these caves had given way.

They talked it over one night in the parlour of the Stag. There was water in these caves, Farmer Wynthwaite knew it; and he expected a further subsidence. If the whole thing collapsed, what then?

'Ay,' said John Marsh. He rose from his chair, and pointed in the direction of the Hall with his thumb. 'What then?'

He walked across to the fire, looked at it meditatively for a moment, and then spat in it.

'A trewly wun'ful owd mon,' said Farmer Wynthwaite as he watched him.

3

In the smoking-room at Mansteth Hall sat Sir Edric with his friend and intended brother-in-law, Dr Andrew Guerdon. Both men were on the verge of middle-age; there was hardly a year's difference between them. Yet Guerdon looked much the older man; that was, perhaps, because he wore a short, black beard, while Sir Edric was clean shaven. Guerdon was thought to be an enviable man. His father had made a fortune in the firm of Guerdon, Guerdon, and Bird; the old style was still retained at the bank, although there was no longer a Guerdon in the firm. Andrew Guerdon had a handsome allowance from his father, and had also inherited money through his mother. He had taken the degree of Doctor of Medicine; he did not practise, but he was still interested in science, especially in out-of-the-way science. He was unmarried, gifted with perpetually good health, interested in life, popular. His friendship with Sir Edric dated from their college days. It had for some years been almost certain that Sir Edric would marry his friend's sister, Ray Guerdon, although the actual betrothal had only been announced that season.

On a bureau in one corner of the room were spread a couple of plans and various slips of paper. Sir Edric was wrinkling his brows over them, dropping cigar-ash over them, and finally getting angry over them. He pushed back his chair irritably, and turned towards Guerdon.

'Look here, old man!' he said. 'I desire to curse the original architect of this house – to curse him in his down-sitting and his uprising.'

'Seeing that the original architect has gone to where beyond these voices there is peace, he won't be offended. Neither shall I. But why worry yourself? You've been rooted to that blessed bureau all day, and now, after dinner, when every self-respecting man chucks business, you return to it again – even as a sow returns to her wallowing in the mire.'

'Now, my good Andrew, do be reasonable. How on earth can I bring Ray to such a place as this? And it's built with such ingrained malice and vexatiousness that one can't live in it as it is, and can't alter it without having the whole shanty tumble down about one's ears. Look at this plan now. That thing's what they're pleased to call a morning-room. If the window had been *here* there would have been an uninterrupted view of open country. So what does this forsaken fool of an architect do? He sticks it *there*, where you see it on the plan, looking straight on to a blank wall with a stable yard on the other side of it. But that's a trifle. Look here again – '

'I won't look any more. This place is all right. It was good enough for your father and mother and several generations before them until you arose to improve the world; it was good enough for you until you started to get married. It's a picturesque place, and if you begin to alter it you'll spoil it.' Guerdon looked round the room critically. 'Upon my word,' he said, 'I don't know of any house where I like the smoking-room as well as I like this. It's not too big, and yet it's fairly lofty; it's got those comfortable-looking oak-panelled walls. That's the right kind of fireplace, too, and these corner cupboards are handy.'

'Of course this won't *remain* the smoking-room. It has the morning sun, and Ray likes that, so I shall make it into her boudoir. It *is* a nice room, as you say.'

'That's it, Ted, my boy,' said Guerdon bitterly; 'take a room which is designed by nature and art to be a smoking-room and turn it into a boudoir. Turn it into the very deuce of a boudoir with the morning sun laid on for ever and ever. Waste the twelfth of August by getting married on it. Spend the winter in foreign parts, and write letters that you can breakfast out of doors, just as if you'd created the mildness of the climate yourself. Come back in the spring and spend the London season in the country in order to avoid seeing anybody who wants to see you. That's the way to do it; that's the way to get yourself generally loved and admired!'

'That's chiefly imagination,' said Sir Edric. 'I'm blest if I can see why I should not make this house fit for Ray to live in.'

'It's a queer thing: Ray was a good girl, and you weren't a bad sort yourself. You prepare to go into partnership, and you both straightaway turn into despicable lunatics. I'll have a word or two with Ray. But I'm serious about this house. Don't go tinkering with it; it's got a character of its own, and you'd better leave it. Turn half Tottenham Court Road and the culture thereof – Heaven help it! – into your town house if you like, but leave this alone.'

'Haven't got a town house – yet. Anyway I'm not going to be unsuitable; I'm not going to feel myself at the mercy of a big firm. I shall supervise the whole thing myself. I shall drive over to Challonsea tomorrow afternoon and see if I can't find some intelligent and fairly conscientious workmen.'

'That's all right; you supervise them and I'll supervise

you. You'll be much too new if I don't look after you. You've got an old legend, I believe, that the family's coming to a bad end; you must be consistent with it. As you are bad, be beautiful. By the way, what do you yourself think of the legend?'

'It's nothing,' said Sir Edric, speaking, however, rather seriously. 'They say that Hal's Planting is haunted by something that will not die. Certainly an old woman, who for some godless reason of her own made her way there by night, was found there dead on the following morning; but her death could be, and was, accounted for by natural causes. Certainly, too, I haven't a man in my employ who'll go there by night now.'

'Why not?'

'How should I know? I fancy that a few of the villagers sit boozing at The Stag in the evening, and like to scare themselves by swopping lies about Hal's Planting. I've done my best to stop it. I once, as you know, took a rug, a revolver and a flask of whisky and spent the night there myself. But even that didn't convince them.'

'Yes, you told me. By the way, did you hear or see anything?'

Sir Edric hesitated before he answered. Finally he said: 'Look here, old man, I wouldn't tell this to anyone but yourself. I did think that I heard something. About the middle of the night I was awakened by a cry; I can only say that it was the kind of cry that frightened me. I sat up, and at that moment I heard some great, heavy thing go swishing through the bracken behind me at a great rate. Then all was still; I looked about, but I could find nothing. At last I argued as I would argue now that a man who is just awake is only half awake, and that his powers of observation, by hearing or any other sense, are not to be trusted. I even persuaded myself to go to sleep again, and there was no more disturbance. However, there's a real danger there now. In the heart of the plantation there are some caves and a subterranean spring; lately there has been some slight subsidence there, and the same sort of thing will happen again in all probability. I wired today to an expert to come and look at the place; he has replied that he will come on Monday. The legend says that when the thing that lives in Hal's Planting comes up to the Hall, the Vanquerests will be ended. If I cut down the trees and then break up the place with a charge of dynamite I shouldn't wonder if I spoiled that legend.'

Guerdon smiled.

'I'm inclined to agree with you all through. It's absurd to trust the immediate impressions of a man just awakened; what you heard was probably a stray cow.'

'No cow,' said Sir Edric impartially. 'There's a low wall all round the place – not much of a wall, but too much for a cow.'

'Well, something else – some equally obvious explanation. In dealing with such questions, never forget that you're in the nineteenth century. By the way, your man's coming on Monday. That reminds me today's Friday, and as an indisputable consequence tomorrow's Saturday, therefore, if you want to find your intelligent workmen it will be of no use to go in the afternoon.'

'True,' said Sir Edric, 'I'll go in the morning.' He walked to a tray on a side table and poured a little whisky into a tumbler. 'They don't seem to have brought any seltzer water,' he remarked in a grumbling voice.

He rang the bell impatiently.

'Now why don't you use those corner cupboards for that kind of thing? If you kept a supply there, it would be handy in case of accidents.'

'They're full up already.'

He opened one of them and showed that it was filled with old account books and yellow documents tied up in bundles. The servant entered.

'Oh, I say, there isn't any seltzer. Bring it, please.'

He turned again to Guerdon.

'You might do me a favour when I'm away tomorrow, if there's nothing else that you want to do. I wish you'd look through all these papers for me. They're all old. Possibly some of them ought to go to my solicitor, and I know that a lot of them ought to be destroyed. Some few may be of family interest. It's not the kind of thing that I could ask a stranger or a servant to do for me, and I've so much on hand just now before my marriage – '

'But of course, my dear fellow, I'll do it with pleasure.'

'I'm ashamed to give you all this bother. However, you said that you were coming here to help me, and I take you at your word. By the way, I think you'd better not say anything to Ray about the Hal's Planting story.'

'I may be some of the things that you take me for, but really I am not a common ass. Of course I shouldn't tell her.'

'I'll tell her myself, and I'd sooner do it when I've got the whole thing cleared up. Well, I'm really obliged to you.'

'I needn't remind you that I hope to receive as much again. I believe in compensation. Nature always gives it and always requires it. One finds it everywhere, in philology and onwards.'

'I could mention omissions.'

'They are few, and make a belief in a hereafter to supply them logical.'

'Lunatics, for instance?'

'Their delusions are often their compensation. They argue correctly from false premises. A lunatic believing himself to be a millionaire has as much delight as money can give.'

'How about deformities or monstrosities?'

'The principle is there, although I don't pretend that the compensation is always adequate. A man who is deprived of one sense generally has another developed with unusual acuteness. As for monstrosities of at all a human type one sees none; the things exhibited in fairs are, almost without exception, frauds. They occur rarely, and one does not know enough about them. A really good textbook on the subject would be interesting. Still, such stories as I have heard would bear out my theory – stories of their superhuman strength and cunning, and of the extraordinary prolongation of life that has been noted, or is said to have been noted, in them. But it is hardly fair to test my principle by exceptional cases. Besides, anyone can prove anything except that anything's worth proving.'

'That's a cheerful thing to say. I wouldn't like to swear that I could prove how the Hal's Planting legend started; but I fancy, do you know, that I could make a very good shot at it.'

'Well?'

'My great-grandfather kept wolves – I can't say why. Do you remember the portrait of him? – not the one when he was a boy, the other. It hangs on the staircase. There's now a group of wolves in one corner of the picture. I was looking carefully at the picture one day and thought that I detected some over-painting in that corner; indeed, it was done so roughly that a child would have noticed it if the picture had been hung in a better light. I had the over-painting removed by a good man, and underneath there was a group of wolves depicted. Well, one of these wolves must have escaped, got into Hal's Planting, and scared an old woman or two; that would start a story, and human mendacity would do the rest.'

'Yes,' said Guerdon meditatively, 'that doesn't sound improbable. But why did your great-grandfather have the wolves painted out?'

4

Saturday morning was fine, but very hot and sultry. After breakfast, when Sir Edric had driven off to Challonsea, Andrew Guerdon settled himself in a comfortable chair in the smoking-room. The contents of the corner cupboard were piled up on a table by his side. He lit his pipe and began to go through the papers and put them in order. He had been at work about a quarter of an hour when the butler entered rather abruptly, looking pale and disturbed.

'In Sir Edric's absence, sir, it was thought that I had better come to you for advice. There's been an awful thing happened.'

'Well?'

'They've found a corpse in Hal's Planting about half an hour ago. It's the body of an old man, John Marsh, who used to live in the village. He seems to have died in some kind of a fit. They were bringing it here, but I had it taken down to the village where his cottage is. Then I sent for the police and a doctor.'

There was a moment or two's silence before Guerdon answered.

'This is a terrible thing. I don't know of anything else that you could do. Stop; if the police want to see the spot where the body was found, I think that Sir Edric would like them to have every facility.'

'Quite so, sir.'

'And no one else must be allowed there.'

'No, sir. Thank you.'

The butler withdrew.

Guerdon arose from his chair and began to pace up and down the room.

'What an impressive thing a coincidence is!' he thought to himself. 'Last night the whole of Hal's Planting story seemed to be not worth consideration. But this second death there – it can be only coincidence. What else could it be?'

The question would not leave him. What else could it be? Had that dead man seen something there and died in sheer terror of it? Had Sir Edric really heard something when he spent that night there alone? He returned to his work, but he found that he got on with it but slowly. Every now and then his mind wandered back to the subject of Hal's Planting. His doubts annoyed him. It was unscientific and unmodern of him to feel any perplexity, because a natural and rational explanation was possible; he was annoyed with himself for being perplexed.

After luncheon he strolled round the grounds and smoked a cigar. He noticed that a thick bank of dark, slate-coloured clouds was gathering in the west. The air was very still. In a remote corner of the garden a big heap of weeds was burning; the smoke went up perfectly straight. On the top of the heap light flames danced; they were like the ghosts of flames in the strange light. A few big drops of rain fell. The small shower did not last for five seconds. Guerdon glanced at his watch. Sir Edric would be back in an hour, and he wanted to finish his work with the papers before Sir Edric's return, so he went back into the house once more.

He picked up the first document that came to hand. As he did so, another, smaller, and written on parchment, which had been folded in with it, dropped out. He began to read the parchment; it was written in faded ink, and the parchment itself was yellow and in many places stained. It was the confession of the third baronet – he could tell that by the date upon it. It told the story of that night when he and Dr Dennison went together carrying a burden through the long garden out into the orchard that skirts the north side of the park, and then across a field to a small, dark plantation. It told how he made a vow to God and did not keep it. These were the last words of the confession: 'Already upon me has the punishment fallen, and the devil's wolves do seem to hunt me in my sleep nightly. But I know that there is worse to come. The thing that I took to Hal's Planting is dead. Yet it will come back again to the Hall, and then will the Vanquerests be at an end. This writing I have committed to chance, neither showing it nor hiding it, and leaving it to chance if any man shall read it.'

Underneath there was a line written in darker ink, and in quite a different handwriting. It was dated fifteen years later, and the initials R. D. were appended to it: 'It is not dead. I do not think that it will ever die.'

When Andrew Guerdon had finished reading this document, he looked slowly round the room. The subject had got on his nerves, and he was almost expecting to see something. Then he did his best to pull himself together. The first question he put to himself was this: 'Has Ted ever seen this?' Obviously he had not. If he had he could not have taken the tradition of Hal's Planting so lightly, nor have spoken of it so freely. Besides, he would either have mentioned the document to Guerdon, or he would have kept it carefully concealed. He would not have allowed him to come across it casually in that way. 'Ted must never see it,' thought Guerdon to himself. He then remembered the pile of weeds he had seen burning in the garden. He put the parchment in his pocket, and hurried out. There was no one about. He spread the parchment on the top of the pile, and waited until it was entirely consumed. Then he went back to the smoking-room; he felt easier now.

'Yes,' thought Guerdon, 'if Ted had first of all heard of the finding of that body, and then had read that document, I believe that he would have gone mad. Things that come near us affect us deeply.'

Guerdon himself was much moved. He clung steadily to reason; he felt himself able to give a natural explanation all through, and yet he was nervous. The net of coincidence had closed in around him; the mention in Sir Edric's confession of the prophecy which had subsequently become traditional in the village alarmed him. And what did that last line mean?

He supposed that R. D. must be the initials of Dr Dennison. What did he mean by saying that the thing was not dead? Did he mean that it had not really been killed, that it had been gifted with some preternatural strength and vitality and had survived, though Sir Edric did not know it? He recalled what he had said about the prolongation of the lives of such things. If it still survived, why had it never been seen? Had it joined to the wild hardiness of the beast a cunning that was human – or more than human? How could it have lived? There was water in the caves, he reflected, and food could have been secured – a wild beast's food. Or did Dr Dennison mean that though the thing itself was dead, its wraith survived and haunted the place? He wondered how the doctor had found Sir Edric's confession, and why he had written that line at the end of it. As he sat thinking, a low rumble of thunder in the distance startled him. He felt a touch of panic – a sudden impulse to leave Mansteth at once and, if possible, to take Ted with him. Ray could never live there. He went over the whole thing in his mind again and again, at one time calm and argumentative about it, and at another shaken by blind horror.

Sir Edric, on his return from Challonsea a few minutes afterwards, came straight to the smoking-room where Guerdon was. He looked tired and depressed. He began to speak at once: 'You needn't tell me about it – about John Marsh. I heard about it in the village.'

'Did you? It's a painful occurrence, although, of course –'

'Stop. Don't go into it. Anything can be explained – I know that.'

'I went through those papers and account books while you were away. Most of them may just as well be destroyed; but there are a few – I put them aside there – which might be kept. There was nothing of any interest.'

'Thanks; I'm much obliged to you.'

'Oh, and look here, I've got an idea. I've been examining the plans of the house, and I'm coming round to your opinion. There are some alterations which should be made, and yet I'm afraid that they'd make the place look patched and renovated. It wouldn't be a bad thing to know what Ray thought about it.'

'That's impossible. The workmen come on Monday, and we can't consult her before then. Besides, I have a general notion what she would like.'

'We could catch the night express to town at Challonsea, and – '

Sir Edric rose from his seat angrily and hit the table.

'Good God! don't sit there hunting up excuses to cover my cowardice, and making it easy for me to bolt. What do you suppose the villagers would say, and what would my own servants say, if I ran away tonight? I am a coward – I know it. I'm horribly afraid. But I'm not going to act like a coward if I can help it.'

'Now, my dear chap, don't excite yourself. It you are going to care at all – to care as much as the conventional damn – for what people say, you'll have no peace in life. And I don't believe you're afraid. What are you afraid of?'

Sir Edric paced once or twice up and down the room, and then sat down again before replying.

'Look here, Andrew, I'll make a clean breast of it.

I've always laughed at the tradition; I forced myself, as it seemed at least, to disprove it by spending a night in Hal's Planting; I took the pains even to make a theory which would account for its origin. All the time I had a sneaking, stifled belief in it. With the help of my reason I crushed that; but now my reason has thrown up the job, and I'm afraid. I'm afraid of the Undying Thing that is in Hal's Planting. I heard it that night. John Marsh saw it last night – they took me to see the body, and the face was awful; and I believe that one day it will come from Hal's Planting – '

'Yes,' interrupted Guerdon, 'I know. And at present I believe as much. Last night we laughed at the whole thing, and we shall live to laugh at it again, and be ashamed of ourselves for a couple of superstitious old women. I fancy that beliefs are affected by weather – there's thunder in the air.'

'No,' said Sir Edric, 'my belief has come to stay.'

'And what are you going to do?'

'I'm going to test it. On Monday I can begin to get to work, and then I'll blow up Hal's Planting with dynamite. After that we shan't need to believe – we shall *know*. And now let's dismiss the subject. Come down into the billiard-room and have a game. Until Monday I won't think of the thing again.'

Long before dinner, Sir Edric's depression seemed to have completely vanished. At dinner he was boisterous and amused. Afterwards he told stories and was interesting.

It was late at night; the terrific storm that was raging outside had awoke Guerdon from sleep. Hopeless of getting to sleep again, he had arisen and dressed, and now sat in the window-seat watching the storm. He had never seen anything like it before; and every now and then the sky seemed to be torn across as if by hands of white fire. Suddenly he heard a tap at his door, and looked round. Sir Edric had already entered; he also had dressed. He spoke in a curious, subdued voice.

'I thought you wouldn't be able to sleep through this. Do you remember that I shut and fastened the dining-room window?'

'Yes, I remember it.'

'Well, come in here.'

Sir Edric led the way to his room, which was immediately over the dining-room. By leaning out of the window they could see that the dining-room window was open wide.

'Burglar,' said Guerdon meditatively.

'No,' Sir Edric answered, still speaking in a hushed voice. 'It is the Undying Thing – it has come for me.'

He snatched up the candle, and made towards the staircase; Guerdon caught up the loaded revolver which always lay on the table beside Sir Edric's bed and followed him. Both men ran down the staircase as though there were not another moment to lose. Sir Edric rushed at the dining-room door, opened it a little, and looked in. Then he turned to Guerdon, who was just behind him.

'Go back to your room,' he said authoritatively.

'I won't,' said Guerdon. 'Why? What is it?'

Suddenly the corners of Sir Edric's mouth shot outward into the hideous grin of terror.

'It's there! It's there!' he gasped.

'Then I come in with you.'

'Go back!'

With a sudden movement, Sir Edric thrust Guerdon away from the door, and then, quick as light, darted in, and locked the door behind him.

Guerdon bent down and listened. He heard Sir Edric say in a firm voice: 'Who are you? What are you?'

Then followed a heavy, snorting breathing, a low, vibrating growl, an awful cry, a scuffle.

Then Guerdon flung himself at the door. He kicked at the lock, but it would not give way. At last he fired his revolver at it. Then he managed to force his way into the room. It was perfectly empty. Overhead he could hear footsteps; the noise had awakened the servants; they were standing, tremulous, on the upper landing.

Through the open window access to the garden was easy. Guerdon did not wait to get help; and in all probability none of the servants could have been persuaded to come with him. He climbed out alone, and, as if by some blind impulse, started to run as hard as he could in the direction of Hal's Planting. He knew that Sir Edric would be found there.

But when he got within a hundred yards of the plantation, he stopped. There had been a great flash of lightning, and he saw that it had struck one of the trees. Flames darted about the plantation as the dry bracken caught. Suddenly, in the light of another flash, he saw the whole of the trees fling their heads upwards; then came a deafening crash, and the ground slipped under him, and he was flung forward on his face. The plantation had collapsed, fallen through into the caves beneath it. Guerdon slowly regained his feet; he was surprised to find that he was unhurt. He walked on a few steps, and then fell again; this time he had fainted away.

The Last Leaf

O. HENRY

In a little district west of Washington Square the streets have run crazy and broken themselves into small strips called 'places'. These 'places' make strange angles and curves. One Street crosses itself a time or two. An artist once discovered a valuable possibility in this street. Suppose a collector with a bill for paints, paper and canvas should, in traversing this route, suddenly meet himself coming back, without a cent having been paid on account!

So, to quaint old Greenwich Village the art people soon came prowling, hunting for north windows and eighteenth-century gables and Dutch attics and low rents. Then they imported some pewter mugs and a chafing dish or two from Sixth Avenue, and became a 'colony'.

At the top of a squatty, three-storey brick house Sue and Johnsy had their studio. 'Johnsy' was familiar for Joanna. One was from Maine; the other from California. They had met at the *table d'hôte* of an Eighth Street 'Delmonico's', and found their tastes in art, chicory salad and bishop sleeves so congenial that the joint studio resulted.

That was in May. In November a cold, unseen stranger, whom the doctors called Pneumonia, stalked about the colony, touching one here and there with his icy fingers. Over on the east side this ravager strode boldly, smiting his victims by scores, but his feet trod slowly through the maze of the narrow and moss-grown 'places'.

Mr Pneumonia was not what you would call a chivalric old gentleman. A mite of a little woman with blood thinned by California zephyrs was hardly fair game for the red-fisted, short-breathed old duffer. But Johnsy he smote; and she lay, scarcely moving, on her painted iron bedstead, looking through the small Dutch windowpanes at the blank side of the next brick house.

One morning the busy doctor invited Sue into the hallway with a shaggy, grey eyebrow.

'She has one chance in – let us say, ten,' he said, as he shook down the mercury in his clinical thermometer. 'And that chance is for her to want to live. This way people have of lining-up on the side of the undertaker makes the entire pharmacopoeia look silly. Your little lady has made up her mind that she's not going to get well. Has she anything on her mind?'

'She – she wanted to paint the Bay of Naples some day,' said Sue.

'Paint? – bosh! Has she anything on her mind worth thinking twice – a man for instance?'

'A man?' said Sue, with a jew's-harp twang in her voice. 'Is a man worth – but, no, doctor; there is nothing of the kind.'

'Well, it is the weakness, then,' said the doctor. 'I will do all that science, so far as it may filter through my efforts, can accomplish. But whenever my patient begins to count the carriages in her funeral procession I subtract fifty per cent from the curative power of medicines. If you will get her to ask one question about the new winter styles in cloak sleeves I will promise you a one-in-five chance for her, instead of one in ten.'

After the doctor had gone Sue went into the workroom and cried a Japanese napkin to a pulp. Then she swaggered into Johnsy's room with her drawing board, whistling ragtime.

Johnsy lay, scarcely making a ripple under the bedclothes, with her face toward the window. Sue stopped whistling, thinking she was asleep.

She arranged her board and began a pen-and-ink drawing to illustrate a magazine story. Young artists must pave their way to Art by drawing pictures for magazine stories that young authors write to pave their way to Literature.

As Sue was sketching a pair of elegant horseshow riding trousers and a monocle of the figure of the hero, an Idaho cowboy, she heard a low sound, several times repeated. She went quickly to the bedside.

Johnsy's eyes were open wide. She was looking out the window and counting – counting backward.

'Twelve,' she said, and little later 'eleven'; and then 'ten', and 'nine'; and then 'eight' and 'seven', almost together.

Sue look solicitously out of the window. What was there to count? There was only a bare, dreary yard to be seen, and the blank side of the brick house twenty feet away. An old, old ivy vine, gnarled and decayed at the roots, climbed halfway up the brick wall. The cold breath of autumn had stricken its leaves from the vine until its skeleton branches clung, almost bare, to the crumbling bricks.

'What is it, dear?' asked Sue.

'Six,' said Johnsy, in almost a whisper. 'They're

falling faster now. Three days ago there were almost a hundred. It made my head ache to count them. But now it's easy. There goes another one. There are only five left now.'

'Five what, dear? Tell your Sudie.'

'Leaves. On the ivy vine. When the last one falls I must go, too. I've known that for three days. Didn't the doctor tell you?'

'Oh, I never heard of such nonsense,' complained Sue, with magnificent scorn. 'What have old ivy leaves to do with your getting well? And you used to love that vine so, you naughty girl. Don't be a goosey. Why, the doctor told me this morning that your chances for getting well real soon were – let's see exactly what he said – he said the chances were ten to one! Why, that's almost as good a chance as we have in New York when we ride on the street cars or walk past a new building. Try to take some broth now, and let Sudie go back to her drawing, so she can sell the editor man with it, and buy port wine for her sick child, and pork chops for her greedy self.'

'You needn't get any more wine,' said Johnsy, keeping her eyes fixed out the window. 'There goes another. No, I don't want any broth. That leaves just four. I want to see the last one fall before it gets dark. Then I'll go, too.'

'Johnsy, dear,' said Sue, bending over her, 'will you promise me to keep your eyes closed, and not look out the window until I am done working? I must hand those drawings in by tomorrow. I need the light, or I would draw the shade down.'

'Couldn't you draw in the other room?' asked Johnsy, coldly.

'I'd rather be here by you,' said Sue. 'Besides, I

don't want you to keep looking at those silly ivy leaves.'

'Tell me as soon as you have finished,' said Johnsy, closing her eyes, and lying white and still as a fallen statue, 'because I want to see the last one fall. I'm tired of waiting. I'm tired of thinking. I want to turn loose my hold on everything, and go sailing down, down, just like one of those poor, tired leaves.'

'Try to sleep,' said Sue. 'I must call Behrman up to be my model for the old hermit miner. I'll not be gone a minute. Don't try to move 'til I come back.'

Old Behrman was a painter who lived on the ground floor beneath them. He was past sixty and had a Michaelangelo's Moses beard curling down from the head of a satyr along with the body of an imp. Behrman was a failure in art. Forty years he had wielded the brush without getting near enough to touch the hem of his Mistress's robe. He had been always about to paint a masterpiece, but had never yet begun it. For several years he had painted nothing except now and then a daub in the line of commerce or advertising. He earned a little by serving as a model to those young artists in the colony who could not pay the price of a professional. He drank gin to excess, and still talked of his coming masterpiece. For the rest he was a fierce little old man, who scoffed terribly at softness in any one, and who regarded himself as especial mastiff-in-waiting to protect the two young artists in the studio above.

Sue found Behrman smelling strongly of juniper berries in his dimly lighted den below. In one corner was a blank canvas on an easel that had been waiting there for twenty-five years to receive the first line of the masterpiece. She told him of Johnsy's fancy, and how she feared she would, indeed, light and fragile as a leaf herself, float away, when her slight hold upon the world grew weaker.

Old Behrman, with his red eyes plainly streaming, shouted his contempt and derision for such idiotic imaginings.

'Vass!' he cried. 'Is dere people in de world mit der foolishness to die because leafs dey drop off from a confounded vine? I haf not heard of such a thing. No, I will not bose as a model for your fool hermit-dunderhead. Vy do you allow dot silly pusiness to come in der brain of her? Ach, dot poor leetle Miss Yohnsy.'

'She is very ill and weak,' said Sue, 'and the fever has left her mind morbid and full of strange fancies. Very well, Mr Behrman, if you do not care to pose for me, you needn't. But I think you are a horrid old – old flibbertigibbet.'

'You are just like a woman!' yelled Behrman. 'Who said I will not bose? Go on. I come mit you. For half an hour I haf peen trying to say dot I am ready to bose. Gott! dis is not any blace in which one so goot as Miss Yohnsy shall lie sick. Some day I vill baint a masterpiece, and ve shall all go away. Gott! yes.'

Johnsy was sleeping when they went upstairs. Sue pulled the shade down to the window-sill, and motioned Behrman into the other room. In there they peered out the window fearfully at the ivy vine. Then they looked at each other for a moment without speaking. A persistent, cold rain was falling, mingled with snow. Behrman, in his old blue shirt, took his seat as the hermit miner on an upturned kettle for a rock.

When Sue awoke from an hour's sleep the next

morning she found Johnsy with dull, wide-open eyes staring at the drawn green shade.

'Pull it up; I want to see,' she ordered, in a whisper.

Wearily Sue obeyed.

But, lo! after the beating rain and fierce gusts of wind that had endured through the livelong night, there yet stood out against the brick wall one ivy leaf. It was the last one on the vine. Still dark green near its stem, with its serrated edges tinted with the yellow of dissolution and decay, it hung bravely from the branch some twenty feet above the ground.

'It is the last one,' said Johnsy. 'I thought it would surely fall during the night. I heard the wind. It will fall today, and I shall die at the same time.'

'Dear, dear!' said Sue, leaning her worn face down to the pillow, 'think of me, if you won't think of yourself. What would I do?'

But Johnsy did not answer. The lonesomest thing in all the world is a soul when it is making ready to go on its mysterious, far journey. The fancy seemed to possess her more strongly as one by one the ties that bound her to friendship and to earth were loosed.

The day wore away, and even through the twilight they could see the lone ivy leaf clinging to its stem against the wall. And then, with the coming of the night the north wind was again loosed, while the rain still beat against the windows and pattered down from the low Dutch eaves.

When it was light enough Johnsy, the merciless, commanded that the shade be raised.

The ivy leaf was still there.

Johnsy lay for a long time looking at it. And then she called to Sue, who was stirring her chicken broth over the gas stove.

'I've been a bad girl, Sudie,' said Johnsy. 'Something has made that last leaf stay there to show me how wicked I was. It is a sin to want to die. You may bring me a little broth now, and some milk with a little port in it, and – no; bring me a hand-mirror first, and then pack some pillows about me, and I will sit up and watch you cook.'

And hour later she said: 'Sudie, some day I hope to paint the Bay of Naples.'

The doctor came in the afternoon, and Sue had an excuse to go into the hallway as he left.

'Even chances,' said the doctor, taking Sue's thin, shaking hand in his. 'With good nursing you'll win. And now I must see another case I have downstairs. Behrman, his name is – some kind of an artist, I believe. Pneumonia, too. He is an old, weak man, and the attack is acute. There is no hope for him; but he goes to the hospital today to be made more comfortable.'

The next day the doctor said to Sue: 'She's out of danger. You won. Nutrition and care now – that's all.'

And that afternoon Sue came to the bed where Johnsy lay, contentedly knitting a very blue and very useless woollen shoulder scarf, and put one arm around her, pillows and all.

'I have something to tell you, white mouse,' she said. 'Mr Behrman died of pneumonia today in the hospital. He was ill only two days. The janitor found him the morning of the first day in his room downstairs helpless with pain. His shoes and clothing were wet through and icy cold. They couldn't imagine where he had been on such a dreadful night. And then they found a lantern, still lighted, and a ladder that had been dragged from its place, and some scattered brushes, and a palette with green and yellow colours mixed on it, and – look out the window, dear, at the last ivy leaf on the wall. Didn't you wonder why it never fluttered or moved when the wind blew? Ah, darling, it's Behrman's masterpiece – he painted it there the night that the last leaf fell.'

END